WARRIOR RISING

SEVEN JOURNEYS
BOOK 1

ANN SHAW

DORRANCE
PUBLISHING CO
EST. 1920
PITTSBURGH, PENNSYLVANIA 15238

Thanks to my friends and family
that have helped me so much to make my dream come true.

Emily Ann Smith

Dorrance Publishing Co
585 Alpha Drive
Suite 103
Pittsburgh, PA 15238
Visit our website at *www.dorrancebookstore.com*

ISBN: 978-1-6491-3377-9
eISBN: 978-1-6491-3605-3

Prologue

The black stoned throne room was covered in thick layers of dust and cobwebs. The once grand and detailed carvings of knights, fair maidens, horses and dragons had begun to weather and erode away. Tattered and shredded tapestries hung from the walls, their remains billowing in the wind that swept through the broken and glassless windows. Somewhere in the distance the steady, hollow plunk of water droplets echoed through the empty space. The air was dank and smelled of mildew. A strange blue light permeated the room, its source coming from a starlike crystal that was imbedded into the gray flag stone floor. As if it were a heart, it beat with a brightness of light in a rhythm sending out waves of electric blue light that spread throughout the cracks of the floors and walls casting the corners into shadows.

Stone statues of military soldiers filled the old chamber. All were carved in a similar fashion as the walls, with fine and intricate detail. A number were chiseled from dark, black marble and others were formed from white alabaster stone. They were all dressed for battle in breastplates and helmets, with weapons of swords and shields. Some were in the form of an attacking stance, while others lay on the floor as though asleep.

One statue that kneeled just over the stone crystal was far more life-like than any of the others. His face was carved upward in a painstaking expression with his hands clasped together as if he were kneeling in prayer.

"So this is what has become of the great Master Shelrin's palace," a raspy and shallow voice rang out and echoed off the chamber walls, "ruins."

zThe man moved forward, struggling to cross the room to where a rotting throne sat on a dais. Above, moth eaten and rat infested curtains hung, once a bright purple, but now they were blackened with age and mold. The old man gazed up at the statue that sat on the wormwood eaten throne. Its head was slumped down upon its chest, with a hood carved over the head, hiding the face beneath in shadow. Draped stone- robes were gathered around, covering the body of the cold stone figure.

"I can remember when the great palace was gilded in gold, now look at it. Wasted away into nothing," the old man spoke, staring up at the statue with pity.

"Master Logan, we c-c-c-can rebuild it," another voice stuttered. "Once we awaken our master again."

A man, thin and pale skinned, dressed in his own dark robes stepped out from the shadows and looked at the throne's figure with caution.

"Yes, you are right Rassworth. The Black Dragons and our great Master Shelrin will rebuild it once more. Then all of us within the brotherhood will take back what is rightfully ours," the old man Logan proclaimed. "Now that we have the Staff of the Dark King, we can wake our dear Master. Those that have betrayed us will feel Shelrin's wrath and they shall know the Master once more," the figure spoke, then raised the staff and brought it down onto the crystal star. The room fell silent save for the echoing of the weapon hitting the stone floor.

"Did it work Master Logan?" the thin man asked timidly.

"Of course it didn't work Rassworth. Why did it not work?" Logan snarled. "Old wizard, tell me why the staff's power failed."

With a cackling laugh a voice resonated out of a dark corner. "Because you do not have what is needed to break the power that holds this place."

With fear in his eyes, Rassworth shifted away from the corner, as what appeared to be a bundle of dirty rags stepped out from the darkness and into the moonlight. Under the tattered and faded clothes, was a wretched looking man, with graying hair and a beard that covered the majority of his face. He looked at Rassworth with cold black eyes that had a glint of red to them.

"The magic that holds this place captive is strong, much stronger than any power that you possess."

"Kayden, blast that good for nothing whelp," Logan snarled with loathing.

"Master Logan, who is this that you speak of?" the manservant Rassworth asked.

"He is the one that cursed our master and turned our dark lord to stone. That is the curse that we of the Black Dragons have tried to undo for these past fifteen years," Logan spoke with venom.

"Then what shall you do Master?" Rassworth asked. "I thought the staff held enormous amounts of power. I thought that it would restore our Grandmaster?"

"So did I," Logan muttered.

The old wizard continued to laugh as he watched Logan pace the court-room in frustration.

"Answer me this old man. Why hasn't the magic within the staff worked?" Logan asked suddenly, pouncing on the old man and grabbing him by his throat.

The old warrior said nothing but put a finger to his lips and continued to chuckle.

"It's a secret," the old man whispered, then continued his maddening laughter.

"Old wizard, or should I call you Lord Kale?" Logan spoke, his words coming out like he was speaking to a child.

The man stopped laughing and looked up into the hood of Logan as he stood over him.

"Long have you lived and no doubt you wish to leave this world. I can do that. I can grant your wish, if you tell me what is needed to unlock the power of the staff."

The old warrior known as Lord Kale looked up at Logan with a wicked smile.

"You cannot give me death, I was cursed to live forever until a true Elfain chooses to release me. But give me food and I shall tell wht you want to know."

From his travel bag Logan pulled out a block of dried out and moldy cheese and some dried bread and threw it at the old wizard.

Kale grabbed at it and tore into it like a starving dog.

"I will tell you what you seek," Kale said, licking his mouth full of the cheese.

"The magic that binds this place and your master is old magic. There is not enough power within the staff to break the curse that is upon this mourn-ful place. The power of a lifespark was willingly sacrificed to imprison your master and this precious palace." Kale spoke spitting bits of cheese from be-tween his lips.

"So a lifespark equal to that power must be given to fully break the magic that binds this place. As for unlocking the power of the staff, only the true wielder, it's owner of the weapon can use its full power," the old man chortled.

Logan's eyes narrowed on Rassworth as he stared at the manservant.

"Rassworth, what would you give to see Master Shelrin back on the throne?"

Rassworth looked up at the tall stone figure, his eyes shining with emotion. "Anything!" Rassworth breathed.

Logan took a step forward to the little man.

"Would you give your spark?"

"My spark?" Rassworth questioned in fear.

With unnatural speed, Logan's hand struck out like an attacking snake and grabbed Rassworth by his throat. Dropping the staff from his other hand he moved towards Rassworth's left side of his chest.

"No! Please!" Rassworth pleaded.

Rassworth fought for his life as Logan's fingers curved into claws that started slipping through skin and bones. The manservant tried to fight, tried to get away, but Logan held tight. The little man's body stiffened as the color of his skin faded away to stone gray. The light in his eyes faded. His mouth opened to let out a scream, but it never came. The old warrior looked on, showing no emotion as the life was being drawn from Rassworth. Logan pulled free his hand from Rassworth's chest, letting the little man's body dropped to the floor. Within Logan's hand was a dimly lit rounded orb that pulsed red with the rhythm of a heartbeat.

"Thank you Rassworth, your sacrifice will not be forgotten."

"To steal a spark for power will send you to the deepest part of the underworld," the old wizard spoke with amusement.

"You speak of the underworld to me old man," Logan mocked. "Is that not now where you are bound?"

With that, Logan placed the throbbing orb into the crater of the silver staff. When he did the staff began to glow a slight reddish color.

With the staff in hand Logan went to the crystal embedded in the floor. With a cry he lifted the staff and plunged the end of it onto the crystal. The staff bit into the stone and a crash of thunder violently shook the room. Red lightning forked out from the staff, streaking out and striking the walls, floor, and ceiling. Using all his strength Logan controlled the wildness of the flashing light. It collected around him and somehow he managed to push it into the crystal. The red light spread through the veins of the stone floor, over taking the blue light. There was a sudden explosion and Logan was thrown back across the room. Lord Kale's laughter vibrated off the walls as the lightning faded and then disappeared. The chamber fell silent.

"Has it worked?" Logan asked breathless.

Kale said nothing but merrily chuckled to himself.

Logan looked towards the statue that sat on the throne, still solid as rock and the blue light returned, though not as bright as it once was.

"Why didn't it work? Rassworths gave his lifespark," Logan cried.

"Not much of a spark that one had," Kale smirked. "But it has done what you wanted it to. The seal is cracked.

Logan's attention was drawn to the throne's statue as he heard the cracking and breaking of stone. The statue began to move. It curled its fingers while a thin layer of dust fell away. Its head came up from its chest, rolling from side to side, and then it fell forward and lay still. Logan looked cautiously at the breathing figure. He stepped forward slowly, not really sure what he should do. Suddenly Logan jumped back as the figure's hooded head suddenly snapped up and stretched out a hand. The staff that had fallen to the floor suddenly whizzed through the air towards the cloaked figure that caught it. Slowly Logan's Master rose and Logan fell to one knee, with his head bowed.

"Master Shelrin at long last you have awakened," Logan announced.

The cloaked figure said nothing but brought up the staff and slammed it down.

Again lightning forked, thunder rolled and the earth beneath Logan shook, causing him to cry out in fear. Mixed with the screaming cries of Logan, Lord Kale started laughing hysterically.

"The Dark Dragon is reborn, the war has started," he yelled and then continued his maddening laugh.

Chapter 1

West of the Moon, East of the sun,
The wind doth whisper when darkness comes.
Dark be the dragon that will rise again,
Seeking out the light and wanting revenge.

Black be the wings that cover the sky,
Red be the ground where dead men lie.
Long will the birds cease to sing their songs,
And the rays of sun will seem far-gone.

All joy will seem lost, all hope will be gone,
Cold is the night that wanes too long.
Fear not my child, for night doth not last,
Look to the old stories that have come to pass.

The Elfain warriors of yester years,
Defeated a darkness that many feared.
Sent from the Haven's they did fight,
Wielding weapons with power and light.

And when that Dark Dragon comes again,
So too will the warriors to fight and defend.
Sleep sound my child, and dream tonight.
The warriors protect you with truth and light…

Cole, are you listening to me?" the old man asked loudly, looking up from the text he was reading to the boy that sat directly in front of him.

The boy was perched on a bench with his books, parchment and inkwell neatly laid out in front of him. However, he did not seem to notice the objects at all, they had been long forgotten. The boy's black haired head was turned towards the open window of the workshop. His pale blue eyes stared blankly out towards the range of mountains to the east. In his hand he held a quill, poised above his parchment. Small droplets of ink were starting to drip onto the paper, spreading down across the page. The old man watched his young apprentice, wondering what adventures the boy was conjuring up.

"Cole!" The old man called louder this time.

The boy's head snapped away from the window to look at his master, suddenly realizing where he was.

"Cole, did you hear anything of what I have said?" questioned the old man.

"Sorry, Master Merryrick, I guess I was just ..." Cole started to say.

"Daydreaming," the old master named Merryrick quirked an eyebrow, finishing Cole's sentence.

Merryrick was a tall sturdy man with eyes that Cole swore changed color everyday. Today they were sea green. A short white beard with tale-tell streaks of red covered Merryrick's chin, the same whiteness with red streaks matched the hair atop his head. Cole's master walked with a slight limp, but that didn't stop him from working the small farm they lived on and his work in his carpenter's workshop.

Cole dropped his head in shame and then noticed the blotches of ink. He tried wiping the ink away but only succeeded in smearing the black ink onto his hand and across the sheet of parchment. He spat on the fingers of his other hand and tried to remove the ink, this however only made the ink spread farther.

Merryrick chuckled softly at the boy's folly.

Cole's pale blue eyes looked up at his master with frustration.

"I still haven't gotten the ink off from last week's schooling day," Cole said with irritation.

"Perhaps you should pay more attention to your lesson, rather than day dreaming." Merryrick replied with amusement playing in his eyes.

Cole quit trying to wash the ink away and sat straight up on the bench waiting for Merryrick to continue the lesson. But as Merryrick went to bury his face back in the ancient text a great gust of wind came sweeping in through the open window of the little cottage ruffling Cole's hair. Cole's head slightly turned toward the window and then whipped back to stare at Merryrick.

"Be off with you, I know what today is," Merryrick announced shooing him to the door, "Your schooling is done. It is a fine day and I doubt you would pay any more attention to an old man than I would. Besides, there is much the outside world can teach you"

"Thank you, Master Merryrick," Cole said, jumping to his feet and knocking back the small wooden bench he had previously sat on, to the floor.

"Sorry Master," Cole said, picking up the bench and placing it back where it belonged.

"Tis alright Cole, go and have yourself an enjoyable time. Say hello to Maggie and Chanlyn for me," Merryrick called after him.

Cole was out of the little workroom, stopping only to grab his bow and quiver of arrows that hung on a peg near the door. He was across the threshold, running for the barn to fetch Gladadear, the horse, before Merryrick could finish his sentence. Merryrick stared after Cole as he rode bare back towards the Forest of Kells, wishing that he were once again Cole's age. He then shook his head taking back the wish when he remembered where he was when he was Cole's age.

THE VALLEY OF KELLS was buzzing with new life. After a long and tiring winter the isolated valley had finally decided to stir. Surrounded by the Elfire Mountain range, the winters in Kells were cold and filled with lonely days and freezing nights. Those who lived in the village had the company of their neighbors, but those who lived beyond the village, on the farms, were shut off, snowed in and often not seen until the spring festival. Cole and Merryrick lived just a few leagues on the outskirts of the village of Kells, but even there the snow piled deep and blocked the road into the village.

But now it was late April and the world was green once more. The farmers had started planting their crops after the first thaw and their fields were now covered in a carpet of green. Meadows were showing off their bright spectrum of colors as flowers bloomed in the mid-afternoon sun.

Cole took a deep breath when he entered the woods. The air was sweet with the fragrance of pine, evergreen and cottonwood. Gladadear knew the woodland so well that Cole did not need to guide her, for the little shaggy white horse knew the way. She carried Cole forward along the path while he let his mind wander elsewhere. Cole's thoughts revolved around his two friends Maggie and Chanlyn. He had not seen them since last fall, right before the first snow. He knew that Chanlyn had started working as an apprentice to his father, Master Goldhill, as a miller and Maggie had spent the winter with her father on their farm. Like Merryrick and himself they too were shut off from the outside world by the snow. Today they were meeting each other after the long months of ice and snow.

Cole kicked Gladadear forward and turned to the right, off the path she had been following. He guided her through a grove of tightly knit trees, and was suddenly standing in a small clearing of emerald green grass.

The clearing was hidden within the vast woodland and was surrounded by sycamore trees that were as ancient as the land they grew on. Few people knew of the clearing's existence. He was certain that the only ones that knew of the place were Maggie, Chanlyn and himself. As Cole came further into the clearing he noticed two horses grazing on the lush grass. The place was peaceful, and silent, even the living creatures of the woods did little to make loud noises here in the glade. Within the clearing was a small pond. Ducks and geese glided across the glass-like surface until, they suddenly burst upward, flying skyward, as a loud CRACK rebounded around the glen followed by a high pitch screech of a scream.

"No...no...no, to the left, it was supposed to fly to the left. I missed my mark by a mere millimeter."

Cole's lips twitched up into a smile as he recognized the high shrill scream.

"It seems Maggie's here," Cole said to Gladadear.

The little horse nodded her head in agreement as she trotted forward.

Cole caught sight of the willowy, strawberry blonde haired girl, not too far off. Although Maggie was a few years younger than he was, Cole considered her to be one of his best friends. Maggie stood with her leather sling in hand, staring defiantly at her target. He pulled Gladadear to a stop and dismounted, then slowly walked forward.

"Wait for Cole, he can show you how to aim more accurately."

Cole knew that was Chanlyn's voice speaking, for it had a civility in it that could only be Chanlyn, but he could not see him. Cole scanned over the clearing and found Chanlyn sitting under one of the giant sycamore trees, book in hand. Maggie didn't reply. She picked up a stone from the ground and looked it over to see if it was suitable then placed it in the smock pocket of leather, she then put the two strings of the sling together and began to whirl it over her head. In a swift and graceful movement Maggie let go of one of the strings and the stone went flying with the familiar CRACK. Cole watched the stone fly through the air and pass the target, which was a fallen tree.

"Oh, now I can't hit a thing!" Maggie cried.

"I'm sure you hit something," Cole replied with a smile, as he stepped forward. "It just wasn't the target."

Maggie jumped at Cole's sudden appearance. To her it seemed like he had come out of nowhere.

"Cole you scared me to death," Maggie whined.

"Sorry," Cole replied grinning.

"You know you could make a little more noise next time. I hate it when you come stalking in without making a sound. And those clothes of green and brown that you wear don't make it easy to spot you" Maggie said, scolding Cole as she came towards him.

"Well it's nice to see you too," Cole said, giving Maggie his best smile.

Maggie gave Cole a small hug and returned the smile.

"You've grown," Maggie stated looking Cole up and down.

"So have you," Cole said, seeing that Maggie had indeed changed since the last time he had seen her. Sure she had her shoulder bag that she always carried with its collection of stones that she gathered for her sling, and her usual sprig of mint that she had placed in her hair but the round baby face that he remembered from last fall had faded away and left a beautiful cream-colored face that seemed to be without fault. Her figure had changed as well. She was no longer the skinny reddish-blonde haired creature that was always trying to best Cole at everything. She had curves and seemed to hold herself differently.

"And what do you mean by that?" Maggie asked, sounding offended.

"I…I was just saying that…" Cole stammered out.

Maggie let out a burst of laughter when she saw the look on Cole's face.

"You haven't changed a bit, Cole," Maggie said, shaking her head. She turned and walked back to stand in front of her target again.

Cole started making his way toward Chanlyn as he watched Maggie pull a stone from her bag and place it in her sling. Maggie whirled it around more than once then let it go. The stone sunk low and hit the ground.

"Don't spin it so much," Cole yelled. "Remember the power from your legs needs to flow into your arm."

"What do you know about sling throwing anyway, Archer Boy," Maggie taunted.

"A far bit, since I taught you."

Maggie turned around and stuck her tongue out.

"You haven't changed either," Cole yelled back.

Chanlyn marked his page and closed his book as Cole came near.

"What are you reading now?" Cole asked, looking Chanlyn up and down. He had grown a few inches since the fall harvest and had developed a few muscles as well. Cole figured he would have after hauling heavy sacks of flour all day. His once sandy blond hair was now a lot lighter, having been bleached by the new spring sun. Most people in Kells thought Chanlyn to be a slow thinker because he did not answer questions right off. But Cole knew that Chanlyn was smart, far smarter than people realized. He could add numbers in his head faster than a rabbit could run. He also could quote books he had read years earlier and he knew every meaning to every word Cole could think of, and no matter where he went, he always had a book with him.

"I'm reading the record of our ancestors, the first ones who settled Kells," Chanlyn said.

"Not my ancestors," Cole mumbled.

The people of Kells prided themselves on their family history. Kells wasn't really that old. Refugees of the Albavarin War had settled Kells nearly one hundred years earlier. They had run, when a warlord named Shelrin, had started taking over the land. They escaped over the Elfire Mountains, into a world of wilderness and woodlands. There were stories told of the difficult crossing. Many people died from climbing over the snow-covered mountains peaks in the dead of winter.

"It is quite possible that you are part of a Kellian line Cole," Chanlyn said.

"You know as well as I do that I'm nowhere near anyone's *line*. You know the story. I was brought here by a man that no one knew and left with Merryrick, without a word of who I am or where I came from," Cole said sourly. "And one only has to look at my eyes and hair color to know that I don't have any ancestry line that ties into anyone in Kells."

Chanlyn didn't reply, he knew Cole was right. Chanlyn could trace his ancestral line back to when his great-great grandfather arrived in Kells, and even further. Everyone in Kells could do that. Cole could not even trace back to who his father was, let alone to his father's father.

"So are you entering this year," Chanlyn asked, changing the subject of families.

"I don't know, are you?" Cole asked, gladly letting the subject slide.

"I don't know if I'm good enough," Chanlyn replied.

"You're better than most," Cole said.

"Not as good as you."

"I'm not that good," Cole said, pulling up a blade of grass and sticking it into his mouth.

"I'll enter if you enter," Chanlyn said, looking at Cole with a smile, "but you and I know who will win."

"Win what?" Maggie asked, as she approached the boys, tying her sling around her waist.

"Chanlyn here is going to win first prize for best archer," Cole said, giving Chanlyn a little punch in the arm.

"No I'm not, you are! We all know you're the best. People talk about your bows and arrows all the time, not to mention your shooting," Chanlyn said, returning the punch.

"That's not all they talk about either," Cole muttered.

"Oh come on Cole, you can do it! If I were a boy I'd enter. It really is a dim-witted idea not to let girls enter." Maggie said looking at Cole with her deep green eyes. "Besides no one wants to see Artemis win again."

"She has a point there," Chanlyn said. "He's won for the past two years."

"And he'll win again, even if I do enter. He is Sir Arthur's son, trained in archery, knife fighting and swordsmanship."

"Then maybe it's time that someone stood up to him," Maggie said, jumping to her feet and looking out across the clearing. "It would have to be someone brave and strong, that doesn't care about titles or riches. It would have to be a hero!" Maggie turned back around to face the boys. "Do you gentlemen know where I can find one?" Maggie asked with a raised eyebrow.

Chanlyn and Cole looked at her with grim faces.

"Very funny Maggie," Cole said.

"I wasn't trying to be funny," Maggie replied flatly.

"Fine," Cole said, "I'll enter, but Chanlyn has to as well."

"Willing and ready!" exclaimed Chanlyn.

Cole nodded, the whole thing seemed to have been settled.

The rest of the afternoon the three practiced shooting, laughing and telling jokes, most of which were at Artemis's expense. Cole gave Chanlyn tips on how to better his aim and to use the wind as an advantage rather than as a disadvantage. It did not seem that long before the sun started making its way toward the western sky and the forest began to grow dark. Realizing how late it was getting, the three gathered up their things and collected their horses and started towards home.

Cole rode with Chanlyn and Maggie until they reached a fork in the road.

"I'll see you at the fair then," Chanlyn said, steering his horse towards town.

"Till the fair," Cole muttered.

Maggie waved at Chanlyn until he was nothing but a speck in the distance. Then she turned and looked at Cole. She said nothing but stared at Cole from atop her saddle.

"What?" he asked getting nervous under her gaze.

"I was just imagining how you will look when you win the archery competition." Maggie said loftily.

"I'll look the same as I always have," Cole said.

"What? Like a scrawny black-haired scarecrow," Maggie asked with a laugh.

"I do?" Cole squeaked out.

Maggie let out another laugh when she saw the concerned look he gave her.

"Well that is somewhat of an improvement from the lop ear rabbit you called me last fall," Cole said, giving Maggie a nudge. "Come on, I'll take you home."

"There's no need, father is at Merryrick's," Maggie said.

"What's he doing there?" Cole asked with curiosity.

"He said that he had something to discuss with him." Maggie answered back.

"Wonder what it could be?" Cole thought out loud.

"Whatever it was, he said that he would be at Merryrick's and that I was to come there and we would ride home together," Maggie said, clicking her tongue, letting her horse Buttercup, know that she could go forward.

"Well, then I bet I can beat you to the cottage," Cole said, crouching low on Gladadear.

"Alright! First one to the well is the winner. Loser has to get on one knee and kiss the hand of the victor and call them the queen."

"Queen! I'm not a queen," said Cole indignantly.

"I didn't say anything about me calling you a queen. It is you who will be calling me queen. I will be winning this race," Maggie said smugly.

"Oh, you think so?" Cole asked.

"I know so."

"Well then are you ready?" Cole started to say.

"Of course," Maggie said.

"Then…"

"Go!" Maggie cried, suddenly tapping Buttercup's side with her feet. The horse took off galloping up the hillside.

"No fair," Cole cried as he tapped Gladadear's side and raced off after Maggie.

The two galloped along the dirt road, each one taking great strides to beat the other. Maggie started out ahead, but it was not long before Cole and Gladadear caught up to her.

As the two came up over the hill, their eyes were greeted with the sight of Merryrick's cottage. Cole thought that it was the most beautiful place in all of Kells. The whitewashed walls and thatched roof cottage stood on a small hill. Rolling green meadows surrounded the place, while wild flowers and a sea of deep emerald grass grew throughout the yard. It would make the most stubborn of men take in a breath of amazement when they came up over the hill and saw the cottage and meadows ahead.

As they were ascending the hill and were making their way to Merryrick's, Cole's eyes flickered towards the eastern sky. In that instance Cole sucked in a breath of air as a searing pain streaked through his head. It felt like a bolt of lightning was striking through his brain and then there was a bright flash of light that blinded him.

After the light cleared, Cole found himself no longer riding towards home on Gladaders back but standing before a great black gate that was locked with thousands upon thousands of linked chains that bore locks of steel. The doors were barred with wood and metal beams. Yet for all its locks and chains the doorway was shaking with a great force from the other side. The chains rattled, the beams cracking and bending. Whatever was imprisoned on the other side wanted to be set free.

The vision lasted only a second, within the blink of an eye, but within that blink Cole was left with a troubling feeling. The bright flash of light came again and when he opened his eyes he discovered that he was staring face down at the ground. The warm rusted iron taste of blood filled his mouth and he could also feel warm blood running down his face. He rolled over and looked up to see that Maggie was still riding up the hill on Buttercup. Gladadear was still running, not realizing that her rider had fallen off.

Maggie let out a cry of triumph when she reached the top and turned to see where Cole was. She saw him getting to his feet and wiping the blood from his bleeding head, on his shirt. With a look of concern and worry she dismounted and ran back down to meet him.

"Are you alright?" she asked

"Yeah," Cole muttered touching the cut on his forehead. "Just got a little dizzy."

"Anything broken?" Maggie asked, pulling a handkerchief from her sleeve and handing it to him. He took it and put it up to his bleeding forehead.

"I don't think so," Cole replied.

"Are you sure you're are alright? You look a little pale," Maggie asked.

"I'm fine, just a bit of a headache," Cole replied.

"Here," Maggie said digging into her belt pouch and giving Cole a gnarled bit of dried out root.

"What am I suppose to do with this," Cole said looking at the root with raised eyebrows.

"It's ginger root. It will help ease your headache."

Cole took a bite of the root and felt a hotness enter his mouth and dance along his tongue.

"No, you don't eat it. You make a tea from it. Just add a little honey to sweeten it. Other wise your tongue will burn like there's a fire in you mouth."

"Too late, the fire is already burning my mouth," Cole remarked sticking his tongue out to try and cool it down.

Maggie let out a laugh as the two ascended the hill. They reached the top of the hill and passed under a small stone archway that led into the courtyard. A short stonewall surrounded the courtyard and the cottage that lay within. As Maggie entered she looked around her, familiar with her surroundings. There was a chopping block and ax, for splitting wood, which sat to the north side of the yard, while the chicken coop, filled with cackling hens was opposite it. In the center of the yard was a drinking well. Further back was another arched gateway that led to the stables and kitchen garden.

Maggie led Cole to the well and threw down the bucket to fetch water. Once the bucket was full she started to pull. Seeing that Maggie struggled with the weight of the water and the rope, Cole stepped in to help free the bucket.

"Has it at least taken away your headache?" Maggie asked, taking back her handkerchief and dipping an end of it in the cold water.

"I suppose it has," Cole answered.

"Good. Now let us see to the gash on your head."

Maggie cleared away the blood from Cole's forehead with the wet handkerchief.

"It doesn't look too deep so you won't need stitches," Maggie replied, her gaze shifting to stare into his eyes. "Keep a cold compress on it and it should stop the bleeding and decrease the swelling."

Maggie's breath caught in her chest, as she looked deep into Cole's blue eyes. She couldn't help think that his eyes reminded her of a cool spring day or a bright winter morn. She felt her cheeks flush and her heart begin to pace a little faster as Cole leaned in a little closer to her.

"So you two are back?" Merryrick's voice asked from behind them.

Cole and Maggie jumped and quickly turned away from one another, with faces red with embarrassment.

"Yes Master Merryrick, we are back," Cole said, finding Merryrick standing next to the well looking Cole up and down.

"I can see that you're back, no need to point it out," Merryrick said with a knowing smile.

"Yes," Cole muttered as he tried to get his heart to slow down.

Merryrick had a way of sneaking up on a person without making a sound even with his limp, causing one's heart to race when he suddenly seemed to appear out of thin air, a talent that Merryrick had taught Cole, although he had never really mastered it yet.

"Master Merryrick, where is my father?" Maggie asked, trying to take the attention off Cole.

"I am right here," said a deep voice.

Coming through the arched gateway that led to the back was Master Wallace. He held the reins of his massive black workhorse, Brom, and the reins of Buttercup, who apparently had found her own way to the stable, in his hands.

Wallace was a big man, tall and strong. The years of working the land on his farm had made him look as hard as the dirt he plowed yet he was kind and cared for his daughter like a mother hen. He was a great man in the eyes of the Kells people. They looked to him as a leader and listened to his advice when he gave it. The children loved to hear the stories he told at festival. The man stood at least six feet tall, a rare thing among the people of Kells. He had deep gray eyes that were full of a lifetime of happiness and sorrow. Wallace's unusual short snow-white hair contrasted with his middle-aged face, making him appear older than he was. In truth Master Wallace always made Cole feel a little nervous. He felt as if Wallace were judging him in some way, as if he were waiting for something to happen. It was quite intimidating.

"Cole, how are you?" Wallace asked in his deep voice.

"I'm well Master Wallace," Cole answered softly.

"That is good. I hope to see you and Master Merryrick at the Festival."

"We plan on going. Yes, I do believe that we will be going." Merryrick replied.

"Good, then I shall see you there. Come Maggie, if we are to make it home before nightfall, we shall have to leave now."

"Yes, Father. I suppose the next time I will see you will be at the spring festival." Maggie said.

Cole nodded in reply.

"Merryrick, will you think on what I have said?" Wallace asked as he pulled himself up into his saddle.

"I shall," Merryrick replied, "and I'll have your plow fixed by then also."

Maggie climbed into her saddle on Buttercup and waved to Cole. "Bye Cole!"

"Bye Maggie," Cole said.

Both Wallace and Maggie lightly kicked their horse's flanks and the horses galloped off towards Wallace and Maggie's home in the west.

When Wallace and Maggie were nothing but a fading silhouette in the setting sun, Cole turned and found Merryrick observing him.

"Had a little accident?" Merryrick asked, taking notice of the cut on Cole's head.

"I fell off Gladadear," Cole replied, "Maggie and I were racing."

"Uh! Wonder how that happened? You are a fairly good horseman after all. Did anything happen to cause you to fall off the horse," Merryrick said, looking Cole in the eyes.

"I don't know," Cole lied. He didn't want to tell Merryrick about the flash of light and seeing those big black-chained gates.

"Master Merryrick, what was it that Wallace was telling you?" Cole said, wanting to change the subject.

"Oh it was nothing," Merryrick said, "just that there seems to be a visitor that has come to Kells."

"A visitor? What sort of visitor? No one ever comes to Kells," Cole remarked surprised, trying to think back to when the last visitor came to Kells. There was no one he could think of.

"I guess this Tinker does," Merryrick said as he tried to hide his smile.

"Really! You mean a real live Tinker in Kells," Cole said with excitement.

"He will be at the fair," Merryrick said nodding.

"That's really great. I just have one question Master Merryrick," Cole said.

"Yes, and what is that Cole?" asked Merryrick.

"What exactly is a Tinker?" Cole inquired.

CHAPTER 2

DAWN HAD YET TO RISE over the Elfire Mountains when Cole woke from a restless nights sleep. He had dreamed of the black gates again. Within the black gates he saw 7 crystal-like stars that were cracked and broken. However as soon as he awoke he remembered it was the day of the fair and he was too excited to fall back to sleep. Merryrick had told him that a Tinker was a traveling artisan or craftsman. He explained to Cole that each Tinker had his own distinctive skills or talents. Merryrick had also explained that the Tinker might be a fire juggler or sword swallower, possibly a healer, a fine woodcarver, or he could even be a master storyteller.

After brushing out Gladadear's shaggy white body, Cole walked her out and hitched her up to the small horse drawn cart. He then went about loading the many pieces and wares that he and Merryrick had built during the long winter months that would be haggled or traded at the fair. Trading and haggling was an artform in Kells and when the spring and fall festivals rolled around each year, the masters of the artforms created a tapestry of their trades.

Merryrick was one of the best. Two summers ago he bartered a pair of boots, pants, shirt and cloak for Cole, with tailor Jenkins for a few needles and thread. Master Jenkins said it was worth it because he claimed that the thread never ran out and the needles never dulled.

Along with the many needles and threads, there were crates of every day items such as wooden bowls, plates, cooking spoons and farmtools that needed loading. There were also the larger things such as tables, chairs, head and footboards, along with shelves and cupboards that all needed to fit within the cart. The larger components took more time and a lot more energy and effort than the small things, but Cole managed to get them in the back of the cart and tied down.

Cole had just finished tying the last securing knot when Merryrick came out of the cottage into the courtyard.

"Are we ready to go?" Merryrick asked as he climbed up into the seat of the cart.

"Yes, Master Merryrick," Cole replied, climbing up after his master.

"Good! Now did you remember everything, your bows, your arrows and quivers?" Merryrick questioned.

"I have them," Cole replied.

"Well, we shall go then," Merryrick said, then gave a loud three-note whistle and Gladadear began to trot forward.

Although Cole sat quietly in the driver's side of the cart, with the reins in his hands, guiding Gladadear along the dirt road, his insides were twisting with excitement and apprehension. Today would be filled with fun, food, dancing, and music. Everywhere there would be the smells of baking, frying, roasting, and cooking of tasty delights. Children would be running around, playing games and getting into mischief. The men would be drinking and laughing, challenging each other to the caber toss, the stone put or the sheaf-toss. The women would gather as well, telling each other the latest gossip that they heard over the long winter. The young ladies would be found dancing and smiling at the young men that had captured their hearts. The farmers would be there with their early crops of fruits and vegetables. Plus there was the Tinker to look forward to.

AN HOUR OR SO later, Cole pulled Galdadear onto the village green, a wide expanse of grassland in the middle of the village. To the west end of the green, Cole could hear the distant roar of the Clearwater River, which emptied into the Gray Lake. The flow of it was so strong that it could sweep a full-grown man under and drag him to white rapids and over the steep rocky falls. Cole hated that river. It had terrified him ever since he was little and he made a point to never go near it if possible. The very sound of the fast moving current gave Cole a spine tingling chill. Pushing the thoughts of the thunderous river to the back of his mind, he concentrated on guiding Gladadear across the field of grass.

It was still early in the morning, yet the Green was already starting to fill with the booths and pavilions of the local artisans, farmers and tradesmen. It was a holiday today and the children of the village ran around with smiles on their faces as they met up with their friends. In the distance Cole could hear a gaggle of girls sing out a skipping rhyme as they jumped roped.

"First comes the mist that turns day into night,
Then comes the howl that fills you with fright.
Cold be the air that freezes the Bone.
Next comes the dead, which once were known.
You want to scream, to run and hide,
But it's too late for a Reaper is at your side.
How many souls will it take?
Will it be two, four, six, eight…"

The girl's voices faded away as Gladadear pulled the cart further away. Cole had never liked the skipping rope rhyme. It had always left him with a feeling of foreboding. Further along, the women of Kells had already gathered around a quilt, under the great oak tree in the center of the Green, cackling like hens about the news of a neighbor or a farmer. As Cole and Merryrick passed them, they all fell silent, smiling suspiciously as they watched them with curious stares. When Cole and Merryrick were far enough away the women started clucking again.

"Probably deciding which girl should marry you," Merryrick said watching the women as they vanished from view.

"Me? I'm not old enough to get married!" Cole protested.

"Ah laddie, you'll be eighteen next year, old enough then."

"No one will want to marry me. I'm…"

"You're what?" Merryrick questioned.

"I'm different," Cole muttered.

"Different is what they like my boy," Merryrick smiled.

As they continued on to where Merryrick would assemble their pavilion, they passed a man dressed in bright purples and reds. Cole's eyes connected with his and he felt a strange feeling pass over him as if he could sense the man's strength. The man nodded as they passed and Cole turned his head to get one last glance of the stranger.

"That would be the Tinker," Merryrick replied.

"What do you think he can do?" Cole asked curiously.

"Hard to tell, but we will find out soon enough," Merryrick answered.

A SHORT TIME LATER Cole pulled Gladadear to a stop, jumping from the wagon, he started to unload.

"Why did the Tinker come this year Merryrick? We've never had one come before," Cole asked as he pulled long wooden poles out from the back of the wagon.

"I do not know. But when a Tinker arrives danger usually follows," Merryrick answered, watching as Cole began to set up their pavilion.

"What does that mean?" Cole asked.

"No idea. Just an old saying," Merryrick answered.

Cole went to work hammering four long poles into the ground and made sure they stood straight and were placed deep into the ground before he tied four more long poles, horizontally to the vertical poles, creating a square like structure. He then laid canvas on top and using ropes, pulleys and stakes he tightened down the canvas, creating a cool and shady spot that would serve not only for selling and displaying their wares but also as living quarters for the next few days. After the canopy was completed, and as Cole started helping Merryrick unload the larger items, he heard a familiar voice calling his name.

"Cole," a cheerful voice yelled.

Cole turned to see Maggie and her father walking towards them.

"Hello Maggie, hello Master Wallace," Cole muttered softly when the girl and her father had come to a stop in front of him.

"Good to see you Cole," Wallace said, "I was beginning to think that you and Merryrick would not be coming. But Maggie assured me you would. She said that you are entering the archery contest?"

"I... ah," Cole started to say.

"Well my bet is on you. Merryrick is here obviously?" Wallace stated and then disappeared under the canopy, leaving Maggie to talk with Cole.

"It's good you made it. Isn't this wonderful? I've never met a Tinker before. "Father said he met one when he was younger,"

Maggie spouted with excitement, only taking a breath as she finished her sentence. "So are you ready?" Maggie inquired looking into the cart.

"Ready for what?" Cole asked as he pulled a wooden chair from the cart.

"The archery contest, silly," Maggie said, following Cole under the canopy.

"Ah… Margaret so nice to see you again," Merryrick said. He abruptly stopped his conversation with Wallace but before he did Cole thought he heard him tell Wallace "It seems he is waking up."

"It's nice to see you too Master Merryrick," Maggie replied, giving a curtsy to Merryrick.

"Come now, Margaret, there is no need to curtsy to me. I am not important enough to receive one such as that," Merryrick smiled. "But since you have given it to me I will take it and give you one in return. Though I fear it will not be as graceful or as delightful as yours."

Merryrick clasp his hands together behind his back and then bent forward, bowing towards Maggie. "There now was that not impressive. I am delighted with myself that I did not fall flat on my face," Merryrick chuckled.

"Now what's this about you entering the archery contest?" Merryrick questioned, turning his attention to Cole.

"Cole said he would enter the contest this year. I know he'll win Master Merryrick!" Maggie cried, stomping her foot on the green grass.

"Did you say that?" Merryrick asked looking at Cole.

"Yes Master Merryrick, but if you don't want me too…" Cole mumbled.

"Nonsense Cole, you are a very fine archer. Why would I not want you to enter,"

"Yes but…what about…" Cole tried to say.

"After all I'm the one that taught you," Merryrick said, ignoring Cole's small protest. "A master should encourage his apprentices to take on challenges and seeing that you are my apprentice you should enter the contest. Well now, what are you standing around here for, you had better go and sign up. We would not want to disappoint our fair young lady friend here, now would we?" Merryrick chided. "Go along Cole, get your bow. Wallace and I will finish unpacking."

"Are you sure Master...I could..." Cole stammered.

"Go, go my dear boy," Merryrick asserted pushing Cole towards Maggie.

"Come on Cole," Maggie said, seizing his hand and dragging him out from under the canopy and into the morning sun.

As Maggie pulled Cole away past the cart, he managed to grab his bow and quiver of arrows before Maggie yanked his arm off. The sign-up for the archery competition was at the other end of the green, at the White Rose Tavern. Maggie pulled Cole along with such force that there was no possibility of digging in his heels, though he made several attempts. As the two crossed the green, they wound through the maze of tents, booths and pavilions and passed a crowd that was gathered around in a circle. Curious as to what was going on, Cole managed to escape Maggie's grip and made his way back to the crowd. Just as he reached the outskirts of the gathering crowd, a large cloud of flames erupted into the air. The shouts and screams of excited boys and girls echoed as they marveled at the youngish man standing in front of them. He held not just one lit torch but three torches. Two in one hand and the other he put up closely to his mouth and blew. Cole stepped back in surprise as another burst of flames exploded into the air. He knew right off that the young man was the Tinker.

After the Tinker had let out another cloud of flames he started juggling the three torches, throwing one torch in the air just as another fell into his recently emptied hand. As Cole watched the young man, he realized that the Tinker was watching him, staring at him with unblinking eyes, as he juggled one torch after another.

"Come on Cole," Maggie said, eagerly pulling at Cole.

"Maggie, I wanted to see him finish," Cole exclaimed in awe.

"You can watch him later. After you sign up for the contest," Maggie insisted.

Cole blew out a breath of air, shrugged his shoulders and followed Maggie, climbing up the small hill towards the village and to the White Rose tavern.

The village of Kells was small with only two dozen or so homes, built around the green and along the main road, the only road in Kells. The houses were made of white stone and red timber, some with thatched peaked roofs, while others were shingled. Smoke rose from most of the chimneys, filling the air with the fragrance of burning wood. Maple, oak and pine trees grew along the roadside creating an alleyway of branches and leaves.

The White Rose was the tallest building in the small village, set in the middle of Kells. It was an impressive building, built from red oak and white stone from the riverbed. The two-story tavern held a few extra rooms and was the only one of its kind. The common room was so large that it fit all the villagers inside and was run by Master Morell and his wife.

When they reached the White Rose a crowd of men of all ages were gathered around. Each man was signing up for certain events in the competitions that they wanted to participate in. Many of the older village men were signing up for the lighter events such as the ring toss or horseshoes, while the younger more robust men, were signing up for the stone throw and caber toss. The farmers waited in line for the sheep-shearing contest and sheepdog herding competitions.

"Come on who's next to sign up," a voice called out.

Maggie pushed Cole up to the sign-up table where he was greeted with the musical voice of Sir Arthur, the mayor of the village.

"Good morning Cole."

"Good morning, Sir Arthur," Cole said softly.

"Signing up at last for the archery competition? That's a good lad," Arthur said. "Do you have a new bow?" Arthur inquired looking at the bow slung across Cole's shoulder.

"No it's still the old one," Cole replied, pulling it off his shoulder and handing it to Arthur.

Arthur took the bow and rubbed his hands across the smooth white wood. It was a unique bow, not like any of the Kell's bows that were made from a single piece of wood like yew, ash or elm. Cole's bow was slightly curved and appeared to be made from several different types of white woods with bluish veins running through them. The handle, which held the grip, was not made from the skins of animals but rather a metal. The grip was molded with finger placments and the handle was waves of different shades of blues.

"It is an amazing bow. The offer I made you for it still stands," Arthur said.

"No thanks, Sir Arthur. I like my bow too much," Cole muttered, taking it back and slinging it back over his shoulder.

"It's alright lad, I understand. Speaking of bows, have you made any new ones this year?"

"Yes sir, I have made two," Cole said, dipping the quill into the inkbottle.

"Wonderful I shall be around to purchase one, along with those fine arrows you make. Now you will be in the last round of the competition. It starts at noon and may I say you have excellent penmanship."

"Thank you, Sir Arthur," Cole said, putting down the quill.

"Yes, far better than my son's, lazy boy. Can hardly write his own name."

Not too far away, Cole spotted Sir Arthur's son Artemis, standing behind his father with a group of village boys. He was a tall fair-haired boy, with cold blue eyes and a hard stone expression on his face.

Cole said nothing but turned and walked away.

He and Maggie started walking across the green, back towards Merryrick's booth. They were silent at first, not saying anything, but then Maggie, not being able to hold her excitement in anymore, suddenly broke the silence.

"So how does it feel?" She asked excitedly.

"How does what feel?" Cole asked with raised eyebrows.

"You have just entered the archery contest! How does it feel?"

"Fine. I didn't see Chanlyn's name on the list though."

"Maybe he hasn't come yet. I haven't seen him all morning. So what will you name the horse that Sir Arthur is offering as the prize this year? I was thinking Cloud or Thunder or…?" Maggie chattered.

"I haven't won Maggie and I don't think that I will."

"Oh pah, you are one of the best archers in Kells. Father even said so himself," Maggie encouraged with pride in her voice. "You are even better than Artemis and everyone here in the village knows it."

"That may or may not be true Maggie. However, I saw a lot of other names on the list and they are all very good archers as well," Cole muttered.

"Cole, you underestimate yourself. I have seen you hit targets hundreds of leagues away," Maggie said.

"You are exaggerating," Cole said calmly.

"Maybe a little," Maggie said, stepping in front of Cole making him stop. "But there is something in you Cole. You were born to do great things. I may not know what they are yet, but be assured you are great."

Cole looked at Maggie. She was smiling at him. Her smile was one of the most beautiful smiles that he had ever seen. When she smiled it showed off her dimples and made her eyes dance. A smile from her and his whole day went right.

"Here, I made you something," Maggie said, pulling out a small object from her belt pouch. It was wrapped in blue cloth and was tied with a red ribbon. Cole took the package in his hands and admired the smooth silky cloth and the bright red ribbon.

"Well go on," Maggie said nudging Cole in the side with her elbow.

Smiling, Cole unwrapped the gift and found that the blue cloth had been embroidered with pink and white wild roses. They looked almost real. Cole rubbed his fingers across the stitching. The thread was soft and smooth to the touch. Putting it to his nose he smelled the flower. Instead of smelling the scent of wild roses, he took in the scent of lavender and honeysuckle. The fragrance reminded Cole of Maggie when she smiled. Pulling the cloth away from his nose he looked at Maggie.

"Did you do this?" Cole asked, letting the blue cloth run through his fingers.

"Yes. I know it's not very good. But it was one of the best I did this winter."

"No, it is very good. They look so real."

"Is that why you smelled them?" Maggie asked with a humorous smile.

Cole nodded his head as he looked down at the flowers again.

The women of Kells took pride in their needlework and Festival was the time to show off their skills. They all dressed in whites, pale blues, greens and yellows, but what caught the eye were the bright, embroidered patterns of flowers and leaves arranged on the skirts and bodices of the girl's and women's dresses. Even the husbands and sons had a few vines creeping up their sleeves and around their collars. The women and girls worked through the long winter months designing and creating elegant patterns.

Cole looked Maggie over and saw that she too had worked hard on embroidering a pattern on her dress. Dressed in green to match the silver and green stone necklace that she wore, Maggie had stitched tiny red roses along the skirt, sleeves and bodice. Each rose sprouted tiny little deep green leaves that grew into thin vines. The vines then wound and curled around the dress. Cole knew that it must have taken Maggie ages to do such small stitching.

"Did you do your dress as well," Cole asked.

"Yes," replied Maggie.

"It's beautiful," Cole replied. "It matches well with your necklace."

"Thank you. Father gave me the necklace just this morning. He said it belonged to my grandmother," Maggie said, as she felt her cheeks burn red with delight.

"It looks nice on you." Cole said.

"Thank you Maggie for the handkerchief. I will always take care of it," Cole said, rewrapping the cloth in the red ribbon then placing the handkerchief in his belt pouch.

"Well, what do we have here?" said an all too familiar sour voice from behind.

Maggie and Cole turned their heads and found Artemis and his band of village boys standing around them, blocking their way.

"We are all going for a swim in the lake. Care to come with us stable boy?" Artemis jeered.

"Ignore them," Maggie whispered.

"Oh, but I forgot the stable boy here cannot swim, he is too afraid of the water," Artemis mocked.

The other boys mocking laughter sung through the air.

Maggie's face started growing red with anger. "Shut your mouth you toad!" Maggie screamed.

"I would suggest you leave them alone," another voice said from behind Cole, and Maggie.

Cole turned to see the Tinker walk up and stop just next to Cole. He was taller than Cole and looked at least five years his senior.

"What's this, you got a girl and a vagrant to fight your battles for you, stable boy," Artemis heckled.

"I don't have any battles to fight Artemis, not with you or anyone else," Cole said, taking Maggie by the hand. "Come on Maggie, as you say just ignore them," Cole whispered softly.

Maggie looked at Cole and then at Artemis, and slowly the rage left and a queen like manner began to appear. "Come Cole, let these foolish little boys have their swim." Maggie said graciously. "You have a contest to win," She said as she pushed her way passed Artemis and his friends, knocking them back.

"How dare you!" Artemis roared.

"How dare you," Maggie said, turning to look Artemis directly in the face.

"My father is the mayor of this town and I shall have you pay for your insults." Artemis spat. He raised his hand to backhand Maggie across the face, but before he could, Cole caught Artemis's wrist in his bare hand.

Blinding light burned before his eyes and he had to close them from the sudden brightness. When he opened them he found himself surrounded by a circle of fire. He saw that he was standing in a room that was swallowed in flames. Somewhere within the room he could hear a child crying. Looking past the smoke that burned his lungs and stung his eyes, he saw a small boy no more than four or five. He sat cowering in a corner, as the flames grew ever closer to him.

"Artemis! Artemis, where are you?" the voice of a young woman wailed. "Artemis!" The voice was frantic, hysterical with anxiety. "Artemis it's not your fault."

There was another brilliant flash of light and Cole was back in his own reality again.

"It's not your fault," Cole muttered dizzily.

"What did you say?" Artemis' voice rang out cold.

"It's not your fault." Cole said again.

Artemis's temper blew as he pulled back his fist and clobbered Cole in the face.

Warm blood ran from Cole's nose and lips as he fell to the ground dazed.

"Get up stable boy. Get up and fight me. Or are you afraid?" Artemis cried, kicking Cole in the gut. "Afraid to fight me?"

"Leave him alone, Artemis," Maggie yelled, jumping up on Artemis' back and pounding her fist into him. Artemis shrugged her off and she fell back hitting her head on the hard ground. Cole saw Maggie fall, but she didn't get back up, and she wasn't moving. The Tinker seeing Maggie fall rushed towards her.

"Maggie!" Cole cried. "What did you do?" he yelled jumping to his feet and grabbing Artemis by the wrist. "What did you do?"

Cole rarely gave into his anger, but when he saw Maggie lying still on the ground, something within him snapped. A cold rage washed over him igniting a fire. The fire burned, running down his arms and into his hands and fingers. It was a rage that he had never felt before, a rage that threatened to consume him.

Artemis let out a cry and twisted his wrist free from Cole. He then threw a punch that made Cole's head jerk to the side. Cole slowly turned his head back around and looked at the mayor's son with a gaze that made the marrow in Artemis' bones freeze.

Burn him, a voice whispered within Cole's head. *Burn him where he stands.*

"Cole your hands!" Maggie cried.

Maggie's cry seemed to break through the wall of anger that surrounded Cole. He looked back at Maggie still filled with anger.

"Cole," she whispered with fear in her voice.

Cole saw the fear in her eyes and suddenly the anger within him faded away leaving him very weak. With Cole's attention turned elsewhere, Artemis took the opportunity to sock Cole in the stomach.

"You really are a freak of nature," Artemis said, looking down at Cole with his cold blue eyes.

The boys of the village laughed and looked at Cole with mocking smiles. Artemis raised his fist to take another strike at Cole but the Tinker stepped in and blocked the blow, catching Artemis's wrist.

"That's enough," the Tinker snapped.

Artemis tried to jerk his hand free from the Tinker's hold but he held Artemis in a vise like grip. Artemis's anger then turned from Cole to the Tinker and Artemis pulled back his other arm to strike the fire juggler. The Tinker anticipated the hit and caught Artemis' other hand. He threw Artemis away from him and the boy stumbled back.

"I said that was enough," the Tinker spoke softly, but there was anger in his voice. "Now get going with you," the Tinker snapped.

The boys that shadowed Artemis bolted and ran, but Artemis stayed and glared at the Tinker and then he let his gaze slide down and he moved away. When Artemis was gone the Tinker turned to Cole, who was still on the ground feeling suddenly dizzy and terribly weak.

"Cole?" Maggie cried, rushing over to his side. "Let me see your hands," she cried.

"They're fine, Maggie," Cole said.

"They were on fire Cole! And they're probably burned to a crisp now. Let me see them," Maggie ordered.

"I told you Maggie they're fine," Cole said, reluctant to show his hands.

"Show me your hands," she demanded.

Cole let out a breath and presented his hands to her. Maggie took his hands and flipped them over examining them.

"They're fine," Maggie said in disbelief.

"I told you they were," Cole said. But Cole was confused himself as to what had just happened to him.

"I could have sworn they were on fire," Maggie said rubbing the back of her head. "I guess I hit my head harder than I thought," she murmured.

"Are you two alright?" the Tinker asked, squatting down in front of them.

"Fine," Cole muttered.

"We should get you to Merryrick," Maggie said softly.

"What about you?" Cole asked.

"It is just a little bump, nothing to worry about. You on the other hand look as though you've been in a fight."

"I have been in a fight," Cole groaned, then made an attempt to stand. He stood for only a second before a wave of dizziness sent him back to the ground.

"That blow must have knocked you right silly," Maggie said digging into her belt pouch and pulling out a small terracotta container.

"More ginger root?" Cole questioned.

"No it's yarrow salve. It will heal your bruises and bring down the swelling from around your eye," Maggie said, as she tried to rub the balm across Cole's blackening eye, but he jerked his head back away, so she gave him the pot and he did it himself.

"I'll give you the ginger for the pain when we get back to Merryrick's tent."

After Cole had finished rubbing the yellow salve on his bruises he attempted to get to his feet again, this time he stayed on them.

"Here let me help you," the Tinker said.

"I'm fine thank you," Cole muttered.

"You most certainly are not fine," Maggie chided. "You look paler than a ghost. Let him help you!"

"No really, I'm fine," Cole said.

But after taking a couple of steps and falling forward he was more willing to accept the help.

CHAPTER 3

"MUST HAVE BEEN some fight," Merryrick's voice rung in Cole's ears. Cole opened his eyes to find Merryrick standing before him as he handed him a mug that was steaming hot.

"Be sure to drink it all. It may smell bad but it will help," Maggie more or less commanded.

Cole sat in one of Merryrick's chairs looking down into the murky brown liquid that was in the mug. She wasn't kidding about the smell. To Cole the concoction reminded him of rotting mushrooms. He wouldn't have been surprise if the tea did contained decaying mushrooms.

He took a deep breath, plugged his nose and put the cup to his lips and filled his mouth with the brown brew. He nearly spit the whole thing out because of the bitter taste, however Merryrick slapped him on the back and Cole swallowed, his body cringing as the potion went down.

"That was foul," Cole said.

"Serves you right. I have told you more than once Cole, to stay away from that boy," Merryrick stated. "He only causes you pain."

"It wasn't really his fault," the Tinker volunteered. "That boy, Artemis, was the one causing trouble. He was about to strike the young lady for insulting him."

"Is that true Maggie?" Wallace asked, turning to his daughter. Maggie looked up from her spot near Merryrick's fire.

"He was so childish. Yes I called him a toad and yes he was going to strike me but then Cole stopped him and they got in a bit of a fight when I hit my head and got knocked out for a minute, then Cole's hands caught on fire."

"Cole's hands caught on fire?" Merryrick asked, turning to Cole to check his hands.

"Well I thought they did but I think that I must have been dreaming it, because Cole's hands are fine," Maggie blurted out.

"Where did you hit your head?" Wallace asked with concern.

"I'm fine father," Maggie squeaked.

With everyone's attention on Maggie, Merryrick bent over Cole as he looked over the boy's cuts.

"Did you touch Artemis?" Merryrick whispered in Cole's ear.

Coke nodded his head.

"With your bare hands?"

Again Cole nodded.

"And your hands did they really catch fire?" Merryrick asked softly.

Cole shrugged his shoulders, "I don't know? I was a little preoccupied trying not to become unconscious. But something strange did happen when I touched Artemis. I felt anger like I never have before. I don't know if it was mine or Artemis'."

"Mmm, we'll talk about this later," Merryrick whispered, seeing the Tinker eyes falling on them.

Maggie perhaps we should have you drink some of your healing tea," Wallace said.

"No. I'm fine," Maggie replied hurriedly.

The smell of the healing tea still lingered in the air and as she looked over at Cole she saw he was looking a little green in the face from it.

"Speaking of Tinkers, Maggie would you like to introduce your new friend," Merryrick replied, turning to the Tinker.

"Oh this is…well I really don't know," Maggie answered.

"My name is Gildon," the Tinker replied. "But you can call me Tinker or Gildon. I answer to both."

"Well, welcome, Tinker Gildon. I am Master Merryrick, and this here is Master Wallace," Merryrick said indicating to Wallace, "and you have already met Maggie and Cole. We are much honored to have you here for the Festival," Merryrick expressed, "and also for helping young Cole here."

"I thank you," Gildon replied with a polite nod.

"If I may ask Master Tinker," Wallace asked, "How did you find us? Not many know that our little hamlet even exists. So we do not get many visitors here in Kells."

"Oh there are stories about you on the other side of the mountains," Gildon said.

"Stories!" Wallace asked, "What sort of stories?"

"Well when I was younger, just a child, I was told a story about a
band of Albavarians that escaped the The War of Shelrin by going
over the Elfire Mountains, and they were never seen again. Ever since
then…"

"You wanted to see if the story was true then," Merryrick asked.

"Yes." Gildon answered.

"But you have another purpose for finding us don't you?"
Merryrick inquired.

"Is it that obvious?" Gildon asked.

"No one comes over the Elfire Mountains when it is still winter
to see if there is a hidden village on the other side. Now please what
is your purpose?"

"I did not go over the mountains that would be foolish. But I rather
went around them, and yes I have another purpose for being here."

"And that would be?" Merryrick inquired.

"Well, I feel you might think me a little foolish when I explain my
reason for coming," Gildon said.

"Try us," Wallace answered.

"Have you ever heard of the foretellings by the great Elfain
Warrior Ayden?"

The Tinker was met with silence.

"You have heard of the Elfain Warriors, have you not?" Gildon
asked.

"I don't believe I have," Maggie injected, as she followed the conversation.

"Of course you have Maggie," Merryrick said. "They were great men
and women that for five hundred years were the guardians of peace and
justice of the old kingdom of Albavar. This was before the dark time, before the rule of Shelrin. Your father no doubt has told you the legend of
the first seven Elfain Warriors the ones that defeated the shadow King."

"You mean with Ayden, Gracelyn, Kirkwell. Skylar, Dresden,
Alberdeen and Lochlynn. Oh yes, father used to tell them to me all the
time when I was going to bed," Maggie replied.

"Well Ayden, was gifted with the foresight of seeing the future and he wrote down what he saw after the defeat of the Dark King. Foresight of visions became known as the Foretellings." Merryrick explained. "Is that not so Master Gildon?"

"Correct," Gildon answered. "Many of the foretellings have already come to pass."

"But I thought that they were just myths and legends," Maggie remarked, "something to tell children to entertain them."

"No they were as real as you and I are now," Gildon said, "for there would be no spirit wielders, who are the descendants of the Elfain Warriors. I believe that there are those that carry the true bloodline of the Elfain Warriors and that through those bloodlines the seven warriors will arise. I have traveled all across Albavar, visiting villages, in hope that I might find those that hold the potential to be the warriors. That is also my reason for being here. In one of Ayden's foretellings it states that a great darkness would arise from the ashes of a black dragon, yet as the darkness arose, so too would the seven Warriors rise. These Warriors would then fight the evil that would rise across the land. It also tells that some of these warriors would come from the shadow of the fire mounts."

"So you think that you will find these foreseen warriors here?" Merryrick asked,

"I believe so," Gildon answered.

"Why?" Merryrick simply asked.

"When Shelrin's empire took control, many of the old families that bore the blood of the seven warriors were killed. Few remained that had the capabilities to wield and fewer that were true Elfains. If some of the Elfain families made it over the mountains, then maybe there is the possibility that there are some among you that are true Elfains," Gildon spoke, his voice rising with excitement.

"And if you find these potential heirs of the Warriors, these true Elfains what would you have them do?" Merryrick asked, with curiosity.

"I will invite them to come back to my home city Aloria. So they can be trained in the old ways of the Elfains," Gildon simply replied. "Even if they do not have the potential of being one of the seven,

I would still invite them to come with me and to learn how to control their gifts of wielding."

"What is wielding?" Maggie interrupted. "What exactly is that?"

"Certain individuals are born with what we Tinkers call spirits. They have the capability to bend the winds or move the earth. Some can control water or fire, others can hide in shadows and not be detected and on rare occasions, very rare, there are some that can see the future. I, myself, am a Fire wielder."

Maggie let out a cry of amazement as small little sparks flew from Gildon's fingertips into the air.

"You might not want to show that gift around the village here," Merryrick said softly. "There are some who might not take kindly to someone with power like yours." The Tinker nodded in acknowledgement.

"So who is it that you train?" Wallace asked, not very impressed with what he saw.

"And who trains these wielders? From my understanding all the Masters were hunted down and condemned to death," Merryrick questioned.

"There are still a few living warriors that remember the old ways. Although they are not full Masters, they teach others what they can. We try and help them learn to control their spirit, so they don't hurt themselves or others."

"These heirs you hope to find, how old would you think them to be?" Wallace asked.

"They could be any age," Gildon responded.

"Could they be my age?" Maggie asked. "Or Master Wilkins? I'll bet he's a wielder. I've seen him do some strange things. In fact, I bet you're a wielder Cole, a fire wielder, like Gildon. It would explain why your hands caught on fire and didn't burn you," Maggie put in.

"I'm not a fire wielder," Cole muttered.

Gildon turned and looked at the boy seriously.

Cole sat slumped in his chair with his head down. He looked tired and drained of energy, a sure sign that he had used too much of his spirit, but then again he was just in a fight and received quite a beating. Yet when he first saw the boy he had felt something, something that he had never felt before. It was as if he could feel the boy's strength within him, and it was strong, like a great furnace burning with a pure white light. But the moment only lasted for a few seconds and then the feeling was gone. It was so quick that Gildon thought that it was just his imagination and paid it no heed. Until he felt that same feeling again when he saw the boy watching him when he did his first performance.

"Could it be?" Gildon thought to himself. "Have I really found one of them?"

Gildon was about to ask about this boy named Cole when all at once Cole suddenly jumped to his feet claiming that his mouth was on fire.

"Ah, the wild ginger has taken effect," said Maggie smiling. "That means the tea is working."

Cole's face turned bright red and tears had started streaming down his cheeks. Maggie placed in Cole's hand another wooden cup, which contained a concoction that she had made before hand. Cole looked down into the cup with caution.

"It is apple tea, Cole. It will quench the fire that burns in your mouth," Maggie answered, seeing his suspicion. Cole quickly swallowed down the amber liquid and the fire went out.

"Better?" Maggie asked.

Cole realized that he was better. He wasn't so tired anymore and the pain in his face and head had gone. He felt as if he had just woken up after a long night's sleep.

"Better!" Cole replied, with a bright smile.

"Good! Can't have you feeling ill for the contest, now can we? How's your eye? The swelling seems to have gone down, but you'll have a black eye for some time," Maggie said.

"If I may, what contest is this?" Gildon inquired.

"The archery contest!" Maggie said proudly. "And Cole is the best archer in all of Kells."

"Indeed he is and not a bad bowyer either," Merryrick remarked.

Gildon looked over at Cole, who sat somewhat awkwardly with all the attention on him.

"I am in need of a good bow," Gildon said. "Perhaps you might show me the ones you have constructed."

Cole looked over at Merryrick as if asking permission.

"Come Cole, show Tinker Gildon your bows," Merryrick instructed.

Cole quickly turned around and exited the canopy to where the cart was parked. In moments he was back with two carrying cases and two quivers with about thirty arrows in each one. Cole opened one case and pulled out a rolled up piece of soft leather. He carefully unrolled the cloth and in seconds the bow was revealed. There was a notable gasp from Gildon and even Wallace's eyes widened in amazement.

"The bow is made of unblemished Yew. The belly is made from the heartwood while the back is made of sapwood. The sapwood is good on the tension while the heartwood is good for compression. Sinew has been glued to the belly giving the bow strength and elasticity," Cole explained, pointing out each part of the bow as he described it. "The yew wood is light weight and holds its shape very well. The bow itself is longer than most bows in Kells but it is stronger and can shoot farther. The bowstring is made of flax, woven together to create strength and is coated in wax to prevent water from seeping in. The nocks on the top and bottom of the bow are made of deer bone."

Cole set down the bow on the cloth and pulled out one of the arrows from a quiver. "The arrow shafts are made of ash wood and are twenty-seven thumbs length. The fletching are goose feathers and the nocks are of the same deer bone," Cole reported, repeating what he did with the bow, pointing out each part to Gildon. "The arrow heads are made by the finest blacksmith in Kells. The quivers are made from deer hide and have a hood cover to protect the arrows from rain and snow. It's worn on the back for easy access to the arrows."

"And the other bow, what of it?" Gildon inquired.

"It is constructed in the same manner. Except perhaps a little taller," Cole replied picking up the second case and revealing the second bow.

With careful hands, Gildon picked up one of the bows, running his hands up and down the length of the bow. It was smooth and the grip felt good in his hands. He could see that there were no imperfections in the wood. He knew that it must have taken Cole ages to find such excellent wood to make such fine bows. Gildon could only imagine the time Cole spent to make the bows themselves.

"Your son is indeed a master bow maker. I have only once before seen one bow like these and that bow was said to have belonged to Kayden, that great warrior we mentioned before. I would be afraid that I would damage it in some way," Gildon said, placing the bow back into Cole hands.

"Oh…I'm not," Cole started to say but Merryrick cut him off.

"Thank you," Merryrick responded.

Cole looked over at Merryrick with surprise. Everyone in Kells knew that Cole was not Merryrick's son, but he had not divulged that information to Gildon and he wondered why as he turned back to Gildon.

"I do not imagine you could do anything to this bow that I have not already done to my own, and mine is still in excellent shape. These bows are fashioned after my own and I have had mine at least six seasons."

"May I see your bow?" Gildon asked.

Cole pulled his bow from its case that hung across his shoulder and handed it to Gildon. The Tinker looked at the bow and ran his hands over the white wood.

"This bow looks very similar to one I saw in Aloria, the one that was Kayden's. Where did you get your bow?" Gildon asked, with great interest as he handed the bow back to Cole.

"It was a gift," Cole replied, "from Merryrick."

"For his birthday, made it myself," Merryrick said. "Oh it was a fine present. Cole nearly flew to the moon with excitement when I presented it to him."

The memory of receiving the bow played out in Cole's mind. He had just turned the age of eight and Merryrick had presented him with the bow. It had been too big for him at the time, but Merryrick had told him that he would grow into it. The day that Merryrick gave Cole the bow he was told that it was time for his training to begin. At the time Cole didn't understand what Merryrick was talking about. In fact he still didn't know what Merryrick had been talking about.

The sudden sound of bells ringing broke through Cole's thoughts and made everyone turn and look towards the green. "The competitions are about to begin!" Maggie cried. "Come on Cole!"

"Maggie, I'm in the last round," Cole said, turning around to look at her.

"So! We have to see who you will be up against," Maggie said.

Maggie had now grabbed on to Cole's arm and was yanking on it. Both Merryrick and Wallace laughed at Maggie's enthusiasm.

"Come! We shall all go and watch the contest. Master Gildon will you please join Master Wallace and me as we watch from the sidelines, I would like to know more about this…school you have," Merryrick asked.

"I would be delighted," Gildon said, raising a hand to his chest and bowing slightly. The flaps of the canopy were quickly pulled down and secured for safekeeping. Cole followed the others as they made their way to where the competitions would take place.

The contests were the main entertainment of the fair. First, there would be the archery contest, then the caber toss and finally the races. Usually the events went on throughout the day. People would come and watch their loved ones compete in certain events, and then leave to go and enjoy the rest of the fair. Today however it seemed that everyone from the village was in attendance. The village green was packed with all the villagers and farmers that had come to enjoy the festivities. Women and men brought chairs to sit on, while the children sat on the grass, waiting for the first round of archers to take their place and ready their bows.

"Good luck my boy, we're counting on you," said Merryrick, patting Cole on the shoulder then went to find a seat with Wallace.

With a lost expression on his face, Cole looked over at Maggie. The girl shrugged her shoulders signifying that she did not understand what Merryrick was talking about any more than he did.

"What did he mean that he's counting on me?" Cole asked, out loud as he watched Wallace and Merryrick.

"I believe that he was referring to the bets that were made," Gildon said. "It seems that there is a wager between you and a man named Sir Arthur, no wait, it is his son they have bet on."

"The whole village is betting on Cole to win?" Maggie said, jumping with excitement.

"Not to win, but to lose."

This reply brought red anger to Maggie's face.

"What's the wager?" Cole asked softly.

"There are many wagers. One in particular is of interest. One man has bet his horse, saying that you will win, while the other man has bet his whole store of ale that you will lose and Sir Arthur's son will win. Apparently the horse is a rather valuable beast and the ale is of great value as well."

"This man that has bet his horse would not be my father, would he?" Maggie asked, with a little terror and anger ringing in her voice.

"I believe it is. And the other is Master Morell," Gildon said. "Now if you'll excuse me the first round has started," Gildon gave a nod to Cole and bowed to Maggie and then departed, walking over to where Merryrick sat.

Cole stood silent. Thoughts raced through his head. He felt a little light headed and sick again. Sweat started to bead across his forehead from nerves and his insides had turned to knots. It only got worse when Maggie spun around to face him.

"You had better win, Cole, or I'll tan your hide so hard your fight with Artemis will be a simple beating to what I'll do to you," she shouted.

Cole did not answer, for fear that something would come up and out that was not supposed to if he should open his mouth. All he could manage was a nod of his head.

"Good, now the first round is over. It will not be long before you show all these people what archery really is," Maggie said, turning from Cole to watch the first round of archers walk off the field.

"Maggie, I don't think I can do this," Cole said shakily.

Once again Maggie whirled around to face Cole. "Of course you can. Just think of it as if we're in the woods practicing," Maggie said, looking Cole up and down with a worried eye, for his face was turning a little greenish in color again.

"This is not the woods," Cole said, wiping his hand across his forehead. "People don't bet on me in the woods, especially your father! Maybe I should not even go out there."

"Cole, look at me," Maggie said, taking Cole by the shoulders so he was forced to look down into her eyes.

"If you do not go out there and at least try, then my father has already lost Brom to that sniffling skin flint Morell."

Maggie words made sense, but they did not stop the butterflies in Cole's stomach from fluttering about.

The names of the next round of archers were called to stand in front of their targets. Cole was feeling as if he were about to run off and be sick in the bushes, when suddenly he felt a great cloud of relief settle over him when he heard Chanlyn's name being announced by Master Wilkins, who was one of the judges. Chanlyn stepped out onto the field and took his stance in front of one of the targets, with his bow and arrow in his hands.

Each contestant was allowed to shoot one arrow each round. Whoever got their arrow closest to the center of the target would then go on to the next round. As each round progressed, the targets of straw would be moved farther back and the same process would continue until there were only two opponents left.

"Gentleman! Take your aim," Master Wilkins yelled. "Fire when ready."

Each man took his time but eventually each one let his arrows fly. It was apparent that Chanlyn would be the one in the second round to move on. Many of the participants were good shots and all got their arrows to the target but not nearly as close to the center as Chanlyn's. As the judges went to examine the targets, Chanlyn came rushing off the field towards Cole and Maggie.

"You entered!" Maggie said, with excitement.

"I told you I would, if Cole did," Chanlyn said, a little out of breath.

"But I didn't see your name on the list," Cole said.

"I waited until I saw you sign up, then I signed up," Chanlyn answered.

"Why didn't you come find us afterwards?" Maggie asked, as she watched the next competitors take their stands.

"I had to help father for a bit," Chanlyn said shrugging his shoulders.

"Oh, well you did very well," Maggie said congratulating Chanlyn on his performance. "Artemis is in this round," she said angrily.

When Artemis' name was called some of the people in the crowd cheered.

"Boo! Boo!" Maggie yelled.

Like before, the men took up their bows and aimed. Maggie watched intently as each competitor let his arrow fly. With Maggie's full attention on the contest, Chanlyn leaned over and whispered into Cole's ear.

"I wasn't really helping father, I was trying to stay away from Maggie. I knew that she would make me nervous."

"I know what you mean," Cole whispered back.

"Oh no!" Maggie suddenly cried out.

Cole and Chanlyn knew what that cry meant. Artemis had won this round and would continue on to the next challenge. Two more rounds went by and out of them came Creed Sanderson and Luke Morell.

Cole's stomach gave a lurch as he realized that he was next.

"You're up next Cole, now remember to aim carefully. Don't rush it and…"

"Maggie!" Chanlyn cried breaking up Maggie's rushing words.

"What?" She asked, looking over at Chanlyn.

"Leave him be, this is Cole, not some child that has just picked up a bow."

Maggie opened her mouth to say more, but before she could get anything out Master Wilkins called out the names of those who were in the last round.

"William McTavish, Todd Hopkins, Clayton Goodfold, Shawn Fairfield and Cole of Fletcher Farm, please step forward and take your stands in front of your targets."

Taking in a giant gulp of air, Cole stepped onto the field. His being the last name called, he got the last target on the green.

"Gentleman, ready your bows," Wilkins cried.

With slightly shaking hands, Cole strung his bow then he pulled out one of his best arrows from his quiver and placed it in the ground, signifying that his bow was strung and he was ready to fire.

"Gentleman take your aim and fire when ready," Wilkins yelled, when all the men had placed their arrows in the ground. Each man pulled free their arrows from the earth and nocked them on their bowstrings. One after another they let their arrows fly until Cole was the only one left who had not let loose his arrow.

Cole's heart was racing. He felt his breath come in great heaves and he started to shake. He stood with his arrow drawn until the feathers touched his cheek, ready at any moment to let it fly; all he was waiting for was that right moment. He knew that all eyes were on him and he could feel their gaze directed at him.

"Calm down, just calm down," he told himself.

Closing his eyes Cole took in a deep breath forcing his body to relax. He started counting in his head, slowly letting out the deep breaths of air as he said each number in his head and gradually he felt the world fade away. He ignored all the people, let them fade away; let them disappear into the back corners of his mind until they were nothing but a small, minuscule thought. Still he waited. Then suddenly the moment came. A small breath of wind came up and tickled his cheek.

Awaken, Cole heard a voice say within his mind.

It was then that Cole snapped opened his eyes and let his arrow fly from his bow. It flew fast and straight. The wind carried it on its back and delivered the arrow into the center of the straw target.

The people sat in silence, looking from Cole to the target and then back. Even Gildon was lost for words. All he could do was stare, wide-eyed, like the rest of the villagers. And at that moment he knew.

After a minute or so the spectators seemed to waken from their amazement. A sudden burst of cheers exploded from almost every mouth of those who were watching. Master Morell however looked as if he was going to fall down to the ground and burst into tears.

Cole let himself smile as he stepped off the field but when he saw the face of Maggie, the smile faded. She looked confused and a little terrified.

"How'd you do that?" Chanlyn asked, as Cole came to stand next to him.

"Do what?" Cole asked, trying not to look into Maggie's eyes.

"Cole, you've never shot like that before. It was as if your arrow….it was as if…as if your arrow was a lightning bolt, striking so fast and so precise. At one moment I thought the target would burst into flames," Chanlyn said, wide eyed. "It was so…amazing! Perhaps you will win," Chanlyn said, slapping Cole on the back.

Maggie's gaze however shifted from Cole with wary eyes.

CHAPTER 4

THE NEXT ROUNDS of the tournament knocked Master Walker, Mark Stonewall, Jake Fisher and Creed Sanderson out of the running. Those that would continue on to the next round would be Luke Morell, the elder son of Master Morell, Chanlyn, Artemis and Cole. Cole stood between Luke and Chanlyn. He kept sneaking glances to the sidelines where Maggie stood to see if she still had the fear in her eyes. The last two rounds Cole had tried to shoot like he normally did. He just nocked his arrow, took aim and let the arrow go, allowing it to land wherever it wanted to. The arrows never landed in the direct center as his first arrow did, but they always landed close enough to the bull's eye that it allowed him to move up to the next level.

"Gentleman! Take your aim and fire when ready," Wilkins yelled. Cole nocked his bow with an arrow and took aim, but he could not concentrate. His fear and worries clouded his vision. He was scared that one incident with the arrow had changed Maggie's opinion of him somehow. Yet Cole had no idea what he had done to make Maggie look at him with uncertainty. He wanted so desperately to know and to make matters worse his head was throbbing.

He was sure that the tea Maggie had given him was starting to wear off, for Cole could feel himself starting to shake and a slight pain in his head was slowly increasing. The strain of him pulling back on his bowstring and holding so long was starting to affect him. He noticed that Artemis and Luke had already fired their arrows and were making their way off the field. Cole made ready to fire his bow, but as Luke was passing him, he seemed to stumble and he fell into Cole. Luke reached out to catch himself and grabbed onto Cole by his exposed wrist.

In that instance when Cole was touched by Luke, his lightning strike of a headache hit him and Cole let his arrow loose. In that short amount of time, from when the arrow left the bow and hit the target the bright flash of light blinded him. Within that flash Cole saw the face of a young boy, his eyes closed, face pale and his lips blue.

A loud groan erupted from the people and Cole was snapped out of his vision. The arrow had flown high and then had dropped, just barely hitting the top of the outer rim of the target. A few more inches to the left and Cole would have missed the target entirely. Artemis had already taken his shot and it was a good one, landing somewhat in the center, yet slightly off. There was no doubt Cole had lost. Still shaking a little from his vision he stepped off the field. He knew he had lost. He wanted to hide and stay hidden until the fair was over. He had disappointed a lot of people and had lost them their bets and worst of all, he had lost Wallace's horse to Master Morell. He said nothing to Maggie as he passed her. He could not stand to look into her eyes and see the disappointment.

"Cole, where are you going?" she asked, stepping in front of him.

"I'm going to go dig myself a hole in which I can hide," he said somberly.

"You can go dig yourself a hole later. Right now you have to finish this contest," Maggie declared pushing Cole back.

"Maggie I lost. Did you not see where my arrow went?"

"I saw it, but it was also announced that Luke was disqualified for purposely bumping into you," Maggie, said putting her hands on her hips.

"What?" Cole said, turning around to see Luke get a slap upside the head from his father.

When Cole stepped back onto the field, he stood in the middle of Chanlyn and Artemis. He also saw the damage he had done to Artemis in the fight. Besides a black eye and a split lip, Artemis had bandages wrapped around one of his wrists.

"It is an insult to me that I have to compete with a stable boy and a miller's boy, for I am the mayor's son," he said indignantly.

Cole said nothing. He gave Chanlyn a nod and told him good luck then turned and took his stance in front of the one target that was left on the Green. The target had indeed been moved back a great distance. Cole could just barely make it out. He figured that the target had been moved at least another ten yards, adding to the hundred yards that it was already at.

"Gentlemen take your aim," Wilkins called out, "fire when ready!"

Cole nocked his arrow and pulled back on his bowstring. He knew he could not mess up on this, for everything depended on this last shot. He let himself breathe in deeply, letting all thought and worry fade away to the dark corner of his mind. All he needed to see was the target. Just like the first time, Cole closed his eyes and waited. He felt the wind tickle his cheek and the stillness surround him.

Opening his eyes, Cole let his fingers start sliding off the nock of his arrow when all of a sudden the world that surrounded him came rushing towards him. He felt his feet on the hard ground, yet the ground, the sky, the trees and the grass were all being pulled into one another creating a blurred mesh of color, and then it exploded with the familiar blinding bright light. Cole forced his eyes closed against the brightness, but when he opened them it seemed that the world had righted itself. Yet something was different, something had changed.

Cole no longer stood on the Green, but by the Clearwater River. The raging and foaming waters that rushed by him turned Cole's blood cold. Instinctively he rushed from the waters edge, up the steep gully to a safe distance away from the river. When he reached the top of the gully he found a crowd of people standing in a circle. More and more came to stand and look down at something in the center.

As Cole stepped closer to investigate, he could hear someone crying. "What has happened?" Cole asked, with foreboding.

When Cole spoke everyone turned and looked at him. He recognized all their faces, for they were the villagers of Kells. Master Goldhill looked at him with a grim stare, but others like Master McTavish and his wife looked at him with loathing and hatred, while others just stared in contempt. As Cole stepped forward, people moved away from him, pulling their children with them, as if he had some sort of plague upon him that they did not want to catch.

Further and further Cole went into the crowded circle until he came to the center. There in the middle was Mistress Morell. She was on her knees rocking back and forth, holding in her arms the lifeless body of her youngest son Thomas. Master Morell sat next to her, his arms wrapped around his grieving wife and Luke stood over them with his head down crying.

Thomas' body was soaking wet. His face was white and his lips blue. His was the face that Cole had just seen moments before, when Luke had touched his bare skin. It was apparent that the boy had drowned in the river.

Cole looked down at the couple, and his eyes began to well up with tears. He reached down to wipe the hair away from Thomas's face, when Mistress Morell grabbed his wrist and looked up at him with her tear filled eyes.

"Why Cole?" she wailed. "Why could you not save him? He was my son. Why could you not save him? You knew this would happen, you knew."

Again the world came rushing at him, blurring into colors and then erupting into pure white blindness...

"Are you going to shoot, or will we have to wait until doomsday?" Artemis' voice burned into Cole's ears.

In confusion Cole opened his eyes and found himself back on the Green, still holding his bow with the arrow still notched. He looked up and down, left and right. He gazed across the people that stood watching and his eyes landed on Mistress and Master Morell. His bicep suddenly give out a singe of pain as he stared at the couple. Cole shook his head and turned back to stare at the target.

"I haven't got all day. Shoot your arrow," Artemis said hotly.

Cole pulled back on his bowstring a little more, ignoring the increasing pain growing along his arm. He looked at the target and let his arrow go. The arrow flew through the air and it hit the target, but Cole did not even look at where it had landed. But by the mocking look on Artemis' face as he rushed by him, it told him he had lost. Cole raced towards the Morells. When he reached them, Master Morell stepped up to face Cole.

"Where is your son?" Cole blurted out.

"I beg your pardon," Master Morell said, with shock and his eyebrow scrunched in confusion. Luke was seated right next to them. "I know he knocked into you and he will apologize..."

"Not Luke! Where is Thomas?" Cole asked a little breathless.

"Why Thomas…"Master Morell started to say.

"He is not here," Mistress Morell's voice screeched out in alarm.

Master Morell spun around to see his wife in a panic.

"He was right here. He was watching the tournament with us, and he had his little boat…" Master Morell said, turning around again to discover that Cole was gone. He had thrown his bow and arrows to the ground and had taken off at a run headed towards the river. Cole only hoped that he was not too late.

Fear coursed through Cole's veins as he headed for the bluff of the river. He dreaded coming to it and finding Thomas's body limp and lifeless on the banks of the river, yet the thought only drove him harder, driving him to run faster. Upon reaching the bluff, Cole let himself exhale a sigh of relief. A small blond haired boy about the age of six, stood standing in the shallows of the river playing with a toy boat.

"Thomas," Cole cried desperately.

The boy gave no response, but kept on playing. The sound of rushing water was the only noise that the boy could hear. Cole tried again, but knew the moment he had headed towards the bluff that he would have to go down to the river and retrieve the boy himself. Taking a deep breath, Cole stepped onto the path of steep stone steps that led to the riverbank. Instantly his stomach twisted into knots, his fear growing more the closer he got to the raging river below, than for Thomas's safety. Sweat began to bead on Cole's forehead as he made his way to the river and he dug his fingernails into his palms to prevent his hands from shaking.

"Thomas," Cole cried again, when he was about half way to the river. This time fortunately the boy seemed to have heard. He looked up at Cole with a smile and waved, then he went back to playing with his boat.

"Thomas!" Cole yelled again.

Thomas looked up again and Cole signaled for him to come in, but Thomas shook his head. By now Cole's nerves were on the edge of a knife and the sound of the water ringing in his ears made his lungs constrict and tighten causing him to heave deep gasps of air. For a split guilty second Cole thought about going back up the stairs to tell someone where the boy was so that they could go and retrieve him. But in that second, the vision of Thomas's drowned body and his wailing mother blazed across his eyes.

Taking in deep gulps of air to calm himself, Cole made his way down the last couple of steps and walked towards where Thomas stood on the shallow banks of the river.

"Thomas!" Cole said loudly, yet unsteadily, so as to be heard above the white water that swept by only meters away.

Thomas looked over at Cole and smiled.

"Have you come to play with me? No one else would. They were all too busy watching the tournament," Thomas said, his lips pursed with a pouty frown.

"The tournament is over," Cole replied, his eyes darting from the water to Thomas.

"So now you can find your friends and play with them up on the Green."

"Oh, but I am having so much fun here, my boat is sailing very nicely," he said as he stared out at his little boat.

One end of a string was attached to the bow of the boat while Thomas held the other end, wrapping the extra string around a stick. The little wooden boat started to drift into the swift current, but with Thomas' watchful eye he pulled in on his string and brought the boat out of danger. The boy loved playing this game, yet Cole wanted nothing more than to be away from this place, spending time with Maggie and Chanlyn, having their annual contest of who can eat the most honey oatcakes. A sudden idea had somehow slipped though the wall of fear that surrounded Cole.

"Thomas, your mother wanted me to tell you that she has honey oatcakes for you and if you don't hurry and claim yours she'll have to give them away."

At the mention of oatcakes, Thomas looked over at Cole and eyed him, as if trying to decide if he was lying.

In the end the boy gave a sigh and started to roll up his string, pulling his boat into harbor. With his own sigh of relief, Cole turned around and was about to place his foot on the first step when Thomas gave out a horrifying scream.

"MY BOAT!"

Cole spun around just in time to see Thomas dive into the river after his boat.

"THOMAS NO!" Cole screamed out in fierce terror, but it was too late. The string on Thomas's boat had snapped and the boat was now caught up in the currents and they were sending it down to the white waters. Thomas, not thinking, threw himself into the river to go after it. The current immediately caught the boy and pulled him away.

Another scream echoed across the bluff. Mistress Morell screamed as she stood in the middle of the stone steps watching her son disappear into the water. Cole's eyes searched the water desperately, trying to find some sign of Thomas. He saw the boy's head bob up over the water and then disappear under the current. Without thinking or hesitating Cole tossed himself into the waters after the boy.

The river received him and swallowed him up, pulling him into the depths of murky darkness. The water was so cold it shocked his whole system. Cole forced his arms and legs to move and pushed himself upward and he exploded out of the water taking in huge gulps of air before he was pulled down again. Again and again he burst out of the water gasping for breath and searching for Thomas. He used his arms, reaching out when the water pulled him under; he kicked and pushed toward the surface. The current was strong and fast. He needed to find Thomas and get to safety before the two went over the falls. As Cole came up for another breath of air, he caught sight of the boy. He was only meters in front of him. With a few kicks and the push of the current, Cole caught the boy's hand and pulled the boy close to him with all his strength.

"Thomas," Cole tried to say, but a wave of water came in over their heads. The unconscious Thomas was dead weight, and it was starting to pull him under.

Again Cole kicked with his feet and the two came up for air. Using what strength he had left in him, Cole tried to keep the two afloat, but the cold water was depleting his strength. He was getting tired and his boots were weighing him down. He knew that he had to get out of the water, not only for Thomas's sake, but for his own as well.

Another wave of water enclosed around them. It pulled them in so many directions, spinning and tossing them like rag dolls. Cole could feel himself fading, sinking into the darkness below. As he and Thomas drifted downward, being pulled by the current, he saw the bright flash of light and when it cleared he saw the villagers of Kells standing around a tomb. Merryrick was there, as was Maggie, Wallace and Chanlyn. Cole could see their faces and see the unbearable sadness in their eyes. He stepped forward, moving between his friends and wondered who it was that had died. He stepped up to the stone marker and read his own name.

"Cole was a good boy, on the verge of becoming a great man. He died trying to save Thomas. Sadly none were saved. We will miss Cole and hope that he is happy on the other side," Wallace said.

"No!" Cole shouted, as he turned to his friends and saw the agony in their eyes. He didn't want this. He didn't want his friends to feel this way.

There was another flash and Cole snapped open his eyes. He was back in the river with the swirling and tossed driven water around him. Somehow, with renewed energy Cole pushed through the water, kicking his legs, dragging Thomas with him. He didn't know if he was imagining it or not, but he felt as if the water was pulling away from him. Cole felt a wave of joy hit him as his feet hit ground. On shaky, weak legs Cole picked Thomas up in his arms and carried him from the water to the shore. There, his knees crumbled and he collapsed. He put Thomas down softly on the damp ground and looked him over. Thomas lay still. His eyes were closed and his face pale, his lips blue. His vision had come true.

"No!" Cole wept shaking the boy. "No you have to wake up!"

Images of his early vision flashed across his mind. He saw the grieving Mistress and Master Morell. He could feel the sadness and despair that would arise from the young Thomas's death. He felt responsible for not going to the riverbank earlier. If he had gone, if he had listened and reacted faster to the vision he had earlier, then maybe none of this would have happened. It was his fault, Cole told himself, all of it.

As Cole wept over the lifeless body of Thomas, a strange feeling came over him. He felt something like a fire of warmth and light rushing through him, yet it wasn't painful at all. His vision had changed. It was as if he could see the light of life that burned in every living thing. The trees, the animals and even the river glowed with a brightness of a white flame. All of them burned with a brilliance that he had never seen nor felt before. He could even see his own flame of life that burned within him. It was bright, as bright as the sun. Yet when he looked at Thomas, he saw that his was faint and was fading fast as the seconds passed. But there was still life there, only a small flicker of life left.

"All he needs is a little more," Cole thought.

Cole put out his hand and touched the boy. He willed some of the life light Cole felt within him be transferred to Thomas.

Thomas's flame began to grow brighter the more Cole fed his light to him. But the more Thomas's light grew bright the fainter Cole's faded. His vision began to blur again. Around the edges it was turning black and his body was feeling very tired and heavy.

He heard a gasp coming from Thomas and heard him stir.

"Cole," the boy whispered. Cole smiled at the boy then closed his eyes and let the darkness take over.

CHAPTER 5

BOOM... BOOM... BOOM! The sound roared like thunder and Cole felt it vibrate through his bones. The angry whacking on the black-gated iron doors continued. It rattled the great links of chain that bound the doors shut. Yet even as Cole stood watching, he saw that the doors were weakening and giving way to the pressure of the continuous onslaught. The strange blue light that once was so bright when Cole first saw the gate in his brief vision had faded and was weakening along with the doors. Cole felt a cold chill run up his spine when he realized that the pale blue light that glowed throughout the gateway's walls, towers, and doors was linked to keeping whatever was behind the gate's doors in. Once the light had faded away to nothing, then the gate would be open and whatever lay behind the double doors would be free.

Cole felt a rush of fear wash over him as the light faded for an instant and went out. At that moment a great flash of red lightning struck the doors and they were blown open. The red lightning continued to flash as clouds of mist spilled out from the open doors. The phenomenon lasted only a few seconds before the doors slammed shut and the blue light returned. Then all fell silent. Cole shivered in the cold silence as the fog surrounded him. The mist quickly grew in thickness and in coldness.

Cole's breath turned to mist as the temperature dropped dramatically. He began to quake, but his chills were not entirely from the sudden frigidness in the air, it was something else. There was something beneath the silence, within the fog, a growing restlessness that stirred inside of him. Flinging his arms about him, Cole moved quickly away from the gate and before long he was running through the fog not knowing where he was going.

Hoof beats thudded in the mist. Cole came to a halt suddenly and spun around, his head turning swiftly from left to right, trying to analyze where the hoof beats were coming from. The baying of a hound howled in the darkness of the fog. Another howl came and another echoed after it. Cole fell back onto the ground terrified as a black horse came bursting out of the clouds of mist. Astride the black beast was a monstrous form. It looked to be the form of a man, covered in robes that were more rags than clothing. Cole's heart raced as he stared up in horror, not into the face of a man, but into the hollow eyes of a metal mask that was shaped like that of a human skull. The creature moved through the mist like a ghost, suddenly there, then gone. The baying and barking of hounds followed the horseman as they too disappeared into the mist.

As Cole pulled himself up from the ground and began to wipe the dirt from his hands he suddenly froze. A pair of red glowing eyes stared at him. They peered through the mist and with those eyes came the deep rumbling of a growl. He suddenly became aware that there was not just one pair of eyes examining him but several. His breath came in sharp, short huffs of terror as the glowing eyes began moving in closer. Cole's eyes widened when the hounds, the owners of the glowing eyes, came out of the mist and began walking around him. Cole ran through the mist without knowing or seeing what was in front of him. He could hear the hounds behind him with their barks and their howls. He let out a cry when he was suddenly pulled down to the ground. One of the hounds had hold of his foot. Cole swung out with his other foot and managed to kick the beast in the face. With his injured foot he struggled to get to his feet. But it was no good. His foot could not hold his weight. With fear and absolute terror, Cole backed himself up against a tree, curled up into a ball, with his knees to his chest, and hoped that the hounds would not tear him apart.

"WAKE UP, COLE. Come on boy, wake up," Merryrick's voice rang out in the dark. Cole's eyes suddenly snapped open as he bolted up right.

"Merryrick?" Cole questioned, his eyes darting around, half expecting to see the red eyes in the dark surrounding him.

They were nowhere to be found. Cole blew out a breath of relief as he realized it had all been a dream. It was nothing but a nightmare. Feeling more at ease, after his heart rate returned to normal, Cole realized that he was in a room in a bed. There was a fireplace with a pleasant fire burning and a few lit candles spread about the bedchamber, providing a little more light than just the fire.

"How do you feel?" Merryrick asked.

"I feel...," Cole started to say as he let himself fall back onto the pillows, then let out a groan when he suddenly seemed to feel pain everywhere, "awful."

He hurt in so many places that he didn't know what hurt worse. It was a hot pain that had started all over him and it seemed that there was no way of extinguishing it. His shoulders, arms, legs and even his hair seem to pulse with pain. He tried to sit up again, hoping that the movement would relieve some of his aches. Instead Cole let out a moan as a shock wave of intense agony hit him.

"That bad, huh?" Merryrick questioned. "Well I can't say that it doesn't serve you right," he replied rather curtlike.

"Is there something wrong, Master Merryrick?" Cole asked, looking around for anything that might cause Merryrick to be so upset.

"Is there anything wrong he asks, when he's lying in bed with a knot on the head the size of a goose's egg and more than one cracked rib," Merryrick muttered. "And he asks if there is anything wrong? Yes there is something wrong my boy. You could have been killed. What in the world were you thinking?" Merryrick scolded.

"I couldn't let him die, Master Merryrick," Cole muttered, "I had to help him."

"You helped him alright. What you did was very dangerous, healing him like that. You could have seriously caused yourself harm or worse killed yourself," Merryrick replied angrily.

Cole sat for a moment lost in what Merryrick was yelling at him for.

"Wait? You're not mad at me for jumping in the river and pulling Thomas from it?" Cole asked bewildered.

"What? The river? No. Yes I am mad about that."

"Then what else is there? What are you so mad about?" Cole asked in confusion.

"I am mad because you healed him! You used your gift right in front of half the village. Your lifespark was so bright anyone that has the slightest talent for sensing lifesparks could have felt it a thousand miles away!" Merryrick ranted. "No doubt we will be having people sticking their nose where it's not wanted or belongs. That Tinker fellow has undoubtly noticed you."

Cole stared at his Master, lost for words. He didn't know what to say, let alone what to think. He wondered if Merryrick had suddenly lost his mind, speaking words that he didn't know the meaning of.

"Lifespark?" Cole said. "What is a lifespark and how was I so bright?"

"I'm sorry Master Merryrick. I have no idea what you are talking about. I had no idea that I did anything wrong," Cole answered. "I don't even know what I did," he said.

Merryrick let out a breath, his anger fading, as he realized that Cole knew nothing of what he was ranting about.

"Tell me when you were on the river bank with Thomas something happened didn't it. You saw something, right? What was it that you saw?" inquired Merryrick.

"I saw flames, white flames burning within every living thing."

"Right, those flames you saw are known as the Flames of Life. Everything that is alive carries it, from the tiniest of insects to the largest of beasts. As long as the living remain alive they carry the Flames of Life with them, once that flame goes out or runs out then you are no longer alive.

"I see," Cole nodded in agreement. "Thomas's flame was going out, so I gave him some of mine."

"You didn't just give him some, Cole. You nearly gave him all of your life, there by making your flame almost go out completely so you could have died!" Merryrick remarked.

"Oh! Sorry! I didn't know," Cole said, suddenly realizing what Merryrick was saying.

"Well now you do. I apologize for being rather vexed with you. But you must promise never to do it that way again."

Their voices died for a moment and the room fell silent for a time as Cole and Merryrick contemplated the words that had just been spoken.

"So how do I heal someone and not risk killing myself."

"By using the life forces around you and letting time do the healing," Merryrick answered.

"What do you mean?" Cole asked.

" Just as we use plants and animals to keep our physical bodies alive we can also use the plants and animals for lifesparks as well. There are plants that have remarkable healing qualities. Trees have an abundant amount of life within them. They have a flame that can let them live for thousands of years. The very ground you walk on is full of life. You can use some of the natural life to help heal those or yourself if you were ever to be injured. But if you must give some of your own life to another, it must be in controlled stages, not all at once. You obviously carry within you a power that gives you more than just your abilities to trace. You must be a seer and thereby have the unique gift to see what others cannot. I for one cannot see a lifespark, but rather can only feel it.

"A seer? How can I be a seer?" Cole asked looking astonished.

"Do remember what the Tinker Gilden said about the Elfain Warriors and their gifts. Obviously they had children and this would have been passed down to them and so on. You must descend from one of those warriors to have such power. This power of seeing is what made it possible for you to give some of your own life flames to Thomas. This power can be used to do many good things. As a seer you can see what causes people pain, physical and mental, whenever you touch them. You can see the out come of choices that people have made.

"You mean like seeing the consequences of their choice?" Cole asked.

"That is a good way of explaining it. We all make choices and all choices have consequences. Whether the choices are good or bad you see the out come," explained Merryrick.

"I don't quite understand," Cole said.

"About what precisely?" Merryrick asked.

"Well, when Luke touched me I saw Thomas' future. How is it that when I touched Luke I saw Thomas' future? You said I see the outcome of people's choices. How could I have seen the outcome of Thomas' choice through Luke when it hadn't even happened yet?

"Tell me what you saw when you touched Luke?" Merryrick ordered kindly.

Cole told his master about the circle of townspeople and Thomas on the riverbank soaking wet and his parents hugging him and Luke stood there crying over his brother's body.

"I see, I believe what you saw Cole, was Luke's future. You saw Luke mourning the death of his brother. Again you saw the outcome of a choice. Perhaps if Thomas had not gone down to the river this whole thing might not have happened. All of the choices that we make, in some way or another, effect everyone around us," Merryrick stated. "Even the simplest of choices have an effect."

"But I saw an outcome before it even happened. How is that possible?"

"Some choices have already been made. Maybe Thomas had made the choice to go play in the river that morning or later in the day. Whenever he made the choice it must have been before you touched Luke so you saw the consequence.

"And Artemis, why did I see his past? It had to have been him caught in the fire as a young boy?" questioned Cole.

"That I do not know. Maybe you saw the out come of a choice that Artemis made and because of that choice he still suffers from the consequences of it today."

"Maybe I could help him in some way," Cole muttered. "Not that he would accept help in anyway from me."

Merryrick gave him a sad smile.

"You are a very kindhearted person, Cole, and I know you would help people in any way that you could. But I must caution you, my young apprentice. What you can do must be carefully guarded. Only help those that you trust with your life. There are those who would try to use your power selfishly, to try to claim it as their own or misuse you for the power you hold. That is why I have been so careful to keep your abilities a secret. You must be cautious my boy."

"Is that why you don't trust the Tinker?" Cole asked, wondering how Merryrick could have known he would have a gift.

"I don't trust a lot of people. As strange as it seems, the Tinker is one that I do trust."

"Who don't you trust"?

"The better question you might want to ask is whom do I trust," Merryrick stated.

"Okay then, whom do you trust?"

"Wallace, Maggie, your friend Chanlyn and his father Master Goldhill," answered Merryrick.

"Do you trust anyone else?" questioned Cole.

"The fewer the better," Merryrick said.

Merryrick was about to continue on but the sound of the bedroom door creaking open brought both Merryrick's and Cole's attention towards it. Maggie's head popped through the opening and when she saw that Cole was awake she pushed the door open wider and rushed into the room.

"Finally! You slept for two days and Festival is nearly over. And what did I have to do? Worry. That's what! You know you could have killed yourself. Here I was thinking that you were terrified by moving water and that you couldn't even swim and you go jump straight into the Clearwater River, without even taking your boots off," Maggie snapped.

Her concern and worry for Cole was revealing itself through her angry ranting.

COLE STARED open mouthed at Maggie. He had nearly died and she was yelling at him for almost doing so.

"I'm sorry Maggie. The next time someone falls in the river, I'll consult you first to see if it's okay if I go and help them," Cole replied.

Maggie stared down at Cole with defiance and then a smile broke across her face and she started to laugh. It wasn't long before Merryrick joined in.

"Well now, after a day and a nights sleep, I would think that you are hungry. I will go and see if Mistress Morell has any soup for you," Merryrick said getting up from his chair.

"Is that where I am then?" Cole asked.

"Indeed! She was most insistent that we bring you here," Merryrick said, as he walked to the doorway. "I think that she is grateful to you for doing her an act of kindness."

Cole gave out a laugh, but quickly stopped when it brought on a rush of pain.

With that Merryrick opened the door and stepped out into the hallway of the White Rose.

The room fell silent when Merryrick left. Cole tried to think of something to say that would break the stillness. In the end it was Maggie that broke the awkwardness.

"You know you scared me?" Maggie said, taking Merryrick's chair by the bed.

"I'm sorry Maggie. I promise I won't go jumping in any rivers anymore," Cole replied.

"It wasn't just the river, Cole, but also the fight you had with Artemis," Maggie said. "Something happened to you. You weren't yourself and it scared me."

Cole took a breath and tried to think of something he could say that would make her feel better, but nothing came to his mind.

"What happened to you Cole?" Maggie asked, as tears fell from her eyes.

"I don't know Maggie," Cole whispered. "When I saw that Artemis had hurt you, I got angry and something snapped in me," Cole explained.

"I saw that anger. It was almost tangible. It filled your eyes and they changed color, Cole. They changed from blue to silver," Maggie whispered. "And then when you shot the arrow, they changed again. We've known each other a long time as friends, and as friends I would hope that you would trust me enough to tell me when something is happening to you."

Cole blinked several times when he heard this. He didn't know what to say. What was he suppose to say? All this was new to him also. He took a breath and let it out slowly, giving himself time to think on how to begin.

"Merryrick calls it the Seer's touch. Honestly this is the first time it has happened. Merryrick thinks I see the consequences of choices that people have made," Cole replied.

Maggie's eyebrows went up and she looked at Cole with a dead stare.

"So when you touched Artemis you saw something in his future or past?" Maggie asked softly.

"I think I saw something from his past," Cole remarked.

"And you saw that Thomas had drowned after Luke bumped into you. That is why you knew he was missing and that he was at the river."

Cole nodded, not daring to look at Maggie for fear of seeing disgust in her eyes.

"And the changing of your eye color and your hands on fire, is that part of the seer's touch?" she asked softy.

"I really don't know about that. It's never happened before," Cole said truthfully. Maggie nodded her head and took a breath in and then blew it out.

"Why didn't you tell me before?" Maggie asked.

"I thought that you might think me peculiar and not want to be friends anymore."

"You were already perculiar, Cole," she said, "and besides, you are not the only one that is peculiar," Maggie remarked, as she got up from her chair and went over to the nightstand where a vase of dying flower was placed. Picking up the vase, Maggie gently blew on the blossoms. Amazingly the flowers began to rebloom afresh. Cole stared wided eyed at the flowers and then at Maggie and then back at the flowers.

"Maggie that's amazing. How come you never said anything?" Cole asked.

"The same reason you never said anything about your gifts," she replied as she placed the vase of fresh flowers back on the nightstand. "I will never not be your friend Cole," Maggie said.

"And I will never not be yours."

Cole looked up at her and saw that she was smiling and he couldn't help but break into a smile himself.

"So how did the archery contest go?" Cole asked.

Perhaps that wasn't the right subject to bring up, Cole thought, as he got a look at Maggie's face.

"You didn't win," Maggie announced.

"Oh," Cole muttered.

"But neither did Artemis," Maggie said.

"Then that means…" Cole trailed off.

"Chanlyn won! And because the bet was for you or Artemis to win, which neither of you did, the bets are all off. Father got to keep Brom."

"He did?" Cole cried with excitement.

"Yes. You should have seen the look on Artemis's face when they pronounced Chanlyn the winner. He looked like he had swallowed a mouthful of bugs," Maggie giggled.

"Oh don't make me laugh," Cole said, chuckling through gritted teeth, "it hurts too much."

"Sorry," Maggie said, with a smile. "If you think that you'll be feeling better enough, Tinker Gildon will be telling one of his stories tonight. He told one last night and it was the most amazing thing I ever saw. He's telling them at the great tree on the green. I'm so excited!"

"What do you mean saw? Don't you listen to stories?" Cole asked.

"Just wait and see," was all that Maggie would tell him.

CHAPTER 6

IT SEEMED THAT ALL the inhabitants of Kells were out and on the Green that night. Lanterns hung off hooked poles that were forced into the ground, encircling the gathering crowd with soft light. A large bonfire burned high and bright enough to be seen for miles around and cries of laughter burst up from the nonsensical conversations that echoed all around throughout the party. The local musicians were playing a lively jig that wove itself in and out of the night's festivities. Little children danced to the beat as they held hands and spun around in circles until they all fell down. Food venders sold their delicacies to the crowd as well. The smells of cooked meat and sweets, wafted in the air adding to the atmosphere of the night.

"Are you sure that you are up for this, lad," Merryrick asked, helping support Cole as they moved slowly through the crowd.

"I wouldn't miss this to own my own kingdom," Cole replied, looking around him as he beheld the scene.

"Cole, Master Merryrick, over here," Maggie yelled, waving her hand in the air so that Cole could see her. She had chosen a spot near where the large bonfire was burning. Beside her were her father, Chanlyn and his father, Master Goldhill.

Cole could see several people congratulate Chanlyn on his win, and by the look that Master Goldhill was giving his son, he showed nothing but pride on his face. As he and Merryrick moved through the crowd towards Maggie, Cole could feel more than one pair of eyes watching him.

"Cole."

Cole stopped when a gentle hand touched his shoulder. He turned and saw that it was Mistress Morell.

"Mistress Morell! How is Thomas?" Cole asked.

"Oh he is fine. He's off with his friends. I just wanted to thank you for what you did. I know it must have been hard for you, what with your fear of the river."

Cole felt his cheeks redden with embarrassment. He knew that it was silly to be afraid of the water. Most children in Kells learned to swim by the time they were six or seven, but Cole had always feared the water and he didn't know the reason for his fears.

"But I also know that if you hadn't jumped in at that moment Thomas would be…" Mistress Morell stopped and sniffled then wiped her eyes. "You have yourself a very good apprentice Master Merryrick."

"Thank you, Mistress Morell, I do have to agree with you," Merryrick said, with a nod of his head.

"I'm glad I could help," Cole smiled.

"Yes, well I wish to thank you," she said, dabbing her eyes with her handkerchief. "So anything you want, anything at all you shall have it," Mistress Morell said.

"You have already given me so much, allowing Merryrick and me to stay in your extra rooms. Your beds are very comfortable."

"They are, are they not? Goose feathers! That is what they are stuffed with," Mistress Morell said proudly. "But come, there must be something," Mistress Morell asked.

Cole just shrugged his shoulders, not being able to think of anything.

"I know! Both of you come to the tavern after the story telling," she said. "I'll have fresh honey oatcakes and a fresh pot of cider waiting for you and anyone you wish to bring. As much as you can eat and drink."

"Ahh, give him a mug of ale. Cole here, I think, is man enough to drink ale. Isn't that right lad?" Sir Arthur's laugh echoed behind Cole, as a hard slap hit him on his back. The force of the good-humored blow almost made Cole's knees buckle. He could feel his eyes water as a sharp pain electrified his spine.

"Come Master Merryrick, come Cole, come and sit with me and tell me of your adventure in the water. I wish to know everything," Arthur said, inviting Cole to sit with him. From out of the corner of his eye, Cole saw Maggie waving at him, summoning him to sit with her.

"If you don't mind Sir Arthur, I'd like to sit with my friend tonight," Cole said, looking over at Maggie.

Sir Arthur followed Cole's gaze and a knowing smile appeared on his face.

"Ah yes, not a bad friend to be with," Arthur said, with a wink, "and what about you Master Merryrick? Will you not join me?"

"I thank you, Sir Arthur, but I fear I must decline. Ale is not a favorite of mine. Whenever I drink it, I seem to loose my wits and I have a hard time finding them again."

"Alright I will excuse the both of you this time but I do expect you, Cole, to tell me all about your adventures sooner or later."

Cole nodded in agreement as he received another slap that brought more tears to his eyes.

"It seems that Sir Arthur has lost a few of his wits already," Merryrick chuckled.

COLE EASED HIMSELF down between Maggie and Chanlyn and greeted them with a smile.

"So you woke up finally? Maggie was very worried about you," Chanlyn remarked. "And when Maggie gets worried her mouth starts going, non stop," Chanlyn whispered into Cole's ear.

"What was that, Chanlyn Goldhill?" Maggie asked, her eyes throwing daggers at Chanlyn.

"Nothing Maggie. I was just asking Cole how he is," Chanlyn said.

"Fine, sore, but I'm okay," Cole replied.

"That's good," Chanlyn said. "I'm glad that you're okay Cole. You gave us a scare, but you really are alright, right?" Chanyln asked.

"I'm fine," Cole replied in a reassuring way.

"Strange though how the water seemed to pull away from you," Chanlyn said.

Cole looked up at Chanlyn with raised eyebrows. "What do you mean?"

"Well, we couldn't find you and Thomas at first and we thought that you had err…" Chanlyn stopped and took a breath to control his emotion. "We thought that you had gone over the falls, but then I saw you come out of the water and it was like the water was pulling away from you, but pushing you to shore at the same time," Chanlyn stated.

Cole looked over at Maggie, wondering if she had something to do with what Chanlyn was talking about, since she had the capability to bring plants back to life. But she merely shrugged her shoulders and shook her head.

"I don't really know what happened," Cole replied, having no explanation for what Chanlyn was describing.

"I guess it doesn't really matter," Chanlyn said.

"Guess you're right. Hey I hear that I need to congratulate you on winning the archery contest," Cole smiled. "I told you, you'd win!"

"Yeah! I was flabbergasted when they announced me as the winner," Chanlyn said. "Da was really pleased. He keeps bragging about it a lot," Chanlyn said, his head turning towards his father.

Master Goldhill had gone off to take in some of the ale that Master Morell was offering. He was standing next to Sir Arthur with a mug in his hand, apparently telling Sir Arthur about Chanlyn's win. Sir Arthur didn't look too pleased as Goldhill put down his mug on a table and had begun to re-enact the whole event.

"Sir Arthur doesn't look too pleased," Maggie muttered under her breath.

"Speaking of Sir Arthur. What did he want just a moment ago," Chanlyn asked.

"He just wanted me to tell him about what happened in the river," Cole said.

"What did happen?" Chanlyn inquired. "I mean just before you ran to the river. You froze on the field. You've never done that before. It was a good two minutes before you loosened your arrow."

"I did?" Cole remarked.

"Yes. And how did you know where Thomas was? One minute you're ready to fire your arrow and the next you're running off the field wondering where Thomas was," Chanlyn asked. "Did you have kind of vision of something," Chanlyn asked with a laugh.

Cole looked at Chanlyn with widened eyes, wondering how he had figured it out. As Chanlyn caught Cole's expression his laughter faded along with his smile.

"Wait! Is that really what happened?" Chanlyn asked.

" Shh," Maggie hissed. "Will you two stop talking?" Maggie said, in a harsh whisper.

"Now is not the time or the place to explain. We can talk later about it. Right now the story telling is about to begin."

"What is Maggie talking about?" Chanlyn insisted.

"He's a seer okay. He saw Thomas go into the water. That's how he knew that Thomas was at the river. Now will you be quiet Chanlyn," Maggie commented.

"Is she serious?" Chanlyn asked.

"She pretty much said it all," Cole whispered.

"Shh," Maggie hissed again.

"Unbelievable!" Chanlyn muttered under his breath

"I said SHHH," Maggie ordered.

The lanterns that surrounded the gathering started to dim and then went out. All of a sudden silence fell over the field. Conversations died and people that were standing found their seats. All that remained of light was the bonfire. The flames twisted and turned, dancing in the darkness. There was a flash, a bright light, so bright that everyone had to look away, but when the audience's heads turned back, there was Gildon. He was dressed in his best robes of red and blue silks that blew around him as the wind came up. He watched the audience with a half-smile. He said nothing at first, just stood there watching and waiting.

"Welcome gentle ladies and fair maidens. Welcome gentle sirs and young lads," Gildon finally spoke. "And what story shall I tell thee tonight?" As Gildon spoke his words he walked around the fire.

"Shall it be 'The tale of Echorus and his Dragon'," Gildon shouted, throwing a handful of what appeared to be sand into the fire. The flames reared up, jumping high. Cole didn't know if it was his imagination, but he could have sworn that he glimpsed a dragon's head within the flames, roaring with might.

The boys in the crowd jumped and howled out for the story of the Dragon.

"Or shall it be 'Ava and her Adventure in Finding her Lost Love?'"

Again Gildon threw a hand full of something into the fire and the flames danced, leaping up and taking the shape of a young woman, then faded away. It was the girl's turn to cry out for the romantic story.

"Or perhaps, there is another story to tell," Gildon said, stepping in front of the bonfire. "A story full of adventure, war and sorrow," Gildon fell silent again. His eyes turned back to the fire and watched the flames. Then he spoke, softly, but everyone heard.

"Our story begins beyond the Elfire Mountains to the east. It starts back beyond the memories of your great-grandfather's father, to a time when the Elfain Warriors protected the kingdoms of Albavar. The warriors were said to be the children of the Seven Great Haven Warriors that came down to defeat the Dark King and his monsters. They were an extraordinary race of men and women."

Gildon stretched out his hand over the flames and tossed a hand full of his dust into the fire. The flames jumped, reaching up toward the inky black sky. They twisted and turned shifting into the shape of a blue dragon that wrapped itself around a sword.

Deep breaths of shock and wonder echoed throughout the night from the spectators.

"For five hundred years the warriors protected the land, fulfilling their mission to bring peace and prosperity across the nation. Their powers were unmatched, for each warrior had his own skills. Each warrior was born with magical abilities, such as controlling the elements, or being great healers, while others were gifted with foreseeing future events."

Cole watched as Gildon's eyes wandered across his audience and when they found him they stopped and held his gaze for a moment.

"They were master swordsmen, archers and fighters."

Within the flames a pair of swordsmen, dressed in full armor, battling with one another appeared. They soon disappeared and in their place appeared an archer, his face hidden in the hood of his cloak. He was pulling back on a bowstring and letting an arrow go. He too disappeared into the glowing fire.

"Upon reaching the highest level of a warriorship, they were given a gift of a weapon, like unto the weapons of the original Seven Elfains. The weapons were said to increase the warrior's power by ten fold. It was a golden age for the people of Albavar when the warriors walked among us. But like all good things in life the peace of the warriors would not last."

The flames reared up exposing the image of a hooded figure.

"Abandoned at birth and found, Shelrin was brought before the council of the Elfain Elders at a young age and was found to hold great power. Thought to be one of the Seven Warrior's heirs of the generation foretold by Ayden, one of the original seven warriors, Shelrin was trained to be a warrior and quickly grew through the ranks. Fellow warriors marveled at Shelrin's power, but one warrior was fearful. Hayden, great-grandson of Ayden, a great warrior himself, was gifted with his grandfather's foretelling of the future. He saw darkness within the young warrior. He saw a cold future before them and he feared Shelrin would bring it upon them. Hayden began to watch the young warrior and saw that there was a great darkness in Shelrin's heart. The warrior abused the powers and laws of the Elfains. Hayden discovered that Shelrin was planning to overthrow the Elders and was going to take control over them. Hayden warned the Elfain Elders about Shelrin's plan. Found guilty of treason Shelrin was banished from all the realms of the Elfains. Where the young warrior went no one could say.

Time passed and all seemed right within the realm of the Elfains. Yet Hayden knew that a dark storm was brewing. Enemies beyond the borders of Albavar were stirring. And enemies within were rising."

Gildon walked around the bonfire's flames and as he did the flames changed in color. The cheerful reds, oranges and yellows turned black and purple. The mood in the gathering crowd changed as well. The small children ran to their parents to be comforted. Even the older ones scooted closer to their friends out of nervousness.

"On a day of celebration, when the Elfain's welcomed the newest warriors into the guild, the enemy known as the Black Dragons attacked. Their leader, none other than Shelrin, who had learned the traditions of the Lonely One, the master of all darkness and claimed to be the heir of the Dark King, went forth destroying all of Alorian, the great city of the Elfains.

The storyteller looked down and continued on, deep sadness and sorrow resided in his voice.

"Many betrayed their fellow warriors and joined Shelrin's army to infiltrate and destroy the Elfain Warriors. Hundreds of lives were taken the day that Alorian fell. With the Elfain warriors destroyed, many other cities fell to the rule of Shelrin. Others were completely demolished. "

Gildon stretched out his arm over the fire and flames began to die, growing smaller and smaller until all that was left were the coals. The people in the audience were silent. They watched Gildon, hoping that that was not the end of the story.

"For nigh unto a hundred years Shelrin ruled over Albavar. People feared for their lives. Those that spoke out against Shelrin would vanish, never to be heard of again. The age of Shelrin's rule was the hundred years of darkness. But fear not, good people of Kells. Shelrin's rule could not last. Hayden foretold that the day would come when Shelrin's rule would end and would be destroyed.

> *The blood of the seven shall cry up from the grave*
> *And they that are chosen shall hear.*
> *They shall rise up from the shadows of the mountains*
> *And will take up the bow and the sword and the spear and the sling*
> *and stones. They shall bring forth the trident and the axe and*
> *the staff and will smite the darkness that comes again.*
> *And it will come to past that that dark dragon of the night shall be*
> *destroyed.*
> *And the old ways will come forth once more.*
> *A new dawn will bring forth peace throughout the land.*
> *Then the seven shall have their kingdoms*
> *And shall rule one with another until the last days are fulfilled and*
> *the heirs of the warriors shall fight in the last battle and shall*
> *conquer the dark once and for all.*
> *So it is foretold so it is written."*

Like the rising of a new sun, seven warriors did come to stand Grant the Strong, Allena the Wise, Kaya the Sage, Tate the Swift, Will the Brave, Sophie the Brilliant and their leader, Kayden the thief, stood up against the powers of Shelrin's empire."

The flames of the fire erupted burning hotter and brighter than ever before. "Thousand upon thousands joined Kayden. Battles were fought and Kaydens's armies won. For the first time in a very long time the people of Albavar had hope. After many battles, Kayden's army marched to the city of Alorian where Shelrin had taken over and had built a fortress. This was the last stand, the final battle, for Kayden and his fellow warriors had found a great weapon that they would use on the dark ruler. This weapon was used to trap the Dark King and seal him away. With it they planned to seal Shelrin away for all time."

The flames split then, one part turning red, the other blue, and as Gildon spoke they fought each other, twisting around one another climbing upward towards the sky.

"Many men's lives were lost in the battle and it seemed that Kayden's army would fail and be lost to the merciless armies of Shelrin. When suddenly within the fortress there came a blinding light and an ear splitting scream that burned through the darkness of the battle and rippled throughout the entire city. Anyone within the confines of Shelrin's fortress began to turn to stone. The dark lord Shelrin was sealed away inside a tomb.

When the captains and leaders of Kayden's armies went to enter the palace they found that they could not, for the great gates of Alorian were closed and none could enter. With that the armies left thinking that if nothing could get in then nothing could get out. Yet still they chained and barred the gates of Alorian and placed enchantments upon the gates and the city was left to crumble and rot away. As for Kayden and his fellow warriors only three of the seven warriors survived the war. William was presumed dead before the battle and Kayden, Allena and Sophie were lost within Alorian. Kaya, Tate and Grant still live and it was they who told me the tale, which I tell you now. It is because of the sacrifice of many that we live in the free world today."

At Gildon's words, sparks from the flames began popping and springing upward. Suddenly a blaze of fire shot up high into the sky and exploded into bright sparkles of color and with it, came a large boom that shook the sky. Gidon fell silent and the story was over.

It remained quiet for some time, and then all at once there was an explosion of cheering and applauding. Gildon flared his robes out around him and he took an elegant bow towards the audience.

"Thank you, my dear friends, it was an honor. But come, the night is still young and there is much to see," Gildon said. There was another explosion of loud booms and several sparkling fireworks in the sky and when it was all over Gildon had disappeared.

CHAPTER 7

THE TAVERN COMMON ROOM at the White Rose was packed to the rafters with villagers, conversations, ale, cider, laughter and music. From his remote table in the far corner, the one furthest away from the door, hidden in shadow, Gildon the Tinker sat watching the room with a careful eye. A single candle had been placed on the table and the Tinker absent-mindedly waved his hand over the flame of the candle. As he did his hand closed up into a fist as if he were catching something. When his hand moved away from the candle, the flame was gone and the wick was smoking. He then waved his hand back over the candle, releasing his fist and the flame would be back on the candlewick. He did this over and over again as he watched the goings on around the common room. The lack of light in his little corner didn't bother him. In fact it allowed him to regard the villagers without being noticed. He sat up in attention however when the door creaked open and in stepped the boy with the dark hair.

Gildon watched him as he and his two friends were greeted by Mistress Morell and then escorted to a table near the large hearth that nearly took up most of the west wall. With a wave of her hand, Mistress Morell shooed away two men who sat at the table. They walked away, slightly tipsy and went to the bar. She seated Cole and his friends and then went off for a bit and came back with three plates stacked high with what were called honey oatcakes. Gildon had enjoyed the sweet dish several times and would have to ask Mistress Morell for instruction on how to make the delicacy before he left. The honey oatcakes were about the size of a man's hand and were round flat cakes that were stacked onto one another with wild raspberries and honey in-between the layers. The thin layers of cake were so flaky and crumbly they melted in the tinker's mouth. Gildon watched the boy dive into his plate of cakes and was not surprised how fast the stack disappeared.

"He's a peculiar one, isn't he?" a voice broke through Gildon's concentration. "Well all three are peculiar really."

Gildon looked across the table to find a somewhat heavyset man with a gray beard that matched his graying hair. He held a pint mug in his hands and he swayed a little as he stood before Gildon. Gildon recognized the man as the mayor of the village, but his name escaped him for the moment.

"Pardon," Gildon said.

"Cole, he's peculiar don't you think?" the man said, taking a seat on the bench across from Gildon.

"Forgive me, but I have forgotten your name," Gildon said.

The man looked a little put out at having been forgotten. He took a swig of his ale and then spoke with a bit of a slur.

"Arthur," he said, with a hiccup, "Sir Arthur, Mayor of the village."

"Forgive me Sir Arthur, I am quite forgetful when it comes to remembering names."

"It is quite alright," Sir Arthur said, with a wave of his hands and a small spill of his drink.

"If I may ask your honor?"

"Sir Arthur, none of that honor stuff. Bit formal considering where we are," Arthur mumbled, before he took a swing of his ale.

"Well Sir Arthur, why do you say that Cole is peculiar?" Gildon asked politely.

"You only need to look at the boy to see the answer," Sir Arthur muttered.

"You mean his dark hair? I know a fair amount of people that have dark hair," Gildon replied.

"Indeed, but watch the boy for a moment, through the corner of your eye without blinking," Sir Arthur mumbled, taking another gulp of his ale.

Gildon did as he was advised and looked at Cole without blinking. Gildon let out a gasp of utter amazement.

"Ah...you saw it?" Sir Arther smiled.

"It is amazing," Gildon said, his eyes returning to watch Cole.

There seemed to be a light surrounding Cole, a pale blue light that glowed in and around him. It was thin, almost invisible. One would not be able to see it if you were looking directly at him. Gildon could only see it out of the corner of his eye.

"Where does it come from?" Gildon wondered out loud.

When Sir Arthur had finished swallowing, he leaned in over the table and signaled Gildon to come in closer.

"Some say he is a *Wildling*," Arthur whispered.

"A *Wildling*?" Gildon questioned.

"Mmm," Arthur muttered.

"Excuse me for my ignorance. But I have never heard of a Wildling?" Gildon questioned.

Gildon considered himself a bit of a scholar. He had searched the entire ancient records within his home city and nothing in them explained a *Wildling* that he recollected.

"A *Wildling* is a person born from the dark blood," Arthur explained.

"Do you mean he comes from one of the seven warrior's bloodlines?" Gildon asked, trying to understand Sir Arthur.

"No! A *Wildling*! He bares the blood of the Dark King. He is of wild magic, dark magic. A *Wildling* can control all the elements. They can control the winds, the earth, the waters and fire. They can see into the future and look into your past and steal the magic from another, with just one touch," Arthur spit as he whispered. "Don't get me wrong, Cole is a good lad and he can track a deer trail that has gone cold after three days and can shoot nearly a hundred and fifty yards with his bow, but the boy is... well peculiar," Sir Arthur admitted.

"And does the boy's father know about the rumors that have been going around about his son?" Gildon asked.

"His father?" Sir Arthur muttered, not understanding. "Oh you mean Merryrick," Arthur said, as he took another huge swig of ale, then smacked his lips. "Merryrick is not Cole's father. Some say that Merryrick found Cole in the forest, while others say that it was a stranger that left Cole with Merryrick, without a word as to who he is or where he came from. No one really knows. Merryrick just showed up one day with a young child in his arms," Arthur said.

Gildon rubbed the beard on his chin.

This is getting interesting the more I learn about the boy, Gildon thought.

"So what about Merryrick? What do you think about him?" Gildon asked.

"Oh, Merryrick is a good man, an even better one to have around for a hunt. The man can track like a hound. Guess he taught everything his knows to Cole. I swear the man is not afraid of anything. He stood up to a raging bear once, happened when I was a far bit younger than I am now."

"Oh really! And how long ago was this?" Gildon asked.

"Oh lets see! I believe it was about eight or ten years ago. It was on a hunting party," Arthur retold. "Yes, we were hunting deer and Merryrick was leading the party. He was also training young Cole. A bear cub came into our camp and the mother bear came running in after it. She stood up on her hind legs and gave out this menacing roar. I was terrified out my head and do you know what Merryrick did?"

"I assumed he killed it," Gildon answered.

"You'd think that! But no! He just roared right back at the bear. Then he threw the bear some of the fish we had caught that night and the bears went on their way. Merryrick told us that the cub had lost its way," Arthur laughed. He took another drag from his tanker still laughing.

Mmm, I wonder, Gildon muttered to himself. "How long has Merryrick lived in the village?" Gildon asked.

Arthur thought for a moment. His brain undoubtedly slowed by the ale seemed to take forever to answer.

"Oh he's been here ever since I can remember, and I've been here fourteen years or more," Arthur said.

"How old do you think Merryrick is?" Gildon asked.

"I have no idea. Perhaps in his fifties or sixties," Arthur said.

"Or maybe older?" Gildon said.

The door to the tavern opened and in stepped the man himself, followed closely behind by the man named Wallace.

"What about Wallace? What is he...?" Gildon started to ask Sir Arthur, but when he turned his attention back on the mayor, Gildon found him with his head down on the table softly snoring. It seemed that Gildon's interview with Sir Arthur was over. It didn't matter to Gildon. He knew he could find someone else that would talk to him, for that's why he was here in the tavern to begin with. There was always someone to talk to, to get information from and most of the time he could find those individuals at the taverns or inns. Gildon decided that he would stay in the village for a few more days. He let out a breath as he sat back in his shadows watching and waiting.

CHAPTER 8

DAYS LATER, after the fair, Cole found himself standing by the well in the courtyard of his and Merryrick's cottage. The sun was setting over in the west and a wind was blowing, foretelling of an on coming storm. Cole picked up his buckets of water he had been fetching, and walked up the small lane to the cottage. Opening the door Cole dropped the buckets as his eyes widened in alarm when he beheld the scene of wreckage. The table and chairs were knocked over and broken. Pottery was thrown on the floor and shattered and the cooking pot was turned over in the ashes of the fireplace, its contents spilled across the floor.

"Merryrick!" Cole cried. He received no reply or response.

Cole moved through the small house, looking for Merryrick, calling his name but still received no answer. There were only three rooms in the cottage, Merryrick's and his bedchambers and the workshop. Cole checked both rooms, but found nothing. He ran down the little hall to the workshop at the back of the house, but Merryrick wasn't there either.

Thinking that he might be in the barn, Cole ran from the cottage and headed across the yard to the back of the house, towards the two-story barn. As he ran, his head turned towards the eastern sky. He suddenly froze in his tracks. His eyes squinted as he tried to make out what was coming in over the mountains.

He knew it couldn't be the storm, because storms came in from the northwest. But as Cole watched, he realized that it was indeed a storm, but not like any storm he had seen before. Great black clouds boiled in the sky, blocking out what little sun there was. Within the clouds, red lightning cracked and forked out splitting the sky. It came up over the Elfire mountain range and covered the land, filling it with a thick black fog.

Cole and everything around him was swallowed up in it. An over powering sense of despair came over him and it grew heavier and heavier as time passed. He ran this way and that trying to shake free of the darkness, but only managed to get himself lost as he sought after Merryrick. All Cole could see was the black fog that seemed to seep in every pore and drain the life from him. Cole fought the fog, pushing it away, but it was a battle that he could not win. He would push away one patch of the fog, only to have it be replaced by another. Feeling as though he was going to go mad, Cole pleaded in his heart for a way out. His plea was answered when seven sources of light burned through the fog.

The fog began to thin and dissipate until it finally cleared. Cole closed his eyes and took in a deep ragged breath and gagged on the foul stench in the air, which reeked of rotting meat. He opened his eyes and let out a cry of horror. He stood in a battlefield surrounded by the dead. The village green was smeared in scarlet. Men and even women lay with empty blank eyes staring at nothing. Before him, no more than twenty feet away, stood a figure dressed in dark robes and carrying a staff of gold. A hood hid his face and even when the wind blew the robes, the face was never revealed.

You did this, a voice said, within his head. You brought this on. *This is your doing*, the voice said, condemning Cole.

COLE BOLTED UP RIGHT, taking in heaving deep breaths of air that made his healing ribs burn. His heart pounded in his chest, ready to explode and he felt like he had run a hundred leagues and yet he had never left his bed. His stomach twisted and turned as the dream still lingered in his mind. It took all his strength not to turn over and vomit. Breathing in through his nose and letting the air out of his mouth, helped calm his queasy stomach and the rest of him. Fearing that he was still in the state of dreaming, Cole pinched himself and was glad when he felt the simple pain of the pinch. He was awake and in the real world. When his heart rate and breathing were back to normal and when he did not feel so sick, Cole wiped the sweat from his brow and fell back onto his bed, wrapping himself in his blankets. He closed his eyes hoping to fall back to sleep, but the dream was still so vivid and so real that sleep would not come. Feeling there was no point in trying to fall back to sleep, he rose from his bed and dressed himself, then stepped out of his room and into the small hallway that led to the kitchen and living area. Feeling a small chill in the air, Cole started a fire and began cooking breakfast.

As the breakfast cooked, Cole made a mental list of all the things that needed to be done, to take his mind off his nightmare. The garden needed weeding and picking. Gladadear's stall needed mucking out and she also needed to be washed and her hair was in need of a brush through. The chicken coop was in need of repair as well as a cleaning, there was wood to be chopped and stacked, clothes that needed washing and a few things that needed mending. The sheep needed to be gathered from the field and their coats sheared off. When living on a farm there was always work to be done and when one task was complete there was always something else that needed doing.

When the sun was just creeping up over the mountains and the first beams of light swept over the land, Merryrick appeared in the kitchen. He looked over at Cole and saw dark shadows under the boy's eyes.

"You look horrible," Merryrick commented, as he took his seat at the table.

"I couldn't sleep," Cole mumbled, serving Merryrick a bowl of cooked oats.

"You haven't been sleeping for the past two nights," Merryrick replied, placing a large amount of honey in his oats from the honey jar that Cole had placed on the table earlier. "Was it another bad dream? Anything we need to worry about?" He asked lifting a spoonful of the honey-sweetened oats to his mouth and blowing on it to cool it down. Cole shrugged his shoulders as he took a seat and started to eat his own cooked oats.

"It was nothing but a dream of a bad storm," Cole muttered.

Merryrick watched the boy as he ate his meal. He could tell that Cole was tired, his head was down and his shoulders were slumped forward. He looked as though he would topple over any minute and he kept rubbing his right bicep as if it pained him.

"Tell me your dream, Cole," Merryrick commanded.

Cole retold his dream to Merryrick of how he was seeking Merryrick and couldn't find him. He told him of the black storm coming with dark fog and red lightning that forked the sky. Then he told of the field of the dead and a figure cloaked all in black holding a golden staff and how he had told Cole it was his fault all this had happened. As he talked he continued to rub his arm. When he finished Merryrick's face had a look of grave concern.

"What do you think it means?" Cole asked.

"I fear I do not know. Let me meditate on this. Is your arm bothering you?" Merryrick asked him.

"It's just a bit sore that's all. Like I said, a storm's coming," Cole replied. His arm had been throbbing with a slight ache ever since that day at the fair when he'd touched Artemis.

"Do you want me to look at it?" Merryrick questioned.

"No I'm fine. I should get working," Cole replied.

"Are you sure you want to work today. I can manage while you go back to bed for a few hours."

Cole's head shot up and he looked at Merryrick with a startled expression, as if the thoughts of going back to bed frightened him.

"No, I'm fine," Cole stated, in a rush of words. "Besides there's too much to do today and they're just normal dreams, like everyone gets."

"But you're not everyone, Cole," Merryrick stated.

"Gladadear's stall needs mucking out," Cole said, changing the subject, "I thought I might start with that this morning."

"Aye, it needs doing, if you're not too tired."

"I'm not tired," Cole said, getting to his feet.

Cole scraped the last of his oats into his mouth, and then walked out the door, glad that Merryrick had not pressed him for details about his dreams. He felt a little foolish to be afraid of dreams.

"Dreams are just dreams, they have no meaning," Cole said, to himself as he walked the short distance across the yard to the back and then to the stables.

Keep telling yourself that, the little voice inside Cole's head whispered. Shaking his head at his own foolishness, Cole entered the stables. The barn was fairly simple. There was the hayloft built above a few stalls, one of which housed Gladadear. There was a wide opened space in the middle of which Cole used when shearing the sheep in the summer. The rest of the time it housed the cart.

Once inside he made sure that he was far enough into the stable that Merryrick couldn't catch a glimpse of him. Cole pulled off his work glove and rolled up the sleeve to his right shoulder and looked it over. Everything seemed normal to Cole. His hands and right shoulder were scarred from a severe burn, that he could not ever remember receiving. His fingers ran across the smooth, and shinny skin that had healed. His arm and hands always throbbed alittle whenever there was a storm approaching. The healed skin ran from Cole's forearm up past his shoulder. The palms of his hands itched with the sensation of tiny needles pricking him. Letting out a breath Cole put his gloves back on and unrolled his sleeve. He tried not to think or look at the disfigurement for it was only another reminder that his life before he came to Kells was lost to him.

Ignoring the slight discomfort Cole led Gladadear out into the paddock. He was just going back into the stable when he heard the beating of horse hooves. Curious as to what was happening, Cole ran from the back of the stables to the front. He was just coming through the back archway to see six horses and riders coming up over the hill toward Merryrick's cottage. Cole recognized the horses before he saw the faces of the riders. He made out the two deep chestnut stallions of Sir Arthur and Artemis. He also saw the dark black skin of Brom and knew that Wallace was among the party. He recognized the pale yellow hide of Buttercup, Maggie's horse and saw the reddish flank of Chanlyn's new horse. There was a white stallion among them, but as to whom its owner was, Cole could only guess. He crossed the farmyard and stood at the well watching the party approach.

When the party reached Merryrick's farmyard, they all pulled to a stop and dismounted from their horses. Cole found out that the white horse belonged to the Tinker Gildon, who apparently had not left yet. Merryrick came out from the house and stood on his porch looking at the riders with eyebrows raised in curiosity.

"Good morrow, Master Merryrick," Sir Arthur shouted, as he dismounted from his horse.

"Sir Arthur," Merryrick said, nodding to the Mayor of Kells. "What brings you here on this fine morning?"

"A hunt, good sir, a hunt," Arthur said, cheerfully as he stepped up to Merryrick. "You wouldn't happen to have any coffee brewing would you? I was up awfully early. Oh and my horse could do with some water if you would be so kind," Arthur asked.

"I'll take care of it, Master," Cole said, crossing the yard to retrieve the reins from Arthur.

"Good lad," Arthur replied, giving Cole a pat on the shoulder as he passed him the reins to his horse. Artemis followed his father and as he passed Cole, he threw his reins at him.

"Be careful of Addis's feet, he likes to step on toes," Artemis commented then purposefully slammed his shoulder into Cole.

It was only a second, a mere blink of an eye, but that was all it took for Cole to see the snapping jaw of a sharped tooth beast. Then just as fast as it had come, the image was gone.

"Are you alright, Cole?" Wallace asked, looking at Cole with raised eyebrows. "You look paler than a ghost."

Cole shook his head and blinked several times before he looked up at Wallace.

"Fine, just got something in my eye," Cole muttered.

"Much appreciated Cole," Wallace said, patting Brom and then gave the reins to Cole as he entered the house as well.

The only people left in the farmyard were Maggie and Chanlyn. They had stayed to help Cole with the horses. They led the horses, two at a time around the back of the cottage to the paddock and to the trough.

"So, what's going on?" Cole asked, letting Sir Arthur's horse drink, after which he put him in the paddock with Gladadear.

"Several sheep were killed yesterday on Master Kent's farm. He came running into the village, hollering about his dead animals. Father went to his farm to investigate. He said it was pretty bad," Maggie whispered, putting Buttercup in with the other horses.

"It was probably a wolf pack come down from the mountains; it was a hard winter," Cole said. He'd seen a wolf or two during harsh winters strike down farm animals.

"A wolf pack wouldn't come anywhere near the village, not with the bonfires that surround it," Chanyln stated. "Master Kent wasn't the only one to have animals killed. Some of the watchdogs were killed as well. Father said that the poor hounds had their throats ripped out." Chanlyn commented.

"Whatever it is, people are getting scared," Maggie put in. "We've never had anything like it in Kells before. Father thinks it's a mountain lion, sickened with the maddening disease," Maggie divulged. "He wants to hunt it down before it kills any more animals or attacks and kills someone. That's why we're here. Father came to ask for your's and Merryrick's help. He knows how good you are at tracking," Maggie replied.

"I'm not that good," Cole muttered.

"From what I hear, you and Merryrick can track a deer from a three day old trail," a familiar voice replied.

Cole turned around to where the voice had come from. Standing just behind them was Gildon. Cole looked at him with a surprised expression. He wondered how the Tinker had snuck up on him.

"How is the eye?" Gildon asked.

"What?" Cole asked.

"Your eye. You said you had something in it."

"Oh it's fine. I thought that you'd be gone by now, what with the end of Festival," Cole said.

"Oh, I thought that I would stay a little longer. It's not every day that you find a secret village that no one knows about," Gildon said, joining the others as they leaned against the paddock's wooden fence.

"Fine horses aren't they, especially that one," Gildon said, pointing out Gladadear. "Your's I believe," Gildon said, looking at Cole.

"That's Gladadear," Cole replied. "She is Merryrick's."

Cole gave out a whistle and in only a few moments the little shaggy horse came trotting up to Cole.

"She's quite a stout little horse isn't she?" Gildon replied. "Mind if I give her a try."

"You can if she'll let you. Gladadear is a bit particular about who climbs on her back. She doesn't even let me ride her sometimes. She really only let's Merryrick ride her," Cole stated.

"You can't ride her?" Gildon asked in disbelief.

"Oh, I can ride her," Cole said, "but I have to say please." He was feeling a bit red in the face with embarrassment.

"That's interesting. You know the Elfain Warriors used to train their horses so that only they could ride their mounts. It prevented horse thieves from taking them."

"Maybe Master Merryrick is a warrior in disguise," Maggie suggested. All three laughed at the idea. But Gildon did not and Cole found that odd.

"You, stable boy," Artemis' voice hollered.

Cole turned around, to find Artemis standing just a few yards away, looking at Cole with loathing.

"What?" Cole barked. Cole could see the fury in Artemis' eyes at being answered to in such a manner.

"My father wishes to see you." Artemis said with ice in his voice.

"Fine. Tell him I'll be there in a minute," Cole responded, turning back around to watch Gildon.

"You will not keep my father waiting," Artemis shouted.

"Perhaps we should go in. Now that the horses are watered and resting in comfort, we can hear what Sir Arthur has planned," Gildon said, taking his eyes off of Gladadear. Cole let out a breath of air and the four of them walked toward the cottage.

They were all seated around the table when Cole stepped into the cookery with Chanlyn, Maggie, and Gildon behind him.

"Ah, speak of the man himself and he appears," Arthur said, looking up at Cole as he entered. "Cole, my boy, how would you like to go on a hunt with me?" Arthur asked.

"I don't know. I have a lot of work to do," Cole said. In truth it was an excuse not to go on the hunt. He had gotten a bad feeling in the pit of his stomach when Maggie described the state of the animals after they had been attacked.

"Are you mad boy? You would choose work over spending the day, possibly two in the woods in my company?"

"Cole go and get your bow. These animal attacks are not to be taken lightly," Merryrick said. "The work will keep until you get back."

"What about you master? Will you not come too?" Cole asked.

"I think not. My old leg is hurting me today. As you said a storm is coming. But you go, I think you are old enough to take the lead."

"Lead?" Cole questioned.

"Yes, the lead," Merryrick replied.

Cole's nervousness disappeared with Merryrick's words. This was a big step for him. He had never been allowed to lead a hunt before and now Merryrick thought him ready. Cole took in a breath and nodded his head.

"Capital!" Arthur said, clapping his hands together. "A merry party of six we will be."

"Seven! I will be coming as well," Maggie said.

Arthur looked over at Maggie with raised eyebrows.

"You wish to go on a hunt young lady?" Arthur said in disbelief.

"I don't see anything wrong with that." Maggie said.

"I suppose that you are welcome, if your father agrees?"

All eyes turned on Wallace.

"I don't know Maggie," Wallace said in hesitation.

"Oh please father. You have to admit that I am a better shot than you and I've always wanted to go on a hunt. Please!" Maggie begged.

"Alright, but if there is any sign of trouble and I feel that the situation is getting too dangerous you will turn around and immediately go back home understood?"

"I understand," Maggie agreed.

"Well now, it is getting late and I do not want to let anymore daylight escape us. Let us begin," Arthur said, as he started to rise to his feet.

"Gildon, may I have a word with you," Merryrick asked and gestured toward the door to the workroom. As Cole slipped past the workroom to his room to gather his things he thought he heard the word "Shelrin" but he wasn't quite sure. Questions rushed into his mind as he remembered that Shelrin was the Dark Lord that had ruled in horror for a hundred years but had finally been vanquished nearly 16 years ago. Why would Merryrick be asking Gildon about Shelrin, when he thought the Dark Lord had been imprisoned where he could never escape? At least that is what he remembered from the story Gildon had told. Could any of this have anything to do with his dream? He would ask Merryrick about it later but for now he had a hunt to lead.

They rode west from the cottage, arriving at the Kent farm where the last attack had taken place just as the sun reached midday. Master Kent and his five sons showed the hunting party where they had found the dead sheep.

Cole dismounted from Gladadear and started studying the surrounding area. Maggie, Chanlyn, Gildon and Wallace followed suit.

"Found anything Cole?" Wallace asked him.

Cole's eyes gazed across the open field where the cattle and sheep grazed. Thick dense woods surrounded the grazing land, showing where the forest of Kells began. Cole moved forward examining the ground as he went. He stopped when he found what he had hoped he would find. He recognized the many sheep tracks that were imprinted in the soft dirt. Yet as he inspected the ground more closely, he found another imprint.

Cole got to his knees and inspected the tracks. It looked like a dog's track yet it was massive, with four toe pads and a heel. The claw marks were splayed out wider than any normal dog's imprint and it was about the size of the palm of a grown man's hand.

"Over here!" Cole shouted.

The four ran over to where Cole knelt.

"You found the trail already?" Maggie asked, impressed.

"Yes, and I don't think this is any mountain lion that we're tracking," he said as he pointed out the obvious trail the dog went.

"What do you think it is then?" Gildon asked.

"It's very big whatever it is. Looks almost like a dog's track but larger," Cole replied, taking notice at how large the imprint of the track was.

"Not like anything I have ever seen," Chanlyn stated.

Cole had never seen anything like it either and he had seen his fair share of animal tracks. As he looked at the track he noticed something funny about it. The four toe pads and heel pad were pressed deep into the dirt, but as Cole looked closer he saw that there was an over lap. There were two sets of prints, one on top of the other.

"There's more than one," Cole interjected.

"How can you tell that?" Maggie asked.

"There's another set of tracks. One on top of the other," Cole responded.

"You are right Cole. They must be smart dogs to walk on each others footprints," Wallace remarked, looking over Cole's shoulder.

"Why would they do that?" Maggie asked.

"To hide their numbers," Gildon responded.

All of them turned and looked at Gildon.

"You've seen something like this before Gildon?" Wallace asked, turning to the Tinker.

"Never seen anything like it," Gildon replied, "But I have heard stories," he muttered looking worried.

"How many do you think there are?" Chanlyn asked.

"Hard to say, from what I can tell there are only two," Cole explained.

"So do we have the beast or not?" Arthur shouted from atop his mount.

"Yes, Sir Arthur," Cole cried, as they all ran back to their horses. "They've headed west," he stated, pointing the direction the animals went.

"They?" Arthur asked, with an eyebrow up.

"There's more than one," Cole replied.

"Excellent!" Arthur cried in excitement. "I shall have two heads mounted on my wall rather than one."

"I want everyone to be on guard. Remember to keep your eyes open and don't take any chances. This is no mountain cat or lion that we're hunting," Wallace announced.

"Oh and what is it we hunt that requires such cautions, Master Wallace?" Arthur asked.

"I don't know, Sir Arthur, but whatever they are, they are smart, they are big and I'm pretty sure dangerous.

"Oh come now, Master Wallace, you cannot think that these things are smarter than we are," Arthur said.

"I have no doubt about it," Wallace answered, as he turned to Maggie and said, "Maggie I think you had better head for home."

"Father I can handle myself," Maggie retorted in such a way that Wallace realized she was no longer a little girl but a rather mature young lady.

Wallace looked at his daughter and nodded then said to the group "Be on your guard." Then he turned his horse and kicked it as he headed towards the woods.

CHAPTER 9

THEY MOVED SLOWLY, riding through the dense forest, while Cole, leaning sideways out of his saddle, studied the trail that the large dogs left behind. The deeper they went into the forest the fresher the trail got and the more nervous Cole became. The feeling in the pit of his stomach grew until he felt like he was choking. The signs that they were catching up to their prey were everywhere. Even a less experienced hunter could see the path of bones of animals that were scattered across the forest floor. Cole knew he wasn't the only one getting more anxious. The ears of Galdadear were up and she pawed at the ground whenever they stopped. She blew out great breaths of air and her flanks twitched in nervousness.

As the party came upon a thick pocket of trees, Cole pulled Glad to a halt, as did the others following his lead, pulling to a stop just behind him.

"What's the matter Cole?" Wallace asked. At first Cole didn't say anything.

"Do you hear that?" Cole asked.

The others fell silent, turning their heads so they might hear whatever it was that Cole heard.

"Its just flies," Artemis said.

"A whole lot of flies," Chanlyn responded.

"What does it mean?" Maggie asked.

"Death," Wallace stated grimly.

They followed the sound of the winged maggots and in a few short minutes they found the decaying remains that attracted the flies. It was a boar. It lay on the forest floor, its eyes not yet glazed over with its throat ripped out. Cole, Chanlyn, Wallace and Gildon climbed down from their horses to examine the beast. Maggie feeling a bit sick and remained where she was.

"Dead," Wallace announced. "Whatever did this has to be very powerful or very smart to bring down a beast like that." The boar was huge, almost the size of a horse, with large curved tusks that were bloodstained.

"Probably both," Cole replied. He'd noticed the tracks of the dogs and could guess how they had managed to corner the boar and then bring it down. "One came from the south, the other came from the north, circled the thing and killed it by crushing its throat."

"How long ago?" Wallace asked walking around the boar.

"No more than a few hours," Cole responded.

Cole took off his riding glove and squatted down. He closed his eyes and with shaky fingers he touched the ground. He felt the rushing sensation of running forward without taking any physical steps. Merryrick had told him that it was part of his gift as being a seer. A talent that Merryrick had called tracing.

To Cole, it was like riding the wind, rushing forward, following the tracks. The trees and brush were all just blurs until he stopped and looked around him. His vision was clouded, much like seeing the world with eyes half closed yet it was clear enough that he could tell that he was still in the woods not far from where his physical body stood. It was silent save for the wind rushing through the trees. He focused on his surroundings that were around him, sensing that something was out there and then he heard a deep growl. He turned in the direction the noise had come from and froze when he saw the great black outline of a hound. Cole let go of the ground and his minds eye rushed back to his body. He took in a breath and snapped open his eyes.

"It's time we were leaving," Cole said, urgently rushing to Glad.

"What is the rush?" Artemis asked.

He had dismounted from his horse and was examining the boar as well.

"The thing that killed that boar is what's the rush!" Cole cried.

With more than terror running through them, they all raced back to their horses and as Cole mounted into the saddle and started to turn Gladadear back around, she jerked her head and sent out a terrifying scream and reared up, kicking at the air. Surprised by the sudden outburst, Cole fell back out of the saddle and onto the hard dirt. There was an explosion of light as Cole's head hit the ground.

When he opened his eyes he was flat on his back staring up at the canopy of trees. He was about to rise to his feet, but a sharp stinging pain in his chest only allowed him into a sitting position. Cole touched his chest as the pain increased. When his fingers came away, they were wet with his own blood. Confusion circled around Cole's mind as he tried to remember how he had gotten this way. He looked about him and discovered that the horses were gone and there was no sign of his friends.

"Maggie!" Cole tried crying out, but it came out as a whisper. "Wallace!"

Something wasn't right. It was silent, too silent and there was a foul smell upon the air. Cole turned his head from left to right. He saw Artemis laying not far from him, his eyes staring, unblinking, up at the tree tops

"Artemis," Cole called his voice hoarse.

There was no answer.

"Artemis!"

Still there was no response.

Bleeding and in pain Cole slowly crawled towards Artemis.

"Artemis, are you?"

Cole had to turn away when he saw the mess that Artemis was in. His clothes were shredded and torn to bits. Deep claw marks were ripped into his chest, and his arms and legs had been bitten many times. But what made Cole beyond sick was that Artemis's throat had been ripped out. Panic filled Cole as he looked around him. He saw it then, the battlefield that lay before him.

Men and horses lay dead. Gildon had fallen, still astride his white stallion, and undoubtedly lay trapped beneath the horse until the very end unable to defend himself. Wallace lay several feet away from the others. The spear he had brought lay close to his hands, snapped in half. He had tried to fight whatever it was that attacked them and had lost. Like Artemis, Wallace's throat had been crushed and his limbs showed signs of being bitten several times. Cole found Chanlyn not too far away, his throat in the same state as everyone else. Sir Arthur was face down and Cole did not dare turn him over for fear of what he might find. He mourned the death of his friends, but felt a small hope when he realized that Maggie was not among the dead.

"Maggie," he called as loud as he could.

"Cole!" a soft voice answered.

It was so soft that Cole thought he might have imagined it. But when he caught sight of a fallen Buttercup, he limped towards the horse. He found Maggie lying on her side. Her dress was torn and blood stained.

"Maggie," Cole whispered as tears began to fall.

"Run, Cole! Run!" Maggie whimpered, and then she went completely limp.

"No! No! No!" Cole whispered taking Maggie into his arms.

He rocked back and forth holding Maggie's lifeless body.

"NOOOO!"

Light exploded around Cole and the world around him was swept away. It was over in matter of seconds and Cole felt himself lying on his back.

"Cole, are you hurt?" Maggie asked.

Cole opened his eyes and found his companions looking down at him with concern.

"Are you alright lad?" Wallace asked.

Cole jumped to his feet, his right arm burning like hot iron, which could only mean one thing. His vision was about to come to pass.

"We have to leave. NOW!" Cole cried.

"Cole, maybe you should take it easy for a bit, you did just fall off your horse," Maggie said softly.

"Maggie, there's no time. Get to your horse!" Cole snapped.

"What are you talking about stable boy," Artemis sneered. "Are we to be attacked by your dogs?" he mocked.

Just as the words left his lips a deep howl resonated throughout the woods and echoed all around them. A few moments later another howl vibrated through the woods, an answer to the first call.

The rest of the hunting party had never heard a cry like it before, a deep whine that bore deep into ones soul and tore at the heart. But Cole recalled the howl, for he had heard it once before, in a dream.

The horses snorted and tossed their heads out of fear.

"What's happening?" Maggie asked in a frightful whisper.

"They're talking," Cole said.

Artemis gave out a cold laugh despite his fear.

"Talking! Dogs can't talk," replied Artemis.

"They're communicating, signaling each other," Cole stated.

"What are they communicating?" Sir Arthur asked.

"How to attack us," Gildon replied.

The howls came again only closer. It froze the marrow in their bones and made the hair on the back of their necks stand up on end. Both Cole and Chanlyn strung their bows and fitted an arrow to the string. Their eyes darted back and forth, not knowing where the beasts would come from. Maggie pulled free her sling and and made ready. Wallace hefted his long spears and Artemis strung his own bow. Gildon pulled free a long sharp blade, that looked sharp enough to cut through anything and Sir Arthur pulled a broad axe free.

"Watch your backs," Cole whispered.

"Maggie I deem this too dangerious and think its time for you to leave." Wallace orderd.

"I would have to agree with you father" Maggie replied "But I think it's a little too late for that."

"What is this sort of devilry?" Sir Arthur asked.

It fell silent. Nothing moved or made a sound. Everyone was now on edge, each breath coming in soft short bursts. Suddenly the horses went mad, rearing up and screaming in terror. Gildon rushed forward to try calming them.

"Gildon, don't!" Cole cried.

But it was already too late.

Out of the shadows a dark shape sprang forward and attacked Gildon, knocking him to the ground. His knife flew from his hands and was lost. The black mass that was a hound sunk its teeth into Gildon's arm that he used to protect his throat. Gildon's screams ripped through the darkened woodland.

"Hellhound!" Wallace screamed, and threw his spear at the hound.

As the spear flew towards the hound, the dog leaped away off of Gildon causing the spear to just barely miss the creature. The blackness of the hound then turned to face them all.

They all seemed to be paralyzed with fear at the sight of the monster. The thing was massive, far bigger than a mountain cat. It was coal black with sleek, shinny fur on some parts of the body while black tough scales covered vitals and exposed parts of its body. It had a huge head, big ears and a large mouth with knife like teeth. Its large deep-set eyes glowed red and long sharp claws extended out from the massive paws as it turned to face Wallace.

Cole knew that they needed to do something. He aimed at the beast and pulled back his bowstring. He didn't know if the arrow would do anything to the massive dog. All he could hope for was that he could distract the creature long enough, so the others could get Gildon to safety. He let out a yell as he let his arrow go. Cole watched it fly towards the hound. The arrow would have hit the beast in its side just above the shoulder blade, but at the last second the beast's head came up, and turned as if it could hear the arrow coming, and ran straight towards Cole.

"Get Gildon!" Cole yelled, as he took off at a run.

He didn't have time to let another arrow go. Gildon was safe but now it was Cole that was in danger. He ran with all his might, trying to put as much distance between the hound and the others. He sprinted forward, knowing that he could not out run the black dog so he made for the cover of a large oak tree. He jumped up and grabbed hold of the lowest branch of the tree and started to pull himself up. His feet were dangling mid air when the dog came upon him. It leaped up and clamped its teeth down on Cole's foot. Cole let out a scream as the beast ripped through skin, muscle and sinew. The heavy weight of the dog pulled him from the tree and he fell, landing at the base of the trunk, right in front of the dog.

Cole's eyes widened in fear as he stared at the hound, its red eyes stared down at him as it let out a low growl, pulling back its upper lips to show its canine fangs. Cole closed his eyes and wrapped his arms around his head, hoping that the hound would not tear him apart.

A deep whistling hiss cut through the air. It was followed by a solid crack and then a loud whinning howl. Cole dared to peek through his arms and he saw the dog had turned its attention toward someone else.

"Maggie! No! Get out of here!" Cole screamed, in agony as he tried to get to his feet, but his wounded foot would not hold his weight. He could not get to her. The dog bounded towards Maggie. She turned to run but her foot caught on a tangle of fallen tree branches and she toppled over.

"MAGGIE!" Cole screamed.

Everything seemed to slow down for a few seconds. Cole watched the beast rush towards Maggie. He saw Chanlyn run for her, but knew that he too would not be able to reach her in time. The horror and fear he was feeling exploded and he felt a rush of energy. His hands ignited with hotness.

Out of the corner of his eyes he saw Artemis pulling back on his arrow that was aimed at the dog.

"Shoot it Artemis!" Cole bellowed. "Shoot it now!"

The last thing Cole remembered seeing was Artemis letting go of his arrow and a blast of blue lightning streaking in front of him. Cole was thrown back, all energy spent. As his vision faded to nothing, all he could hear was the sound of distant thunder.

CHAPTER 10

COLE WOKE TO THE SOUND of a blue jay's cry. He opened his eyes and found that he was staring up at the distant treetops. The green foliage gently swayed in the cool refreshing breeze. The vision of him waking and finding his friends dead, shot through his mind. He bolted up right and looked around him. His heart jumped into his chest when he saw the forest empty of his friends.

"Maggie!" Cole cried.

There was no answer. He took in great breaths of air as he realized that his vision was all coming true.

"Maggie! Chanlyn!" Cole yelled again.

"I'm here," Maggie called, from across the way.

"Chanyln?" Cole shouted.

"Fine!" Chanlyn's voice echoed not too far away.

Cole fell back with relief when he heard Maggie and Chanlyn's voices.

"Artemis," Cole hollered. "Artemis!"

"Quit shouting stable boy," Artemis yelled back as he sat up.

"Oh my," Maggie gasped after she had risen to her feet.

She stood stunned with a shocked expression on her face.

"What the…" Artemis trailed off. He too had gotten to his feet and was looking confounded.

"I have never seen anything like it." Chanlyn exclaimed.

"What is it?" Cole asked as he tried to stand. He got to his feet and leaned up against a nearby tree and stared.

The hound was dead. Artemis's arrow penetrated its chest, right where the heart lay, but also the thing was smoking and the smell of burnt hair drifted through the air. The ground cover surrounding the dead animal was black and it too smoldered with smoke.

"What happened to it?" Maggie questioned.

"It looks like it's been stuck by lighting," Chanyln added.

All four of them turned their heads up to look at the heavens. Dark thunderclouds had rolled in over the sky. Artemis, Maggie, Chanlyn and Cole stared at the thing in silence; all of them thinking that it had been lucky that the lightning had not hit anyone of them.

"Maggie!" Wallace cried out, breaking the silence.

Maggie jumped a little but turned to see her father running towards her, with Sir Arthur on his heels. When Wallace reached her, he grab her in his arms and his breath came in deep sighs of relief. After a few moments he turned from Maggie to Cole.

"What were you thinking boy?" Wallace shouted. "You could have gotten yourself…" Wallace started to say, but stopped when he caught sight of the corpse of the beast. His eyes went wild and his head darted from side to side as if he was looking for something.

"Is it dead then?" Arthur asked, seeing the large black body. "Well, I suppose the hunting party wasn't a total loss. The head of that thing will look quite nice over my mantel, whatever it is."

"Do you not see what lies at your feet, Arthur? That is not just a creature that roams the forest like a bear or a mountain cat. That is a Bargest! Arthur! A Hellhound!" Wallace cried.

Arthur's face suddenly paled as he looked down at the black monster.

Artemis let out a laugh, as a wide smile appeared on his lips. "Hellhounds are just made up, told in stories to frighten children into behaving."

Wallace turned and stared at Artemis with such a cold hard gaze that the smile disappeared. "Where do you think stories come from boy? There is truth in everything for the proof lies at your feet."

"That means…"Arthur stuttered.

"That means their masters the Reapers are near," Wallace replied. "Arthur, Artemis gather the horses, Maggie help Cole with his foot"

"I'm fine. Gildon needs attending to," Cole said, hobbling towards the others.

"Maggie see to Gildon, help heal him if you can. Chanlyn help Cole get to his horse. We need to get away from this place and quickly," Wallace said in distress.

"Father, what is it?" Maggie asked, seeing the fear in her father's eyes.

"Questions later Gildon first?" Wallace said.

Maggie nodded her head and went to the Tinker. Wallace followed in his daughter footsteps. Gildon was sitting up against a tree when Maggie came upon him. His eyes were closed and he was deathly pale. If it had not been for the shallow breathing, Maggie would have thought that death had already claimed him.

"Is he alive?" Wallace asked.

"Yes," Maggie sighed as she knelt down next to the Tinker.

Maggie gently looked over Gildon and saw that his arm was the worst of his injuries. She could see that several of the bones in his hand were broken. The skin was horribly torn and ripped away so that some of the muscles and bone were exposed. The side of his face was marked from the beast's claws.

"Master Gildon," Maggie whispered.

Gildon eyes fluttered open and he looked at Maggie and then his gaze shifted over to Wallace.

"Bargest," Gildon whispered.

"Yes I know. It is dead."

"How?" Gildon asked hoarsely.

"I do not know," Wallace said, as the corner of his eyes looked over at Cole. "Gildon, we can bind your wounds as best we can, but we must leave. Can you ride?" Wallace asked.

Gildon nodded.

"Maggie quickly," Wallace ordered then he went off to help Artemis and Arthur gather the horses.

Maggie nodded then took hold of Gildon's hand. She closed her eyes and breathed deeply. She scrunched her eyebrows together, as if she were concentrating on something difficult. Gildon's back suddenly straightened as he sucked in a huff of air. His mouth opened as if he was going to scream, but nothing came out. If anyone had been around to watch what was happening, they would have seen the claw marks on Gildon's face begin to heal and scab over. They might have also witnessed the torn skin and broken bones begin to mend. But as it was there was no one to see the miracle that was taking place.

After a few minutes Maggie let go of Gildon's arm. She was breathing hard and perspiration began to bead on her forehead. She tore a strip from her dress and bound Gildon's arm as best she could with it.

"You're a healer!" Gildon whispered, looking at Maggie with wonder.

"I have done what I can for now," Maggie said, trying to ignore Gildon stares.

"Thank you!" Gildon whispered.

"Are we ready Maggie," Wallace asked, looking from her to Gildon.

"Yes," Maggie replied wiping the sweat from her face.

"Cole, are you able to ride?" Wallace inquired.

"Yes," Cole said, as Chanlyn supported him and they went to his horse.

"Good, I don't know how much time we have," Wallace announced.

"Time for what?" Artemis asked.

"Cole, do you know where we are?" asked Wallace, ignoring Artemis's out cry.

Cole looked around him, looking for any landmarks he might recognize. "We are about a two hours ride from home," Cole replied. "And an hour's ride from Kells."

Wallace nodded.

"We ride for Kells then and the White Rose," Wallace ordered.

The frightened horses, which were still a little jittery, had been gathered and found to be unharmed. Cole gave out a low whistle. Gladadear's head shot up and she obediently came to her master. He had to have help mounting her, from Chanlyn, because of his wounded foot.

Gildon, like Cole let out a low whistle and his milky white horse came to him also. He whispered a few words to the horse and amazingly the horse knelt down to the ground, allowing his master to climb up into the saddle. Once Gildon was mounted, the horse climbed back up onto all four legs. Cole, Maggie and Chanlyn stared awestruck and amazed at the horse and its master.

"It is a Tinker trick," Gildon said, when he saw their faces. "I'll show it to you when we are safe," Gildon smiled weakly.

"Cole, which way to Kells?" Wallace nearly shouted.

Cole pointed in the direction of the village.

"We ride hard. We do not stop until we have reached Kells," Wallace said, looking around him to make sure everyone heard. "Now move!" he cried.

In a wild rush they kicked their horses forward and raced as best they could through the woods. They reached the road into Kells just as the sun disappeared behind darkening storm clouds. Only when they arrived on the outskirts of the hamlet did they slow their horses. Cole let out a sigh of relief when he saw the chimneys and rooftops of Kell's houses. Wood smoke drifted in the air and all thoughts turned to a warm fire and a good meal at the White Rose.

But as they drew closer, Wallace pulled to a halt, making the others stop as well.

"Something's happened!" Wallace replied his head turned upward towards the sky.

Cole turned his gaze up and saw what it was that concerned Wallace. Thick columns of smoke rose into the air, too thick to be from chimneys. Wary of what they had already experienced and fearful of what was before them, the party kicked their horses forward, moving up the avenue of trees and into the village to find a scene of destruction.

Piles of rubble stood in place of half the homes in Kells. What used to be walls and roofs, had become nothing but fragments of what they once were. The houses looked as if they had been blown to bits. Remnants of timber and brick lay scattered in every direction. The ground glittered in the fading light with shattered glass and broken crockery. The destruction seemed to be random, with no particular pattern. While one house was totally demolished, the neighboring houses, in twos and threes, were left alone. At the end of the lane the men of the village dug through the rubble that had once been the mill where Chanyln and Master Goldhills lived.

"Father!" Chanlyn cried. He flung himself from his saddle and raced towards his home.

"What has happen here?" Sir Arthur called out.

"Strangers! Sir Arthur," Master Morell cried out, "came this afternoon. They said they were looking for Wielders. We told them there were none here and that they were all dead. They didn't believe us. So they did this," Morell said, gesturing towards the wreckage. "I think they would have pulled the whole village down had it not been for the lightning in the sky. They took off then, one going south towards the woods while the other went west."

"Has anyone been hurt?" Arthur asked.

"Master Goldhill is trapped within the rubble of the mill, sir. We believe he's still alive. The injured are at the tavern."

Wallace and Arthur immediately jumped from their saddles and went to help at the crumbled mill.

"Maggie! Artemis! Get Gildon and Cole to the White Rose," Wallace yelled back.

But it was already too late. Cole was long gone by then. He had felt an overwhelming feeling the moment Morell mentioned one of the strangers heading west. West was the direction of his home. He immediately turned Galdadear around and kicked her into a run for home.

Cole's mind flashed back to his dream that he had had that morning, of his home in ruins and Merryrick nowhere to be found. As he rode his stomach was twisting into knots, and his heart almost stopped completely with fear at what he might find. Somehow he knew that Merryrick was in danger. Whoever these strangers were, they wanted Merryrick. Master Morell said that they wanted Elfain Warriors. Gildon had come looking for Warriors and now these strangers were also looking. This was no coincidence.

They had joked just that morning, laughing at the thought that Merryrick could be an Elfain Warrior. Old Merryrick, the carpenter! Old Merryrick, who had a bad leg and could barely stand, let alone fight like a warrior. As Cole's thoughts revolved around Merryrick the tighter the knot became.

"Run, Gladadear run," Cole thought as he wished the old mare to go faster. Galdadear must have read Cole's thoughts because she sped up her pace and they arrived at the house in what seemed like only minutes.

Cole guided Gladadear into the front yard just as a clash of thunder broke across the sky.

He reined in Gladadear and she came to a stop just in front of the cottage. Pulling his bow from his saddle he nocked an arrow to his string as he scanned the yard. He could see nothing out of the ordinary. Cottage, well and chicken coop looked to be untouched. A few chickens still remained outside, scratching at the ground looking for a worm or two. The door of the cottage was shut and the shutters had been closed and locked and bolted for the oncoming storm.

"Merryrick!" Cole cried.

He received no answer.

Cole climbed down from Gladadear, looping his quiver over his shoulder and limped up to the door, still holding his arrow to his bow. When he was sure there was no one about, Cole lowered his bow and returned the arrow to its quiver and slung his bow across his shoulder.

Taking a breath he lifted the latch and pushed on the door, but the door would not budge. He pushed again and this time it moved an inch. Cole put his shoulder to it and leaned against the wood with all his strength. The door opened but only enough to allow him to squeeze in through a small gap.

He felt his mouth drop when he beheld the mess. There was nothing left that had not been destroyed or damaged. The cooking pot, which had once held a hearty stew for Merryrick's dinner, now lay in the flames of the fire, it contents mixed with ash and charcoal. The table was over turned and shoved against the door, explaining why Cole could not get in at first. The table bore deep gashes and half of it was hacked to pieces. The legs of the chairs were broken; one was completely crushed into splitters. Shattered pottery and glass crunched under Cole's feet as he entered. Shelves and cupboards were pulled from the walls and lay face down adding to the destruction.

"Merryrick?" Cole whispered.

Cole turned and looked down the short hallway, which led to the back of the cottage. "Hello. Is anyone there? Merryrick?" Cole called out.

His only answer was silence. Cole feared that Merryrick was not answering him because he couldn't. He was terrified that he would find Merryrick hurt or worse dead. Swallowing down his fear, Cole pulled his bow free and fitted an arrow to it and moved slowly down the darkened hallway. The stone and wood cottage consisted of four rooms. The living area with the fireplace and tables and cupboards, Merryrick's room which was behind the living room, separated by the fire place and Cole's room which was directly across from Merryrick's room. Then there was the workroom, located at the back of the house.

Cole reached Merryrick's room first. He kicked open the slashed door and stood before the room. It too was trashed. The mattress and sheets were torn to shreds and feathers from the pillows covered the floor, a few still drifted in the air, falling gently like snow. Half of a chest of drawers that once stood along one side of the bed had been tipped over. The other half lay on the bed. It had become nothing but splinters of wood. The washstand was only recognizable by the fact that the mirror had amazingly not been destroyed. However the pitcher and basin had been smashed, tiny bits of it were scattered in with the feathers and wood. Finding no Merryrick, Cole withdrew stepping out into the hall and went down the hall next the workroom.

This room was the largest of all the rooms in the cottage and it was trashed just like the others. It once was crammed from ceiling to floor with the woodwork that they had been working on. Now there was nothing left recognizable. Half made chairs and tables were broken and crushed. Tools were all about the room, some buried deep in the doorframe as if they had been thrown.

The bookcase that had contained Merryrick's large leather bound books, books that Merryrick used for tutoring Cole, were pulled down from the bookcase. They were torn apart. Pages lay everywhere, scattered across the floor. Drops of blood stood out against the stark white background of the torn pages.

Cole backed out of the room feeling as though he was about to fall down in despair, when he suddenly felt the cold steel of a blade across his throat.

"Who are you?" a hoarse voice whispered in his ear.

"Merryrick, it's me, Cole," Cole replied, his own voice turned hoarse from having a cold blade at his throat.

"Prove it," Merryrick commanded, digging the blade deeper into Cole's neck.

Cole thoughts whirled around in his head as he tried to figure out what was going on. Had Merryrick gone mad?

"You have five seconds," Merryrick whispered.

"Merryrick it's me. Cole, your apprentice," Cole said his heart racing.

"If you are Cole, how do I like my ale?" Merryrick questioned.

"You don't like ale. You say it makes you loose your wits and you have a hard time finding them again."

Merryrick removed the blade from Cole's throat, and he found that he could breath again.

"Sorry lad, I had to make sure you were you. Those things can fool a man into thinking that his wife is alive and well," Merryrick replied.

Cole turned around and beheld his master. Blood ran down the side of his face from a cut on his forehead. In his hands he held a silver steel sword.

"Merryrick, you're hurt," Cole cried.

"Hush boy! Unless you want to bring that foul demon back to finish us off," Merryrick whispered.

"Merryrick, what's going on? Who did this to our home and to you? And where did you get that sword?" Cole said, taking notice of the silver blade in Merryrick's hand.

"Never you mind where I got the sword and now is not the time for answering questions. There is a Reaper about," Merryrick replied, his eyes peering into every dark shadow of the house.

"Reaper?" Cole questioned. "Wallace mentioned them when he saw the dog that Artemis killed."

"Dog?" Merryrick asked, forcing his attention back to Cole. "What dog?"

"The animals that killed the sheep and the watch dogs turned out to be Bargests or Hellhounds. That's what Wallace called it. When he saw it he got all frightened and that's when he said there was a Reaper nearby," Cole explained.

"As well he should be," Merryrick answered. "For if there are Hellhounds there are sure to be Reapers around and death is soon to follow."

"Master I don't understand. What are these Hellhounds and these Reapers that you speak of," Cole asked in a whisper.

"The hellhounds are creatures that have an unusual sense of smell. They can sniff out Spirits, and the Reapers are the hunters that capture those that have the gifts of Spirits."

"The Reapers only had one master and that was Shelrin, and they were sealed away with the Dark Lord nearly fifteen years ago. If the Reapers are here then…" Merryrick muttered to himself. "Cole tell me again about your vision of the black gates," Merryrick commanded.

"Which one?" Cole asked timidly.

"You've have had more than one vision about these black gates."

"I dreamed about them."

"What did you see?"

"I uhh…" Cole stuttered.

"Quickly boy," Merryrick ordered.

"The doors were black, with chains and metal bars across them. There were markings on the gates and there was a strange blue light that glowed within the walls."

"Tell me Cole, tell me about the gates? Were there two bird-like creatures with their wings spread wide just above the gate? Were there two towers?" Merryrick asked.

"I…" Cole started.

"Yes or no Cole?" Merryrick asked, grabbing Cole by the shoulders.

"I can't remember."

"Try Cole, try to remember," Merryrick said, shaking his apprentice.

Cole closed his eyes and thought back to his nightmare. He saw the dark gates before him. They were shaking, the chains were rattling. Within the strange blue light he saw the two birds above the gateway, their eyes aglow. Cole opened his eyes and swallowed hard then looked at Merryrick.

"Yes, there were two birds, wings wide spread. They were phoe-nixes."

"And?" Merryrick asked, wanting Cole to continue.

"And the blue light went out and one of the markings on the door cracked and part of the gates cracked. A strange mist came out and I couldn't see anything. I could hear horses and dogs and then I woke up."

"The doors to the gate cracked?" Merryrick asked.

"Yes."

"When the blue light went out?"

"Yes." Cole reported. It cracked with the markings."

"How could I have been so foolish!" Merryrick cried.

"What is it Master, what does it mean?" Cole asked not under-standing.

"It means that the gates of Alorian are open. It means that Shelrin has awakened."

Cole swallowed again. He started to say something but then fell silent.

"Did anyone follow you Cole, Wallace, Gildon, anyone at all?" Merryrick asked.

"No, I don't think so. The whole village looks as though it's been blown to pieces and Master Goldhill was trapped in the rubble of his house and everyone was trying to get him out and..."

Merrick held up his hand for silence and Cole quickly shut his mouth.

"You should have never come here Cole," Merryrick whispered. "We need to be away from here," Merryrick said. "Where's Gladadear?"

"Just outside, in the front," Cole whispered.

"We'll have to go for the front door. I put all the shutters over the windows, thinking that a storm would be coming."

"But we always put the shutters up when a storm comes," Cole said, hoping this would make Merryrick feel better.

"Aye, your right lad, but something told me not to do such a thing tonight, but I did not listen. Always listen to that little voice inside your head and it will never lead you astray," Merryrick said, leading the way to the front of the house and to the door. They tried to push the table away from the door but managed to get it lodged between the fallen cupboards and the doorframe.

"Hold my sword Cole," Merryrick said, handing his blade to Cole.

Even though there was the threat of danger, Cole could not help but be awestruck by the sword. Never had he seen such an elegant weapon before. It was a straight sword except for a slightly curved end. It held no gems or gold, only a star-like crystal encased in silver attached to the pommel. There was a thin vein of blue silver worked into the blackened leather hilt, making it almost look like streaks of lightning, which was its only decoration. There was nothing significant about it, yet as Cole held it he could feel that there was a certain kind of energy around it, almost electrifying. It was cool to the touch and yet as Cole continued to hold it the hilt seemed to get colder.

"Is it supposed to get colder when you hold it," Cole asked.

It was now almost so cold that Cole could barely hold it any more.

"What?" Merryrick asked, snapping up the blade from Cole's hands.

As Merryrick held the sword, his eyes darted around the room.

"Merryrick?" Cole cried out and pointed at the shuttered closed windows. Cole's eyes widened in complete wonder as he beheld a strange mist leaking in from outside.

"It's back," Merryrick whispered.

"What?" Cole asked.

"The Reaper."

The mist continued to seep in from the outside. It crawled in like a snake, moving up the walls and across the floor. It swirled around the room as if in search of something. It collected heavily near the hearth, around the still glowing remains of the fire. It split into smaller curls, encircling the flames then swallowed them completely, extinguishing the warmth and the light.

"Merryrick! What's going on?" Cole asked, seeing his breath in the air as the temperature dropped dramatically. The mist continued to roll in becoming thicker and heavier.

"Cole, it's not real, whatever you see, it's not real," Merryrick said, grabbing Cole by the shoulders and forcing him to look into his eyes. "Say it!" Merryrick shouted.

"It's not real, it's not real," Cole repeated.

"Keep saying it," Merryrick yelled.

The mist continued to fill the room and before long Cole could see nothing in front of him.

"Move!" Merryrick yelled, as Cole felt himself being shoved aside. The door and the table suddenly blew apart, throwing Cole from his feet to the floor. His head hit something hard and Cole remembered nothing more.

CHAPTER 11

COLE OPENED HIS EYES and found he was lying on a frozen lake surrounded by mist. He looked at the ice beneath him in panic. He didn't like ice any better than fast moving water. In fact, when it came right down to it, he liked ice even less than water. Ice, although it was frozen water, was unpredictable. It could break just as easily as a sheet of glass.

"Merryrick!" Cole called out.

"Cole!" Merryrick's voice echoed around him, but it was distant, far away.

Cole looked earnestly around searching for Merryrick. A few clouds of the mist cleared and Cole could see the banks of a shore appear, with green leafed trees swaying in the wind. On the shore stood Merryrick, or at least Cole thought it was Merryrick, but as he squinted his eyes he saw that it wasn't Merryrick at all, but a woman, dressed in a white grown with her long silver colored hair hanging over her shoulders.

"Hurry Cole! Come on," the woman shouted desperately.

The woman stood there with her hands reaching out to him, looking out at him pleading for him to come to her. Cole rose to his feet, desperate to get off the ice and on to the firm ground. But as he took a step the ice let out a groan. Cole took another step and he felt pure terror rush through him when he heard it. It was like the sound of thunderclaps, a sharp snap that repeated over and over again. He looked down and saw the ice was breaking, splitting underneath him. He ran for the shore, only getting a few meters before the ground fell out from under him and he was plunged into a river of white water.

Water was everywhere. It rose up around him, pushing and pulling him. It filled Cole's mouth, choking him. The water rose over his head and then fell away. He could still see the woman on the shore; she had sunk to her knees and was reaching out to him. The waves pulled him under again, pulling him away from the woman. Cole fought the waves and tried to swim to her out-reached hand.

"Cole!" Merryrick cried from out of nowhere. "Cole, remember what I said."

Cole tried to bring back the memory of what Merryrick had told him, but he was trapped in a swirl of water and he was fighting for his life.

"It's not real Cole! It's not real!" Merryrick's voice shouted.

"It not real," Cole whispered.

The woman began to cry, a desperate plea on her face, reaching for him to take her hand.

"Say it again," Merryrick's voice shouted.

"It's not real," Cole replied, as a wave covered him.

"Again!"

"It's not real," Cole screamed, as he came up out of the water.

The woman was there, so close now that Cole reached out and almost touched her fingertips.

"No Cole!" Merryrick yelled. "Say it. Keep saying it," Merryrick shouted his voice just next to him.

"It's not real. This isn't real. Nothing is real," Cole said.

The mist was back, swirling in and eating up the trees and the water. The walls of the cottage began to fade in as the mist itself faded away as well.

"It's not real," Cole repeated, his hand still reaching out for the long haired woman. But she too was beginning to change.

"It's not real," Cole shouted.

All at once Cole was no longer looking at a woman, but was staring into the face of a cold iron mask. He opened his mouth to scream as he beheld the mask that was molded to look like a skull with a sharp dagger-like crown encircling its head. Before him was a figure dressed in decaying, shabby black robes. One flesh peeling boney hand was reaching out to Cole's still out stretched hand. In the other hand, the figure clutched a black jagged sword.

Horrified Cole snapped back his hand and tried to crawl back away from the creature. Angered by the fact that Cole was no longer under its spell, it raised up its hand that held the sword and brought it down. There was a loud clang and sparks flew as Merryrick's sword blocked the blow of the Reaper.

"Run Cole," Merryrick hollered.

Without any further thought Cole obeyed the order. He dashed for the destroyed doorframe as fast as he could and out into the farmyard, his heart racing in terror. The moment he was out the door, Cole felt ashamed of himself for leaving Merryrick on his own. But fear was in his heart and in his legs, and they carried him out the door as if they had a mind of their own. Like a scared rabbit running from a fox, Cole limped for the woods. Rain and mud splattered and soaked him as he raced for the safety of the trees. Thunder rolled so deep that he felt it vibrate within his bones. The heavy clouds blocked out any light from the moon, making the world around him as black as shadows. He was nearly to the trees when the hair on the back of his neck stood up on end and his right bicep sent out a burning pain. All at once there was a blinding flash, an echoing boom and Cole was sent flying forward through the air.

He landed face down, knocking the breath from him. Letting out a groan, he rolled over and let the rain fall on his face. Still fairly dazed by the fall, he blinked up at the sky and was amazed at how many fireflies there were. The fireflies flew in the air their soft orange glow flickering as they flew high and then disappeared into the darkness. But then as Cole's mind began to clear he realized that the flickering red and orange lights weren't fireflies at all but bits of ember. He darted up and felt his mouth drop when he saw what remained of his home. Half of the cottage was on fire and the other half wasn't there at all. It looked just like the houses in Kells, as though it had been blasted apart. The remains of the cottage were strewn everywhere. What used to be walls, windows, chimney and roof were nothing but broken brick, shattered glass and splintered wood.

"Merryrick," Cole cried, rushing towards the remains of the cottage, hoping Merryrick had not been in the cottage when it was destroyed. As he reached the wreckage a silhouette figure rose up from the rubble.

"Merryrick?" Cole questioned.

A flash of lightning cracked the sky revealing a shadowy figure that was not Merryrick but the Reaper.

Cole froze, panicked that the whole mist and false visions would occur again. But the Reaper didn't move. He didn't seem to have seen or heard Cole. It just stood there still as a statute, it's back turned to him. Cole hardly dared to move for fear that it would turn around and spot him. His heartbeat so fast and so loud he was sure that the Reaper would hear it.

Then he felt his heart stop completely when a hand covered his mouth and pulled him back, away from the remnants of the house.

"Stop fidgeting boy, we have only a few moments to escape," Merryrick whispered.

Cole stopped his fighting and felt relief over take him.

"Merryrick," Cole whispered, overjoyed at seeing Merryrick alive and somewhat unharmed.

Merryrick put a finger to his lips signaling for Cole to be quite. Together, with Merryrick leading the way, the two sprinted across the farmyard towards the woods. Looking back Cole saw the Reaper still standing disturbingly still.

"What is it doing?" Cole asked.

"Gathering his strength," Merryrick replied. "Remember what I told you about the lifesparks? It's pulling the life from the plants and trees and any living thing that is near it."

Looking around, even in the darkness, Cole could see that all around the Reaper the grass and trees started to shrivel up and wilt away.

With his eyes else where, Cole did not see the remains of what was once part of the roof sticking out of the mud. His bad foot caught on it and he toppled over, letting out a cry of pain.

The Reaper's masked head went up and with impossible speed he was racing towards them, his dark sword in hand. Merryrick pulled his own sword from his sheath and jumped in front of Cole, just in time to meet the Reaper. Steel meeting steel rang out through the night as sparks flew and its sounds mixed in with the thunder and lightning that shook the night sky. Paralyzed in terror, Cole watched as the Reaper and Merryrick fought each other throwing strikes and blows that would crush any normal man and all the while, Merryrick was slowly drawing the Reaper away from Cole. As the fight continued on, Cole could see that Merryrick was in trouble. He was weakening and he was now only blocking the blows from the Reaper, instead of attacking. Seeing Merryrick weakening, the Reaper raised his sword and brought it down hard, cutting Merryrick on his shoulder.

Merryrick let out a grunt then fell to his knees, his sword falling from his hand and sinking into the mud. The Reaper seeing his opponent disarmed, raised his black sword above his head, ready to bring it down.

"No!" Cole yelled.

Cole pulled out his hunting knife then and flung it at the Reaper. The knife flew end over end and sunk deep into the chest of the Rider. Yet it did not fall or cry out in pain. It only staggered back from the impact of the knife.

Cole stared in disbelief as the cloaked figure pulled the knife from his chest and let it fall to the ground. It stepped over the wounded Merryrick and made its way towards Cole.

Cole pulled his bow free from his shoulder and loosened an arrow at the Reaper. The Reaper didn't stop when the arrow hit, he just kept coming. Cole loosened another and another until his quiver was empty. Yet the arsenal of arrows did little to slow the Reaper down.

"You're a fool boy," a hollow voice echoed inside Cole's head, "To think that your sticks of wood can harm me," the voice continued.

Cole looked up at the Reaper, knowing that it was its voice talking inside his mind.

"You cannot harm us," the Reaper stated. To prove its point it grabbed hold of the arrows that penetrated his cheat and ripped them out, then crushed them into splinters. It then stretched forth its hand and before Cole could even blink his bow was ripped from his own hand. The Reaper caught it and proceeded to squeeze it.

"No!" Cole cried.

He could hear his bow cracking and breaking under the pressure of the Reaper's hand. Then like the rattling of thunder, the bow snapped in half and the Reaper let the pieces fall to the muddy ground.

Anger filled Cole and he felt the familiar rush of energy burn through him like a raging river. He ran at the Reaper and slammed into him and pulled back his fist and clobbered it into the middle of the mask.

Cole let out a cry of pain when his hand hit the mask.

The Reaper's head was jerked to the right.

"A fool indeed," the Reaper's voice echoed in his head.

"You can not hurt us with mortal means," the Reaper said, as its hands moved up to the mask and pulled it away from its face.

Cole's eyes widened and his mouth opened to let out a scream as he beheld the true identity of the Reaper. He was looking into the face of a rotting corpse. Bits of ash gray skin pealed away from its face, revealing bone and decaying muscle. The eyes were glazed over and opaque, holding no color at all. There was no nose, just a hole in the center of the face. Frozen in horror and disgust, the Reaper grabbed Cole around the neck with one hand the other moved to the left side of Cole's chest.

"You see boy, nothing can hurt us, because we are already dead," the voice echoed inside Cole's head as its hand sunk into Cole ribs.

Cole tried to scream as an agonizing pain encompassed his body. He felt like his life was being ripped from him. He fought, punched at the Reaper, he kicked out, slammed his arms against the one hand that held him, but nothing worked. His limbs were going weak and his vision was starting to fade, turning black around the edges.

Then all at once the Reaper let go of him and Cole crumbled to the ground, coughing as he sucked in great breaths of air. He looked up at the Reaper and stared at the tip of a sword coming through him from the back. The Reaper also looked down at the blade that was sticking out of him. It pulled its self off and turned around. Merryrick stood holding his injured arm at his side and in the other was his sword.

"Merryrick!" Cole yelled out hoarsely.

"I behold another fool. Your time is at an end Warrior." The voice echoed both in Cole's mind and in Merryrick's.

"I know!" Merryrick breathed out, "but so is yours!"

And with that Merryrick lifted up his sword, the blade pointing up. Lightning touched down and hit the sword, turning it electric blue. Merryrick slammed the sword into the Reaper with all his might, stabbing it through its heart. Cole had to look away, blinded by the brightness of the lightning that coarsed through the Reaper. When he looked back the Reaper stood frozen like a black twisted statue. Smoke was rising from him and it smelled horribly like burnt flesh. Cole rose to his feet with a stunned expression on his face. Merryrick let out a deep breath of air and then sank to the ground. Cole ran over to Merryrick, fearing the worst.

"Master Merryrick," Cole cried, reaching his master. Blood oozed from the wound in his shoulder, soaking into his shirt.

"Merryrick?" Cole asked softly.

"Cole," Merryrick said, his breath coming in huffs. "The Reaper? Where is it?" Merryrick choked out.

"Over there," Cole replied, as he pointed to the statue.

"Help me get to my feet," Merryrick said.

Cole pulled Merryrick to his feet and they both stared at the blackened form that was once the Reaper.

Cole reached out a hand and was inches away from touching it, when Merryrick's own hand caught his.

"Don't touch it!" Merryrick said, out of breath. Cole looked at his master with awe struck eyes.

"I told you to run," Merryrick said, almost in anger.

"I couldn't. I couldn't just leave you." Cole answered.

"When I say run, you run."

Cole nodded glad that Merryrick was still alive.

"Master how did you?"

"Now is not the time," Merryrick interrupted.

After he was certain that Cole understood him, Merryrick stepped forward and pulled free his sword from the burnt Reaper. As he did the statue of the Reaper started to disintegrate until all that remained was a pile of ash and the metal mask.

"Come, we are not safe here anymore. We need to find a place to hide," Merryrick stated.

They made their way to the barn and as they entered Merryrick wavered in his step. If Cole had not been holding Merryrick's uninjured side, he would have hit the ground.

"You need to rest Master and your wound needs tending to," Cole replied, lowering Merryrick to the straw covered floor.

"It's just a scratch, we have to keep going," Merryrick insisted.

"But why Master, the creature is dead?"

"One Reaper may be dead. There are more. You said so yourself. There were dogs correct?"

"Yes," Cole replied.

"More dogs, more Reapers," Merryrick breathed out. "The other Reapers will undoubtedly be here soon. They will know what happened and we must flee to the forest. It is the only place where they may not be able find us," Merryrick said, trying to rise to his feet but fell back down onto the straw.

"But then again perhaps you are right…" Merryrick said, as his eyes closed.

Cole kneaded his fist into his thigh, trying to figure out what to do. Gladadear was gone, undoubtedly scared off by the Reaper. With her were the supplies he had for the hunt. Supplies they would need if they were going to spend the night in the woods.

Taking in a breath, Cole stood, but as he did Merryrick caught him by the hand.

"Where are you going?" Merryrick asked breathless.

"Master, we need supplies. I'm just going to see what I can salvage," Cole answered.

"I'll be back," he whispered his promise.

As silently as a creeping mouse, Cole slid out of the barn and into the darkness. The rain had stopped, leaving a cold and frosty night. He moved slowly, creeping from shadow to shadow, his eyes scanning the farmyard for any movements. The moon rose up from the drifting clouds and shone down its glowing light, illuminating the yard. Cole could make out the pile of ash that had once been the Reaper only minutes before. He stared at the mound, his thoughts turning back to the moment when Merryrick had thrust the sword into the Reaper and the lightning striking the rotting corpse.

Had Merryrick really summoned the lightning? Or had it just been a coincidence that lightning struck at that very moment. The more Cole thought about it, the more he knew that it was unlikely.

Which only left the fact that Merryrick had indeed summoned the lightning bolt. Cole wondered what else Merryrick could do that he didn't know about.

The deep cry of an owl sent Cole jumping and he fell to the ground covering his head and began shaking unconsciously. Taking in deep breaths he settled his nerves as best he could, and darted to what remained of the cottage. The downpour of rain had put out the fire, allowing Cole to dig through the rubble. Where once was the kitchen, he found a wineskin which had some how survived the explosion and the fire. He came across several cracked iron pots and a few utensils, scraps of wet blankets, twisted carpenter's tools and scraps of burned paper. Other than that, there wasn't much more that had escaped the destruction. Taking the waterskin and some of the carpenter's tools as weapons, Cole ran back to the barn.

Merryrick was right where he had left him, sleeping; at least he thought he was sleeping. Fear gripped at Cole's heart and he dropped the supplies and placed a hand on Merryrick's head. He was still alive, but hot with fever. The touch of Cole's hand on Merryrick's forehead roused him but only in a half conscious way.

"Cole, we must leave, they will know what I did, they can read the air," Merryrick babbled.

"No time…to…"he muttered then drifted back into unconsciousness. Cole was worried. The wound on Merryrick's shoulder wasn't as deep as Cole first thought. The jerkin that Merryrick wore had taken most of the impact from the blade, but the layers of skin had been penetrated. What concerned Cole most was that Merryrick had a broken arm. He knew men had died from broken limbs. With the water from the waterskin, Cole quickly washed and bandaged Merryrick wounds. He cursed himself for not having paid more attention to Maggie when she talked about caring for wounds in her ramblings.

"Now what?" Cole thought.

They needed to escape, but with Merryrick the way he was, there was no way they could walk. Frustrated, Cole looked around him for anything that might help him with Merryrick. His eyes fell on the small cart, but he knew instantly getting Merryrick into the back of the cart would be hard and the cart would leave tracks. He also knew that the cart would be no good in the forest and the forest was his escape route. Cole rubbed a hand through his hair trying hard to think of what he could use to carry Merryrick away from the danger that was coming. It was then that Cole's eyes fell on the ladder that led up to the hayloft.

Pulling it free, Cole managed to quickly rig the ladder into a makeshift litter. Using ropes and leather straps from around the barn, Cole managed to tie them across the open spaces, making it a little more comfortable. Gathering the thick saddle blankets and horse blankets, Cole wrapped Merryrick in them, taking care of his wounded shoulder, and as gently as he could he dragged Merryrick on to the ladder, tying his broken arm to his chest so it would not move. He slid in behind the first wooden rod, pulled the cowl of his cloak over his head and with a deep breath he pulled Merryrick out of the barn and into the darkened forest.

CHAPTER 12

RAIN CAME AGAIN and it continued to fall. At first Cole was grateful for it. It washed away the trail that the ladder made in the wet earth. But as the night passed on, the rain made pulling the ladder harder, as it sunk into the sticky mud.

Cole made for his hidden meadow, hoping that the twelve large pines would hide him and Merryrick from the other Reaper and his hounds. But as the night wore on Merryrick got worse. His fever climbed and soon he started muttering incoherent words that Cole could not understand. He knew that Merryrick needed a bed to rest in, with a warm fire. He also needed Maggie and her skills in healing.

Changing his course Cole headed towards Kells. He knew urgency was required to get Merryrick to Kells, but he dared not take the road, although it was the fastest and easiest route. Cole didn't know how many Reapers and hellhounds were out there. He feared that the road would be patrolled by the shadowy nightmares. He also knew that if he did meet another Reaper, he could not protect himself and Merryrick from another attack. Instead he moved through the forest, hidden amongst the trees and the foliage, moving as fast as he could while pulling the ladder with what little strength he had. His foot had felt like he was stepping on nails with every step he took, but as time passed the pain faded to a numbing feeling in the back of his mind.

The silence that surrounded Cole was oppressive. He imagined that the Reapers were hiding everywhere, waiting for him. His fears made him peer into every shadow until his eyes burned. His ears buzzed from straining them, listening for any sound that might give warning to an attack. He froze with every scrape or snap of a twig. Only when he was sure that it was just the wind or a nocturnal animal on the hunt did he continue on. Weariness and exhaustion crept in on him and Cole found it hard to keep to his feet. Unseen roots and branches grabbed at his feet and ankles and threatened to bring him down. More than once he groaned in pain when a branch or vine caught around his sore ankle. He continued on in the dark for another hour until he could see the first few houses that had escaped the destruction of the Reapers.

Overjoyed that he had finally made it, Cole was about to step out of his tree covered hiding place, when all at once he heard a sound that almost completely stopped his heart. It was a howl. The very howl he heard just hours before. He didn't know where it had come from. The shifting wind made it seem that it was coming from every direction. Cole turned his head from side to side trying to distinguish from which direction the cry was coming from. He couldn't help wondering where its keeper was and as that thought whirled around through Cole's mind a sweep of movement caught the corner of his eye.

The remaining clouds from the thunderstorm shifted with the wind allowing moonlight to filter through, illuminating the dark black horse and its single cloaked rider as they moved slowly along the road towards Kells.

Cole's heart seemed to jump into his throat as he beheld the rider.

"Another Reaper," Cole thought, as he backed up going deeper into the trees, hoping that their branches, along with the darkness of the night would conceal him. However as Cole stepped back, his foot stepped on a fallen branch and a loud snap thundered throughout the darkness.

The rider intently pulled his horse to a stop, his head whipping around towards the direction of the snapping branch. Clamping his hand over his own mouth to stop his panicked breathing, Cole closed his eyes, imagining the Reaper's hollow gaze penetrating the forest foliage and finding him. Too frightened with fear Cole remained where he was unmoving and after a while, silence fell and Cole dared to open his eyes and chanced to take a step closer to the road to see if the Reaper had gone. His heart beat only increased in panic when he saw that the rider had not left but instead had dismounted from his horse and was now moving soundlessly towards where he was hiding.

Nervous muscles and tendons grew tight as the intensity of the situation grew. Cole unconsciously placed a hand on Merryrick's sword and pulled the sword from his scabbard. The cloaked figure must have heard the hiss of steel as the sword came free, for he froze and laid his own hand on the hilt of his sword.

The hilt under Cole's sweaty hand grew warmer as a plan formed in his head. If he attacked the Reaper, surprising him, he might be able to end this night of cat and mouse. Taking in a deep breath, Cole slipped from his hiding place and into the shadow of another tree, moving away from the Reaper so he could sneak up behind him. He stood against a large oak tree waiting and watching. He was so close now that he could see the mist coming out from under the Reaper's hood as he breathed.

Do Reapers breathe, Cole thought, but he pushed the idea aside.

The Reaper turned his back towards Cole, and started to walk away back to his horse. Silently, as if he were hunting, Cole snuck up on his prey and raised the sword over his head, ready to run the Reaper through, when all off a sudden Cole let out a cry and dropped the sword as a searing pain burned his hand.

The Reaper spun around, pulling his sword free and at the same time sent his fist flying. The hard fist hit Cole in the face and he fell back, his knees crumbling underneath him. He felt warm blood flow from his nose and slide down his lips. Dazed and half blinded by the pain, Cole looked up as the cloaked figure stood over him.

"Master Wallace!" Cole sputtered in astonishment, as he looked up into the stupefied face of the farmer.

"Cole! I could have killed you, boy," Wallace said angrily, as he sheathed his sword and then reached down to help Cole to his feet.

"What were you thinking?" Wallace asked, ripping part of his cloak to give to Cole to stem his bleeding nose.

"I thought you were a Reaper," Cole sniffed, stuffing the material up his nose.

"Reaper?" Wallace asked worried. "Where's Merryrick?"

"He's over there," Cole pointed towards the tree line.

Cole picked up Merryrick's sword and led the way back through the trees to where the litter lay with Merryrick on it.

"What has happened?" Wallace asked, getting to one knee to look Merryrick over.

"It was a Reaper. It cut Merryrick," Cole stated.

"The Reaper did this to him?" Wallace asked, more concerned as he examined the wound in Merryrick's shoulder.

"Yes! Wallace, he will be all right won't he?" Cole asked with fear in his voice.

"I don't know Cole. Perhaps you got him here in time," Wallace replied.

"Time? What do you mean?" Cole asked.

Wallace looked at Cole with a sad expression, and that expression sent threads of terror into him.

"The wound is infected Cole," Wallace replied.

"But it's just a scratch. It not even that deep," Cole shouted.

"Shhh," Wallace ordered. "The Reapers!" Wallace continued. "They dip their blades in poison Cole. It's called Black Venom. If they don't kill a man right off, the poison will. Sometimes the Reapers will wound a man just to watch him die from the poison."

"So Merryrick's going to die?" Cole asked, fear welling up in his eyes.

"Not necessarily Cole. Some men have survived the poison. Merryrick's strong and a fighter. If anyone can pull through this it will be him, but he could use all the help he can get," Wallace stated. "Come, there is no time to waste. Maggie is at the tavern."

Wallace pulled the litter free from the brushes and trees and using Brom's reins and bit, tethered the make shift litter to the horse saddle. No longer burdened with the ladder and Merryrick, Cole moved along the road more quickly. They entered into what remained of Kells, and Cole felt himself relax a little. He was in Master Wallace's company and now that they were close to Kells, he had the hope that everything would be all right. Wallace however, seemed to tense up even more as he walked with Cole. His hand was always on the hilt of his sword, never moving it. Even when they reached the middle of the village, Wallace did not let go. He was not the only one feeling the tension in the air. The village men, bearing weapons of pitchforks, axes and scythes, walked up and down the avenue that was lined with burning torches.

"The stories are true then about the Reapers and their hounds?" Cole asked.

"Aye lad, so they are," Wallace grunted.

"Master Merryrick said that the Reapers only served one and that was Shelrin."

"That is true as well," Wallace commented.

"But I thought that Shelrin was dead," Cole questioned.

"Not dead lad. Sealed away or at least he was," Wallace muttered.

The two walked in silence for a time until Cole saw the remains of the mill.

"How is Master Goldhill?" Cole asked. When Wallace didn't answer right off, the feeling of dread rose up in his throat and he had to swallow it down several times.

"Is he dead?" Cole asked.

"He's alive! He was lucky though," Wallace answered. "Master Goldhill's leg is pretty torn up. The two support beams came down on top of one another, stopping the roof from caving in on top of Goldhill. It most likely saved his life, but his leg was caught under one of the beams," Wallace explained.

They pulled to a stop in front of the tavern. Maggie came out from the tavern and ran to Cole.

"You're okay? We thought the worse when Gladadear came back without you," she said into Cole's shoulder.

"She came here then?" Cole asked.

Maggie pulled away and wiped the tears from her eyes and nodded her head.

"Terrified she was. We got her to calm down and I put her in the tavern's stable and..." Maggie voice suddenly stopped and she truly looked at Cole through clear eyes. "Cole what's happened to you. Your hair! It's gone completely white!"

"What do you mean?" Cole asked, reaching up to touch his hair.

"Did the Reaper touch you Cole?" Wallace asked.

"Yes it..." Cole swallowed, as the terrifying memory came back to him. "It tried to take my heart. It felt like it was ripping the life from me."

"Not your heart, but rather your lifespark. And as for life being ripped from you, they did just that," Wallace replied. "They took some of your life, hence your white hair."

Cole didn't know what made him more surprised, the fact that Wallace knew about lifesparks or that he knew so much about the Reapers.

"What has happened to Merryrick?" Maggie asked.

"He was cut by a Reaper's blade. He's been poisoned. Can you help him Maggie?" Cole asked desperately.

As Maggie bent down to check Merryrick, the rumbling of hooves made Cole turn his attention towards three galloping horses that came flying down the road. He felt his heart speed up when he saw three black hooded riders coming towards them.

More Reapers, Cole instantly thought, but then his heart slowed its pace and he took in a breath of relief when he heard Sir Arthur's voice come from one of the hoods.

"There's no sign of them," Sir Arthur cried, pulling his dark hood of the cloak from his face. "The house has been destroyed and I fear poor Master Merryrick and young Cole have been either killed or…" Arthur said, as he dismounted from his horse. His words fell short however when he saw Cole and Merryrick, "…captured. Good gracious boy, you look worse than death, and your hair. I'd say you've seen death and it scared you so much that it turned your hair completely white!" Arthur sputtered. "And Merryrick what's happened to him?"

"Cole, how long has he been like this?" Maggie asked, as she looked over Cole's master.

Sweat from his fever dripped down the side of his face and even though he had thick woolen blankets wrapped around him he was shaking uncontrollably.

"I don't know. Maybe a few hours or so," Cole answered.

"Cole, what happened?" Gildon asked.

Cole explained what happened again and Gildon's facial features turned grim just like Wallace's.

"We need to get him inside," Maggie ordered.

"You can help him then?" Cole asked, fear climbing up to his throat when he saw Maggie's expression.

"I will do what I can," Maggie replied.

Wallace and Arthur took the corners of the ladder that Merryrick lay on and carried him inside the travern. Mistress Morell saw the state Merryrick was in, and quickly led them to a comfortable back room. As Cole followed, he saw the common room of the tavern. The tables that once cluttered the floor had been pushed back to make way for the many makeshift beds that scattered the room. Here and there people lay or sat with bandages wrapped around their heads, arms, legs or hands looking dumbfounded or stunned. Those that had not been injured ran around helping care for those that had suffered an injury.

"Mistress Morell, would you bring hot and cold water please?" Maggie said, as she started to strip away Merryrick's jerkin and shirt. "And fresh linens" she shouted after Mistress Morell as she left the room.

Wallace started to pull Cole towards the door but he dug in his heels.

"I want to stay. I can help," Cole stated, looking at Maggie for support.

"Let him stay father. I will need his help."

Wallace nodded his head and left the room, looking sad as if he knew that Merryrick would not last the night. They bathed Merryrick in cold water to cool his body temperature down. After cleaning the wound, Maggie applied a poultice of charcoal.

"What will that do?" Cole asked.

"The charcoal will pull out and absorb some of the poison," she explained.

When they were finished, they bound Merryrick's arm after they had, what Maggie called, set the bone" then wrapped Merryrick in blankets and placed a wet cold cloth on his forehead.

"All we can do now is wait," Maggie replied, as she took a seat and exhaled a breath of exhaustion. "Do you know what they mean? The bands on his arm?" She questioned.

When they had stripped Merryrick of his shirt, Maggie took notice of a tattoo of seven bands that were intertwined with one another in the shape of an eternal braid.

"I asked him once about them. He said that it was a part of his past and should remain that way," Cole stated. "I never asked him again and he never mentioned them."

"Wonder what they mean? Father has similar bands on his arm, but he won't explain them to me either."

COLE SAT BY Merryrick's sick bed hour after hour, keeping the washcloths fresh with cold water, wiping his fevered brow and changing the charcoal poultices every few hours. Maggie had gone hours before to check on Master Goldhill's leg and the others that had been injured during the attack and had not come back. Cole sat slumped in his chair half asleep, when Merryrick suddenly let out a cry and bolted up in bed. Cole was so surprised from shock that he froze.

"They've breached the western gate. They're heading for the keep. Get his majesty out." Merryrick shouted.

Cole stood staring at Merryrick, struck dumb by what he was saying, and then as if someone had shaken him awake he rushed to calm Merryrick down.

"Master Merryrick! It's all right! You're safe!" Cole said softly, leaning over Merryrick.

Merryrick looked at Cole his eyes burning with fever.

"How did they get in? How? The gates were locked," Merryrick wailed, grabbing Cole by the shirtfront and pulling Cole towards him, with unbelievable strength, until they were nose to nose.

"You let them in," Merryrick said coldly, as he grabbed Cole by the throat and started to squeeze.

"No, Master Merryrick, it's me, Cole," Cole choked, as he tried to break Merryrick's hold.

"Cole?" Merryrick said, as if he were trying to recall a memory.

Cole started seeing little black spots forming in front of his eyes for a second time that night.

"Cole?" Merryrick said, suddenly remembering who Cole was, as a light of recognition came into his eye. His hands fell from Cole's throat and laid them on his shoulders.

"By the great warrior of old, your hair Cole, its gone white," Merryrick gasped.

"Yes, Master Merryrick," Cole muttered.

"They tried to take you from me. They tried to take your spark. But I made a promise, so long ago. I will admit mistakes were made

Cole. We were foolish and arrogant, thinking that nothing could touch us, but we were brought down. I see now that I was given a second chance. I could fulfill my promise I made by raising you, in training you. She saw it too. She saw what you could or would become and what you would do."

"Who are you talking about Merryrick?" Cole asked softly. "Who saw what I was to become?" Cole wondered.

"Your mother," Merryrick responded.

Cole fell back away from Merryrick, a look of pure shock on his face. He felt like he had been punched in the stomach. He was breathless, shaken.

"Merryrick, who is my mother? When did she tell you this?" Cole asked, making Merryrick look him in the eye. But the light of recognition was gone and Merryrick was lost somewhere in a different time.

"My sword! Where is my sword?" Merryrick yelled, desperately trying to get to his feet.

"It's here Master Merryrick," Cole answered, and then went to the corner where it stood up against the wall and retrieved it for him.

Cole gave it to Merryrick and he grabbed the sword.

"His Majesty gave this to me. Said I was to protect it for it was the key," Merryrick whispered to the sword. Merryrick's eyes widened and his head snapped up as if he was hearing something. "They're coming."

"Take it. Take it and promise you won't let anyone know of it. It is the key. His Majesty said so." Merryricks words came out rapidly as he twisted the sword's pommel 'It is the key to finding the lightning."

"Merryrick what do you mean? Lightning?" Cole shouted.

"I'm sorry my boy, but it's time for you to see," Merryrick whispered as he pulled the crystal star from the swords hilt.

Merryrick grabbed one of Cole's hands in a vice like grip.

"It's time for you to know where you come from," Merryrick said, then pressed the star into Cole's hand. The moment he did, that familiar flash of light blinded Cole.

When he could see, Cole found himself not in the sickroom within the White Rose, but in a solarium, with an indoor garden.

Bright warming sunlight filtered in through a green-glassed paneled ceiling. Ionic columns held up a balcony that looked out over the garden. On the far wall was a stone carving of a tree. A great white living tree, much like the carving on the wall, with blooming silver leaves, grew within the center of the solarium on a small grass covered island surrounded by a pool of spring water. Exotics plants and flowers grew in pots, their blossoms the color of sunsets, and rainbows. Standing guard over the solarium was a white marble statue of an archer. He stood looking out over the view of a vast city. His left arm was pulled back while his right arm held a bow. A stone-carved arrow was nocked to the bow and the archer was ready to let it fly.

The bright flash of light came again.

Cole jerked up and snapped open his eyes. He was back in Merryrick's room, within the White Rose, sitting by the bed. He looked around him in confusion. Merryrick lay in the bed with the blankets pulled up to his chin. His sword was sheathed and stood in the corner. It appeared as if nothing had happened, that Cole had just dreamed it all. Yet his one hand was clenched in a fist and as he he opened it up, there was the crystal star, glowing softly in the firelight.

"Cole? Are you alright?" Maggie asked. She stood over Merryrick checking his wound.

"Sorry I didn't hear you come in" Cole said tucking the star into his jerkin pocket and then pretended to wipe the sleep from his eyes.

"You were sleeping. I didn't want to wake you," she smiled. Cole noted that she appeared very tired and worn out.

"Have you had any sleep?" he questioned.

"A little," she replied.

"How is he?" Cole asked, getting up from his chair to join her.

"He's not doing as well as I would have liked," Maggie answered, her brow scrunched up in worry.

"The poultice hasn't helped?" Cole wondered.

"No," Maggie muttered.

"Then what else can we do?" his voice shook with emotion.

"Something I should have done when I first saw Merryrick."

Maggie took a seat on the bed next to Merryrick. Then Maggie placed a hand over Merryrick's wound. She took a deep breath and closed her eyes.

"What are you doing?" Cole asked.

""Shhh!" she commanded.

"Maggie?" Cole questioned.

"I said shh!"

The room went quiet, all but for the sounds of the fire burning in the hearth. Cole watched Maggie wondering what it was that she was doing. Suddenly Merryrick's eyes snapped open and he started shaking like he was having a fit.

"Maggie what are you doing?" Cole cried, grabbing Merryrick to hold him down.

Cole looked over at Maggie, who still had her eyes closed. His own eyes widened with fear as he stared at her. She was very pale, almost the color of marble. Her skin was so pale and thin he could see her veins under it and they were turning black.

"Maggie stop!" Cole cried, and pulled her hands from Merryrick's wound.

Maggie let out a grasp. Her eyes rolled up into her head and she fainted into Cole's arms.

"Master Wallace!" Cole called, "Master Wallace!"

Wallace came bursting through the door and saw Maggie in Cole's arms.

"What happened?"

"I don't know. She was helping me with Merryrick. She placed her hands on his wound and then she went all pale and her veins went black. I tore her away and she fainted," Cole explained.

"She tried to heal Merryrick?" Wallace asked.

"I don't know?" Cole sputtered.

Wallace said nothing as he took Maggie from Cole and then left the room.

Cole didn't know how long he paced back and forth within the confines of the bedchamber, but it felt like hours. His head whirled with what Merryrick had said. Did he really know who his mother was, or was it his high fever causing him to imagine things? Merryrick did try to choke him, thinking that he was someone else. The more

Cole thought about it, the more tired he became. Not only was he occupied with the ramblings of Merryrick but he was also concerned about Maggie and Merryrick seemed to be getting worse. He felt like he was going out of his mind with worry. He didn't even notice the door to the room opening until he heard his name being called.

"Cole!"

Cole looked up, surprised to see Wallace and Gildon standing before him.

"How is Maggie?" Cole asked.

"She is fine. Just over did. You however are not fine," Wallace answered. "You look worse than death. You need to rest," Wallace said, stepping forward and taking Cole by the arm and nearly dragging him towards the door.

"No! Merryrick needs me!" Cole said, trying to break free of Wallace's grip.

"You need to take a break and get some rest yourself. Have someone see to your own wounds. It won't do Merryrick any good if you became sick yourself," Wallace stated.

Cole tried to fight off Wallace but he was tired and Wallace had a firm grip on him.

"It's alright Cole, I'll stay with him," Gildon said, managing to place the wet cloth on Merryrick's forehead despite the sling on his arm.

Grudgingly, Cole let Wallace lead him out of the room and down the short hallway of the tavern to the common room. The aroma of baking bread and roasting meats drifted around the room. Cole's stomach gave out a growl of hunger as he took in the smells.

"Take a seat, I'll see what Mistress Morell has for you to eat," Wallace ordered.

Cole did as he was told, taking a seat at one of the tables and rubbing his eyes of the weariness that was in them.

The taverns large fireplace was lit with a great blaze, making the common room warm and comfortable. Before Cole knew it his head was down on the table and his eyes were closed. When Wallace came back with a tray of food in his hands, Cole was sound asleep.

CHAPTER 13

"COLE!" Merryrick's voice called out waking him.

"Master Merryrick?" Cole muttered still somewhat half asleep.

"Cole it's time. You need to leave this place. They are coming."

Rubbing the sleep from his eyes, Cole sat up in a bed that he had obviously been moved to. Looking down he found Merryrick standing at the foot of it.

"There's not much time Cole. You have a day, maybe two at the most. You must go to Aloria. Gildon will take you there," Merryrick ordered.

"What about you?" Cole asked. "I can't just leave you."

Merryrick smiled, a sad sort of smile. "I am alright Cole. I am beyond the realm of pain now. My time is over," Merryrick said simply.

"I don't understand," Cole responded.

"You will Cole. For now, know that I will never leave you and that I am watching you. There is much I have not told you, much that I feared to tell you. I had hoped that you could live a life without anyone knowing of your gifts, but I was wrong and I hope that you can forgive me for that," Merryrick said, his voice starting to fade as he himself started to disappear.

"Merryrick! Wait!" Cole yelled.

"Aloria, Cole, it is the only place where you will be safe."

COLE SUDDENLY JERKED AWAKE, sitting up in bed within a darkened room. He looked down at the end of it but did not find Merryrick standing there. He threw back the blanket that covered him and was on his feet and through the door, running down the short hallway to the stairs. He took them two at a time regardless of his now cleaned and bound injured foot. He felt his heart flutter with grief when he saw the door to Merryrick's room open. Cole rushed forward and saw Maggie. She looked up at him and he could see the tears sliding down her cheeks.

Cole stepped into the room and was nearly blinded by the brightness within it. Lighted candles were scattered around, illuminating the room. The lighted candles were a tradition among the people of Kells. It was said that it helped the spirit of one who had just died to see their way through the darkened land of death into the light to paradise. Merryrick lay resting peacefully on the bed, a slight smile upon his lips. He was dressed in fresh linens and his hair had been combed. His hands were folded around the hilt of his sword. He looked as though he might just be asleep, except for the paleness of his skin. Cole took in a breath and then sunk to his knees before the bed.

"No!" Cole breathed out in grief.

Cole's shoulders shook as the tears started to fall. "You said you'd never leave," Cole cried. "You said that, remember?" Cole yelled, shaking Merryrick.

"Cole," Wallace comforted, coming up behind him and putting a hand on his shoulder. "I'm sorry".

Cole jerked away from Wallace's touch.

"I can bring him back," Cole muttered. "I can bring him back just like Thomas. I just need to find his flame, his spark" Cole said, remembering how he had saved Thomas at the river. Cole reached out with his hands and placed them on Merryrick arms. To his utter disappointment everything remained as it was.

He closed his eyes, trying to concentrate on how he had felt that day. He dug deep within him, searching for the firelight energy. But no matter how hard he dug, it wasn't there. All he felt was darkness and emptiness.

"Cole! You can't help him. He's gone," Gildon said. "I'm sorry, Cole, but Merryrick's flame has gone out."

Cole didn't hear. He was too lost in his own grief and sorrow. He knelt by Merryrick's bedside and cried until there were no more tears to shed.

COLE SAT BEFORE the flames of the fire within his small room at the White Rose, the remaining pieces of his bow in his hands.

The bow was a visual reminder of what had happened to his world. Once whole and strong, it now was broken and shattered into pieces.

They had buried Merryrick that morning, placing him in a tomb of earth with his hands gripping his sword. Wallace had said a few words about Merryrick that were nice but they did not fill the hole that had suddenly appeared within Cole's heart. The villagers that attended made their condolences to Cole and then went on their way. For the rest of the world the sun was shining and the birds were singing yet within Cole's world, it seemed that it was ending.

What was he to do now? He felt lost and alone. In one small moment he had lost his master, he had lost a friend and in truth he had lost a father. All that remained of his life with Merryrick was Gladadear and his memories. A fresh flow of tears swept over Cole as he tried to find some ray of light that could break through the darkness and guilt that enclosed him.

It's my fault. It's all my fault, the words kept repeating over and over again inside Cole's head.

"If he had not gone to the house would Merryrick still be alive? If he had run like Merryrick had told him to would he still be alive? If… if…if…all of the if's swirled in Cole's head causing him to fall into a pool of self guilt.

Everytime he closed his eyes he could see that fatal moment when the Reaper had stabbed its sword through Merryrick shoulder, thereby poisoning him. It played out over and over again in his mind. As it did, the grief, the guilt and the pain that Cole had been feeling, seemed to increase and a cold savage anger began to boil within. He wanted vengeance for what the Reapers had done to Merryrick, what they had done to him. The thought of hunting down the remaining Reapers and destroying them, burrowed deep into his consciousness. The idea of revenge was frightfully comforting. He couldn't help thinking of the satisfaction he would receive by destroying them. Yet there was a thread of doubt running through him. It was a desperate thing to do. He didn't even have a bow or a weapon to fight with. His bow was broken. He nearly threw the pieces of his bow in the fire but thought better of it and slipped them into his quiver. If he didn't even have a bow how was he going to fight the reapers?

"Does that matter?" a little voice inside his head whispered. *The Reapers hurt you, in more ways than one. They deserve to be obliterated from this world.* That fatal moment of Merryrick and the Reaper flashed across his mind again.

Cole stood from his chair, a grim, cold expression on his face as he made his decision. It was time to go on another hunt. Although he wanted to rush off to track down the rest of the Reapers at that moment, he made himself stop and forced himself to focus on what he needed for this quest. He didn't know how long it would take, a day if he was lucky or possibly a week or more.

"Food, bedding, water skin." Cole thought, making a mental list in his head. He remembered that he had a water skin, the one that he pulled from the wreckage of the house but the other things, the food and bedding, he had no such things anymore so he would have to make do with what he could find. He rolled up the blankets from the bed and put them under his arm. Then as silently as possible, he opened his door and slipped down the stairs.

It was early in the evening and the tavern was busy with customers. Most everyone there had come to the White Rose to mourn Merryrick's death with a pint or two. It was full of noise, of yelling, singing and cheering. Sir Arthur was the loudest amongst the crowd. Cole was pleased with the uproar. It allowed him to sneak away more easily and unnoticed.

The kitchen was empty when Cole crept in, which he was glad of. He didn't want to explain himself to anyone, certainly not to Mistress Morell. He found a few loaves of bread and a wheel of cheese that he wrapped in cheesecloth and then tucked under his arm along with the blankets. He felt guilty for taking stuff that did not belong to him and he hoped that Mistress Morell would not hate him too much for stealing from her. He told himself that he would pay her back oneday. When he thought that he had everything that he would need, he slipped out the back door and into the kitchen garden.

A short distance away, further back from the tavern, was the barn where Galdadear was being kept. The white mare had come running into town that fateful night, without her rider. That was how Wallace and the others knew that something had befallen Cole and Merryrick.

When he entered the tavern stable, he felt a wave of panic rush through him. The stall where Gladeader was kept was empty.

"If you're looking for Gladadear, she's not here at the moment."

Cole whipped around and found Gildon, standing on the threshold of the stable; his arm still wrapped in bandages and hung in a sling.

"Where is she?" Cole snapped, his anger flashing.

"She's safe," Gildon answered. "Going somewhere?" he asked, taking note of Cole's supplies.

"It's none of your business," Cole raged back.

"No, I suppose it's not," Gildon said, "but I have to wonder what you're running away from when Merryrick has only been laid to rest."

"I not running way," Cole shouted.

"Really! Sure looks like you are," Gildon responded calmly.

"I told you," Cole said through clinched teeth, "I'm not running away."

"No? Then where is it that you are going?"

"Hunting!"

It became quiet as Cole and Gildon stared each other down.

"It won't bring him back Cole," Gildon suddenly said, softly breaking the silence.

"What?" Cole grunted.

"Going after the Reapers won't bring Merryrick back," Gildon stated.

"How do you know that I am going after those murderers," Cole asked.

"Because it's what I would do, if someone close to me was murdered by those dark creatures," Gildon responded.

"Then let me go," Cole said.

"I can't do that."

"Why not?"

"Because of who you are. Because of what Merryrick told me," Gildon spoke.

Cole froze. He looked at the tinker hard, trying to detect any facial expression that would tell him if the man was lying.

"What?" Cole barked.

"Merryrick never told you?" Gildon replied acting truly surprised.

"Told me what?"

Gildon looked at Cole with raised eyebrows.

"If I tell you Cole, you have to promise me that you won't go after the Reapers."

"They killed Merryrick!" Cole shouted. "They murdered him and you want me to promise not to go after them?"

"Yes," Gildon plainly said.

"Tell me what Merryrick said," Cole demanded.

"Not until you promise," Gildon ordered.

"Tell me!" Cole shouted.

"Promise me first!" Gildon shouted just as loud,

Without really thinking about what he was doing, Cole dropped his supplies. His hand went to his belt as he pulled a dagger from his belt. He heard the steel coming free from the sheath and saw the tip of the blade pointed at Gildon's throat. Cole heard the distant sound of footsteps running towards the barn but his eyes never left Gildon.

"Cole, what are you doing?" Maggie's voice screamed.

She had come running to the barn when she heard all of the yelling.

"Cole stop!" Maggie screamed again, but Cole ignored her.

"Tell me or I'll kill you!" Cole threatened, his hands starting to shake.

"You won't kill me, Cole," Gildon said calmly.

Gildon grabbed hold of the dagger with his good hand and ripped the blade right out of Cole hands.

"You don't even know how to use this," Gildon said, turning the blade on Cole.

"Master Gildon, leave him alone," Maggie cried, running to Cole's side.

"Maggie get back," Cole hollered, as he looked down at the blade and then back at Gildon, his blue eyes throwing daggers at the Tinker. He stepped back away from the blade and managed to trip on his supplies. He landed on his backside looking up at Gildon.

"Promise me, Cole!" Gildon whispered.

"They killed Merryrick!" Cole said angrily

"And they will kill you too, Cole. If you go after them right now, they will cut you down and not even give you a thought. You saw what they did to your village, what they did to Merryrick. Do you think that you can go up against them by yourself? You could barely manage to hold this dagger," Gildon remarked. "Even if you did somehow manage to destroy one Reaper without getting yourself killed, it wouldn't matter, more would just come. But if you come with me to Aloria, there are those that can teach you how to fight, they can teach you how to defend yourself and defeat the Reapers. Come with me to Aloria and learn how to fight and you can not only protect yourself but so many others as well."

"And if I don't go with you, if I make the choice to go after the reapers? What then?"

"I cannot let that happen, for that is what the Reapers want. They came here for you and the others."

"Others?" Cole asked, blinking at Gildon. "I don't understand. What others?"

"Do you promise not to go after them at this time?" Gildon inquired.

Cole weighed his options. His desire for revenge still burned within him like a fire, but he desperately wanted to know what Merryrick had told Gildon, him being the last person who had talked to Merryrick before he died.

"I promise," Cole muttered in defeat.

"Good," Gildon said, taking Cole by the hand and pulling him to his feet. He gave Cole back the knife and he sheathed it.

"I think now its time that I told you the real reason why I am here. Maggie," Gildon turned and looked at the girl.

"Gather your father as well as Chanlyn, Artemis and Sir Arthur. If Master Goldhill is able to stand have him come too. Have them come to the tavern, for this concerns them all."

CHAPTER 14

COLE WAITED IMPATIENTLY in the private room of the White Rose with Maggie, Chanlyn, Artemis, Sir Arthur, Master Goldhill, and Master Wallace. They were seated at a small square table with Gildon at the head. The room was dark, for it held no windows and what light there was came from the small fire in the little fireplace and the few lamps that had been lit. The room wasn't big. The room was one of the smaller rooms near the back of the tavern and from the look of it it wasn't used very much. It smelled musty and it seemed that there was still quite a bit of dust. It looked to be more for storage than for entertaining.

Trays of food, provided by Mistress Morell, had been placed on the tabletop and were now being consumed by those that sat around the table. Cole, however, ate nothing. He sat with his foot tapping on the floor waiting for the others to finish their meal. He had no appetite for food at all. He only wanted to consume the information Gildon had.

"Cole, you must eat something," Maggie insisted. She offered him a roll and he took it, but merely tore it to pieces while he waited.

"Now, Master Tinker, why have you summoned all of us here today?" Sir Arthur finally asked, after he had finished his mug of ale and had placed it on the tabletop. "It is a day of mourning. We have lost a great man by the hands of those monsters, the Reapers."

"It is because of those Reapers that you are here," Gildon said. "Have you not wondered why the Reapers came here, when they have not been seen since the time when Shelrin ruled?" Gildon went on.

"They came because they are looking for something or rather someone," Gildon continued when no one answered.

"Oh and who is this someone?" Sir Arthur asked.

"The warriors' heirs that will defeat the black dragon," Gildon answered, "the ones that will completely destroy the dark Lord Shelrin."

"I thought Shelrin was dead?" Maggie stated. "You said that Shelrin was destroyed by Kayden."

"Not killed but sealed away," Gildon answered. "After ruling for over a hundred years, all of Shelrin's armies and the dark masters were captured by Kayden. Then the whole palace was locked within a hard-wall barrier that let no one in and no one out," Gildon explained. "It has lasted for these last fifteen years,".

"What do you mean 'has' lasted?" Sir Arthur asked.

"The barrier must be weakening, " Gildon responded.

"What proof do you have of this?" Arthur nearly shouted.

"The Reapers are the proof, Sir Arthur," Wallace spoke for the first time. "They and the Hellhounds were locked away with Shelrin at the last battle, frozen in time," continued Wallace. "And the Reapers are here for a reason, the same reason that you are here, Master Tinker."

"You are correct. Master Wallace. The Reapers are here for one purpose, and that is to collect you four," Gildon said, his eyes falling on Cole, Maggie, Chanlyn and Artemis in turn. "Perhaps I should start at the beginning and introduce myself properly. I am Master Gildon of the House of Kirkwell and I am a fire master. I have journeyed across the land of Albavar to find those that have the bloodline of the Elfain warriors in them in hopes that I might find the Warriors' Heirs who have been foretold would come and vanquish the darkness. I believe that one of you or all of you might be an heir."

No one spoke for a long time. They all looked around at each other, wondering if this someone was their neighbor.

"How is it that you think that it is one of us?" Sir Arthur asked.

"It was not you they were after Sir Arthur, but rather your son, along with Cole, Maggie and Chanlyn." Gildon answered.

"Me why me?" Artemis cried.

"Because a Hellhound is dead and one of you four was the only one that could have done it," Gildon answered.

"True it was my arrow that brought the beast down," Artemis bragged, "but it was just a dumb dog."

"You think so?" Wallace asked.

"I know so," Artemis announced.

"Then you're a fool," Wallace remarked. "Hellhounds are not just merely dumb dogs, they are near indestructible. They are linked with their masters, both in spirit and in power. They have the incredible gift of scent. They can sniff out a wielder thousands of leagues away. They cannot be killed just by a mere arrow, it takes an incredible amount of power to kill a Hellhound and even more power to kill their masters," Wallace spoke.

"Which brings us back to you four. The Hellhounds sniffed out Spirit wielders, that's why they are here and I'm guessing it was you that alerted them of your presence."

" It's not my fault they're here?" Artemis protested.

"I'm not saying that it is any of your fault. It just happened." Gildon responded.

"Spirit wielders?"Goldhill questioned.

All heads turned to look at Master Goldhill. Cole was amazed that he was even up, let alone talking. He had a few cuts and scrapes across his face, but his right leg was braced and was wrapped in bandages and he looked extremely pale, like he was a ghost in the darkened room.

"Forgive me, where I come from, wielders are those that have Spirit."

"What do you mean Spirit? I'm not haunted by any spirits," Artemis said in distain.

"I don't mean the spirits of the dead. No, rather the elements that you can wield, what you can control, such as fire, earth, water or wind," Gildon explained.

"Yes, well whatever Spirit you think I have, I don't," Artemis announced.

"I don't think I can agree with you, young Artemis. The Reapers are interested in you as well or otherwise they would have not destroyed your home, like they did with Maggie's, Chanlyn and Cole's. It is fortunate that you were all on a hunt when the Reapers attacked."

Cole let out a cold laugh.

"Fortunate?" Cole said bitterly.

He couldn't help think that if he had been there when those cloaked demons first attacked, Merryrick would still be alive.

"If you had been there Cole, you probably would have been killed or perhaps taken," Gildon said, as if reading Cole's thoughts.

"But we are only farmers and millers," Chanlyn said.

"Are you really just a miller Chanlyn? And you Maggie are you just a farmer's daughter?" Gildon asked, "You are all unique aren't you?"

Cole looked around at his friends. He knew about Maggie's talent of healing. But what of Chanlyn and Artemis, what was Gildon talking about. But none would meet Gildon's eyes. Even Artemis looked away from Gildon.

"Show him boy!" Master Goldhill said to his son. "Show him what you can do." Chanlyn looked up at his father and nodded his head. Chanlyn closed his eyes, and he took in a breath. He then opened his eyes and clapped his hands. A gust of wind swept around the room, blowing out the candles and the fire in the hearth throwing them into darkness.

Cole looked towards Chanlyn with wide eyes and open mouth.

"How did you do that?" Cole asked.

"The boy's been able to do that since the day he was born," Goldhill said. "Had a heck of a hard time keeping candles lit when he was little," Goldhill chuckled.

"You hold the spirit of the wind," Gildon said. "Artemis, I believe that it is now your turn."

"Me! I can't do anything. I'm not like him," Artemis said angrily, as if the thought insulted him.

"Look," Maggie said.

A small flame of fire had flickered to life on one of the candles and was steadily growing.

"Well done Artemis!" Gildon said.

"That wasn't me. I told you I'm not a freak," Artemis cried angrily. The fire in the hearth suddenly burst into flames and the candles re-ignited, the wicks burning with a bright flame. Everyone stared at the flames surrounding them and Artemis stared with a look of horror on his face, then he darted from the room, opening the door and running out as if he was terrified of what he had just done.

"The Spirit of fire," Gildon announced.

"Well, what do you know, he's not a complete waste after all," Sir Arthur said, watching his son storm out.

"Your turn Maggie," Wallace whispered, giving Maggie a nod of encouragement.

Maggie nodded her head. She turned to the flowerpot that Mistress Morell had brought into the room for a centerpiece. Some of the blossoms were fading and had begun to wilt and their heads were drooping. Maggie took a breath in and began to blow on the flowers. Miraculously the withering flowers began to grow healthy and strong. Their bright colors of green and yellow returned until they were in full bloom.

"The spirit of earth," Gildon responded.

"I can heal most things back to life," Maggie whispered. "But if the injuries are too great I can only extend life for a short time," Maggie whispered, her eyes filling with tears as she looked at Cole. "I tried to help Cole. But Merryrick…"

"It's alright Maggie. It wasn't your fault," Cole whispered.

It took Maggie a couple moments to wipe her tears away and give Cole a smile.

"So, what is it that you can do Cole?" Sir Arthur asked, "You must be able to do something.

Cole looked up and saw that everyone was eyeing him.

"I can't do anything like that," Cole replied. I can't make the wind blow, I can't start a fire, I can't heal anyone," Cole said bitterly, "I can't even fight."

"You have other gifts Cole," Maggie said softly.

"You can trace? Can't you?" Gildon asked.

Cole's head snapped over to Gildon and wondered how much the Tinker or who ever he was, knew about him.

"Trace?" Sir Arthur asked curiously.

"I believe when Cole touches the ground with his bare hands he can see about a league ahead, or behind. If he's has been to a place and knows the area he can see further." Gildon said.

"And you can do this just by touching the ground?" Sir Arthur asked.

Cole nodded his head, hoping that Gildon did not know what else he could do. He didn't want to explain that when he touches someone he could see their past or their future, nor did he want to share the fact that he had strange dreams that made no sense to him.

"If you were to touch the ground right now what would you see?" Sir Arthur asked, clearly wanting a demonstration.

"How far do you want me to go," Cole asked.

"Oh let's say to the kitchens," Sir Arthur replied.

Cole blew out a breath, bent over his chair and touched the floor.

He felt the familiar rush forward as he passed through the door and out into the common room. He saw people talking and heard conversations as he moved passed the bar. He pushed his mind to the back of the tavern where the kitchen lay. There he stopped. He felt the warm fire from the great hearth, and then saw Mistress Morell move around the large table placing plates of honey oats cakes on a large tray and then followed her as she left the kitchen and made her way to the room at the back.

"Mistress Morell is bringing us honey oat cakes," Cole said, pulling his hand free of the ground.

Just as Cole sat back up in his chair there came a knock and Mistress Morell stepped into the room bearing a large serving tray that was filled with the delicious delicacies.

"Amazing!" Sir Arthur said wide-eyed, as he looked at Cole.

"Oh it's not that amazing, Sir Arthur, just the regular honey oatcakes," Mistress Morell said, as she placed a plate before each of her guests.

"Thank you, Mistress Morell, you are very kind," Gildon said.

Mistress Morell nodded her head then left the room while everyone dug in. Yet Cole only looked at his. The sweet cakes didn't even tempt him.

"It's no wonder you're so good at tracking, Cole," Sir Arthur said, his mouth full of cake. "I would love to have your gift," he announced. "The next time I go hunting I shall surely have you come along."

"I am afraid that Cole won't be going hunting, at least not for a long while," Gildon commented. "He, like all of you, must leave Kells. You must all leave tomorrow if possible."

"Leave? Why would we leave?" Arthur cried.

"You must leave. The fact remains that your son and all the others within this room are in grave danger and they've become more endangered as the hours go by," Gildon replied.

"What would you have them do, Master Gildon?" Wallace asked.

"As I said leave Kells, Master Wallace. Their only hope is if the four of them leave," Gildon said, looking all of them in the eyes in turn. "It would not only make you safe but also the village."

"Where would we go?" Wallace asked. "The Reapers found them here in the mist of the Elfire Mountains. What's to say they won't find them anywhere else?"

"There is a place that I know of where you will be safe. It is to the north of here, it is the city of Aloria."

"Aloria!" Arthur cried. "Aloria is the city where the Elfain warriors were slaughtered. The city no longer exists."

"That city was called Alorian, Sir Arthur, the new city of Aloria was built by those that fought against Shelrin. We tinkers that live in the city have tried to keep the traditions of the Elfain Warriors alive, for we are of the bloodline of the Elfains Warriors just as much as you are, though most of the knowledge the Warriors possessed was lost in the destruction of their city. We have gathered others from across the land with their own gifts of Spirits. We are training many to learn how to use their Spirit. With the Tinker Masters, each one of you would be very safe. You could learn more about your gifts and become stronger in them as well and learn how to fight, at least those that wish to," Gildon said. There was silence in the room as everyone soaked the information in and thought about Gildon's words.

"I don't know how far Aloria is but I gather it is a long way from here. Whose to say that we won't be attacked along the way," Arthur spoke breaking the silence. "If we stay here we can at least defend ourselves. Here we know the strengths and weaknesses of the land. We can stand up against whatever may come our way. Are we not Kells people?"

An image of the village in ruins, danced in Cole's head. Nothing remained but the skeletons of buildings and the Green was covered with markers of the dead.

"No?" Cole spoke. "If we stay there will be nothing left of Kells. If I leave, if we all leave, the Reapers and the hounds won't come back. We have to leave."

"The boy speaks wise words for one so young," Wallace stated.

"Are we to leave our homeland on words of a boy and a Tinker? No offense Cole. What if they are wrong?" Arthur cried out.

"And what if they are right?" Wallace asked. "I am not willing to bet the lives of the people of Kells that Cole is wrong. Are you Arthur?" Wallace asked.

Arthur opened his mouth to say something but nothing came out.

"I believe that Master Gildon tells the truth. For the safety of my daughter and for the safety of Kells we will leave and travel with you, Master Gildon," Wallace proclaimed.

"As will Chanlyn," Master Goldhill replied.

Chanlyn looked over at his father with astounded eyes.

"You will becoming as well father," Chanlyn commanded.

"I wish I could son. But if I am not mistaken, Master Gildon wishes to leave as soon as possible. I cannot travel. Even if I could go lad, I would only slow you down and endanger not only you but also your friends. Your safety is what I desire most," Goldhill replied.

"But..." Chanlyn started to say.

"Chanyln, there is a time when every young lad must leave and make his own way in the world. I believe that this is your time. Although it is much sooner than I wanted, the fates have spun their threads and have begun to weave your tapestry of life. You must go. Besides it is not as if you cannot come back when the danger has ended. Now if you will excuse us, Master Gildon, I wish to return to my bed and spend the last few hours with my son. I would think that you would want to leave before the first rays of light on the morrow."

Gildon nodded his head.

With Chanlyn's help, Master Goldhill and he left the room.

"Well, it seems that Artemis and I have no choice but to follow," Arthur stated, when the door had closed behind Master Goldhill and Chanlyn. "As Master Wallace has said, he is not willing to bet the lives of the people of Kells on a chance that Cole and you are wrong, and nor am I. We will prepare for the journey," Arthur said, rising to his feet. "How many days shall we pack for?"

Gildon thought for a moment. "Two weeks more or less, but pack light. It will be hard going around the mountains."

"We should go too. There is much to do, before the morrow," Wallace said, rising. "We will return to what is left of our home and see what we can salvage. Perhaps Mistress Morell can help us with food supplies."

Maggie rose from her seat and looked over at Cole.

"Coming Cole?" She asked.

"Cole will be along shortly," Gildon answered. "I believe that he has something he wants to ask me."

Maggie's eyes darted from Cole to Gildon and then back to Cole, her mind wondering what it could possibly be that Cole wanted to ask Gildon.

"Come on Maggie, there is much to do," Wallace said, guiding his daughter out of the room.

When the door closed, silence fell in the room. It stayed that way until Gildon took a breath and began. "He would be proud of you," Gildon said.

"Proud of me?" Cole chided. "I'm a coward. I'm running away."

"I don't think he would say that about you," Gildon responded.

"What did he say about me?" Cole asked, picking at his shredded pieces of bread.

"You have heard about the foretelling of the Warrior's Heirs?" Gildon asked.

"Yes," Cole replied.

"Then you have heard of the foretelling of the lost heir of Ayden, have you not?" Gildon questioned.

Cole nodded.

"What Merryrick told me is that he seemed to think that it is you Cole."

At hearing that Cole let out a cold laugh.

"Merryrick must have been out of his mind. I am just a carpenter's apprentice, a nobody."

"You don't think a carpenter can change the fate of a nation or perhaps even the world?" Gildon asked.

"Not me!" Cole replied, getting to his feet.

Cole walked to the door and opened it. He was about to walk out but stopped when Gildon started speaking again.

"And the day doth come ever closer when a great servant of darkness shall rise and bring forth much bloodshed and horrors upon the land. And many souls will fall into darkness and lose the light of hope. But fear not. For I shall tell you this, I have seen the day when one will rise. And it shall come to pass that from my blood shall come forth, a mighty man, with the power of the gods, but have the heart of a human. He shall come forth from the shadows of the great mountains and will defeat the servant of darkness. And this shall be a sign unto you, he will be marked with the brand of a true Elfain and he shall burn bright with wings of fire, like that of a phoenix and he shall be called a king, a warrior, a grand master," Gildon proclaimed.

Cole shook his head in disbelief.

"I am not your lost heir or anything else," Cole replied. "I'm just an apprentice to…I was an apprentice to a carpenter, now I'm no one."

"You're wrong, Cole, Merryrick was not just a carpenter he was an Elfain Warrior and you are also wrong in thinking that a carpenter cannot change the world. For it has been done once before."

Cole said nothing as he left, but Gildon's words resonated in his ears and would not leave him even when he fell asleep that night.

CHAPTER 15

THEY LEFT THE NEXT MORNING before the gray dawn had yet to appear. They planned to take a route that Gildon had followed to get to Kells and ride all day and into the night, resting when the sun was up again. Wallace hoped that escaping the village in the wee hours and riding through the night would give them enough of a head start that they could out run the Reapers. The path the company planned to travel would take them around the mountains, rather than over the mountains. A path much easier by far but it would take longer.

Cole sat on Gladadear waiting for the others to ready themselves. Master Goldhill had come to say his goodbyes to his son, giving him a great hug as tears filled his eyes. Cole looked away then, his jaw clenching to stop the oncoming emotions. If Merryrick still lived, he might have given Cole a hug of goodbye or perhaps he would be coming with them.

"Are you alright, Cole?" Maggie asked, looking at Cole with concern.

"I'm fine," Cole replied stiffly.

With nothing left to do, the group set off heading north towards the Elfire Mountains. As they were about to disappear among the trees, Cole pulled Gladadear to a stop. He turned in his saddle and looked back at the village. The feeling that he would never see his home again weighed heavily on his heart.

Letting out a breath of air, Cole kicked Gladadear forward.

"Goodbye Merryrick," Cole thought, looking over his shoulder to see what he could still see of Kells.

They continued on, hour after hour, going deeper into the forest. It was the farthest Cole had ever gone before. The trees were so tall and grew so close to each other that they blocked out most of the sun, letting only shafts of light through. A thin layer of mist drifted lazily throughout the forest, encircling the trees and the ground. The smells of dirt, dew and pine hung in the air, mixing in with the clouds of mist, creating the feeling that the forest was very old.

"Can you feel it?" Maggie whispered.

"Feel what?" Chanlyn asked.

"The life that flows through the trees. They are very old. I'll bet if they could talk they would tell us of how the world came to be," Maggie commented.

"Probably be a very boring story," Artemis replied curtly.

Wallace and Gildon chuckled at the comment, which seemed to surprise Artemis a little. "I didn't think it was that funny," Maggie muttered angrily. "Beside we could learn a lot from trees…"

Cole wasn't listening to Maggie's chattering for his attention was drawn elsewhere. His eyes darted left and right. The mist that swirled around them was making him nervous and he feared that it hid the Reapers within. It only got worse when nightfall came. They continued to move through the forest by the light of the full moon. Its shifting light filtered through the breaks in the treetops. All moved with caution, steering their horses around trees that looked more like shadowed monsters with their branches reaching outward looking more like claws and talons than tree limbs.

"I don't suppose we could rest for a bit?" Maggie asked, in a breathless sigh.

"Quite right," Arthur muttered. "The young ones are in need of rest."

"There is a place not much farther that I found quite comfortable," Gildon responded.

He led the way in, past a spring and to a place where several large pine trees had been up rooted and had fallen over, one ontop of another. The fallen trees had created a den of sorts and it was here that Gildon stopped his horse and dismounted.

"We are to rest here?" Maggie asked.

"It is more than it appears," Gildon replied.

"What if there are unwanted creatures within?" asked Maggie, looking at the future campsite with raised eyebrows.

"You might have a point," Gildon commented. Then he got down on his hand and knees and poked his head inside. "It is free for the taking," he replied.

So tired were they that there was not a complaint about the accomadations. They dismounted their horses and began to make camp. Cole was exhausted. His eyes burned with weariness and his body felt like a lump of iron. He wanted to fall out of his saddle, crawl forward into the den, wrap his blankets around himself and fall asleep, but he knew that Galdadear was just as tired as he was and would want to have the saddle taken from her back. Climbing down from her, he made sure that Gladadear was all right. Finding that there was nothing wrong, he turned to the job of taking off her saddle and rubbing her down.

He started undoing the cinches under Galdadear's belly, when he heard Artemis give out a command. "You will do Addis! Then you can move onto your own bag of bones."

Cole stood up and turned to look at Artemis to see whom he was talking to. Instantly Cole's eyes flarred with anger as Artemis flung his reins that were linked to his chestnut stallion at him.

"You will make sure that Addis is brushed out thoroughly," Artemis said, with higher authority. "And be wary of his hooves, they often find themselves stomping on feet and breaking toes."

Cole looked at Artemis with disgust as he threw back the reins. "Do your own horse, Artemis," Cole said, through gritted teeth, "I have my own work to do."

"You are a stable boy and stable boys take care of horses. Addis is a great and noble horse and is far more important than your flea bitten old nag over there."

Cole suddenly felt the sensation of an enormous amount of energy running through his body. His hands were balled into fists as he took a step closer to Artemis.

"You may insult me if you wish, but if you ever call Galdadear a flea bitten old nag or anything that is remotely like it, you will find yourself…"

"What is going on?" Wallace grunted, as he came running towards them. Artemis looked at Wallace with his usual superior look, one that he used to indicate he was of high and of noble blood.

"I was just telling the boy he was to brush out Addis's coat and to make sure…"

"You take care of your own horse, boy," Wallace said, interrupting Artemis. "There's enough work to be done as it is. You're not in Kells anymore. There's no one here to pamper you and do your work for you. Now get to it," Wallace said, looking at Artemis with an unnerving stare.

Cole turned back to Gladadear and once again started to undo the cinches letting the anger and the energy slowly float out of him. A half an hour later Gladadear was saddle free, rubbed down and brushed out until her white, creamed-colored coat gleamed in the forest nightlight.

Taking the saddle, Cole crawled in under the trees and tucked himself in a nock near the back. The place was cool and smelled deeply of dirt and old vegetation, but it was as Gildon said. It was comfortable yet somewhat of a tight fit once everyone one was in.

Wrapping his cloak around him, Cole leaned his head back against the earthpacked wall and drifted off to sleep. He didn't know how long he had slept, but when he woke there were bits of morning twilight dipping into the den. The sound of murmuring voices was what had awakened him. After rubbing his eyes, Cole opened them and saw a small fire burning in the center of the campsite. Seated around it were Maggie and Chanlyn, listening to Gildon as he spoke to them.

"Earth, fire, wind and water are the four main spirits that are always around us," Gildon explained, drawing four vertical lines in the ground with a stick. "From them spring forth other spirits, such as life and death, light and dark, hot and cold, snow and ice." He said drawing more lines that extended from the four main lines. "And from these spirits springs forth more and so on and so forth. These spirits, no matter how great or small they may seem they are the elements that make nature work. For you it is the same," Gildon spoke looking into Maggie and Chanlyns eyes, each in turn. "As descendants of the Elfain Warriors you have the inate ability to call these spirits to your aid and wield them for the good of others. That is your gift."

There was a short moment of silence as Gildon let his words sink into his young students, before he went on. "With the ability to wield the earth one can heal wounds, bring forth life, and summon the very earth itself," Gildon spoke, looking at Maggie.

"Maggie, as a child of the earth, you have the ability to use the life of the plants to heal others, not just physically but also mentally. Although that is very difficult and takes years to master it"

"With the ability to wield the winds," Gildon turned to Chanlyn, "One can call forth storms, walk on air and bring the winds to their needs. Chanlyn, as a child of the winds, you have the capability to summon the winds, you have the power to bring in the rains that can bring life or slay fires that can destroy. And yet you have the power to destroy as well. Both of you do. Both of you can give aid to the life and light of mankind, but you also have the gift to bring forth death and misery. The powers that lie within you are great and therefore you must learn to control them by learning to control your emotions.

"Our emotions?" Maggie asked.

"Yes,"said Gildon.

"I don't understand," Maggie commented.

"Maggie when you heal someone how do you do it" Gildon asked.

"How do I do it" Maggie muttered more to herself. "Well I suppose that I have to touch the injured or sick person and in a way I can see were they are injured or why they are sick and then I just know how to help them and how to heal them. It is like I get a picture in my head of what to do. So I follow it and it usually works," Maggie replied, "sometines I see a plant I have to use to bring down a fever or sometimes it is letting the mana flow through me to the area of injury" Maggie replied.

"Mana? "Gildon questioned. "Do you mean Spirits," Gildon asked.

"I suppose. It's the word mother used to describe what you called the lifespark, I think," Maggie said. "Anyway, mother said that everything that was living had mana surging through them. The stronger the mana there is, the stronger the energy that comes from humans. But if we use too much of our own mana or the sick or injured person's mana, one or the other could die. She taught me to use a balance. The healer uses some of their mana, or lifespark and some of the patients, but mostly the healer should use the mana that comes from plants and trees that are around you, because they were created for our use," Maggie explained.

" Interesting," Gildon replied,"we shall have to talk more."

As Cole listened, he understood a little more of what Merryrick had told him before, about using nature's life rather than his own.

"And you Chanlyn, what is it that you feel when you wield the wind?" Gildon wondered.

"Well I guess I feel powerful, as though nothing can touch me. It's as if I could…"

"Walk on air," Gildon interrupted.

"Yes, like I have the power to walk on air," Chanlyn stated. "It feels wonderful."

"And you probably can and will. Once you get strong in wielding."

Chanlyn looked at Gildon with widened eyes.

"It is said that the old Wind Masters could walk in mid-air and even fly. You have the aptitude to do so Chanlyn. But besides blowing out candles and fires you can also tumble mountains, create storms and can wipe out entire villages. When you wield it feels good. As you said Chanlyn, you feel untouchable. Both of you can help people. All of you can. Your unique gifts allow you to do so but as much as your gifts can help they can also destroy."

"And that is where our emotions come in?" Maggie asked.

"Correct," Gildon answered. "As I said before the Lifespark or Mana, is the power source and our emotions control that power. It is most important to always have control. If you cannot control your feelings then you cannot control your power. Do you understand?"

Both Chanyln and Maggie nodded.

" I think so," Maggie said, "you always have to keep calm when healing. If you feel anything other than calm you might do something that could endanger the patients," Maggie responded.

"You are correct Maggie. Now I have a little exercise for you that will let me know how much control you have over you emotions," Gildon said, scooping up a handful of dirt.

"Maggie, hold out your hands."

Maggie did as she was told and Gildon dropped the dirt into her cupped hands, Maggie looked at it with raised eyebrows, wondering what Gildon had in mind,

"Chanlyn your turn."

Chanlyn held out his hands, expecting Gildon to drop a pile of dirt in his hands as well, but instead he got a simple small white feather.

"Maggie what lies in your hand is a simple pile of dirt. Or is it? Whether you can see it or not there is life within that soil. Search through it, find a lifespark and help it grow," instructed Gildon.

Maggie's eyes widened and her eyebrow went up and her lips twisted to the side, a clear sign that she was thinking about how to achieve Gildon's task. Gildon then turned to Chanlyn.

"You hold a simple bird feather Chanlyn. What I want you to do is levitate the feather within the palm of you hand. Try to keep it in your hand for as long as you can. Don't let it float away."

Cole watched as both Maggie and Chanlyn stared down into their hands. Their eyebrows scrunched together and they concentrated on their dirt and feather. After a time Chanlyn let out a cry of frustration because for all his concentration, his feather remained in his hand.

" I can't do it," Chanlyn said.

"Why not?" Gildon asked, "it's only a feather, it's not heavy at all. I have seen you take out hundreds of candles and fire."

"I suppose it's because … because…oh I don't know," Chanlyn cried out.

"Perhaps you're just thinking too much. Try not to think at all. Just let the spirits flow through you," Gildon replied.

"Huh!" Chanlyn asked.

"What I know about you Chanlyn is that you are smart, thoughtful and you're a thinker. Which is good in some cases, but in others, thinking too much can cause you to freeze up and hold back. Try feeling, rather than thinking," Gildon advised.

Letting out a deep huff, Chanlyn closed his eyes, held out his hand and for a few seconds nothing happened, then slowly, ever so slowly the feather rose. It stood straight up. The tip of the hollow shaft was the only thing touching Chanlyn's hand. The feather stood straight for a few seconds more before it fell back down. Chanlyn opened his eyes looking hopeful at Gildon.

"Well done Chanlyn," Gildon said, slapping him on the back.

"Thanks," Chanlyn said breathless.

"Maggie! Your turn," Gildon said, turning his attentions to the girl.

Maggie took in her own breath and closed her eyes. Like Chanlyn nothing happened at first, but then within the small pile of dirt a small green sprout began to emerge. At first it was just a small little thin strand of green, with no leaves. But as Maggie kept at it, two little leaves began to spring forth and a small bud was beginning to appear. Its second leave popped open and the stem was growing longer. It looked as if it were going to bloom when Maggie suddenly let out a gasp of air and her eyes snapped open.

"That was incredibly hard," Maggie breathed.

Maggie looked down at her hand and frowned at the little sprout.

"I thought that it would be bigger," Maggie said, a little disappointed.

"Oh and why did you think that? I thought you did wonderful for your first time," Gildon replied.

"Well I imagined it bigger," Maggie said.

"What do you mean?" Gildon asked.

"Well, when I found that there was a seed in the dirt you gave me, I imagined the seed growing. I saw it within my head as a great, large tree and so I fed it just a bit of lifespark and asked it to grow for me. That's how I have always done it. Is that not wielding?" Maggie asked. "Its what I have always done. Seeing things returning to life. Seeing what you want them to be."

"Yes that is wielding in a way. But..."

"But you can't expect a wind flower to be an oak tree," Cole said.

"How long have you been awake?" Maggie asked, surprise on her face.

"A while," Cole muttered, crawling out of his nook to join the others.

"Oh? So you heard my little lesson?" Gildon asked.

"Yes," Cole answered.

"Then I suppose you should give my little exercise a try," Gildon said, pulling from his pocket a small blue pebble and placing it in Cole's hands.

"I can't make it float or grow like Maggie and Chanlyn," Cole said, looking down at the pebble.

"I know," Gildon responded.

"Then what do you want me to do with it?" Cole asked.

"Touch it," was Gildon's answer. "Tell me where I got it from."

Cole looked at Gildon and saw that he was serious. With a sigh, Cole took the pebble from Gildon and placed the small rock in the palm of one hand. Without much of an effort on his part, Cole closed his eyes and touched the ground with the other. Seconds passed and in those seconds Cole's mind shot backwards along the trail they had passed over just hours before. He saw the large oak tree they had rested under for a few moments during the day and he saw the rock formation that looked somewhat like a cow. He continued to run back, retracing his steps. The sound of a babbling brook pulled Cole towards the running water. He remembered that they had rested there the afternoon before. This was where Gildon had gotten the stone. Cole was ready to pull his hand away from the ground when he was startled by a flock of birds taking off from the trees. They scattered, flying high and fast, as if they were scared of something. Cole looked around him. And his back stiffened. A gust of wind had come up and with it came a howl that made the hair on Cole's neck stand up on end. Everything was still and quiet, not even the call of the sparrows resounded through the forest. Cole remained where he stood, his instincts telling him to do so.

As swift as the wind itself, a large sense of blackness swept past him. Cole spun around and saw to his utter horror a hellhound coming to a stop in front of him. Its head turned and Cole swore the hound was staring at him even though the hound could not see him. After a moment it let out a deep crying howl. Not long after, there was another one that echoed the first. After that there was a chorus of hellhound cries, each one responding to the first. Cole knew instantly that the hounds had found their trail and it was calling the others to him. He also knew that not far behind the Hellhounds would be the Reapers. Cole let go of the ground and he returned to his body.

"They've found us," Cole replied urgently. "They know we've left Kells and they are on our trail."

"That was fast," Gildon said. "Did you find where I picked up the pebble?"

"At the stream, yesterday afternoon," Cole replied. "But we have a problem. The Reaper's have found our trail."

As the words left his lips a resounding chorus of hound howls broke through the daybreak, awakening Sir Arthur and Artemis from sleep.

"But how could they have found us? We left no trail," Maggie whispered, her voice shaking with fright.

"No physical trail," Wallace replied, coming into the den. "I have made sure of that."

Cole looked up at Wallace in surprise. He had not noticed that Wallace had gone anywhere.

"Cole is right, they found us. Did any of you wield?" Wallace asked. Chanlyn and Maggie hung their heads showing signs of guilt.

"What did you do?" Wallace asked.

"We tried doing an exercise with Gildon," Chanlyn replied.

"What was the exercise?" Wallace asked again.

"I asked Chanlyn to levitate a feather and for Maggie to help a wind flower grow. Cole was to find where I found a pebble," Gildon answered.

"That wouldn't have alerted them to our position. They're not strong enough in Spirit wielding yet. Something else must have alerted them to our position," Wallace answered. "Did anyone else beside Cole, Maggie and Chanlyn use their gifts?"

No one answered but they all turned, their eyes darting a glance at Artemis.

"I was asleep the whole time. I only woke up when those blasted hounds started howling."

"Perhaps we should not stand about accusing one another, but maybe rather we should run," Sir Arthur spoke.

"I agree with you Sir Arthur," Wallace said. "Gather your things," Wallace ordered.

A very short time later the companions had their horses saddled and were ready to leave. But before they galloped off, Wallace stood before the den of trees looking at it.

"Hadn't we better go?" Sir Arthur muttered.

"One moment," Wallace replied.

Taking in a breath and closing his eyes, he then stretched out his hands, palm side up. Cole's mouth dropped and his eyes bulged as the earth beneath his feet began to moan, and then slipped right under where the den of tree was. Gladadear gave a snort and stomped her feet.

"Easy Glad, easy," Cole said, reassuring her.

The den and any trace of the campsite disappeared as it was swallowed into the earth. The ground folded back in on its self and there was nothing there to give away that there had ever been anything there,

"You're a wielder!" Gildon exclaimed.

"I am, but now is not the time to explain," Wallace remarked. "There is another matter to think upon, mainly the Reapers," Wallace said, and kicked Brom into a run.

THE LATE MORNING came slowly for Cole and the others. Deep howls of the hounds reverberated around the forest. Some were distant while others were closer, seeming to be only a league or so behind them. Tension was upon every man and the horses trembled as they trotted through the forest. It wasn't until the rays of sunset came filtering in through the trees that the tension eased a little. After the sun had started to sink on the horizon, Wallace had the group stop for a few hours rest. Cole flung himself under a tree and closed his eyes. It seemed that only minutes had passed when he was woken and told that they were moving on. He rubbed the sleep from his eyes and stood and stretched out the knots and pains from his body.

"We've gone too far. This early morning's wandering has made us loose our directions. I'm completely lost," Gildon exclaimed, when the early gray morning revealed the landscape. "I have no idea where we are. I won't be able to guide you around the mountains," he said in a near panic.

"We won't be going around the mountains," Wallace answered, "but rather we will be going over them."

"You're not suggesting that we take the Path of Sorrows are you?" Arthur asked in shock.

"Indeed I am," Wallace replied.

"What is the Path of Sorrows?" Gildon questioned.

"It is the path that our ancestors took to get here and settle Kells," Chanyln responded. "The path runs through the Elfire Mountains, past Sorrows peak and then down into the Valley of Tears. It is named the Path of Sorrows because many who traveled it died along the way, leaving those that still live to mourn the loss of their loved ones," Chanlyn said, freely giving the information.

"And you wish to take this route?" Gildon asked disbelieving.

"What other choice do we have? Judging by the distance of those howls it won't be long before we are found. These woods are swarming with Reapers and Hellhounds," Wallace replied.

"If we go into the mountains we may meet our deaths, "Arthur stated.

"If we stay here we will most certainly meet out deaths," Wallace stated. "We have no other choice."

"Then if we are to go to the mountains, we had better get going. Sundown will come too fast as it is and we must put as many miles as possible between us and those that are hunting us." Gildon replied.

CHAPTER 16

THEY RODE HARD each day, riding to the point where not only they themselves were exhausted, but also their horses. Then darkness of night forced them to stop. They made camp under a thick grove of trees and there was no fire for warmth, for the flames would give away their position and so they ate cold dinners each night. In the mornings the company rose early, rising even before the sky had yet to turn gray.

Five days after they had left Kells, Cole realized that they were getting closer to the Elfire Mountains. All around them the scenery was beginning to change. The compacted and tight knit trees gave way and were soon replaced with high climbing hills. Instead of ferns and ivy taking over the ground, it was short-stemmed grass, with the occasional shrub or bush that covered the ground. Large boulders and rocks stuck up from the ground as if they had grown there.

Cole had mixed feelings about leaving the forest. He and the others were out of the dark woods and finding oneself in wide open space and being able to see clear blue sky with the sun on their faces again was wonderful. Yet it was the wide-open spaces that had him worried. If they were in need of a place to hide, their only option would be the few scattered rocks and boulders that were strewn about the hillsides.

Once they were out of the woods, Wallace increased the pace even more, racing across the hills. What with so few trees now and more grass, the horses could move at a run and be easily guided around any tree, rock and bush that was in their path. By mid afternoon, they reached the base of the Elfire Mountains. Wallace pulled his horse to a stop atop a hillside. The others followed, each pulling their horse to a halt. Looking down the hill, they all saw the winding path that wound its way up the face of the gray rock until it disappeared from view in the far distance.

"Is this the Path of Sorrows?" Gildon asked.

"It is," Wallace replied.

"After a hundred years, you would think that nature would have destroyed any signs of it by now," Arthur muttered.

"I believe it's because so many people traveled the route when they were escaping the war that it has been permanently cut into the earth. It will probably take another hundred years or even more for the trail to disappear completely," Chanlyn chimed in. They all stared at the ancient path and wondered how far it went and how long it would take them to travel it.

"Best get moving. I want to find shelter before the storm hits," Wallace announced. Cole looked up at the sky. From what he could see there was not a puff of cloud in the sky.

"Storm," Arthur asked. "What storm? I see not a cloud in the sky. Surely we can take a moment to rest. We have been riding for hours on end."

"The storm is fast approaching, Sir Arthur, I can feel it," Wallace replied.

"It's true," Maggie whispered to Cole. "He can tell when a storm is coming. I think he can read the air."

Cole looked at Maggie with raised eyebrows. He remembered Merryrick saying something similar, *they can read the air, Cole.*

He understood now what his Master was saying.

"That's how they're tracking us isn't it?" Cole announced.

"I don't know how they really track anyone. But it is believed they can sense wielding, by reading the change in the air," Wallace reported. "And if wielding is involved it only makes the scent stronger and the Hellhounds can find it."

"But what you did back there, at camp?" Cole questioned.

"I covered up our trail. It may confuse the hounds for a while. And if we are lucky my wielding will fade and the hounds won't ever find our trail again, but I wouldn't count on it. Hellhounds are very good at what they do," Wallace muttered.

What do you mean by fade?" Chanlyn asked.

"Its like animal trails or any other trail that you are following," Wallace answered. There are signs that are left where animals or humans have been, tracks are left, branches are snapped or the dirt has been unsettled. Wieiding leaves signs as well. When caught fresh it is easy to follow, right Cole."

"Yes." Cole answed.

"As time goes by the trail fades and the chances of finding the trails is less likely. So the more distance we can put between us the more of an advantage we have. Also the storm that is coming will help wash away our scent, but it may also deture us. So if you don't want to sleep out in a downpour I suggest we get going," Wallace advised.

Although Cole was tired and sore from riding so many hours, he wasn't too eager to spend a night on the mountainside in a pouring rainstorm and it seemed he wasn't the only one. Chanlyn, Maggie and Gildon, kicked their horses and followed Wallace down the hillside and onto the trail that looked like nothing more than a goat trail. Sir Arthur and Artemis had no other choice but to follow.

Wallace turned out to be right. Two hours after they had started ascending the mountain, the storm began to show its ugly face. The wind had picked up and brought with it dark gray clouds, that turned an almost purple black with every minute that passed. Not long after the clouds appeared, rain started to fall. As if to mock them, the wind picked the rain up and threw it hard in their faces. The small path that they had been following was soon lost from sight. The freezing wind ripped at them, tearing away any warmth from their bodies. The horses could no longer be ridden but they had to lead them. The rain soon turned to snow, which clung to their faces and clothing. Cole tried to keep his cloak wrapped around him but he only had two hands, one was used to lead Gladadear and with the other he tried to keep the snow from coming into his face.

The snow began to stick to the ground, and after what seemed like only minutes the level of the snow doubled from ankle deep to knee deep. Any dry patches of clothing that had managed to escape the wind and rain were now soaking wet and the companions were now shaking with cold as their teeth chattered uncontrollably.

"We cannot go on Wallace," Arthur yelled, trying to be heard over the howling wind that tore at them.

"Just a little further," Wallace yelled back.

Cole didn't know how long they kept on moving. To him it felt like hours. His fingers and toes burned with cold. His bones hurt so bad he was sure the marrow within was frozen and he could no longer feel the muscles in his face. All he wanted to do was just sit down, close his eyes and fall asleep and he was ready to so when suddenly Wallace let out a yell.

"I found it," he yelled, as he disappeared into a mountainside.

Wallace's voice echoed around them and as the last call faded away there came a great moan and the sound of rolling thunder surrounded them. The thunder didn't dissolve away but rather grew louder and louder as if it were rolling towards them. Through the shower of snow, Cole could see a large white cloud moving towards them. He watched it with curiosity. He had never seen anything like it before. It moved so fast.

"Avalanche!" Wallace screamed, coming out of the mountainside. "GET INSIDE!" He grabbed Maggie's hand and dragged her towards the mountain.

"MOVE! GET THE HORSES," Wallace hollered at the top of his lungs.

Cole and the others ran then, pulling their horses with them when they realized that it wasn't a cloud at all but a raging storm of snow coming down off the mountain at a speed that was as fast as the Clearwater River flowed.

Wallace shoved Cole into the mouth of a cave, with Gladadear right behind him and then threw himself in, before the cave was flooded with snow. The snow came in so fast that Wallace, and even Gladadear were knockled off their feet and thrown into total darkness.

Cole must have been knocked out for short time, for he woke with a screaming headache. He grabbed the side of his head and felt warm blood. Opening his eyes he found he was in darkness, darkness so thick that he could not even see his hand in front of his face.

"Is everyone alright?" Wallace was saying. "No one hurt?"

"Father where are you?" Maggie's voice came out of the dark.

"I'm here," Wallace answered. "Chanlyn you alright?"

"I'm alright, just a few bumps and bruises," Chanlyn replied, from somewhere.

"Gildon what about you Arthur? Artemis?"

"A little shaken but fine," Gildon responded. "How about giving us some light?"

"We are alright," Arthur's voice came out of the darkess.

The darkness was suddenly blown away when the flicker of a flame burned to life, illuminating the companions and their surroundings as Gildon wielded his fire spirit.

From what they could see they knew that the cavern was somewhat large. The noise that they made as they entered the cave, along with their voices, echoed off the walls. Cole figured as he walked around the cave, that his and Merryrick's cottage could fit within the cavern and there would be room to spare. Thinking about Merryrick shot a pain of grief through Cole. He gritted his teeth and squeezed his hands into fists as his hatred and contempt for the Reapers rose within him. A great moan echoed throughout the cave and everyone froze as the earth beneath them gave a slight shake.

"What was that?" Maggie asked.

"If that's a bear, I am not staying in here. I would rather face the snow than a bear," Artemis said.

"You don't have a choice but to stay in here," Wallace announced. "We are trapped in here by the avalanche. So you might as well get comfortable because we are going to be here for a few days."

Further into the cave they found a stack of wood piled against one of the caves wall and an old abandoned water skin that had a hole in it. There where other signs that the cave had been occupied before.

"Looks like someone has been here before us," Gildon said, taking notice of the stack of wood.

The wood was quickly used to start a fire and the temperature of the cave steadily increased. Cole thought about the wood, wondering where it had come from and who could have stacked it. He also wondered if he were to touch it, would he be able to find out. He had found where Gildon had picked up the pebble from. Cole moved towards the wood ready to pick up a piece when he was suddenly interrupted.

"Cole, go and help with the horses. They need food, water and warmth just as much as we do," Wallace ordered.

Cole left the pile of wood and went to the back of the cave where the horses had been taken. With cold numb hands, Cole worked to take Gladadear's saddle from her. After removing her saddle, Cole noticed that one of Gladadear's legs was bleeding. She must have gotten hurt when she fell. Cole's fingers gently touched the wound and Glad let out a snort.

"Hey old girl I know it hurts," Cole said, consoling the horse.

After examining the wound, he found that the cut was deeper than he expected. This worried him,

"Something wrong with Gladadear," Maggie asked, as she bent down to examine the horse.

"She's hurt. I think it happened when she fell. Do you think you could heal her?" Cole asked, biting his lower lip.

"I don't know Cole. I've never healed a horse before. What if I did something wrong. I could cause her more trouble," Maggie replied.

"Please Maggie. You know what will happen to her if her leg gets any worse," Cole begged.

Maggie knew. She had lived on a farm most of her life. Maggie looked at Cole, his eyes were filled with hope and she wanted to help him. He had already lost so much with Merryrick.

"I'll try, but horses are a lot different than humans".

Maggie closed her eyes and let out a breath. She placed her hands on Gladadear's legs. Again the horse let out a snort and Cole calmed her, stroking her mane. As he did Cole felt Glad suddenly stiffen and her large black eyes seemed to widen. She stood like that for a few moments then she suddenly relaxed.

Maggie let go of Glad and she stood up.

"It is done. At least what I can do," Maggie said breathless.

Cole bent down and examined the wound once more and found that it had started to scab over already.

"Thank you Maggie. Thank you so much," Cole said, looking into Maggie's eyes.

In them he could see that they were tired and her face was pale. Yet even though she was exhausted she still smiled at Cole.

"You're welcome Cole. But now I think I should look at your wounds," She said, her fingers touching the cut on the side of his head.

The flash of light came and Cole stood before two great wooden doors. Around him there were rose petals fluttering in the wind. There were crowds of people dressed in their finest. Next to him was Chanlyn, dressed for a wedding. Cole's eyes widened as he looked down at himself, he too was dressed in his finest. Turning around Cole's eyes widened as a much older Maggie, dressed in white, with a veil of lace flowing from her back, walked down a red carpet towards him. She smiled her smile at him. Brilliant light flooded Cole's vision and he was back staring down at the here and now Maggie.

"I'm sorry Cole I didn't mean to touch you," Maggie said.

"No. It's okay. It wasn't bad or anything," Cole replied.

"Really what did you see?" Maggie asked with curiosity.

"Um…nothing," Cole muttered, his face blushing terribly.

"Must have been something, your face is as red as a blushing bride," Maggie laughed. This comment only made Cole turn a deeper shade of red.

Although the cave was by far warmer than the outside world, that did not stop the cold from seeping in through the hard surface of the rocks, that Cole and the others slept on. Even though Cole had changed into dry clothes and laid on his bedroll in a ball with his cloak and blankets wrapped tightly around him it still was a long cold night. Besides the cold making the night horrible for Cole, he was haunted by dreams of the past. He was lost in the woods of Kells, searching for Merryrick. He knew he had to get home, that something was wrong. Now every turn he took seemed to take him away from home. He wandered in the woods, hearing the baying of the hounds. He could hear and feel hoof beats around him. The mist was thick and blinded his way. Finally after it seemed that he had wandered the woods all night, he came out of them and found himself standing before his front door. Reaching out, Cole pulled the door open. Standing on the threshhold was Merrytick. He smiled at Cole. It was a welcoming smile. Then suddenly the smile faded and he let out a cry of pain. Cole looked down and saw the blade of a sword being stabbed through his master. Standing behind Merryrick, was the cold hollow face of a Reaper.

"Merryrick!" Cole bolted upright, his master's name still on his lips.

For a moment he was disoriented not really knowing where he was. But after a moment his world, his reality came crashing down on him. Tears came to Cole's eyes. He wrapped himself up in his blankets and cloak and let himself grieve for Merryrick.

When all his tears were shed, he pulled himself free from his blankets and looked around him. The camp was quiet for it appeared that all were asleep. Gildon lay on Cole's right side, using his saddle as a pillow, sleeping with his sword at his side. Chanlyn and Maggie lay on Cole's left, buried in their cloaks, sleeping noisily. Every few minutes a large snore would escape from Maggie's mouth.

Artemis was asleep on the other side of the ember glowing fire pit, with his mouth open. Cole smiled as a large bug crawled in and then disappeared. Once that bug was inside, Artemis unconsciously closed his mouth and swallowed. Cole felt sorry for the bug for having been eaten by such a nasty person.

Arthur lay next to his son. He was sound asleep and did not move an inch.

Cole's heart skipped a beat when he discovered that Wallace was nowhere in sight. Since there was no way to get out Cole knew Wallace had to be around somewhere. He found Wallace near the entrance of the cave, with a small torch. In his hands was his sword and he was chipping away at the wall of snow and ice.

"Why are you doing that?" Cole asked.

Wallace stopped his work and wiped the sweat from his forehead.

"The longer we stay in here the more dangerous it will become," Wallace answered.

"You mean with the Reapers?" Cole asked.

"Not just them. We could run out of food or firewood, or one of us could get sick," Wallace said, picking up his sword and resuming his hacking again.

"Can't you just wield us out?" Cole asked.

"Not without causing more damage. I could set off another avalanche and bury us in deeper, or cause a cave in. Wielding can help in most situations but you must understand when to use it. You must feel your surroundings and know when is the right time to use it," Wallace added.

Cole thought about what Wallace was saying and wondered how he was supposed to feel his surroundings. He posed the question to Wallace.

"You already know how to do it," Wallace answered after taking another swing at the snow. "Merryrick taught you. I believe when you went hunting he taught you a skill called Reading, like reading a book but to read the surroundings, correct? "

"Yes" Cole replied. "He said that I was to listen and feel, read the surroundings then to fade all things that didn't matter to the back of my mind and to only focus on what I was hunting or wanting to achieve," Cole replied, remembering his first and many lessons Merryrick had given him on the subject.

"And you achieved it. Did you or did you not use Reading when you were in the archery competition," Wallace asked, "what did you feel?"

Cole thought back to that day so long ago. "I remember letting everything fade away to the back of my mind and waiting. Waiting for the right time, the right moment to let my arrow go and when it came I knew that was the moment to let it fly."

"That was Reading. You were taking in your surroundings sensing the change in the air, the right time to react. It is the same with wielding, to sense the right time to wield or not to wield. But the skill must become an instinct rather than a skill. Much like the instinct to fight or fly. It is a very useful technique in many situations," Wallace huffed, "and can often be a means to determine life or death."

"How can it be a means to determine life or death?" Cole asked.

"Try reading the cave's surroundings," Wallace suggested, "find the cave's strengths and weaknesses. Try to understand why I have chosen not to wield us out of here," Wallace spoke, this time giving Cole more an order than a suggestion.

Cole let out a breath and closed his eyes.

"Listen to the wind as it blows through the caverns. Hear the groans of the rock as it changes," Wallace muttered in a low voice. Cole slowed his breathing until it was soft and even. He let Wallace's low murmurs fade to the back of his mind and he concentrated on the wind and groans of the vast cavern. He felt the bitter cold stab into him like a knife. He heard water droplets seeping into the cracks within the stone. Within his mind he saw water freezing and heard the water cracking as it turned to ice, expanding the stone and weakening it. He saw the tons of snow falling, creating a great heavy load for the rock's surface to bear. Whether or not it was the future that he saw, Cole watched the ceiling of the cavern grow weaker and fall in on itself.

Cole let out a breath and opened his eyes to look at Wallace.

"I see why you don't want to wield," Cole replied, "the rocks surface above us is weakening. Any movement or disruption could cause a cave in, like you said."

"Aye, you understand now," Wallace stated. Then took another bite into the snow with his blade.

"Do you want any help?" Cole asked.

Wallace stopped again and turned to look at Cole.

"You should be resting. These past few days have been exhausting for you no doubt."

"I have had enough sleep," Cole said.

Wallace seemed to understand. He nodded and gave Cole his sword. Wallace's sword was heavier than Merryrick's. He hefted it in his hands then struck the ice. Bits of it flew into Cole's face and the blade did little damage to the frozen water.

Wallace smiled from where he rested, and then rose to his feet.

"Merryrick never showed you how to hold a sword did he?" Wallace asked.

"No," Cole muttered. "Why would he?"

"Mm," Wallace took back his sword to demonstrate the proper way to hold the blade. "Spread your feet apart. Place one foot in front of the other and hold the blade with both hands then strike," Wallace ordered, giving over the blade to Cole.

Cole took it back and copied the stance that was shown him. He realized that by placing one foot in front of the other in a lunge position he found it easier to control his blows and the sword did not seem so heavy. But after only striking the wall a few times, Cole felt as if his arms were going to fall off.

They made some progress with hacking away at the ice. They would take turns, one resting while the other worked. But even with all the work they did there was no sign that they were close to getting out of the cave any time soon.

"You did well for you first time holding a sword," Wallace said.

"You knew that he was a swordman?" Cole commented "Otherwise you wouldn't have asked if Merryrick had ever taught me how to hold a sword. Why would Merryrick have a sword in the first place. He was a capenter, a tradesmen," Cole asked. That question had been on his mind ever since he found Merryrick in the ruined cottage bearing a sword.

"There was more to Merryrick than met the eye," Wallace replied.

"Like what?" Cole asked

"I believe that Merryrick was or is an Elfain Warrior."

"Merryrick an Elfain Warrior," Cole said in disbelief.

"Indeed. And he still is an Elfain Warrior," Wallace answered. "Death from this world does not change that."

"If that's true why didn't he tell me something like that?" Cole asked a little anger in his voice.

"If he had told you, would you have believed him?" Wallace questioned.

Cole thought for a moment, asking the question to himself.

"Would I have believed him?"

From what the legends said, the Elfain Warriors were thought to be myths with wielding weapons of great power and users of magic and thought to be long dead. To think that Merryrick was really one of the legends was almost impossible. The Warriors lived hundreds of years ago. If Merryrick had told him that he was a legendary warrior, he would have thought that Merryrick had gone mad.

"No, I guess I wouldn't have believed him. I think that I might have even laughed at him. In fact I did laugh at the thought, just that morning, the morning of the hunt. Even after he had done what he did with the sword and summomed the lightning that killed that Reaper, the thought still didn't come to me as a possiblity," Cole finally answered. "If Merryrick was an Elfain Warrior, how old do you think he was?" Cole asked.

"No idea. I don't even think Merryrick was his real name. After the slaughter of Alorian, warriors like Merryrick had to disappear.

They had to become someone else. If they were ever found out they would have been hunted down and killed. Gildon could be right. There may be more warriors out there that may have survived," Wallace replied. "Perhaps there are some in Aloria."

Cole's questions fell silent as he thought about what Wallace had said. He thought about what Merryrick's real name could have been, and how old he really was. In his hallucinations, Merryrick had cried out, yelling something about getting people out. Cole wondered if his master had been at Alorian when the slaughter happened.

"When did the slaughter of Alorian happen?" Cole asked.

"That is something you need to ask Gildon. He would know better than I," Wallace replied. "But I can give you a guess. I'd say it was just over a hundred years ago, give or take a few years. Shelrin destroyed Alorian and then took over the kingdom of Albavar."

Cole did a few calculations in his head and figured that Merryrick had been over a hundred and sixty years old or older. That notion was hard for Cole to grasp.

CHAPTER 17

LIFE IN THE CAVE was not a pleasant experience. It was gloomy, cold and depressing. It was always dark. Even when the fire was lit there was always the cold empty space of darkness surrounding them. Cole felt that his toes and hands were always freezing and never seemed to have any feeling in them. It was only when he was hacking at the ice, in hopes that they would get out, that he felt warm. But once he stopped, the moisture that he sweated out would bring a sharp chill afterwards. Cole wasn't the only one to wander around the cave with his cloak and blanket wrapped tightly around him. They all did and when the fire was lit they sat close to the small flames, hands out stretched, in order to catch what little warmth they could and even then it still wasn't enough to melt the bone chilling cold

Fuel for the fire was a problem. The stacked wood that had been stored in the cave was a limited supply. The fire was only lit to keep them from freezing to death. Breakfasts, lunches and dinners were eaten cold. The only good thing about being trapped by tons of snow and ice was that there was always plenty of water to drink.

Gildon gave Cole, Maggie and Chanlyn lessons on wielding and had them do small exercises and challenges to practice their wielding, nothing big because of the fear of attracting the Reapers. Not only was it to help them strenghten their powers of wielding but it also helped pass the time. Chanlyn and Maggie seemed to be growing in their abilities for they could do far more than the simple excersizes that Gildon had started them off with. Chanlyn could move small stones instead of a feather. Maggie had started shaping stones into little figurines of animals. Cole was happy for them but at the same time was frustrated. He spent hours looking at a small pebble and nothing seemed to happen to it. It remained in his palm, shapless and unmovable. Even Artemis was making progress and he never took part in the exercises. Cole had gone into the cavern where the horses were being kept and found Artemis sitting by his horse Addis levitating a pebble in the palm of his hand. A small flame of fire surrounded the stone. He only managed it for a moment, then the pebble dropped to the ground and the flame went out. At that point Cole slipped away, not wanting Artemis to see him and receive a lashing from his tongue. They spent three days and four nights in the cave with every man and boy working to dig them out. It wasn't until the fourth morning that they escaped their darkened prison.

Cole had woken from another nightmare of wandering the woods, trying to out run the reapers and their hounds. There were still a few flames eating at the few twigs of wood. It was the last of the wood. Tomorrow they would be sitting in complete darkness. Feeling very depressed Cole looked over at his companions. Everyone was huddled close to the fire and to each other. Wrapped tight under blankets and cloaks and rolled up in balls, his companions looked like pill bugs folded in on themselves. Maggie let out a moan as she shivered in the fading firelight. Cole pulled his blanket and cloak from his shoulders and laid them on top of Maggie, hoping it would give her extra warmth. He then got to his feet and moved carefully around them, so as to not to step on anyone, as he made his way to the opening of the cave. Tons upon tons of snow had fallen in the avalanche covering the mountain and the cave with at least thirty feet of snow. They had dug and dug, chipping away the ice and snow, hoping that they might breathe in fresh air from the outside world.

Gildon had tried using his gifts of fire wielding to melt their way out. All that did was make puddles of water and made everything more uncomfortable and dangerous. Then suddenly the heat caused a cave-in, which brought the snow down upon them and then it had to be dug out again.

Cole stood staring at the solid snow wall. He had lit one of the few torches that remained and began tearing at the packed snow. He, like everyone else, was tired of being in the constant darkness of night. He wanted out so badly. He felt like he was slowly being suffocated by the dark, that he had a sickness that was driving him insane. He was determined to free himself and find the light of day. But the more he hacked, the more snow there seemed to be. Hot and sweaty from his efforts, Cole let out a scream of frustration and slammed Wallace's blade into the wall of snow. Cole felt a burning heat run up from the sword and into his hands and arms just as the blade was plunged into the snow. The sword, arm and even his body went through the wall and Cole toppled forward and landed face first in a pile of cold wet snow. Cole pulled himself free of the chilly whitness and let out a cry of joy when he got to his feet and felt sunbeams of light and a blast of shockingly cold wind strike him in the face

Blowing warm breath into his hands to keep them from freezing, he looked out towards the west at the wide valley they had come from, that stretched out below him. Somewhere down there was Kells, and he missed it. He realized then that he had been gone from the little hamlet for only a fortnight yet it seemed a lifetime ago.

He wondered what the people were doing. He wondered if they had noticed that he and the others were gone. Cole smiled to himself. He could imagine the circle of wives talking about their disappearance and how they were making up stories about why they had to leave.

"Probably none of them are correct," Cole muttered to himself. Taking in a breath, Cole looked towards the east, towards the way they were going. His breath was taken aback as he looked out at one snow-white mountain range after another. To anyone else that sight would have been almost magical, but to Cole it was overwhelming and disheartening. He felt that once he descended those mountains, the whole Kells valley would disappear behind him and there would be no going back.

You can never go back Cole, you can only move forward, Merryrick's voice echoed in Cole's head.

Cole didn't know how long he stared but when he started losing the feeling in his fingers, he went back into the cave. When he came back in Wallace was attending to the fire placing the last bit of wood in the flames.

"That's the last of it. Well be sitting in the dark soon enough," Wallace muttered.

Cole lips turned into a smile as he was about to tell Wallace that they were free of the darkness at last, but then Maggie rolled out from under her hideaway of blankets with a large groan.

"How did you sleep?" Cole asked looking over at her.

"I will never complain about my bed back at home again," she said grumpily. "I thought that was hard."

"Cold hard rock not to your liking," Cole asked with a smile.

"Not at all," Maggie replied.

"I told you, you should be grateful that you have a bed," Wallace said with an amused smile on his face. "I told you, you could be sleeping on a hard cold dirt floor." Maggie turned to her father and stuck out her tongue at him like a little child.

"You know when I was young, I did not have…"

"Yes, yes, father we all know, when you were young you had to walk five miles up a hill in a snowstorm just to be born," Maggie replied, as she wrapped her blankets around her more tightly. "It feels like it's gotten colder in here," she uttered. Gildon's deep laugh echoed off the walls of the cave, waking Sir Arthur who gave out a large snort.

"Well you won't have to sleep on the cold ground anymore," Cole said. "I guess I can't say that, because you still have to sleep on the ground just not this one," Cole remarked.

"What are you talking about Cole?" Maggie asked.

"We are free. No longer do we have to stay in this hole in the rock," Cole said.

"What is going on?" Chanlyn asked, rubbing his eyes.

"The mouth of the cave is open. We can leave," Cole replied.

"What?" Chanlyn cried out. "We can leave? We can be free of the oppression of the dark?" Chanlyn cried. Like the others he jumped to his feet and ran to the opening.

It was a while before the others came back with their hands tucked under their armpits but had bold smiles on their faces.

"Well done Cole, well done indeed," Gildon said

"I say this calls for a celebration," Sir Arthur cried.

"Oh and what did you have in mind Sir Arthur?" Wallace asked.

"I propose that we have a hot breakfast," He cried.

They all agreed and the last of the wood was thrown onto the fire, snow was melted into a pot and breakfast was cooked over warm flames. Their breakfast was only cooked oats with dried berries but no one complained about the porridge not even Artemis.

They ate their food in a hurry, partly because they were so hungry and partly because they were trying to swallow the oatmeal before it lost its warmth. When everyone was done, they washed their bowls in the snow and then quickly rolled up bedrolls and blankets and saddled horses. They had to dig the opening in the cave a little bigger to allow for the horses to fit through but by midafternoon they were on their way.

The sky was clear and the sun shown bright, almost too bright. The light reflected off the snow making it rather hard to see, but they were grateful for the sun nonetheless. It wasn't much warmer out of the cave, nor would it be at a higher elevation. It may have been spring in the valley, but it was still winter in the mountains and it made their progress slow. There was more digging. A path had to be dug to allow the horses through. By the end of the day Cole felt as though he had plowed a long stretch of land by hand. And when they stopped for the night, he had barely enough strength in him to lift his food to his mouth. That night they slept in a snow cave about which Maggie protested loudly. Cole was so tired from the days work that he sank deep into the depths of sleep where nothing, not even the haunting sounds of hounds or Reapers could touch him.

ANOTHER WEEK PASSED AS THEY traveled across the mountain ranges. Cole had no idea where it was they were going. He often wondered how it was that Wallace knew which direction they were to take. Yet it seemed that Wallace did know, as if he had walked the land before. They had passed through the rest of mountains without too many serious complications or storms to hinder their way. More than once he and the others had fallen along the way hand and knees were scraped but no one had any serious injuries.

As the days worn on, Cole noticed that they had started descending downward onto the lower elevations, moving from the high country to the foothills. The drifts of snow disappeared and tufts of grass began to appear through the melting whiteness. As they traveled onward, signs began to appear that the foothills had once been inhabited. Every so often the ruins of a barn, or a cottage would appear within the growth of vines of ivy, twisting up and around the remains. A solemn feeling fell over the group after the sun had turned westward and started setting. They pulled their horses to a halt when they came to the center of what used to be small village. A dark cloud fell on each of their hearts as they inspected the hamlet. Every building in the small village was nothing but ruins.

But what made Cole swallow back tears was the village green. Markers of graves filled the grass-covered land. Row after row of stone markers told of the deaths that the village had suffered.

"What happened here?" Cole asked softy.

"Shelrin," was Wallace's only reply, as he gazed across the field of worn down stone markers. "This village was once known as Shepherds Hollow," Wallace spoke. "It was known for its fine weavers and good wool. The grass that grew here gave the sheep thicker wool.

"How do you know all this?" Gildon asked.

"A massacre happened here," Wallace replied softly. "This is the village that Kayden was born in and where his parents were murdered."

CHAPTER 18

THE COMING OF NIGHT did not change the mood of the group, if anything it made it worse. A rainstorm blew in, cracking the sky with lightning and crashing thunder. They had to make camp in one of the abandoned cottages that still had part of its roof. The wooden door having rotted away long ago looked out across the graveyard.

Gazing out, Cole felt a shiver run up his back as sat near the fire. "How do you know this is the village Kayden was born in," Maggie asked her father, wrapping her cloak around her tightly.

"His story is well known to those who fought with him."

"You were in Kayden's army?" Cole asked, in astonishment.

"Yes," Wallace answered. "Most everyone in my generation was in an army and fought for one side or the other."

"But why would Shelrin do this?" Maggie asked softly.

"Because of *The Foretellings? They will rise from the shadows of the great mountains.* Elfire means *great* in the old tongue," Chanlyn answered.

Everyone turned to look at Chanlyn. Cole and Maggie had the same expression of amazement on their faces, each one wondering how it was that Chanlyn would know something like that.

"Grandfather wrote about the persecutions in his history," Chanlyn said, answering the unasked question. Maggie turned her gaze from Chanlyn to Gildon.

"*The Foretellings* are the visions that Ayden had right?" Maggie asked.

Gildon took a breath and began speaking low and soft. "Correct. They are Ayden's prophetic dreams. They were recorded and they foretold what was to come. In his last vision, he foretold of a great man, rising up from the ashes that a black dragon created. He would destroy the evil that ruled the land. Because of this vision Ayden had, Shelrin attacked the mountain villages, killing the boys and young men. Shelrin was not taking any chances."

"But Shelrin didn't stop it," Maggie burst out. "Kayden came and destroyed Shelrin, so the prophecy was fulfilled."

"That could be argued," Gildon responded.

"Whether the prophecy was fulfilled or not hundreds of lives were taken. Fathers protecting their sons were cut down, mother's perished holding their young sons and sisters watched their siblings lives stolen from them," Wallace grunted coldly. Cole heard the deep anguish that was behind Wallace's words as if he had experienced seeing someone close to him die in the rampage.

"The towns were burned and the women were left to bury their husbands and their sons and then they themselves died of broken hearts. Now no one dared come back for fear that the ghosts of the dead haunt these places," Wallace recounted. Wallace fell silent and Cole watched him as the flames of the fire threw shadows on his face. He knew that Wallace was seeing a world that he wished he could forget and yet that world was the one that always plagued Wallace's dreams.

The silence that fell on the group lasted through the night. Cole watched the flames until he eyes grew heavy and he fell back onto his bedroll to fall into a restless sleep.

COLE WOKE AT THE SOUND of someone sobbing. He sat up and pulled the blankets from his head and rubbed the sleep from his eyes. His eyebrows rose in surprise however when he discovered a bright blue pair of eyes staring at him. They were the eyes of a young girl, no more then five or six. She stared at him with her thumb in her mouth and a half smile showing off her pink tear-stained cheeks. Sitting next to Cole was a boy, and he was just a few years older than the girl, probably no more than nine or ten. In his hands was a cloth doll. The head had been ripped open and he was busy sewing it up with a needle and thread.

Curious as to where he was, Cole looked around him and saw that he was in a cottage, not unlike the one they had made camp in, yet this one was still intact. The roof was whole and the shutters of the windows were closed. From what Cole could see it was early evening. The room he was in was small, the table and chairs took up most of the room. A single shelf hung on the wall, holding plates and cups. A warm fire glowed brightly in the hearth.

"There Ally. Next time be more careful," the boy said, holding up the doll, with its new repairs. Some of the stitches were very large and some very small, but the girl still took the doll from the boy and hugged it in her arms.

"Thanks William," the girl replied, taking her thumb from her mouth.

"Alright. It's time for supper, father will be here any moment, let's set the table," William said getting to his feet.

William pulled the wooden plates, cups and knifes from the small shelf and set them on the table and Ally went to work.

"William, I need another plate," Ally said. William turned from the fire and looked at the table. Ally had set out three cups, three plate and three spoons.

"You set the right amount Ally, there's only three of us," William replied, turning back to the fire to check on the meal.

"The boy needs a place too," Ally replied.

"You already set one for me," William responded.

"Not you silly," Ally said with a laugh, "the boy sitting in the corner". Ally pointed to where Cole sat.

William turned his head to look at where Ally was pointing. William looked right through Cole, not seeing him at all.

"There's no one there, Ally." William laughed.

"Yes there is. He's right there," Ally insisted, her small finger pointing directly at Cole.

"I cannot see anyone," William said, taking delight in teasing his sister.

Ally began to cry and Cole felt bad that no one could see him except the little girl. He wondered about that, this was obviously a dream and yet somehow this little girl could see him.

"William Shepherd he's right there!" Ally yelled.

William looked at his little sister with raised eyebrows but gave in and pulled another plate, cup and spoon from the shelf and handed it to his little sister. As Ally was setting the extra dish, the door to the cottage suddenly burst open and a dark headed man rushed in.

"William, Shelrin's soldiers are coming. Take Ally to the woods, hide there until I can come for you," the man said in a panic.

The mood suddenly changed. No longer was it the light happy spirited home. It quickly changed to be filled with apprehension and fear. There was a mad rush as William grabbed his sister's hand and ran for the door, stopping only to sling bags over his shoulders. Their father grabbed his sword from their mantel. William put a cloak on Ally's shoulders then held her tightly to him. William's father was about to open the door but had to throw Willam and Ally back inside and slam the door shut when they heard the sound of horses running past.

"Carry out the order of Shelrin. Leave no man or boy alive!" A cold voice echoed through out the night.

Cole was right there with the family, standing next to William, with his sister on one side of the door, while their father was on the other side. He could see the sweat rolling down the boy's face and he could hear his heart beating madly in his chest and the rapid intake of breath.

The door suddenly burst open, pushing William and Cole off their feet and Ally toppled to the ground. Both boys looked up and stared in complete horror at the man that stared back at them. He was dressed in chain mail armor and a black tunic. His face was hidden within the shadows of a helmet.

William let out a cry as the black soldier raised his sword and was going to bring it down on him. But then the soldier froze and the sword fell from his hands, and all at once he clattered to the ground.

"Run!" William's father ordered, as he pulled his sword from the dead man's back. The family fled into the night and Cole with them.

It was a scene like nothing Cole had ever witnessed before. Houses began to burn as the soldiers threw lit torches onto the thatched roofs. There were people everywhere, running from the fire, running from the soldiers. There were bodies in the lane, that of the old men and of the young boys.

As Cole ran with the family he looked back and watched as a soldier and its horse cornered a young man with his back up against a wall. Cole could see that he was just a few years older than him. The young man looked terrified as the solider and his horse went back and forth in front of him. The soldier held a long sword in one hand while he laughed, as he played with the young man, much like a cat plays with a mouse just before it goes in for the final kill. William's father suddenly pulled William and Ally behind a large rock as a horse and its rider passed. Although Cole was never touched by William's father he felt the force of being pushed and was thrown behind the rock as well. They all four huddled there and waited till the soldier raced past them. Cole looked up over the edge of the rock to what had happened to the young man. The horse and soldier were gone but the crumpled body of the young man lay in a heap on the ground. Cole had no choice but to follow as the family raced off for the darkness of the wilderness. It was like something was pulling him with them as they ran. Ally's little feet ran as fast as they could but she stumbled and fell letting out a cry. William reached out and grabbed her little hand and pulled her up. But her cry had alerted the attention of the enemy.

"Stop them Corporal, they're getting away!" A cold voice shouted.

Cole felt a chill run up his spine as he heard a familiar sound vibrate across his eardrums. He knew the sound immediately. It was the sound of an arrow leaving its bow and rushing through the air. Cole turned around and it was as if time stood still. He saw the arrow coming not at him but at William.

William eyes opened wide with terror, but as the arrow came at him something stepped in front of William. At that moment time caught up and the arrow slammed into William's father, square in the chest, knocking him off his feet.

"NO!" Both William and Cole cried. William fell to his knees at his father side.

"Papa, get up!" William pleaded.

But it was no use, the arrow had hit William's father in the heart and great amounts of blood were starting to pool around him.

Cole, who stood next to William, looked back and saw two soldiers walking towards them. Their bloodstained swords were out and with each step they took, the smiles of their faces grew wider.

"Go… William," his father said in great huffs.

"No I won't leave you!" William said, his eyes filling with tears.

"You have to my son....for...for if they catch you...you will die too."

"Then I'll die!" William responded.

"No Will… you have to protect your sister… you and she are the only ones now. GO!" William's father shoved William away and then fell back and lay still.

"NO!" William screamed seeing his father close his eyes forever.

The rain began to fall then. As it did the scene that Cole was part of started to wash away. William and his dead father smeared together.

COLE WOKE with tears in his eyes. The soft sound of his slumbering fellow companions became clearer and he realized that he was back in his own world, in his own time. He wiped the tears that fell from his eyes as he sat up. His gaze fell out of the open doorway of the cottage and looked out across the field of headstones. He shivered in the dark as the last few moments of the dream still lingered, like a thin mist, within his mind.

His dream had been of the past he was sure. A somber vision that showed the tragedy that had taken place years ago. Cole rose to his feet and went to the field. He wandered amongst the memorials to those long since gone from the world. The names of the dead were chiseled into the stones; some were so weather beaten that the words were barely legible. Cole bent down at one that was covered in ivy. He pulled the choking vine from the stone and traced the engraving with his finger. The name on the stone was Edward Millson, son on Edison Millson who died by the hands of Shelrin. By the dates given on the stone, Cole figured the math and concluded that Edward was only in his sixteenth year when the soldiers of Shelrin took away his life. He was just one year younger than Cole was. Like Edward there were so many more. Cole wondered if William and his father were buried on the field. Or had William run, like his father ordered him to do.

"There are so many," a voice came from behind Cole.

Cole jumped at the voice. He turned seeing Wallace standing not too far from him. He held a bunch of grass and weeds in his hands. He looked out across the field of stone markers, his eyes so full of sadness. Cole looked down and saw that Wallace had started to clear away the gravestones, the reason for the grass and weeds in his hands.

"So many innocent lives lost," Wallace replied.

The rain had long since passed during the night and now the full moon was out. The moonlight cast a bluish glow on the earth, making everything look as though it were part of a ghostly world. Even Wallace looked more spirit than mortal.

"Shepherds and farmers, that's all they were. They were poor country folk. The only worry they had was whether or not it would rain enough for their crops to grow so they could feed their family. Killed because they lived near a mountain."

"I'm sorry Master Wallace," Cole replied softly.

"You must never let it happen again, Cole," Wallace pleaded in desperation. Falling to his knees he looked deep into Cole's eyes. "Promise me that you won't let it happen again."

Cole looked at Wallace strangely; the man wasn't acting like himself.

"Do you promise?" Wallace asked, shaking Cole's shoulders.

"Yes. I promise," Cole replied, fearing what Wallace might do if he didn't.

Wallace gave a sigh of relief and then went back to his cleaning of the graves. Cole watched Wallace wondering if he had gone mad.

CHAPTER 19

"WE ARE WITHIN the realm of Aloria," Gildon said. "Our journey will soon be at an end."

Two days they traveled, climbing down the mountainside to come across a glen full of luscious grasses, rushing streams and green forest.

"If you look out, just as far as you can, you can see a sliver of silver. That is Seadeth River. We follow her until we reach the cliffs of Moyor and then onto Aloria!" Gildon pointed out happily, from on top of a rising hilltop. "Three days maybe four."

They had stopped to rest on an outcrop of rock that looked out over the lowlands below. Cole stood gazing out to where Gildon pointed and he could just make out the glint of silver that shone in the late afternoon sun. He let out a breath and felt a great wave of relief flood over him, for the running was almost over.

As Cole pulled back his vision, he took notice of several other rock outcroppings. The outcroppings surrounding them took up the whole of the mountaintop. Some stood tall and somewhat straighter than others, while some were wider and longer. "As if it were a wall," Cole murmured to himself. Cole turned around and looked more closely at the outcrop that they were sitting on.

He wasn't surprise to see that what they were sitting on was not just one big hunk of rock, but rather it was stones stacked on stones with mortar in between. Cole turned back around and as he did so he took off his riding gloves and touched the ground and his vision began to change. No longer was he looking at stacks of stone but rather a fully constructed castle. He beheld the many towers, turrets and archways. He saw the curtain wall with the guards making their rounds. Blue flags flayed out in the wind as they stood on top of the gatehouse and the Keep. Then it slowly faded away. The towers and turrets turned back into old ruins. The great curtain wall was rubble and the gatehouse and Keep no longer stood, save but for a few stone formations. When his vision was gone, Cole put his riding gloves back on and turned to Gildon.

"Was there ever a castle here?" Cole asked.

Gildon looked up at Cole with raised eyebrows.

"Well done Cole. Your eyes seem to see what others cannot. This land was once part of one of the ancient kingdoms. There are old ruins scattered about all over this part of Albavar."

"What ancient kingdoms?" Maggie asked with curiosity.

"The seven Kingdoms of the Elfain Warriors," Chanlyn replied, as if the answer was as clear as the nose on his face.

"Perhaps the history lesson should be told from the beginning," Gildon said.

Chanlyn nodded his head and took a dramatic breath, much like Gildon did whenever he started to tell a tale.

"Far beyond the lands of Albavar, across the Sea of Stars and farther, past the Northern Way lies the homeland of the Elfains, the Havens. It was before Shelrin's rule. During the time of the first Elfain Warriors, just after the fall of the Dark King, the Elfain Warriors established kingdoms, so more than one man ruled Albavar," Chanlyn tried to explain.

"What are you jabbering on about?" Artemis snapped.

"Don't be so rude," Maggies snapped back, and then turned to Chanlyn, "he does have a point though. What are you talking about?"

"The seven Kingdoms of the Elfain warriors," Chanlyn replied, as though it was obvious.

"Perhaps you should start at the beginning, it would make it a little easier to understand," Gildon replied.

Chanlyn nodded his head and began again. "As I said before, beyond the oceans that surround Albavar, far across the Sea of Stars and miles passed the Northern Way, lies the homeland of Elfain Warriors, the Havens." Chanlyn paused for a moment so his words would sink into those that were listening. "Ruled by a kind and merciful king, the land was filled with peace and prosperity. The man who ruled the Havens was known as King Elfain, the name that his warriors took upon them. Within the days that King Elfain ruled he bore two sons,

Gavin the elder and Christoff the younger. Both were good and great in the eyes of the people of the Havens. But Christoff was the one that the people loved, for he was kind hearted, and understanding, yet fair."

When Chanlyn next spoke his voice had changed, decreasing into a low pitch, foretelling that nothing good was coming. "Even as a child, Christoff had a way with the people. They knew within their hearts that he cared for them and loved them and they in return loved him. It was because of the people's love for his brother that a small seed of jealously was planted within Gavin's heart, and as he grew into manhood the seed of jealously turned into hatred."

"Now in those day it was tradion for the people of the land to choose their king, rather than having the kingship passed down to the eldest. King Elfain, having grown in years, knew that some day he must pass the kingdom on and he wished to hear the voice of the people as to whom they wanted to be their next king. There were many names that were presented including Gavin's, for many supported him, but the people cried for their king to be Christoff, and so it came to pass," Chanlyn announced.

"But because of his hatred and jealousy for his younger brother, Gavin planned to assassinate his brother and then take the kingdom by force. The day of the asassination was to be on the day when Christoff was to be crowned as king. The great court of the Havens was filled and was made ready and as the crown was placed on Christoff's head, Gavin struck and would have killed his brother, had it not been for the sharp eyes of a young page named Ayden."

Here Chanlyn stopped and looked around him. Everyone had their eyes on him. Maggie was leaning, waiting impatiently for the story to continue.

"It seemed that while the young page was going about serving his master, he had over heard Gavin and his supporters plan to assassinate Christoff and it was he who shot the arrow that caught Gavin in the shoulder as he was about to raise the knife that would have murdered his brother.

"Deemed as a traitor and a murderer, for Gavin had spilled much blood in his obsession, he and his followers were banished from the Havens and sent adrift in a ship that was never to be seen again. As for Ayden, he was given the honor of protecting the King," Chanlyn stopped, letting out a breath as he finished his sentence.

"That's a very nice story Chanlyn," Maggie said, "but what does it have to do with the seven Kingdoms here in Albavar."

"I'll tell you, if you let me finish the story," Chanlyn snapped.

"Sorry. I didn't know you hadn't finished yet," Maggie muttered.

"The years passed and King Christoff was a good and wise king and the land of Havens prospered even more. Ayden grew in grace and stature in the eyes of the king. He became a great wielder, a wise scholar, an excellent warrior, and was much loved by King and country. But all was not right with Christoff for news had reached him about his brother. In his banishment Gavin had found another land to become ruler over, the Kingdom of Albavar, which Gavin, now the Dark King, ruled with cruelty. He had used his powers of wielding to conquer the people of Albavar. Christoff's heart was full of sadness and sorrow for the people of Albavar, so much so that he called his most trusted advisers and generals to him and asked them what should be done. Christoff felt that it was his doing that the people of Albavar were in such dire circumstances. Most told him that it was not his concern and that it should be left alone. But Ayden asked if he might go to Albavar to protect the people against Gavin's rule and that he might also capture the Dark King and bring him back to the Havens where they might imprison him. Christoff feared that if he were to let his dear friend go and fight his brother that he might never see him again. But because it was the desire of Ayden's heart, the King agreed. When the people of Havens heard of Ayden's journey many of the warriors volunteered including Ayden's six friends, Kirkwell, Lochlynn, Gracelynn, Skylar, Dresden, and Alberdeen." Chanlyn licked his lips to gather moisture back into his mouth then continued on.

"To help them on their mission King Christoff gave the Warriors great weapons of power. And so it was that Ayden and his warriors took their leave of the Havens and journeyed across the Northern Way and through the Sea of Stars until they landed upon a land covered in mist. They had reached Albavar. There they collided with their adversay Gavin, known to the Albavarians as the Dark King. Battles were fought and men and warriors perished in the confrontations with the Dark King. The weeks, months and years went by and as the time passed the Dark King's power was fading at last. Ayden stood against the Dark King. It was said that even in the distant land of the Havens they felt the rolls of thunder and saw the flickers of lightning as Ayden and the Dark King fought. Badley wounded, Ayden nearly fell to the Dark King's blows, but history was about to repeat itself. Rayden, Ayden's young son took up his father's bow and shot an arrow that struck the Dark King in the shoulder thereby giving Ayden the time to disarm the king and capture him. The Dark King was defeated and Albavar was free.

Both the people of the Havens and Albavar celebrated the defeat of the Dark King, but when it came time for Ayden and his Warriors to return to kingdom of the Havens to be with Christoff, Ayden declined. He had come to love the people of Albavar and the land. His friends declined to return home as well. And so it was that Ayden and the Elfain Warriors stayed and became leaders of clans from which the Seven Kingdoms were born," Chanlyn said finishing his story.

"Well done, young Chanlyn, well done indeed," Gildon said with an approving smile. "I think you have the talents to become a fine storyteller. Might I ask how it is that you know the story so well," Gildon asked.

"Merryrick told it to me a few times," Chanlyn responded.

"Then he told it and you remembered it well. Although there are some differences from the story I grew up with, every storyteller tells the stories differently each and every time he tells it."

"Merryrick told the story the same way each time. He never added anything different," Chanlyn said. "Nor did he change the way he told it."

Artemis snorted, "It's just a story. It didn't really happen."

"Ahh, but like all stories there is always some truth to them," Gildon responded. "Obviously they were true because you and I exist.

"You sound like Merryrick," Cole stated.

"Thank you Cole. I take that as a great compliment. Merryrick was a good man," Gildon responded. "But come, there is still several more hours of daylight left. The further we get today the closer to Aloria we are."

...

AS THE COMPANIONS traveled the next few days through the glen, Cole noticed that Gildon became more and more excited. He also noticed that Gildon was not the only one. All of them seemed to smile more often and they would marvel at the stories that Gildon told around the campfire at night. Wallace even smiled at the jokes the storyteller told. Cole, himself felt different, in the two days since they had made camp within the small valley he had not had one nightmare. He had slept through both nights without waking drenched in his own sweat. The grief he had been feeling over Merryrick seemed to be lifting from his shoulders. He still missed Merryrick terribly but the world around him was brighter and warmer. He felt that there was a feeling of peace. His feelings however were short lived. When they started to travel through a dense patch of woodlands, he immediately felt unseen eyes watching him. More than once he twisted in his saddle looking for what could be causing his uneasiness, but he could never directly see anything. Even touching the ground and tracing never revealed anything or anyone.

On their fourth day in the valley they stopped to rest when they came to a lazy stream with cattails growing tall along the banks. Not far from the stream were the ruins of an old watchtower. One half of the stone wall had fallen down, while the other half of it still stood.

"I think we'll stop here tonight," Wallace announced.

"Are you sure Master Wallace, there are still a few more hours of daylight?" Sir Arthur asked.

"This is a good place. There is plenty of fresh water and this tower will give us shelter for the night. It's going to be a cold one," Wallace informed them.

"Master Gildon what do you think?" Sir Arthur asked.

"Sounds good to me. I'm beat," Gildon replied, throwing himself out of his saddle.

So there within the remains of the tower they made camp. Cole had climbed the few stone steps that had escaped the years of neglect, to look out across the land through an archer's slit window. As he stood before the window he imagined himself pulling back his bow and letting an arrow loose.

"It used to be a great watch tower. The records that I have studied called it the great watch tower of Athera," Gildon said, standing next to Cole as he studied the land that he could see through the archway.

"I can see why," Cole said. "You can see for miles, even at this height."

"Do you know what Athera means?" Gildon asked.

"Not what, but who," Cole stated. "Athera was a great warrior and it was said that she had the eyesight of a hawk," Cole replied. "She was one of Ayden's friends. It was said that she could see for miles."

"I am amazed that you know so much about the old stories. Not many people remember them anymore."

"Merryrick was one for telling great stories. He would tell me about the Elfain Warriors when I was little, when I couldn't sleep. We would sit by the fire at night and…" Cole swallowed hard. It still tore him up inside to think that Merryrick was gone.

"It does get easier Cole," Gildon said. "It's hard at first but time does heal your heart."

Cole nodded but excused himself, not wanting to talk about Merryrick anymore, and joined Maggie and Chanlyn near the stream.

With some convincing from Maggie, Wallace allowed them to go fishing. Cole was glad to have something to take his mind off of his conversation with Gildon. Happily he took off his boots and waded out until the water was up to his knees and then stopped. The three splashed and kicked water at each other until they were soaked through. Once their water fight was finished the boys got down to business. Maggie would have helped but she hated touching fish.

"They are slimey and scaley!" Maggie complained, when the boys noticed Maggie wading back to shore.

But you were the one who wanted to go fishing in the first place" Chanlyn commented

"I like to eat them, not catch them," Maggie responded.

It was a warm and clear day and the sun had started its descent to the west. Cole was bending down to a catch a fish in his hands when a gust of wind came up; bringing with it the sense that they were being watched. Feeling the hairs on the back of his neck rise up, Cole suddenly stood straight up and looked around him. He saw no one save for Maggie on the bank. He could make out Wallace and Gildon a few meters from the camp, most likely scouting.

"These are very nice fat fish," Maggie commented, after Cole and Chanlyn had caught several by hand and thrown them on shore. "It will be nice to have a fire tonight. I am so tired of stale bread and moldy cheese," Maggie replied forlornly.

"We probably won't have it for very long," Chanlyn stated. "The Reapers could still be out there."

"But we haven't seen hide or hair since we left Kells. And even Cole hasn't seen them through tracing. It would sure be nice to have a hot meal don't you think Cole?"

"What?" Cole asked, not really paying attention to what Maggie was saying. He was still looking around them.

"A hot meal, don't you think it will be nice?" Maggie said.

"Yes," Cole said, pulling himself from the river.

Cole told himself that he was being foolish, that there was no one out there. No one knew where they were, even he didn't know where they were. Trying to make himself feel better Cole pulled his hunting knife free and started gutting the fish. He had just stuck the blade into the belly of the dead fish when out of the corner of his eyes he saw a wisp of green and red rush by.

"Ouch!" Cole cried, as he felt a sharp pain run across his hand.

Looking down, Cole saw that the fish, the one he once held, had slipped out of his hand and had fallen to the ground and instead of cutting the fish he had cut the palm of his hand. Little droplets of blood slowly spilled from his wound and were lost in the grass. Cole didn't know why but he was overcome with an uneasy feeling about the blood.

Maggie rushed forward grabbing hold of Cole's wrist, being careful not to touch his bare skin, and looked up with scrunched eyebrows.

"It is fairly deep, we need to stop the bleeding."

Maggie snapped off a few nearby cattails and stripped the top of the flower from the stem. She then bent down to mix water in the fluff from the cattails. She placed the poultice on top of Cole wounded hand and had him make a fist.

"Come on back to camp," Maggie said, leading the way.

When they got back to the camp, Wallace and Gildon were still gone. Sir Arthur lay on his saddle and blankets snoring softly, while Artemis sat stretched out on his own blankets, hand behind his head.

"Finally got the nerve to take a bath have you stable boy," Artemis remarked when he saw Cole and the others walking back from the stream.

"Can't you see Cole's bleeding, Artemis. Get off your duff and please go find me some firewood."

Artemis' face turned red with anger as he rose to his feet and took a step towards Maggie, but he stopped when he saw that she was smiling at him.

"Fine!" Artemis muttered then stormed off.

Both Cole and Chanlyn looked at Maggie with admiration.

"He just needed to know who's in charge," Maggie replied, with a smile.

Wallace and Gildon soon returned and agreed that Cole's cut was deep and that it needed to be thoroughly cleaned. A small fire was agreed upon and water was brought from the stream and the pot was set on the coals.

"Can't you just heal it using your Spirit wielding," Cole asked.

"Yes! I could do that, but the cut still needs to be cleaned," Maggie said. "I don't want to heal it with dirt or anything in it that could cause you to get an infection."

"But what about the Reapers, they might see the fire?" Cole asked.

"We haven't seen them for weeks now. There's no way they could have followed us over the mountains in that storm." Arthur said. He had woken up when the others came back. "We barely survived."

"We won't make the fire too big," Gildon assured Cole. "And with the tower surrounding us, a fire will not be seen from far away. Plus no evil thing can enter Aloria."

Cole tried to take comfort in Gildon's words, but he still felt uneasy.

"Well since we have a fire it would be pointless to waste the fish the boys caught." Arthur commented. "We can have a real meal for once."

"Very well, but once they are done the fire goes out," Wallace ordered.

Cole clenched his teeth as Maggie washed the wound in his hand. Then she closed her eyes and told Cole to hold his hand out. She took a breath in and slowly let it out lightly blowing on the wound. Cole felt a cold chill run through him. He watched with utter amazement as his skin started scabbing over. As the wound started healing Cole felt a wave of heat pass through him, starting from his finger and then burning through his body, making his back stiffen with discomfort.

"Amazing." Arthur muttered as they all watched.

"Try not to cut yourself anymore, Cole," Maggie said, a little out of breath.

"Thank's Maggie," Cole said, as he opened and closed his hand. As he did, the scab broke open and his hand started bleeding again. Maggie's eyebrows went up as she saw the blood. With permission from Cole, Maggie took his hand and examined it more closely. The familiar light came, but the only thing Cole saw was Maggie on horseback along with one other rider on horses. He couldn't make out the face of the other rider before his vision cleared and he was back in the camp.

"I can't understand it," Maggie said in disbelief "I healed it again and it still bleeds."

She dragged Cole closer to the fire to get a better look. "It looks as if I have done nothing," Maggie cried out, twisting Cole's hand this way and that.

"Maggie you're hurting me," Cole replied, his face contorted in pain.

"Oh sorry," Maggie said, letting go.

Cole took his hand back and worked his wrist to ease the pain, even though his hand was still bleeding.

"Right. If I can't heal you we'll have to do it the old fashioned way," Maggie said, digging into her saddlebag.

"What's the old fashioned way?" Chanlyn asked curiously.

Maggie turned around from her bags and held up a rather larged curved needle that gleamed in the firelight.

"Stitches!" Maggie replied with a smile on her face.

"Oh!" was all Cole said.

The sewing up of Cole's hand didn't take very long, but it was more painful than getting the wound. Maggie had pulled one of Buttercup's hairs from her tail, boiled it in hot water, threaded the needle with it and worked stitching Cole's hand. Cole had to bite down on his lip everytime the needle was pulled through his skin.

"There!" Maggie said tying a knot and cutting the thread. "It will work," she said admiring her needlework and then she bandaged Cole's hand with a clean white strip of linen.

"Now keep it clean and dry. I don't want it getting infected," Maggie ordered. "And try not to break the stitches."

During Cole's small operation the small fire was not wasted. The fish were filleted and placed over the flames. When the fish were done, they all devoured the flakey white meat. Maggie added a few herbs to the fish and it indeed made a fine meal. After dinner Maggie begged Gildon for a story, and Gildon being the storyteller that he was, obliged them.

"The ruins that we are camping in was once a watch tower of Athera," Gildon told them. "She was a great warrior who lost her love."

He recounted the sad tale of the young warrior Athera, who died of a broken heart. Legend said her spirit still haunted the land. Whether the story was true or not Maggie, Chanlyn and even Artemis were captured by the storyteller's fanciful words. Cole however was too uneasy to listen. The feeling that they were being watched continually pestered him. He wondered if he should tell Master Wallace about his feeling, but when he touched the ground with his ungloved fingers and traced the camp he found no one there so he kept quiet. The night dwindled and Cole's dreams were filled with glowing red eyes that stared out at him behind clouds of darkness. When the moon was full in the sky Cole awoke with drops of sweat sticking to his face. Not wanting to go back to sleep, he threw off his blankets, borrowed Chanlyn's bow and quiver of arrows and went to take his turn at standing guard over the camp.

He found Artemis sitting on the ground just outside the watch-tower rubble, his chin on his chest, bow on his knee.

"Artemis!" Cole said, kicking Artemis's booted foot.

Artemis let out a moan then fell over and started to snore. Cole let out a breath as he pulled the cowl of his cloak onto his head and sat down within the shadow of the tower. He placed three arrows on the ground next to him and waited with bow in hand. He sat motion-less for more than an hour just watching. Every now and again he would see movements out in the darkness, but it would turn out to be a rabbit or a small creature out and about in the night. Cole started to wonder if he had just imagined the feeling that they were being watched.

"But that is the sign of a good hunter Cole," Merryrick's voice echoed in his head as he remembered the memory. "To not be seen or heard but to be a mere shadow." Cole felt himself fall back in time to when he was ten years old. Merryrick had taken him into the woods and they had played a game of hide and seek with his Master.

"Walk softly so even the wind cannot hear you and move slowly so that a hawk cannot see you," Merryrick had told him.

From that day on Cole and Merrryick would always play their game of hide and seek when they went into the woods. Both would camouflage themselves in greens, grays and browns and try to hide in the foliage of the forest, and then try and stump the seeker. Merryrick would usually find Cole in a matter of minutes. There were a few times that he stumped his old master, but rarely. It took Cole, however, a fair amount of time to find Merryrick even if he used his gift of tracing.

Cole was pulled from his memory when he thought he saw some-thing move out of the corner of his eyes. He concentrated on the spot where he saw the movements. He sat so still and quiet, staring out into the darkness so hard, that his eyes were going blurry and his mus-cles were starting to stiffen up.

"Always remember Cole," Cole recalled. "Never put all your at-tention in one spot. If your focus is too intense on one spot you will miss what's going on around you. You will never see your target as a whole, but more as movements. Always be aware of your surroundings as well, because you might think that you're looking at your target directly when really your target is behind you."

Cole pulled back his gaze and kept a wide range over the land and kept his eyes moving. But even that seemed to fail him. The gray light of morning was fading and in less than an hour the sun would be streaming in through the branches and they would be on their way, possibly heading into danger. He was ready to admit that he was just being a little paranoid and was ready to go back to camp when he saw it. A pine branch was swaying back and forth. There was a little wind but not that much. He removed his riding glove and touched the ground. He ran forward in his mind, combing through the night searching for anything out of the ordinary. He nearly had a heart attack when he turned and found a hooded form still hiding in the shadows of a pine tree no more than two yards from him.

"Got you at last" Cole replied with a cat like smile

CHAPTER 20

COLE BLINKED his eyes and turned back to the spot where he had seen the cloaked form only to discover it gone. Cole's eyes darted back and forth looking for the shadowy figure but it had somehow disappeared.

Cole pulled his hand away from the ground and was pulled back to his spot under the tower. He was about to sound the alarm, but as he watched the figure he found him not to be a threat, in fact as he watched him he found him quite amazing. He was stooped over with the cowls of their cloaks pulled over their heads. They had started moving, slipping in and out of the shadows, disappearing for a few moments and then reappearing to slip into another shadow. The quivers of arrows they had strapped over their shoulders rattled as they moved. Cole shook his head, knowing full well that a sound like that would spook the prey you were hunting. Merryrick had told him that more than once.

The two had their bows in their hands with an arrow to their bowstring as if they expected to find themselves in trouble. They moved closer toward the camp. Cole stood, picked up one of his arrows from the ground and with a slight ting of pain from his hand, nocked it to his bowstring. He aimed the arrow high and let it go. The arrow flew toward the two figures dropping suddenly as it slammed into the earth just inches away from their feet.

Cole chuckled as he watched the two hooded people jump backwards, their hooded heads snapping up as they looked around them in the darkness. Cole imagined their surprised faces as they realized that they could not only be seen but also heard. He could see the figures peering out into the darkness, no doubt wondering where the arrow had come from. He was readying another arrow to fire, hoping this arrow would scare the two off, when he suddenly froze. He felt the sharp tip of a blade pressed against the small of his back.

"You know it's not nice to fire arrows at children." A smooth cool voice whispered behind him. "Now drop your bow." The voice continued as he forced a cold steel blade to Cole's back.

Cole dropped his bow and waited for the next order, as his mind raced trying to figure out a plan that would get him out of this predicament. The hood of Cole's cloak was suddenly pulled off his head revealing his mop of white hair. His captor suddenly let out a sharp intake of breath as though surprised.

"Turn around," the voice ordered.

Cole slowly turned around to face his captor with hands raised out to the side of him. Another cloaked figure with its cowl pulled forward so much so that the face could not be seen, stood in front of him. The form was about Cole's height. He too had a bow and a quiver of arrows, which was strapped over his shoulder. The knife was now pointed at his chest, the tip pressing into his clothing.

"Who are you and what are you doing here?" the figure questioned.

Cole remained silent. He was angry with the man that had snuck up on him but even more angry with himself for allowing the hooded man to come upon him unnoticed.

Never take a fool for a fool, Merryrick's voice rang in Cole ears. *If he is distracting you then you won't notice the other man cutting the* strings to your purse.

Cole understood now. The two that he thought were bumbling fools were the distraction. Cole felt like a fool himself for falling for one of the oldest tricks in the book.

"You're trying my patience," the cold voice stated. "Who are you and what are you doing here," he pressed the knife in a little harder.

Still Cole said nothing. The knife was moved from Cole's chest to his throat.

"Ayla," a young voice cried out of the darkness.

The figure that stood in front of Cole turned his head in the direction of the call. Realizing the mistake, Cole took his chance and stepped back from the knife. He grabbed the hooded figure's hand that held the knife and twisted. His enemy gave out a cry of pain and dropped the knife. With the blade gone, the figure sent out a frontal kick, which Cole caught in the gut. Bent over and taking in deep breaths of air, the figure sent out another kick that would have connected to Cole face, but seeing what was coming Cole caught the leg and in one swift movement he swept the other leg out from under his opponent, knocking him off his feet. All of this took less than a second and Cole was suddenly grateful for the hand-to-hand combat lessons that Merryrick had taught him. His opponent fell and landed on the sleeping Artemis.

Artemis's eyes snapped open wide as a large amount of weight suddenly fell on top of him.

"What the heck are you doing stable boy?" Artemis yelled, shoving the body that fell on him off.

Cole said nothing but just stared at the figure now on the ground.

"Answer me!" Artemis screamed walking over to Cole.

Still Cole said nothing, he was too shocked too reply.

"What are you staring at you dumb oaf?" Artemis yelled. Artemis turned around and felt his mouth fall open.

By this time the others had woken from their sleep and were now charging in with knifes drawn and swords out. They all came crashing to a halt when they saw what was in front of Cole and Artemis.

The hood of the figure's cloak had fallen back and sitting on the ground rubbing her cheek was a girl. She stared at Cole through angry emerald green eyes. She had an abundant amount of fiery red hair that was braided back and had fallen over her shoulder. She was dressed in greens and browns and the cloak that she wore was speckled with all different shades of greens. Cole stepped forward, bent down and offered her his hand. She stared at him with a stone cold expression.

"Sorry I didn't know," Cole muttered.

The girl looked at Cole's hand and then like a striking snake, punched him in the face. Cole was knocked on his backend, feeling dizzy.

"Hey! He was only trying to help," Maggie yelled rushing to Cole's side.

"Get back all of you. You are all surrounded by the best archers in all of Aloria," the girl commanded, picking up her knife from off the ground and pointing the blade at anyone that started moving towards her.

"By the best archers, do you Toefur and Rayden?" Gildon said, stepping in and helping Cole to his feet.

This time it was the girl's turn for her mouth to fall open.

"Gildon? Is that really you?"

"Ayla what are you doing out here this far from the city?" Gildon asked. " Does father know you're out here?"

"I'm scouting, and yes he does," Ayla replied, putting her knife back in its sheath. "Master Grayson sent us out last week. He sent all the Green cloaks out."

"Why?" Gildon asked.

"The whole guild of Greens have been sent out to scout all around Aloria and beyond," the girl Alya replied. "We're to report anything strange. Finding you out here with a bunch of," here she stopped and looked around at each one in the group, "outlanders is strange enough."

"Has something happened?" Gildon asked, concern in his voice. Ayla opened her mouth but stopped herself from speaking.

"You can trust them Ayla."

"There are some strange things going on around Aloria. There is talk that says there are Reapers about and that people are disappearing. Rumors from the south say that they have seen strange lights coming from the Grimhold and that the seals on the palace has been broken," Ayla whispered.

Gildon took a breath and nodded his head.

"I tell you that the Reaper's rumor is true. There are Reapers and Hellhounds about," Gildon said more to himself.

"Reapers?" Ayla whispered, her hand reaching for her knife.

"I don't mean to be rude or anything," Maggie interrupted, "but who are you, and who are these green cloaks and what is a Grimhold?" Maggie voiced everyone's questions.

Cole noticed that Maggie's hands were now clenched into fists and they were shaking slightly. He also knew that it was her way of trying to keep her temper from exploding.

"Ahh forgive me. My friends, this is Mistress Ayla Goldfeather 3rd Rank of the Green Cloaks, one who never misses a shot and the most important aspect about her is that she is my little sister," Gildon said, with a smile gesturing to Ayla. "Ayla this is Mistress Maggie, Master Chanlyn, Sir Arthur, Master Wallace, Master Artemis and I believe you have met our young Master Cole already," Gildon said, pointing everyone out to Ayla. "Now come we'll have breakfast which will give us some time to talk. Invite Toefur and Rayden in as well," Gildon said, after the introductions were made. Ayla nodded, then placed her thumb and pointer finger to her mouth and let out a short high-pitched whistle. She turned then and followed Gildon back to the camp.

Breakfast was cooked oats with sprigs of mint, dried berries and nuts, with a bit of honey for sweetening, thanks to Ayla and her cohorts. They all sat around the campfire waiting for Gildon and Ayla to explain things to them. Toefur and Rayden turned out to be boys that were in training, according to Ayla. They were dressed much the same way as Ayla but were obviously not in the same rank as the fiery red head. Cole automatically liked Toefur. He was a sandy haired boy that looked to be about ten or eleven, with wide-eyes that had the look of curiosity. He talked really fast, and Cole had to concentrate on what he was saying. He ran just as fast as he talked. Rayden seemed to be Cole's age, but Cole wasn't so sure about his own age. He always kept the hood of his cloak up over his head and he gave Cole the impression of a cat ready to pounce. When Gildon introduced Rayden, he seemed to disappear within the shadows of the tree. It startled Maggie. Ayla laughted at her then explained that that was Rayden's gift or talent, he could slip into shadows and disappeared, yet he never disappeared to Cole.

"So are you going to explain what all of this is about?" Maggie asked, placing her empty bowl on the ground. Her face was still a little red with anger after being laughed at.

Gildon nodded his head and swallowed the mouthful of oats he had been eating, and rubbed his hand together. Little sparks flew out of his hands, landing in the fire, which grew from coals to flames.

"You asked, Maggie, what the Green Cloaks are. They are Aloria's scout, spies, and our rangers. They patrol the land of Albavar and report anything out of the ordinary to their head master."

"What about this Grimhold?" Maggie asked. "What is that?"

"Grimhold is the gates to Shelrin's palace that were shut and sealed when Kayden imprisoned Shelrin's army and Shelrin inside." Wallace answered.

Both Ayla and Gildon looked at Wallace with a surprised expression. Both wondered how an outlander could know about Grimhold palace.

"And the seals that have been broken?"

"There were seven seals placed upon the black gates, each one powerful enough to last for hundreds of years. They were sealed by the last known warrior's heirs and they were supposed to be unbreakable," Gildon explained.

"It was also said that only the warrior's heirs themselves could break the seals. That is what kept people from going in and from things coming out," Ayla responded.

Maggie's head jerked over to Cole. She looked at Cole with an expression that said, "*tell them*".

Cole shook his head back at Maggie. Now was not the time to expose his nightmares. Gildon, however, noticed the shake of Cole's head, but said nothing.

"The sun is past its morning mark," Rayden said, making everyone jump a little, "we had better get going."

"Your right, Rayden. We'll be going back to Aloria with you then, Master Gildon," Ayla replied.

"Do you think you can keep up with us?" Sir Arthur asked, as they all rose to their feet.

"What do you mean?" Ayla asked.

"Well, we have mounts and you are on foot," he explained.

Ayla gave him a smile and again she put her two fingers to her lips and blew. This time instead of a long high-pitched whistle, she made a short three tone whistle. Rayden and Toefur did the same, only their songs were slightly different from each other. Cole stood stone still. Their whistles were almost the same whistles that Merryrick had taught him to call Gladadear.

In a few seconds, three shaggy horses, ranging in color from white to brown, came bounding into the camp, each one stopping in front of their masters. The horses were the same breed as Gladadear was.

"You see Cole. There was more to your Master Merryrick than met the eye. Would you not agree? I think Merryrick was in Aloria at one time and I have no doubt that he was one of the Green Cloaks," Gildon said, seeing Cole's utter amazement.

"I believe that we can keep up just fine," Ayla replied to Arthur as she rubbed her horse's forehead.

"Right! It's time that we were off. All of you gather your things and saddle your horses. We will be in Aloria by night fall," Gildon said excitedly.

The camp was quickly pulled apart as everyone gathered their gear and made ready to leave. Cole was bending down to buckle the cinch around Gladadear belly, when Maggie and Chanlyn came over to him.

"Cole, you should tell Gildon about your dreams," Maggie whispered. "From what father said about the Grimhold, it sounds like that was what you dreamed about."

"I'm not going to tell them anything," Cole muttered back.

"Cole, your dreams could be warning you about something," Maggie whispered, "You are a seer after all."

"She's right Cole," Chanlyn whispered.

"Just leave it alone," Cole whispered, going around Gladadear to make sure everything was tied on tight.

"Cole, you need to say something to someone. You saw the seals breaking I'm sure if it."

"Maybe I did and maybe I didn't, but I'm not going to tell them and have them go into a panic, that's if they believe me," Cole suddenly snapped.

Maggie and Chanlyn both looked at Cole with surprise. He had never snapped at either of them before.

"Sorry," Cole muttered. "What if I tell Gildon and he doesn't believe me. What if he thinks that I've gone mad? Heck! I think I'm mad!" Cole said.

"Cole you're dreaming about the Grimhold, I'm sure of that. But also your dreams might have something to do with the Dark Master Shelrin."

"What?" Cole cried. "That's impossible, Shelrin was destroyed by Kayden. Your father said so himself."

"Father said that Shelrin was imprisoned not destroyed," Maggie said, speaking very fast. "What if your dreams are telling you that Shelrin is going for a prison break?"

"Shh!" Cole hissed as he checked Gladadears hooves.

"I think you should tell, Cole," Chanlyn whispered.

"And be thought of as a fool. No one would believe me."

"It's better to be thought of as a fool and be wrong, rather than keep quiet and be right," Chanlyn muttered.

Cole realized the sense that Chanlyn made and he let out a breath realizing that his friend was right.

"Fine I'll tell. But not right now. Later when everyone isn't staring at us," Cole replied. Maggie and Chanlyn turned their heads and saw that everyone was indeed staring at them.

"Is there something wrong?" Gildon's voice asked, as he came upon the group on top of his horse.

Maggie looked over at Cole and bit down on her lower lip.

"No nothing's wrong," Cole responded, not daring to look at Gildon.

"Are you sure? It sounds like the three of you are having a bit of an argument."

"Its nothing," Cole said.

"Are you sure? Maggie is there any thing that you need to tell me? Chanlyn anything at all?"

Maggie's eyes darted from Cole to Gildon and then back at Cole. Chanlyn merely rubbed his toe in the dirt not daring to make eye contact with Gildon for fear that he might spill out everything they had just talked about.

"No everything's fine," Maggie replied.

"Yeah everything's fine," Chanlyn replied.

"Well okay. We need to get going then. I want to make it to Aloria by sundown if we can," Gildon said.

He took one last look at Cole and then clicked his horse forward.

"He knows we're hiding something," Chanlyn said.

"I know, but you two have to promise not to tell," Cole said.

"We will. But one of these days, Cole, you're going to have to tell before things get worse," Chanlyn declared.

"I know," Cole muttered, feeling Gildon's gaze upon him.

CHAPTER 21

PALE ORANGE SUNLIGHT slanted through the trees when the company came to a halt. They could go no further, for a great wall of jagged rocks stood before them blocking them from continuing on.

"The Cliffs of Moyor," Gildon said, pulling his horse to a stop. "Long have I wanted to see them again."

Cole tilted his head back and looked up at the layers of large rock formations that stretched up towards the heavens, and then disappeared in thick clouds of mist. Wild hawks darted skillfully to and fro from their nests that were perched precariously on narrow ledges. A creeping sort of vine spilled over the lower part of the cliffs, growing wherever it could take root. It grew so well along the cliff's surface that it was covered in curtains of the vegetation, completely hiding the sandstone rock.

"What do we do now?" Sir Arthur asked, "Can we go around the cliffs?"

"We could," Gildon stated. "But then we would find ourselves getting lost in a maze of slot canyons. The cliffs of Moyor are the entrance to a place that Alorians call the Thayden's maze. It's the landscape the surrounds Aloria, that provides a good defense for the city. Enemies cannot attack if they don't know where the city is."

"So then how do we get to Aloria?" Chanlyn asked. "We go up and over the cliffs?"

"No," Gildon said. "We go through the cliffs."

Gildon walked to the face of the cliff and pulled back a curtain of vines, revealing nothing but a solid rock wall.

"Blast! I can never remember where the gateway is," Gildon cursed.

"Hey! Fire Master, over here," Ayla called out.

Ayla, Rayden and Tofer had moved a little further up from where Cole and the others stood. She pulled back a curtain of vines like Gildon had, but instead of finding a solid wall there was a great stone gateway that had been carved out of the wall. The gateway was framed with carvings of eternal braids that had no beginning nor ending. Within that framework were two carved trees that stood opposite each other. Their branches twisted and intertwined with each other, outlining a rounded stone doorway. Seven swirling stars shown in between the intertwined branches,

"Aye, thank you Ayla. You were always one to remember where the gateways to Aloria are," Gildon said, with much relief in his voice.

"I am a Green Cloak after all. You think I can't find where a gateway is," Ayla replied, rolling her eyes.

Gildon placed a hand on the stone door and muttered a few words that no one understood. Maggie and Artemis jumped back in surprise when Gildon's hand suddenly burst into flames.

"How's he doing that?" Artemis asked.

"He is a Fire Master," Ayla said, as if that were an explanation.

The sound of stone grinding against stone echoed around them as doors slowly opened inch by inch until they had swung inward, revealing nothing but semi-darkness ahead.

"Not another cave," Maggie muttered as she saw the deepening blackness within.

"Scared of the dark?" Ayla asked, with a smug smile before she threw herself into the darkness. Tofer and Rayden followed, stepping into the gloom without so much as a thought, right behind them were their horses. Maggie clenched her fists in fury as she watched the three green cloaks disappear.

"In you go. Come on, it's quite safe, I promise you won't be trapped." Gildon said.

Maggie stepped in with a determined expression on her face. After her went Wallace, followed by Sir Arthur and Artemis. Chanlyn went in next and then Cole stepped in, each leading their horses. Gildon was last and when he stepped in, the door rumbled closed throwing everyone into blackness that was deeper than the night.

In the dark the sound of someone snapping their fingers echoed around them. Suddenly flames of firelight burst forth from torches that hung along the walls. Within the pale pools of light Cole could see a bit of his surroundings. He could see that he and the others were in some sort of passageway. Even though the walls were far enough apart that Cole could stretch out both his arms and have his fingertips of his middle fingers touch the walls, he still felt a slight panic run through him. He didn't like the thought of being underground.

"Go on, just follow the torches," Gildon said, his voice resounding off the walls.

Following the path of the torches, the passage twisted and turned a few times and then continued to descend downward. The air around them was cold and damp, smelling of mildew. Every so often Cole felt droplets of stone cold water fall from the darkness above and land on his head or down his neck, causing goose bumps to appear on his arms. From the light of the torches Cole could make out stairs and arched tunnels shooting off in other directions or sloping downward and disappearing into the blackened darkness. He pointed them out to Gildon.

"Built by the rebels nearly a hundred years ago," Gildon responded to Cole's questions. "Aloria was just a few caves when the rebels came here. They lived in them and made tunnels that are all around the citiy. It was the underground headquarters for the rebellion against Shelrin. But if you go wandering off, you could get lost for days."

As they moved, a distant rumbling sound could be heard under their feet and as they followed the path the sound became increasingly louder. To Cole it was like listening to an on coming thunderstorm that sounded far off but was fast approaching.

"What is that?" Cole asked.

"You will see," was all Gildon said.

Time seemed to pass very slowly underground. Cole felt like he had been walking for hours when their path leveled out for a time and then started ascending upwards. The air around them began to smell fresher and a faint stream of orange sunlight peeked in through cracks and small openings in the stone ceiling. The noise however was so loud now that nothing could be heard above it.

The group came out of the passageway and out onto a ledge. All stood staring with their mouths agape in astonishment and their eyes wide with surprise. With hands over their ears they stood watching a thick curtain of water, fall before them. They had come up behind a powerful waterfall and the sound of it was overpowering, far more powerful than any thunderstorm. Thousands upon thousand of tons of water, free falling hundreds of feet, pounded down on the rocks below and then spilled into a river that flowed down into a hidden valley. A thin spray of water swirled up and around the company, dampening their clothing.

Ayla led the way along a stone ledge, which came out from behind the waterfall and onto a dirt pathway that switched back and forth down the face of the Moyor's cliffs and into the valley below.

"Welcome to Aloria!" Gildon said, taking in a great breath of air. "Can you not smell it? Smell the pine, the oak and the birch, the flowers, the river and the oncoming night. No place in all of Albavar smells like this," Gildon said happily.

Once they were free of the ledge and on the dirt path, they mounted their horses and started downward towards the valley. Gladadear let out a snort and then suddenly picked up her pace, trotting down the path, following it with out any guidance from Cole.

"Easy Glad," Cole said, trying to slow the horse down.

Gladadear ignored Cole and just kept trotting along, the little horse only slowed when she reached the beginning of a stone bridge.

By the time the others had caugth up to Cole and Gladadear, the sun was just setting, throwing shadows across the valley, yet sunlight still touched the higher cliff tops. Ayla and her comrades had long since left Gildon and the others, riding homeward to report to the head of the Green Cloaks of their findings.

"It seems that Gladadear has been here before," Gildon commented when he had pulled to a stop next to Cole.

"I don't know when," Cole responded. "I've never been here."

"Perhaps she has been here with Merryrick," Gildon replied, "getting off his horse.

A cobble stone road replaced the dirt path when the party came to a stone arched bridge that spanned the width of the river. Carved stone lanterns lined the bridgeway, each one holding a bright flame of fire that illuminated the road ahead. On the other end of the bridge, Cole could make out two personages standing within two pools of light opposite each other, wearing cloaks of black. From what Cole could see the two men, at least he thought they were men, were tall and broad shouldered with the hoods of their cloaks pulled over their heads. Although the cloaks were decorated with gold trimming around the hood and edges, Cole could not help but think of the Reapers black robes.

The pair stood with naked swords, tips resting on the ground, their hands folded one on top of the other resting on the pommel of their blades. They didn't move and Cole would have thought that they were stone statues, save for the rising of their chests as they breathed. Gildon was first to step across the threshold of the bridge, and as he did the fires within the lanterns burned a little brighter. The others followed closed behind him and even Wallace seemed a bit skittish when he saw them. When they reached the other side of the bridge, Gildon stood before the two Black Cloaks.

"Who stands before us?" one black cloak asked in an ice-cold voice.

"Gildon, a tinker and a wanderer, with a few new friends," Gildon announced in a voice of command.

"If you are Gildon, who be thy father?" The same black cloak asked.

"My father is Master Godfrey King of Aloria," Gildon answered.

"King… that makes Gildon…" Maggie started to say.

"A prince," Chanlyn muttered.

Cole looked at Gildon as he crossed the bridge and felt his insides melt. He had attacked a prince. The Black Cloaks were deadly quiet as their hooded heads rose up from their chests. The sound of their swords scrapping across the cobblestone as they were brought up over their heads rang out through the night. Cole feared they were going to attack and he was ready to pull his hunting knife free from it sheath but all the Black Cloaks did was cross the blades of their swords over Gildon's head.

"Enter Master Gildon and guests of Aloria. But know this, to walk under the swords is to agree to the laws and rulings of Aloria. Betray us and both blades of justice and mercy will fall down upon you," both the Black Cloaks said in unison.

"I agree and will follow the laws and rulings of Aloria. If I betray Aloria then let the blades fall upon me," Gildon stated and walked under the crossed swords. They all stepped forward repeating what Gildon had said and then joined him on the other side of the blades.

Cole was so nervous that when he stepped forward his mind went totally blank. The words that Gildon and the others had just spoken only moments before were gone. Cole stood there, his mouth open, staring up at the swords, trying to recall the words, thinking that any second they were going to come down on him. Then all at once Cole remembered what Merryrick would say every evening before he went to bed.

"I promise to be true to my words and good to all my fellow mankind. I will honor and keep the laws of the land. I will strive to seek after the light and fight against the dark," Cole said in a rush, the words falling out of his mouth.

The guards stood silent and for a moment Cole thought that he would not be allowed to cross under the swords.

"Enter," one guard said. With a breath of relief, Cole crossed under the swords and joined the others. The black-cloaked guards sheathed their swords and then pulled the hoods from their heads. Cole's eyes weren't the only ones to widen in surprise as one of the Black Cloaks turned out to be a woman just a few years younger than Gildon. The other black-cloaked guard was an older man, in his later forties with graying hair along the edges. He turned and bowed to Gildon, which Gildon returned.

"Prince Gildon it is good to see you. Your father and Mistress Kaya have heard of your return and wish to see you, all of you," the older of Black Cloaks stated.

"It is good to be home, Master Clayborn, but please don't call me prince, it sounds so formal."

"As you say Master Gildon."

"Thank you Clayborn. Now will you escort us and tell me all that has happened since I have been away," Gildon asked.

"I would be honored," the Black Cloak Clayborn replied, and then turned to his colleague. "Willow, go and find Master Hail, tell him to send four grooms to the Grand Staircase."

The woman nodded then rushed off, vanishing into the night as her black cloak concealed her from human eyes. Gildon and Master Clayborn turned and began to follow a gravel path that was shadowed by elder trees that were so tall their branches disappeared in the ink black sky. Carved stone lanterns much like the ones on the bridge lined their pathway, leading them forward through the city. As they wandered along the pathways that wound around the city, Cole and the others couldn't help notice the layers of flags and banners that hung from rooftops and in the windows. As they passed the Village green they saw hundreds of paper lanterns hung within the branches of an elder tree.

"What are all the lanterns for?" Maggie questioned with curiosity.

"You are all very fortunate in arriving tonight, for tomorrow we are celebrating Victory day," Master Clayborn answered.

"Victory day? And what pray tell is that?" Arthur asked.

"Why it is the day we celebrate when Shelrin's empire fell and all men were free once again," Clayborn said proudly.

"It is much like your Festival back in Kells, but is also a day when we remember those that fell fighting for our freedoms," Gildon added.

"Yes, off course we remember those that fought for us so that we might live as free men, and we will light a candle for all at the Remembrance Ceremony tomorrow night, but it is also a day of celebration where one can enjoy the sights, sounds and smells of Victory Day," Clayborn said, with a smile on his face.

They continued along the path with Gildon and Clayborn recalling past Victory Days in which they remembered the smells of honey apples, getting into mischief with friends and competing for prizes in games and contests.

The moment they reached the Grand Staircase, Cole knew why it was given that name. It was carved from the stone of the cliffs. It started as a straight path of stairs with great stone newels on either side. The two newels had a sculpture of a tree standing atop of them. Small glass bulb lanterns hung within the branches, making the trees look as if the bulbs were small glowing flowers. The light also gave more illumination to the impressive staircase. The staircase was carved with much skill. It turned gracefully upward then split into two separate staircases, one leading to the east and the other to the west. The railing was made of polished wood while molded iron, formed into vines, climbed and curled with blooming flowers creating the balusters.

As the party grew closer to the base of the stairs, they were greeted by four young boys, dressed in velvet blue vests with silver lining, and Willow her sword belted around her.

"Willow, you have returned I see. And you have brought 4 grooms as requested. Good. Boys take the horses to the stables, make sure that they are fed and watered and give them a brush down if you please," Master Clayborn ordered.

Reluctantly Cole gave over the reins of Gladadear to one of the boys then turned with the others to climb the Grand Staircase. The group mounted the stairs and followed the path that led to the west.

After a short climb the group stood before a set of double wooden doors. Two other Black cloak guards stood on either side of the doors. They however did not raise their swords over their heads but opened the door as they approached.

"They are waiting for you," one guard said.

"Thank you Master Readford," Gildon replied, and stepped over the threshold. As they all stepped in, the guards behind them shut the door and followed the group as they moved forward.

Torches and candles lit a flagstone-paved hallway with great columns of stone holding up the vaulted ceiling. Around the Great Hall hung the flags of green, black, white, red, blue, brown and yellow.

Ahead was a pool of light and as they got closer to the pool the hallway wound and transformed into a circular room with a domed glass ceiling above them. Situated in the center of the room was a dais where a half circle of seven white stone chairs stood. Two of the chairs were occupied. In one of the chairs sat a gentleman of some years and an old woman, much older than the gentleman.

The gentleman wore a beard of graying brown that matched the hair on top of his head. He wore a necklace of silver and a great cape of red around him. The woman wore white and held a staff in her hands and sat in her chair with stooped shoulders and a bent back. A woman dressed in white as well, stood near the woman's chair. When the company approached they rose to their feet and greeted Gildon with a smile. Gildon bowed and the others bowed in return.

"So young Gildon, you have returned and I feel that you have brought a few others with you," the old woman spoke, her voice rough from years of speaking.

"I have Mistress Kaya," Gildon said.

"Come, let me see how you have changed," Mistress Kaya said, her hands reaching out towards Gildon.

Gildon stepped forward and took the old lady's hand. He then placed her hand on his cheek. It was then that Cole realized that the woman was blind with large white cataracts covering the iris of her eyes. Cole was suprised that she was not as old as he had originally thought. Her stooped figure and long white hair had given him the impression of an elderly woman, yet Kaya's face only bore a few wrinkles.

"You have grown a beard," Kaya said in surprise.

"Yes. When wandering the lands, one doesn't have much time to shave, Mistress Kaya."

"Well it suits you," Kaya said with a smile. "Now go! I sense that your father wishes to speak to you," Kaya commented and pushed Gildon over to the gentleman.

"Gildon my son. It is good to see you home!" the gentleman said, taking his son and hugging him. "Tell me my son of your adventures and introduce us to your friends," the gentleman said, pulling away from his son.

"Father! Mistress Kaya! As you may know, I left here over a year ago on a mission and I believe that I have fulfilled that mission, in a manner of speaking. I will tell you all that has happened to me over the past months but first I think you would have me introduce to you my friends. May I present to you Master Wallace and his daughter Maggie, Master Wallace, may I present Mistress Kaya and my father King Godfrey."

Wallace and Maggie stepped forward and bowed to the King and then stepped to Kaya, who felt Maggie's face.

"Oh a beauty stands before me," Kaya said. "You are very welcome my dear." She then felt Wallace's face.

"Master Wallace, as a word from the wise. You cannot hide from your past much longer. Things that you wish to remain hidden will come out," Kaya whispered. Wallace said nothing but merely nodded his head.

"This is Sir Arthur and his son young Master Artemis."

Arthur and Artemis stepped forward and bowed to Godfrey. Both went to Kaya and she touched Artemis face like with Maggie and Wallace.

"A good man stands before me," Kaya said, "but take heed young Artemis, your journey will be hard and many choices will stand before you," Kaya stated.

Kaya reached out to touch Sir Arthur's face, but he stepped back away from her hands and placed his hand in hers.

"It is good to meet you Mistress Kaya. I am Sir Arthur," he said shaking the old women's hand. "We are very grateful for your hospitality."

"You are quite welcome," Mistress Kaya said, pulling her hand from Arthur's. "If there is anything you require don't hesitate to ask."

When Arthur and Artemis stepped down from the dais, Chanlyn stepped forward and bowed to them. "May I present Master Chanlyn," Gildon said.

"Oh now Chanlyn, a smart one you are," Kaya said, rubbing his cheek, "full of intellect and gifted with a long memory."

"And finally may I present to you young Master Cole," Gildon said, when Chanlyn stepped back.

Cole stepped forward and bowed to King Godfrey, then went to Kaya, but when she felt his face an expression of what seemed like fear came upon her. She grabbed hold of his hands and wouldn't let go.

Your coming has been foretold, Kaya's voice whispered inside Cole's head as she grasped tighter onto Cole's hand squeezing it harder. *The last wild Spirit nearly destroyed our world. Will you do the same?*

As if suddenly woken from a dream, Kaya released Cole's hand and looked at him with a smile. "You will do well here I think," she said to Cole then turned her sightless gaze on all her company.

Cole stepped back away from Kaya, holding his sore hand, and rejoined the others.

"You are all very welcome here. Come, you must be weary from your journey. Master Clayborn, if you would please show our new additions to my home. My household has prepared rooms for you all," Godfey said, his booming voice echoing around the hall. "There you will find food, drink and warm fires waiting for you."

"Yes Master Godfrey," Clayborn replied then bowed to both Mistress Kaya and Master Godfrey.

"Gildon stay and tell us of your adventures and what you have found," Kaya said softly. Gildon nodded and turned and bowed to the company.

"I'll say goodnight to you all. I shall see you in the morning." Everyone bowed again to the Mistress and King of Aloria.

"What was that all about?" Maggie whispered, as they were being led from the great hall.

"I don't know," Cole whispered.

He looked back over his shoulder and he saw that Kaya was watching him. Even though she was blind he could feel her eyes on him.

CHAPTER 22

RAYS OF LIGHT streamed in from the bay window of Cole
and Chanlyn's small room that they shared, and fell across Cole's
closed eyes, waking him from a restless sleep. Dreams had haunted
him during the night, most of which he could not remember save for
one about black birds, with feathers that looked like steel blades, flying
across the skies on a hunt.

Cole let out a moan and pulled the covers over his head and rolled
over, turning his back to the sunlight. He wanted to find a little more
sleep before his day started. But his change in position did little to
block out the growing sunlight. With a sigh Cole gave up and rolled
over and sat up, throwing the pillow and blankets from him.

The bed where Chanlyn had spent the night was empty. Now that
he was awake and could see the angle of the sun through his window,
he realized how late it was. By this time back at home he would have
been done with his morning chores and would be working in the
workshop with Merryrick. A hard lump of emotion filled Cole as he
thought about what once was. A few tears filled his eyes before he took
a breath and swallowed back his grief. Taking in another deep breath
and letting it out Cole got to his feet. There was a city to explore and
a celebration to attend. Cole quickly scrubbed the tears from his face
and dressed.

The house in which their rooms were located was the house of
Godfrey. It was a nice three-story house with many windows and bal-
conies that overlooked the Great Falls.

Cole raced from his room, down a long hallway to a winding stairway that led to the second floor. Taking the stairs two at a time he
hurried down to the parlor where he thought his friends would be.
When he entered the room he found it almost empty. The girl, Ayla,
Cole remembered, the one that had punched him in the face the day

before sat in a chair with her arms resting on the armrest with her fingers drumming impatiently.

"Finally!" the girl breathed when Cole came into the room. "You've slept most of the morning." She sounded irritated as she rose to her feet.

"Where are all the others?" Cole asked, looking around to see if there was anyone else within the room.

"At the fair," Ayla said. "Where I should be, instead I get orders that I have to show you, an outlander, around the city!" Ayla complained.

Cole clutched his fist in anger towards the girl. It wasn't like he couldn't explore the city on his own. Yet he was also feeling a bit of anger towards his friends, they could have woken him.

"Well are you ready?" Ayla asked crossly.

"Lead the way," Cole said coarsely.

With her chin up and her nose stuck in the air, Ayla marched from the room and out the door of Godfrey's house. They crossed a bridge that led out onto the main street of the city. Cole had experienced fairs and festivals before. He had grown up in Kells and they had their yearly festivals every spring and fall, one to celebrate the planting of a good crop and the other the harvesting of a good crop. Cole had fond memories of these festivals but all the fairs that he had ever been to throughout his lifetime could not compare to the one that Aloria was celebrating.

Now that the sun was fully up and shining on the city, Cole truly saw Aloria for the first time, and it was smothered in blue, white and silver, the colors of Aloria. Blue flags printed with a great silver tree were placed anywhere and everywhere that they could be seen. They swayed in the wind above towers and turrets. There wasn't a building that did not have the kingdom's colors hanging from it somewhere. They were sold by street venders, were placed in windows of taverns and homes and were carried by people of every age. So many more had been hung since the night before.

Cole learned from Ayla that the silver tree with its great intertwining branches in the center of the flag represented the seven Warriors and the many other warriors that followed after.

Aloria was much larger than Cole had initially thought. The cliff-side city was built on both sides of the gorge, with the Great River running between them. Bridges of stone and wood connected the two sides together. The Toplands were also considered part of Aloria as well. The many levels of homes, shops and public building were connected together by paths and staircases that zigzagged up and down the cliff-side and were, like everything else, carved out of the gorges of sandstone face.

Ayla explained, as she moved through the city, that Aloria had been just a bunch of caves and holes in the rock wall when the first rebels founded it nearly a hundred years before, and for the first few years they lived in the caves. She spoke of the years the stone- cutters and carpenters worked to build the city.

"Aloria was named after the first Alorian, the warrior's city that Shelrin destroyed." Ayla shouted, as they moved through the crowded streets.

To Cole the city looked a lot like a castle he had imagined once when he was a small boy, with its many towers, turrets, bridges and stairways and Cole marveled at the sight of it all.

"What is that?" Cole asked pointing to a large building with columns and stained glass windows.

"It is the Library. It is where they keep all the records of the warriors. That is what is left of the warriors," Ayla said, acting annoyed.

Cole looked at the building thinking that they would never get Chanlyn out if he ever went in.

Ayla seemed to be in a hurry, for she was pushing her way past people as she hurried through the crowds of festival patrons heading for the toplands where the games for victory day were to take place. As she shoved her way forwards she received more than one cold stare and a few harsh words. All Cole could do was follow and apologize to those that she had offended. They climbed a path of stairs that wound its way up the gorge's cliff face. When Cole reached a landing he had a cramp in his side and was panting as though he had run for miles. He stopped and bent down to catch his breathe. When he looked up Ayla was gone. Cole looked out over the heads of the crowd that were climbing the stairs, looking for a ginger headed girl, but when he didn't see any ginger-heads he merely shrugged his shoulders and didn't really mind that he was left alone. He turned back around and went down the way he came. He wandered through the maze of walkways and streets. In truth he was somewhat glad he was left on his own. He really didn't like Ayla and he got the feeling that she really didn't like him.

Cole roamed the levels of streets without any cares in his mind. He explored the little shops that dotted the sidewalks with awnings out front, protecting goods of clothing, kitchenware, rugs, furs and books. He lost himself up and down the avenues and streets, quite enjoying himself. It seemed that all the guilds of the tinkers were out showing off their talents. He saw fine works of stone cutting, weaponry, weaving and sculpting. He stopped at a woodworker's workshop and watched him carve a horse's head out of a chunk of ash. Cole took in the smells of sawdust and glue and realized that he hadn't touched a piece of wood for nearly a month. As he watched, his fingers itched to touch the tools of his trade again. The woodcarver must have seen Cole's eagerness for he stopped his carving and look up at Cole through storm gray eyes.

"Know anything about wood, boy?" the woodcarver asked.

"Aye sir," Cole responded.

"Mmm, let's see about that," the woodcarver muttered under his breath, as he got up from his workbench.

He walked around his workshop, pointing to different types of wood asking Cole to identify which tree they had come from and what they should be used for.

Cole identified walnut, oak and mahogany.

"They are harder woods so they last longer. Those woods should be used for making furniture."

Cole continued to identify the softwoods, basswood, which came from the Lindon tree, cedar, sugar pine and chestnut, considered both softwood and hard wood.

Satisfied by Cole's knowledge, the woodcarver invited Cole into his workshop and put him to work.

"See those planks of wood," the woodcarver Grayson said, pointing to a stack of rough looking wooden beams.

Cole nodded seeing the wood.

"Take the jack plane and plane the boards smooth. When you're done with that, you can sand that chest. Make sure you don't scratch the wood boy. That chest is for Mistress Kaya."

"My name is Cole, sir," Cole said.

"And I'm Grayson," the woodcarver said introducing himself.

"You're the leader of the Greencloaks," Cole said, having a face to match with the name.

"That I am," Grayson said.

"May I ask a question?" Cole inquired.

"I believe that you just did," Grayson said. But go ahead and ask another."

"Is Lady Kaya the Kaya who was with Kayden?"

"The very same," Grayson replied returning to his carving.

Cole nodded his head and started his planing.

Cole didn't know how long he worked, but the moment he picked up the planer he was lost in his work. He had been working for only minutes it seemed. He remembered that he used to complain to Merryrick about the relentless movement of going back and forth over the wood. Now he liked hearing the sharp thin blade scraping over the wood and the ringlets of wood shavings coming up off the wooden beam and falling to the ground.

"I see you have picked up an apprentice, Master Grayson," a familiar voice said, stopping Cole from working.

He looked up from his planing and began feeling uneasy. Mistress Kaya was standing before him.

"I wouldn't know about that Mistress Kaya. But the boy is a good worker and he knows his woods," Grayson said, standing and bowing to Kaya in respect.

"I believe that he learned the skill from his late Master. A Master Merryrick. Is that not right Cole?" Kaya's said, her sightless eyes turning to Cole.

Cole stared with eyes open.

How does she know that, Cole thought. He hadn't told her.

As if she were reading Cole's mind, Kaya answered.

"Gildon has divulged much to me of you and your friend's adventures. Speaking of your friends I believe they are looking for you and have found you," Kaya said with a smile.

No more than a second went by after Kaya had finished her sentence, when Cole heard the very familiar cry of Maggie calling out his name.

"Cole!"

Cole looked up and saw Maggie and Chanlyn running towards him with Gildon, and Wallace in tow.

"Cole, we've finally found you!" Maggie said, a little out of breath. "We've been looking for you everywhere, ever since Ayla lost you."

"I wouldn't have been lost if you would have woken me up and I could have gone with you," Cole said, a little put out by his friends.

"That was my doing Cole," Wallace said. "I told them to let you sleep, since you have had a hard time coming by it. Please forgive them for following my orders."

"Well now that we have found Cole, shall we all go to the lake, the sun is making its way to the west and the Remembrance Ceremony will begin," Kaya said. "Master Grayson will you join us?" Kaya asked the woodcarver.

"Aye I will light a candle for James and Carla," Grayson said. It took but a moment for Grayson to close his shop and hang his closed sign in the window.

They all followed a zigzag path down to the bottom of the gorge and took a short walk through a small but dense forest and came out on the beach of a small lake. The lake was aglow with small lightweight glass bulbs that floated on the lake's smooth surface. Within the bulbs were small-lit candles that reflected the flames on the water. There were hundreds of the little glowing bulbs and more were being added every minute as more and more Alorians lit the candles and released the lights into the water.

When Cole and the others reached the beach, Gildon produced a few glass bulbs from his satchel. He blew into each of them and amazingly the candle within was lit. Gildon then handed one to each of his companions.

"Each light represents the soul of someone that was lost during the war, not only on the battlefield but also those that were murdered in the slaughter of villages and towns. Think of someone you lost and place the bulb in the water. Then hopefully those that have gone to the other world will see that we are remembering them," Gildon explained.

Cole watched the others send their light out to join with the other bulbs. He watched Master Grayson light two bulbs and with tears in his eyes wade out in the water and gently let his Remembrance Bulbs go.

Cole couldn't help wondering who James and Carla, that he had spoken of earlier, were.

Kaya leaned over and softly whispered the answer to Cole.

"They were his son and wife. They like so many others were killed during the slaughter of his village."

Cole looked out across the lake and wondered how many of the floating lights were for the souls of the young that had been taken away so horrifically. He wondered if one of those bulbs was for William and his sister.

Cole also thought of Merryrick and wondered if he could really see him from the other side of the veil and would know that he was thinking of him. Taking a breath Cole stepped to the waters edge and placed his Remembrance Bulb in the water and gave it a little push. Then he quickly stepped back to a safe distance away from the water. His fear of the water still made him nervous. His gaze followed his little light as it moved towards the center of the lake then became lost in the mist of all the other floating lights.

There had been a soft loll of conversation as people softly talked amongst themselves, but then the talking suddenly died. As Cole turned to look for the reason for the sudden silence he saw that Godfrey had come down to the lake and was placing his own bulb into the water. When he had finished he stood and silently looked around him, then with a great voice he spoke.

"My friends, we stand here this night on the fifteenth anniversary of when the Empire of Shelrin fell. We owe our lives and our children's lives to those that fought and died for that great cause of freedom. Today we've celebrated and have given thanks for the blessing of our children, who can live and grow without the threat of having their lives taken from them, which many of our older generations lived through and lost loved ones because of Shelrin's treachery.

I believe that we must pay homage to Kayden, a great man and leader, for without him and his sacrifice, the world that we live in now would not have ever existed. It was prophesied long ago that a man of small beginning would one day rise up from the ashes of hope and would bring about the ending of the darkness that had taken over Albavar. Kayden was that man and may our children and grand-children and great-grand-children and many more generations beyond, know the history of their land and of the great deeds that Kayden and so many others did to give us our freedom. Let us now have that moment of silence in which we can all remember those that have gone before us and are now safe on the other side of this earthly veil," Godfrey said, as his voice rang out through the audience.

Godfrey bowed his head, as did all those that surrounded the lake's shores. Cole too lowered his own head, lost in his thoughts of what had happened to him and his friends over the past month.

"The fools," a cold voice said.

Cole's head rose up and looked around him to see who had spoken such coarse words. But is seemed that all heads were bent down in reverence and all eyes were closed, or at least he thought so, from what he could see. Then Cole's head suddenly exploded with a sharp cold, hot pain and blast of light. For a moment his vision was blurred then came into focus. He stood on a balcony gazing across a wide river over looking what appeared to be a city lit up in firelight as they celebrated. There was a slight breeze and it picked up the sounds of music and laughter.

"The fools, all of them, to celebrate the demise of me, Shelrin, ruler of them all. They shall all pay!" The cold voice echoed. There was a great flash and Coles was back at the lake. People were staring at him but he didn't care because his arm burned as if it was being stabbed by hot pokers.

"No, not now," Cole muttered, rubbing his forearm.

"Cole, is everything alright?" Maggie's voice whispered somewhere near him.

"Maggie he's awake!" Cole gasped.

"Who?" Maggie asked.

"Shelrin!" Cole groaned.

Then Cole felt his whole body shear up in hot pain, as if a rod of hot steel had been thrust into his spine and was melting into every muscle and vein. He could hear screaming in the distance while the world around Cole blurred and the flash of bright light blinded Cole and folded around him.

LIGHT EXPLODED in front of Cole blocking out his vision. He bolted up right taking in great breaths of air. A hand fell on his shoulder. Terrified Cole jerked away and scooted back until his back came up against a wall.

"Easy boy. I will not harm you," a voice said somewhere near him.

Cole looked around him disoriented as to where he was. He was on a bed near a small window. Roots and herbs hung on exposed beams all around the room. He could smell the sweetness of incense burning. There was a fire in the hearth and a kettle boiling over the flames. For a moment, Cole thought that he was back home in Kells.

"Merryrick?" Cole questioned through blurry eyes at the figure that stood before him.

"No boy. I am Kaya. Do you remember me?"

Cole nodded his head. His mind worked slowly but after a moment he could remember that he was in Aloria.

"Where am I?" Cole asked, still breathing hard.

"You are in my quarters. You've been quite ill," Kaya replied, going over to the fire and fetching the kettle that hung there. She moved to the table that sat in the center of the room and poured the contents of the kettle, which looked to be water, into a wooden goblet.

"Drink this up, Cole," Kaya said, bringing the goblet to Cole. "It will help with the nausea."

Cole drank the warm liquid and tasted honey mixed with tartness. Instantly he felt his heart begin to slow and his head begin to clear and his stomach settle.

"How did I get here?" Cole asked, handing the goblet back to Kaya. "The last thing that I remember was standing near the lake and…"

"And there you collapsed and have been laying unconscious with a fever for a night and a day," Kaya explained, taking the goblet from Cole and placing it back on the table.

Still slightly shaking, Cole wiped the sweat from his forehead and took in slow even breaths.

"How long have your nightmares haunted you, Cole?" Kaya asked. Cole looked over at Kaya wondering how she had known he had been trapped within a nightmare.

"It's was not hard to guess that you were locked within a dream during your days of unconsciousness, Cole," Kaya said softly, taking a seat on his bed. "You are a seer are you not?"

Cole didn't answer.

"All the signs are there, Cole, you needn't hide it from me. Even Gildon is aware of your gifts," Kaya said. "When you touch someone with your bare skin do you see things?"

"I don't always have to touch them," Cole whispered. "Sometime they just happen, like when I was at the lake."

"Then tell me Cole. Tell me of your dream."

Her voice was soft and comforting. He felt his fears calm and the shadows fade. Cole licked his lips and swallowed several times to try and work moisture back into his mouth. He knew now it was time to tell. He took in a few ragged breaths and began to tell his dream.

"At first I stood on a balconey, across a river, over looking a city. There was a voice that called everyone fools and said they would all pay. There was a great flare of light and pain that made my head whirl and my arm burn and I had to close my eyes. When I opened them again I stood in the city. It was night and the people were celebrating. There was music and laughter, bonfires and lanterns hung around the town square. Then there was a loud sound of bells ringing from a tower," Cole recalled. "Across the river I could see the silhouette of a fortress. It was dark and abandoned, almost in ruins. I…I didn't like the look of it."

"This town that you were in, did it have a name?" Kaya asked.

Cole shook his head. "I don't recall. It was a city of white I think, with a fortress on a hill, " Cole replied, seeing his dream within his minds eyes.

"Whiteguard City. What happened next Cole?" Kaya asked softly.

"Everyone was enjoying themselves. That's why they didn't notice the fog that was rolling in from across the river. Thick and black, like the fog from another dream," Cole replied.

"You have had others dreams like this before this recent one?" Kaya asked.

"Yes. I dreamed of the fog when I was in Kells and black walls shattering like panes of glass releasing the Reapers and their hounds."

Kaya was silent for a moment.

"Will you continue with the telling of your dream Cole?"

Cole swallowed again, knowing that the next part of his dream was hard to tell.

"The fog was strange, it moved like ink in water and it came in and covered the beaches of the city and there was a sound, like thunder breaking overhead. Someone yelled that the boats were on fire and many of the menfolk ran out into the fog to try and extinguish the flames. There were cries of pain that echoed in the night that came in with the fog. One man came running out of the fog yelling about an attack, but then he was struck down, with an arrow in his back," Cole said, his voice shaking. "Everyone was in a panic and the doors to the city were shut, men at arms were called. The locked doors did little good. They were blown apart as was half of the surrounding wall. A figure, dressed in a black cloak with the hood pulled over his face came out of the smoke and fog, carrying with him a staff of gold.

The men that survived the blast from the door stood and pointed their swords, spears and bows at the figure. "You fool!" the cloaked figure said. "Do you think your mere weapons of steel can hurt me, for I am Shelrin come back to take what is rightfully mine." The cloaked figure raised the staff and the fog cleared," Cole said, now rocking back and forth. "When it cleared an army stood behind the figure, the staff was brought down again and the army attacked. But it wasn't an army of living men," Cole said, his voice rising, "They bore no faces, there was nothing there but shadow and when one was struck it would shatter like breaking glass, only to reform again." Cole said terrified. "The people could do little but run and try to escape, but many couldn't. Screams of terror and pain echoed out into the night. Somewhere a fire began to burn and the city was engulfed. When it was all over bodies lined the streets and blood ran along them," Cole said, seeing the scene of carnage.

"I think I'm going to be sick," Cole muttered. Kaya retrieved a bowl and rubbed Cole's back as he threw up.

When he had emptied his stomach, Kaya rose from the bed, taking the basin with her and retrieved the goblet from the table and put it to Cole's lips. He drank the honey sweet tea and felt his nerves and stomach calm again.

"Is there anything else Cole?" Kaya asked.

Cole shook his head.

"No. I woke up then."

It remained quiet for a time. Kaya worked grinding roots and leaves. Cole lay back on his pillows, feeling tired and weak but he forced himself to stay awake. He didn't want to face the dream again.

"Do not try to fight sleep. Your mind and body have been through quite an ordeal and you need to rest," Kaya said, sensing Cole's edginess.

"I...don't want too," Cole muttered.

"You are scared. It is understandable considering the vision you just had. But if I promised you that you would have no more nightmares tonight, would you rest?" Kaya asked.

"How can you promise that?" Cole asked.

"There is a song that I can sing that will catch your nightmares and take them away," Kaya said, as she took a seat in her rocking chair by the fire.

Cole looked over a Kaya with raised eyebrows.

Sensing Cole's disbelief Kaya began to sing.

"Lay down your sweet and weary head.
The day is done and night has come.
So do not fear my little one
For you are safe in my arms.

Where dreams cannot harm you
and darkness cannot find you.
So sleep, sleep, until the dawn."

The melody was a lullaby and Kaya voice was soft and gentle. It wasn't long before Cole began to fill his eyelids grow heavy and he felt his stiff body loosen and relax. There was something familiar about the song Kaya was singing. It was a tune that he had heard before but he couldn't quite place it. As the words and melody sunk in a memory began to form. But just as the memory seemed to come to light, Cole faded into the darkness of sleep where no dreams of any kind touched him.

CHAPTER 23

KAYA FINISHED SINGING her lullaby and looked over to where the boy lay. By the sound of his steady breathing, she assumed that he was asleep. As the slow hours of the night passed Kaya thought about Cole and what Gildon had told her and Godfrey about him. She was saddened, knowing full well what was going to happen to him, it happened to all of his kind.

A knock at the door echoed around the room, breaking Kaya from her thoughts. "Come," Kaya responded.

The door opened and Master Godfrey, Master Gildon, Master Clayborn and Master Grayson entered the room. Grayson and Gildon's eyes roamed over to the bed where Cole slept.

"How is he?" Grayson asked.

"He sleeps peacefully for now. The draft I gave him will help keep the nightmares at bay for a few hours more."

"So my suspicions were correct then?" Gildon asked.

"Yes. He is a descendant of the Elfain bloodline, a seer," Kaya said. "That is his Spirit. He is capable of seeing the past, present, and future of any person he touches. He also dreams of what is to come."

"The poor boy," Godfrey said.

"What do you mean father?" Gildon asked.

"To see what is to come. To know that…" Goldfrey replied.

"But surely it is a gift, to know what your enemy plans," Clayborn spoke.

"Being a seer comes with great power true, but it also comes at a cost," Godfrey answered.

"And that cost it," Gildon asked.

"Because Cole is a seer, he will continue to dream of things, causing him to loose his ability to differentiate between reality and dreams. It is more than likely that he will loose his mind and go mad. He might have already gone mad had it not been for the block that is upon him," Kaya explained.

"A block," Godfrey asked with surprise.

"Aye. A block that prevents him accesing all of his powers."

"Can it be removed?" Gildon asked.

"Yes and no, the block is almost unbreakable," Kaya replied. "It would have to be an incredible amount of power thrown at him to do so."

"And if his block were ever to be broken." Godfry asked.

"It is most likely that his powers would overwhelm him, he wouldn't be able to control them. It would be a very bad thing. Think about Cole's block like a dam. A dam allows a flow of water to move continuously. If that dam were ever to break, then a great wave of water would rush forward and swallow everything in its path. If the block were ever to break on Cole, it would swallow him and more than likely break the world."

"How do you know this?" Gildon asked, his voice rising in alarm. "How do you know that Cole will go insane or break the world?"

Cole let out a moan and rolled over on his side. All within the room fell silent as they waited for Cole to settle.

"Calm yourself, Master Gildon," Kaya said.

"We know this, son, because there was someone like Cole before him. Her name was Alleana," Godfrey said.

"Alleana? You mean Kayden's wife?" Gildon asked.

"Yes. She was gifted much like Cole, a seer. She could see events before they happened and she was a great instrument in winning battles against Shelrin. But as she grew older, her mind faded. She could not tell the difference between her reality world and her dream world. She went mad, Gildon. She was so lost in her mind that she threw her own child into the river and the child was lost over the falls," Kaya continued her story.

"But that doesn't mean it will happen to Cole," Gildon said.

"His mind and powers are linked, when one goes so will the other," Kaya said, "but the block has bought him time and his madness won't happen all at once. However he will slowly decline," Kaya said softly.

Gildon was quiet for a moment. He looked over at Cole and couldn't believe that he could go insane. The boy was young, no more the seventeen and from what Gildon had seen of Cole, he knew that he was bright, clever and courageous.

"Can you help him?" Gildon asked.

"I can give him honey and nightshade for his worst nightmares, but as time passes the remedy will not help him and he will slowly fade into madness," Kaya said sympathetically.

"Are you sure that he is a seer?" Grayson asked.

"I have no doubt about it," Kaya said. "I have seen the boy's dreams myself."

"He is," Gildon said, recalling the times when Cole saved the boy from the river and the warning he gave just before the hounds attacked.

"Then has he seen anything?" Clayborn asked, a little tactless.

"He has," Kaya responded, her blind eyes throwing daggers in Master Clayborn's direction.

"He told me of a dream he had. Master Clayborn, I suggest you gather a company to send to the Whiteguard Fortress. Search for survivors."

"Survivors Mistress?" Clayborn asked.

"If Cole's dream is correct, Whiteguard has been attacked and was burned on Victory night," Kaya said mournfully.

"Whiteguard couldn't have been attacked. It is one of the strongest holdings in Albavar," Clayborn answered.

"It has been attacked, Master Clayborn," Kaya replied strongly and evenly.

"Who dares do this? Who can do this?" Godfrey asked angrily.

"It is an old enemy of Albavar, one that we believed to have perished many years ago at Kayden's hands."

"You cannot mean…" Godfrey started to say.

"Shelrin? Yes." Kaya said, with sorrow and anguish in her voice.

"That is impossible. Shelrin was trapped in Grimhold along with his armies," Clayborn answered.

"Grimhold has been broken, the gates shattered even," Kaya said. "Cole has had more than one dream."

Godfrey took in a breath and let it out slowly.

"These things that the boy dreams have not been confirmed. For all we know the boy is suffering from a delirious fever," Clayborn cried incredulously.

"You would dismiss a threat of Shelrin so easily? Claiming that it is a delusion of a boy that happens to have the blood of a warrior running though his veins?" Kaya asked.

Clayborn didn't respond.

"Master Godfrey, I would hope that you have learned from history. The early leaders of Albavar were warned much in a similar manner we are being warned now. They did not listen once before and you must admit that was a mistake. Do not make the same mistake again," Kaya said.

Godfrey sat for a moment in silence contemplating what Kaya had said.

"So, what do you wish to do, father?" Gildon asked.

"We should do as Kaya suggested. Clayborn, prepare a company of your men and go to Whiteguard City. Then we will have our confirmation about whether Cole's dream is right or not. If the city has indeed been attacked, then we will prepare for war. If you leave tomorrow, Master Clayborn, before noon, you will arrive in a week's time. Master Grayson, send your fastest green cloaks with them as messengers. I want word of Whiteguard's situation within ten days," Godfrey ordered, rising to his feet. "Also I want word sent out to Lord Grishem and Lord Huntswell, at Failsgate and Northhall. Tell them to be on guard, and prepared for an attack." Godfrey's voice faded as he exited Kaya's quarters with Master Grayson, and Master Clayborn following.

Gildon did not leave with the others instead he sat looking over at the sleeping Cole, letting out a breath of air his eyes turned towards Kaya.

"Is there something more Gildon," Kaya asked sensing the Gildon had not gone.

"I don't know? Is there?" Gildon questioned. "I feel as if there is something that you have not told us."

You are wise young man Gildon. I have taught you well, Kaya thought and was silent for a moment as she gathered her thoughts.

"You have heard Sir Arthur say that the boy is a *Wildling*?"

"Yes, back in their village. I do not think he meant to tell me. Rather he let it slip, he was after all under the influence of ale."

"Do you know what a *Wilding* is young Gildon?"

"I suppose I don't."

"A *Wildling* is a word use to describe a child born with no magic of their own. Rather they take on spirits by touch. Not only can Cole see a person's future or past with touch but if they have a spirit, a *Wildling* takes on that spirit, they can wield fire, water, the winds, anything.

"So if I were to touch Cole he could."

"He could wield fire. But I suspect he could only wield it for a short time, seeing that he is still quite young."

"But as he gets older and stronger," Gildon asked.

"As he gets older and stronger he will be able to keep the powers he comes in contact with. The more spirit he comes into contact with the more he will be able to wield. In three or four years Cole could be able to wield every spirit in existence, that is if he stays sane that long." Kaya said sadly.

"Cole's powerfully strong. The strongest I have ever felt and that includes his mind. I believe his master taught him that as well."

"The very same master you believed to be an Elfain Warrior?" Kaya asked.

"Yes," Gildon remarked.

"THEN LET US pray that you are right, for I believe the more spirit that Cole comes in contact with the more his mind will go. If his mind were to ever go he would loose all control of his powers."

"And you're so sure of that? Can a Wildling never be healed?" Gildon questioned.

"It has happened once before, in the reign of the Dark King," Kaya informed.

"Anyone that was that cold and evil would surely loose their minds."

"It was not the Dark King that lost his mind, but rather it was Ayden."

Gildon said nothing more and after a time sitting in silence he rose to his feet and left without so much as a farewll. After Gildon had gone Kaya checked on Cole.

"You will need more nightshade," she said, when she saw that his eyes were half open.

Kaya mixed her herbs and lifted Cole's head as he swallowed down the sedative. Softly singing to him as she rocked back and forth in her chair, he was soon back asleep. She wondered as she rocked whether Cole had heard any of the conversation.

CHAPTER 24

A FEW WEEKS LATER, Cole stood in the stable brushing
Gladadear out. As he brushed her creamy shaggy hair, his thoughts
turned over the conversation he had heard a few weeks before.

"Do you think that I will go mad?" Cole asked the horse.

The little horse rolled her eyes and snorted, *like you haven't gone
mad already*, Gladadear seemed to say.

"Thanks," Cole muttered.

He continued stroking the horse with the brush, feeling as though
a great heaviness was upon his shoulders. He had just finished combing through Gladadear's mane when he heard someone coming
towards the barn.

"Cole, are you in here?" Maggie yelled, her voice echoing off the
timbers.

Cole dropped the brush and looked around for a place to hide. He
ducked behind a pile of hay and waited in silence.

"Cole are you in here?" Maggie yelled again.

Cole said nothing, but continued to hide behind the hay.

"Guess he's not in here," Cole heard Chanlyn's voice, "maybe he's
in the library."

"You always think your answers are in the library," Maggie said.

"Well, aren't they?" Chanlyn said.

Their voices faded away as they turned and left the stables. When
all was quiet, Cole rose from his hiding place and went back to
Gladadear. He bent down and picked up the brush he had dropped.
When he straightened back up, Chanlyn and Maggie stood in front
of Gladadear's stall with their arms folded.

"I knew you were in here!" Maggie exclaimed angrily. "Why were
you hiding from us?"

"I wasn't…" Cole stuttered, trying to think of an explanation of why he was hiding.

"Did we do something wrong, Cole?" Chanlyn asked.

"What…No!" Cole replied.

"Then why are you avoiding us? Ever since you woke up, you won't talk to us. You go off on your own and we don't see you for hours on end," Maggie replied hotly.

It was true that Cole had purposely tried to avoid them. If he was going to go mad he didn't want to do it in front of his friends. Those few weeks that he had not been around them had been difficult. He looked into his friend's eyes and saw the hurt he had caused them. Cole took in a breath and made up his mind to tell them.

"I didn't want to hurt you," Cole said, in a huff of words.

"You didn't want to hurt us! Well you failed!" Maggie said coldly.

"I'm supposed to go mad, Maggie."

"Forget about you going mad. I'm mad at you already," Maggie huffed.

"I don't think that's what he means, Maggie," Chanlyn said. "I think he's referring to going insane."

"Yeah, you know loosing my mind, going crazy. Becoming putty in the head," Cole released his fear.

"Is that why you were avoiding us? Because you thought you were going crazy?" Chanlyn asked.

"It's a fate that happens to all seers," Cole told them.

"Cole, you're no madder than any of us are," Maggie's voice changed with sympathy.

"But Mistress Kaya said that eventually I won't be able to tell the difference between reality and dreams."

"Mistress Kaya doesn't know what she talking about," Maggie said. "Not all seers go insane." Cole looked down at Maggie with raised eyebrows.

"Okay, maybe she does. But she doesn't know what she's talking about when it comes to you," Maggie said, stepping close and taking Cole by his hands.

"I have known you all my life Cole. You're stubborn, shy beyond belief and a little dumb at times, but one thing that you're not, you're not mad. And if you do start going mad, Chanlyn and I will stop you," Maggie replied.

"How?" Cole asked.

"I don't know how. But we will," Maggie smiled.

"I don't know how you can stop me," Cole replied.

"Believe me Cole, if Maggie says she going to do something, she's going to do it. And if she says she going to stop you from losing your mind, she will," Chanlyn said all too seriously.

Maggie and Cole looked at Chanlyn for a moment and then suddenly burst out laughing. It wasn't long before all three were laughing so hard tears streamed down their faces.

"It's good to hear you laugh," Maggie commented with a bold smile. "It's been weeks since I last saw you smile."

Cole's smile faded however when Ayla stepped into the stables with her eyes falling on him.

"Godfrey wants to see you," Ayla spoke.

"Why does he want to see me?" Cole asked.

"Not just you. All of you." Ayla turned about to walk out the doorway. "You've been summoned to a war council."

CHANLYN AND MAGGIE looked at Cole with questions in their eyes as they followed Ayla along the winding paths through the city to the Great Hall. Upon entering the great hall, Cole and the others were met with a crowd of people gathered together. Men and women, bearing emblems of the six different kingdoms, stood around the room conversing with those closest to them. Cole recognized Master Grayson, Kaya, Godfrey and Clayborn among the party. Gildon too was there and when Cole, Maggie and Chanlyn entered the hall, Gildon greeted them and brought them further into the room.

"What do you make of this Cole?" Gildon asked.

"I don't know what to make of it," Cole answered.

"Who are all these people?" Maggie asked, surveying the room.

"They are representatives of the five remaining warrior clans," Gildon replied.

"Why are they here?" Chanlyn asked. "Has something happened?"

"All will be revealed when the council begins."

King Godfrey's voice rang out above the low hum of conversation.

"No finery is required, Wellsly," Godfrey yelled at his steward, a skinny sort of man dressed in brown robes, "Just start the council." The man in brown bowed to his king and took a stand on the dais.

"Ladies and gentlemen," Wellsly announced. "Please, if you would take your seats, my lord Godfrey wishes to begin."

The hum of conversation died as everyone went to take a seat around a great circular table.

"Look, there's father," Maggie said, pointing out Wallace.

"He's back then," Chanlyn whispered.

Ever since Cole had told Kaya his dream and Kaya had relayed the dream to Godfrey, there seemed to be a cloud of anxiousness in the air. The company of men captained by Master Clayborn had set out for Whiteguard the morning after Cole woke from his foretelling nightmare. Master Wallace, at hearing about the possible attack on Whiteguard, asked permission to accompany Master Clayborn and Master Grayson, and he was given it. He had obviously returned with the rest of the company.

Seated next to Wallace were Sir Arthur and Artemis.

As Cole moved forward with Maggie and Chanlyn, he accidentally knocked into someone and was thrown to the floor. Cole looked up at a giant of a man that stood over him. He was young, perhaps the same age as Gildon, and he was tall and lean. He wore a breastplate over his tunic and bore a purple cap along with a sword at his side. He looked down at Cole with cold gray eyes.

"This must be some great war council if little boys are invited to them," the man laughed, looking down at Cole.

Cole's anger flashed as he stared up at the brute of the man. Gildon stepped forward and helped Cole to his feet then turned to the young soldier.

"Lord Cornwall. I would not call Cole a mere boy. He has done his share of fighting. He has placed his own life in danger to save me and if anyone has the right to be at a war council, it is Cole," Gildon replied.

Cornwall looked Cole up and down and then gave a smirk in unbelief as he turned away.

"Are you alright, Cole?" Gildon asked.

Cole nodded then quickly followed Gildon to the table were he found a seat next to Chanlyn.

All fell silent as Wellsly stood and the war council began.

"Gentleman and Ladies," Wellsly started. "We welcome you. Welcome Lady Purnella of the Alberdeen clan," Wellsly said, nodding to an older woman, "Lord Cornwall," the fair haired lord that looked to be in his later twenties, the same man that had knocked Cole down, "representing the mortal kingdom of Larkshire, Master Conner of the Dresden clan, Lord Wales of the Kayfelt clan and Lord Failsbane of the mortal Kingdom of Walesburge. We wish to thank you for coming so quickly and..."

"Enough of the pleasantries there is no time for such nonsense," Godfrey interrupted taking to his feet. "My good kinsmen many of you have wondered why I have called the council. The reason for this assembly is that a fortnight ago, Whiteguard and its fortress were attacked and destroyed."

There was a momentary outburst of surprise and shock from those in attendance. Godfrey waited until all fell silent again. "The attack on Whiteguard is an attack on all the people of Albavar, not just warriors but also mortals."

"Mortals?" Cole whispered, leaning over to Gildon for an explanation.

"Mortals are those that are not of the warrior's bloodline," Gildon whispered back.

"Whiteguard was the stronghold that has kept watch over Grimhold prison and the forbidden palace since the fall of Shelrin's empire. It is occupied by both mortals and warriors," Godfrey continued.

"Who would do this?" shouted a small monk like man that Cole thought to be Lord Wales.

"It was probably those of southern lands," Lord Failsbanes shouted, rising to his feet.

"We did no such thing," Cornwall yelled as he stood. "It was more than likely you, Walelings, that did it." Cornwall sneared.

"It was no one from the southern lands, nor any one from the north lands" Godfrey cried. "Neither was it any of the warrior clans within Albavar. I believe that it was an old enemy from the past that has returned, that has attacked the Fortress," Godfrey announced. "I believe that it was Shelrin." There was a stunned silence that fell over the room.

"No! Shelrin was captured," Lord Wales voiced rising to his feet. "Defeated by Kayden and his army and trapped within a prison of rock."

"The seals have been broken. The Grimhold has awakened," Godfrey said.

"How have you come by this information," Lord Wales asked.

"I sent out Master Clayborn, upon receiving a warning that Whiteguard would be or had been attacked. When my men returned, they told me of the city's destruction," Godfrey reported.

"And who gave you this information?" Master Cornwall asked.

"A seer," Godfrey said simply.

There was another outcry of surprise and conversations stirred among the clan representatives.

"Who is this seer?" Lord Wales cried out.

"Are you sure Master Godfrey?" Lady Purnella questioned. "Seers are rare. Not since Alleana has there been a seer."

"I shall have silence," Godfrey commanded and the room fell quiet.

"I will not divulge who the seer is. It is not up to me to reveal his identity," Godfrey said. "Just know that his foretelling has come to pass. Now we must decide what is to be done."

"I do not wish to doubt this seer, whoever it may be. But I must say that the likelihood that it was Shelrin who attacked Whiteguard is unlikely for I was there at his demise. I stood on the blackened hills fighting for my life. I saw the wave of Power that went out across the battlefield and the armies of Shelrin withered away and turned to dust," Lord Wales recounted. "Then I saw the gates barred and chained. Shelrin and all were trapped within. The magic that was used to trap Shelrin was powerful and I do not think that it could have easily been broken," Wales said.

"You are right, Lord Wales. It could not have been easily broken, but it could be broken," Mistress Kaya said. "I too was there, Lord

Wales, as were many. Before my eyesight left me, I also witnessed the gates barred and chained with the power of the six clans. But because of recent events, I regret to tell you the barrier has fallen and Shelrin lives. There were survivors from Whiteguard. They tell the tale of a figure dressed in a cloak, wielding a staff of gold, rising out of a dark mist and claiming to be Shelrin, just before the city was attacked," Kaya said.

"Many have claimed to be Shelrin returned," Cornwall said. "And we have put a stop to their falsehoods."

"I must agree with Godfrey and Lady Kaya," Lady Purnella spoke. "Long have I sensed a shadow growing across Alberdeen, and every day that shadow grows longer. I have heard rumors of great black horsemen, roaming over the land and then disappearing over the mountains."

Cole felt a chill run up his spine as Lady Purnella described the Reapers.

"Would you believe rumors my Lady Purnella?" Cornwall asked.

"Lord Cornwall, Lady Purnella speaks truth, for there are those in this very room that have encountered the black horsemen. And they have lost a loved one because of their encounter," Gildon said.

Cole lowered his head. He could feel all the eyes of those who knew his story looking at him.

"I do not doubt your words Master Gildon. But where is your proof."

"If it is proof that you want, Cornwall, I have it," Gildon said. He signaled for a servant that stood behind him to come forward.

The young page brought Gildon's leather traveling bag and then stepped back to stand at his post again. Gildon took the bag and reached into it. From within he pulled out an object and tossed it onto the table.

The sound of clanking metal hitting the wooden table sounded throughout the room and then the object came to a halt. It was the helmet of the Reaper that Merryrick had destroyed. The cold black steel of the mask carried an air of malice and cruelty, which seemed to quickly spread around the room. Its black hollowed eyes penetrated Cole's very heart and he literally recoiled from it, pushing his chair away from the cold steel.

"A Reaper's helmet," Lady Purnells whispered. "The dark horsemen."

"That is impossible. The death riders were captured within the Grimhold," Lord Failsbane cried out in a panic.

"Grimhold is broken," Kaya broke in. "All of Shelrin's servants are released." Silence fell as each man and woman stared at the helmet, trying to understand the meaning of it.

"Take it away Gildon," Godfrey ordered.

At his father's command, Gildon covered the helmet with the bag and took it off the table.

"Godfrey what can we do?" Master Conner asked, "Shelrin's rule was merciless and unforgiving."

"We can gather our armies and fortify our strong holds. We can also warn the mortal kings of what has taken place, though I believe they have received word of Whiteguard as well. They will more than likely gather their armies as well," Godfrey said.

"A lot of good they will do," Master Conner replied. "Mortals are weak and cannot withstand the power that is Shelrin's. Whiteguard was the strongest fortress in Albavar and if it was destroyed, as you say, then we have no chance of defending our lands or ourselves. If Shelrin has returned and is as strong as before we cannot hope to stand," Master Conner continued.

"Then what would you have us do Master Conner? Nothing?" Grayson asked, slamming his hand on the table.

"Peace, Grayson," Godfrey said, seriously. "You forget, Master Conner that we defeated Shelrin before and we can do it again."

"We had Kayden, the last true Elfain Warrior, on our side and now that he is gone, we cannot hope to even stand against Shelrin," Wales said desperately. "If the Lord of Darkness is alive, what are we to do? Shelrin's forces brought us to our knees before."

"What would you have us do, Lord Wales? Would you have us surrender and have life go back to the way it was before?" Lady Purnella shouted. "I remember well the days of Shelrin. My family and all our kind were hunted down and destroyed because we were born with magic. No! I will not surrender. I will die before I do that."

"I will not see my people die fighting a war that they cannot win," Wales shouted.

"You would live as a coward," Cornwall shouted.

"Yes! I would live as a coward for I would still live," Lord Wales asserted.

The Lords and Ladies rose from their seats, shouting at each other, trying to be heard. As Cole watched, he felt the room grow hot as the temperature rose. His eyes widened as flames of a furious fire began to burn around the room. The more the Lords and Ladies argued the higher the flames grew, consuming everyone in the Great Hall and yet no one noticed the flames. A soft cackling laughter sounded within the flames of the fire and as the flames grew so did the laughter, until it filled the room. It rebounded off the walls and grew in strength until it grew so loud that Cole had to cover his ears.

"Stop!" Cole cried.

But the flames still grew, reaching the ceiling and igniting the curtains around the window, catching the table and the servants on fire. The laughter felt as if it were the wave of the ocean, crashing down on him.

"STOP!" Cole shouted at the top of his lungs.

The cackling laughter continued growing louder, yet deeper in pitch until the laughter had mutated into a rumbling roar. The fire burned around Cole, enclosing him in a circle of flame. His world spun. The Great Hall continued to burn, as did all the people within its great walls. Where Cole stood, he knew not. It was dark. The sky burned with a thousand blazes and the land below him burned as well. The flames that had encircled him, now burned on a field of white. A cold bone chill went up into the sky and Cole beheld a dragon. Its scales were as black as pitch, its eyes glowed yellow and the teeth that protruded from its mouth were as sharp as a sword and just as long. The dragon breathed out red lightning and fire at the knights that surrounded it. There were seven knights in all. They were not dressed in armor or helmets. They wore ordinary clothes of boots, cloaks and jerkins. But the weapons they held in their hands shone like moonlight, starlight and sunlight.

"West of the Moon, East of the sun,
The wind's doth whisper when darkness comes.
Dark be the dragon that will rise again,
Seeking out the light and wanting revenge."

Cole heard Merryrick whisper in his ear.

Cole turned his head to the side thinking that Merryrick was near him, but there was no sign of him.

"Black be the wings that cover the sky,
Red be the ground where dead men lie.
Long will the birds cease to sing their songs,
And the rays of sun will seem far-gone."

The Dragon spread out its giant wings, and the light of the moon and the stars, were hidden from the Elfain warriors, throwing them into a darkness far blacker than night.

"All will seem lost, all hope will be gone,
Cold is the night that wanes too long.
Fear not my child, for night doth not last,
Look to the old stories that have come to pass.

The Elfain warriors of yester years,
Defeated a darkness that many feared.
Sent from the Haven's they did fight,
Wielding weapons with power and light.

The darkness that once surrounded the Warriors did not last. Light from their weapons lit the way. The warriors could see the attacks the Dragon was about to drive. One warrior, bearing a bow, shot two arrows at that dragon's wings. The arrows suddenly burst forth from the bow, not as arrows but as lightning bolts, which burned through the thin membranes of the Dragon wings. The black dragon roared and had to fold it wings for fear of more lightning bolt arrows.

"And when that Dark Dragon comes again,
So too will the warriors to fight and defend.
Sleep sound my child, and dream tonight.
The warriors protect you with their weapons of light."

The Seven Warriors all struck the dragon together, their weapons burned through the dragon, destroying it. As the dragon lay dying it began to shrink, withering away into the form of a human. And as it withered away the darkness of night faded and the dawn's morning light peeked up to the east. As the sunrise flooded over the land, plants began to grow and flourish, the wind blew clear, fresh air and Cole closed his eyes and let the wind sweep past his face.

The next time Cole opened his eyes. He was no longer on the battlefield but back in the garden that he had dreamed of before. He stood in front of the stone archer, looking up and down. His eyes caught an inscription at the base of the statue. But the words made little sense to him.

"In honor of Ayden our once great King.
Though he is gone, his bow remains.
It waits for he, who is the rightful heir."

Cole felt the world turning in on itself, the colors blurring together until it was nothing but a muddle of colors and then a sudden blast of bright light.

Cole shook his head and rubbed his eyes. He was almost getting used to the blinding light that seemed to end his visions. But it was still a surprise to find himself back sitting in the Great Hall with the others still arguing.

"And I suppose we should just follow you into battle Lord Cornwall," Wales was shouting.

"I would not have such a coward amongst my men," Cornwall tossed back. "You would squash the spirit of my men with your gloom and doom."

"You know nothing of Shelrin's power, boy," Wales shouted. "You were not but a baby in your mother's arms when the Massacre at Dunlow occurred. Thousands upon thousands were killed by Shelrins's army," Wales hollered, "and the power that was wielded that day....no weapon or warrior exists today that could take on that amount of power," Wales mourned.

"Your wrong," Cole muttered.

"What was that Cole?" Gildon asked, hearing the boy speak.

"I was just saying that Master Wales is wrong, there are weapons and even warriors that can be used to wield much more power than Shelrin could wield. There are seven weapons, the ones that destroyed the Dark King."

"You speak of the seven weapons that our ancestors brought from the Havens?" Godfrey asked.

"I do!" Cole replied quietly.

"Don't speak of myths and legends to me boy," Wales mocked.

"I believe Cole is not telling us legends or tales, Master Wales, but rather the answer that we seek," Kaya interrupted. "He is telling us to search out the weapons of the Elfain's. Is that not right Cole?"

Cole nodded his head in agreement.

"What do you mean Cole?" Gildon asked.

"The seven weapons destroyed a darkness once before. Why can they not do so again," Cole responded.

"Because those weapons have been lost for thousands of years," Cornwall jeered.

"Then we find them," Cole simply replied

"And how are we to do that? There are no records of these weapons. Shelrin destroyed any and all records of the Elfains. What remains are only bits and pieces. There is nothing that can lead us to those weapons. You cannot be thinking about sending men out to try and find these...these fabled weapons?" Cornwall asked Godfrey.

Godfrey sat in silence for a while, looking at Cole. He saw something in the boy's eyes that told him Cole was not making up stories, or trying to make fools of them all. What he saw was truth in him that made him finally speak.

"Cole if I may asked, what makes you think that these weapons are still in existence," Godfrey asked. "As pointed out no one knows where they are."

The words were out of Cole's mouth before he even knew what he had said. Though he merely whispered them, everyone heard.

"I do."

CHAPTER 25

AN UNNERVING SILENCE had fallen on the room. It was like Cole had suddenly gone deaf. The silence seemed to last forever, dragging on for hours, but in truth it was only mere moments. They all sat there, gaping at him with their mouths open. Even Maggie looked at Cole with astonishment. Then all at once the sound returned to Cole's ears as an explosion of voices buzzed throughout the room. Everyone had suddenly gotten over their shock and they were now talking all at once.

"The boy jests," Lady Purnella voiced.

"This cannot be possible."

"The boy has gone mad," Cornwall mocked.

Cole's head turned toward Cornwall and glared at him with such intensity that the great general had to turned his own gaze away from Cole.

"Silence!" Godfrey cried over the commotion.

All the voices fell silent but they still looked at Cole.

"Now Cole, what do you mean?" Godfrey asked.

Cole took a huge breath, allowing him time to think about what he was going to say.

He looked at Maggie and she nodded giving him encouragement.

"I…" Cole started to say but was interrupted by Mistress Kaya.

"Stop Cole! I will not have you speak until the room is cleared of all servants, pages and what have you and then each lord and lady will swear upon his or her life that nothing that is about to be revealed to you will ever leave this room," Kaya spoke "If you do your life will be forfeited."

"Surely there is no need for that, Mistress Kaya. The boy can know nothing that would require that sort of action," Cornwall said with a mocking smile.

"You will swear Korbin Cornwall of the house of Korin, or you will leave," Kaya's voice said coldly. "As will all Lords and Ladies."

It was apparent that no Lord or Lady wished to leave, for after the room was cleared of servants and other personel they all swore that no matter what happened, the information that was spoken of would not leave the room, nor would it ever leave their lips. As each person stood and swore on their lives that they would never tell, Cole felt a sudden rush of energy hit him and then sink away. It happened every time.

"If you would, Cole, continue," Kaya said.

Cole stood for a moment, thinking how best to begin. Finally he took a breath and spoke.

"From the time I was little I could see things, events that took place in the past or sometimes I can even see the future. Master Merryrick called it the seer's gift. I can see the outcome of certain choices that people make. Usually I see them by touching someone. I can see a person's life, where they have been and where they are going if I touch them. Other times it is just a feeling," Cole said, "and sometimes I have dreams."

"Are you telling us that you are a..." Lady Purnella started to say.

"Cole is our seer," Kaya finished.

Everyone sat in silence, lost in his or her own thoughts.

"And are we to believe him? That he knows where these weapons of power are," Wales asked. "What if the boy lies?"

"Cole has never lied in his life," Maggie cried, jumping to her feet.

"Calm down Maggie," Wallace said, rising to his feet.

Seeing that her father had stood, Maggie folded her arms and took her seat.

"I am Wallace of Kells. I have known Cole most of his life and I can stand here today and tell you that what my daughter has just told you is true. Cole has never lied, not even as a child. If he says that he knows where these weapons are, then he knows," Wallace said calmly, then took his seat. After Wallace had spoken the room broke out again with conversation as questions were thrown out. But it all fell quiet when Godfrey took to his feet.

"What I have heard here today only confirms my fears, for there are whispers that the Dark Palace has awakened and I believe you,

Cole. I believe what you have said." Here the king took a breath of air. "And so I must ask you Cole, if you would do your King and the Kingdom of Kirkwell, the Northlands and the Land of Albavar a great favor. Would you, Cole, go and search for these weapons. If they do exist, gather them and bring them to the place where they will destroy Shelrin and the enemy."

Cole sat in his chair taken aback. He looked all around him searching for an answer.

"We cannot tell you what to do, Cole," Kaya replied, "this choice is yours and therefore you must make it."

Taking a breath, Cole rose to his feet.

"I am honored that you have asked me, your highness, but would it not be wiser to send another man that is more capable of doing the job?" Cole said softly.

"For once I agree with the boy," Cornwall voiced.

"There is no other man that knows the way," Godfrey replied, ignoring Cornwall's comment.

"I can draw a map," Cole said.

"A map can fall into the wrong hands and thereby destroy our chances of winning this war," Grayson said, looking up at Cole from his chair. "Since you are the only one that knows where the weapons are, that leaves no physical evidence for anyone else to find so they can retrieve the weapons and use them against us. Then it would make our chance of winning far greater."

"What we ask is great, but I fear it must be asked," Godfrey said solemnly. "Help us Cole. Help us find what only you can find."

Cole said nothing. He just stared at the table.

"He's scared," Artemis said, getting to his own feet.

Cole's head snapped up from the table and whipped over so he could stare Artemis in the face. Artemis stood there proud, with his head held high and his chest expanded outward.

"Only a fool would not be scared," Kaya said, getting to her feet again. "He has seen what so many take for nightmares. He knows how powerful the darkness is."

"But that is not why you hold back," Kaya said gently.

"No," Cole whispered.

"Then what is it?"

"I am scared. I'm scared of Shelrin and what the future might hold. But I fear one thing above all," Cole voiced.

The room fell silent as they waited for the explanation.

Cole took a breath and let out the words that dug deep in his heart.

"It is that I might fail, and the world that I dreamed of will come to pass," Cole said solemnly.

There was no answer to what Cole had just said, for no one knew what to say.

"You doubt yourself too much, Cole," Wallace finally spoke. "You have too much determination in you to fail. Merryrick taught you that every journey begins with one step and if that step is not taken, then you have already failed," Wallace spoke.

Again Cole said nothing. He was too lost in his own thoughts to say anything. Wallace's words had struck him hard. He knew what he had to do however hard it would be.

"If you lead Cole, I will follow and do everything I can to protect you. I would see Shelrin fall once and for all," Wallace announced getting to his feet. He took his sword and placed it on the table.

Everyone looked at Wallace in surprise. The man was laying his sword on the table as a sign that he would lay down his life for Cole. Cole was astounded that a man like Wallace would offer him such a great gift.

Gildon was next to rise. He too placed his sword on the table. "As Wallace has just done, so do I. I will go with you and see that you do not fail."

Next to give his life to Cole, was Grayson.

"I have lost much because of Shelrin and if I can prevent others from suffering the same fate as I, then I too will stand and protect you," Grayson said, as he laid down his sword on the table.

Chanlyn was next to rise to his feet, "Although I have no sword to lay before you Cole, I will do what I can to help." Cole and Chanlyn's eyes connected and Cole saw in the bookworm a good and trusting friend.

It was quiet for a moment and then Sir Arthur spoke.

"You hold a hope for all us, Cole. If these weapons are real, then I too will help you find them," Arthur said bowing to Cole.

He did not lay his sword on the table nor did Artemis when he said that he would be going as well. But Cole had not expected the two would. Cole looked at the men that had volunteered to give up their lives for him. He knew that he could not refuse. With a great knot of fear that burned deep within him Cole spoke.

"I will do as you ask."

There were no cheers of joy or cries of happiness, just nods of understanding and the knowledge that events were now in motion that would change the course of everyone's lives, for good or bad.

Godfrey nodded his head and once again took to his feet. "I too would go with you on this quest. But I cannot. The armies of Aloria need to be gathered and our people protected. So the six of you..."

"Seven!" Maggie interrupted, "I am coming as well." Wallace gave his daughter a grim look that told her they would be talking about this later.

"The errr ...seven of you," Godfrey announced, "will leave as soon a possible. In fact I would have you leave on the morrow," said Godfrey. "As for you, my fellow lords and ladies of the clans, I would advise you to go back to your realms and tell all that Aloria has called her armies together to fight against the dark storm that is rising. You would be wise to do the same. And so I hearby declare that this council of war over," Godfrey said, looking at one another.

Once the council was over everyone started to disperse. Cole left the meeting feeling drained of energy and a little lost. He reached his room just as the sun was fading down in the west and the city was already lighting the street lamps. He threw himself on his bed and closed his eyes. Question after question raced through his head like bees in a hive.

Can I really do this? Can I do what they have asked me to do, Cole thought. Could he find these weapons? What if he did find them, then what? What if he didn't find them? Was the vision he saw of the statue and the garden real?

Cole shrugged his shoulders as a chill of fear and doubt ran up his spine. Not wanting to think anymore, he jumped up from his bed and began to busy himself with packing, to take his mind off his thoughts. Cole packed the few belongings he had into his saddlebag. He was rolling up his cloak in his bedroll when he heard voices arguing just outside his door.

"I am no longer a child to be ordered about," Maggie's angry voice yelled.

"I will not have you coming. This journey is not going to be safe. It will be dangerous!" Wallace cried back.

"I know of the dangers father," Maggie hollered. "Do you think that I could stay here and watch you and Cole go off without me by both of your sides."

"I am telling you, Margaret, that you are not coming. You do not know how to defend yourself," Wallace said rather harshly.

"Defend myself," Maggie screeched. "You of all people should know that I can defend myself just fine. Was it not you who taught me how to handle a knife and I am useful enough with the bow and I can use my sling better than any man or boy. I will be coming whether you agree or not."

"Margaret, you are not coming. You will be staying here where it is safe and that is my final word," Wallace replied, with a tone in his voice that told Maggie the conversation was over. "Heed your father," Wallace ordered.

It was quiet for a bit then a knock on his door told Cole that it could only be one person.

"Yes," Cole responded.

The door opened and Maggie stepped into his room, fuming.

"I suppose you heard our argument?" Maggie said, walking over to where Cole was.

"I did," Cole said, as he folded up his shirt and packed it into his saddle bag.

"And what do you think?" Maggie asked. "Do you not think that I should be allowed to come?"

Cole didn't answer right off. He wanted to say yes. He wanted her to come. He wanted to know that he had her support and friendship. But he also knew what he and the other searchers would be facing. Letting out a breath of air, Cole looked at Maggie.

"Maggie, one day, if not already, Shelrin will learn of our journey and whether or not he does, it would kill me to see you get hurt in any way. So… therefore I must agree with your father," Cole said in the softest way.

Anger instantly rose up in Maggie's eyes. She balled her fist and threw a punch at Cole, but missed.

"I thought that you would agree with me. I am just as capable of fighting as any man," Maggie shouted.

"No one said you were not," Cole said back.

"Then why will you not let me come?" Maggie asked as tears started to appear in her eyes.

"Because I do not want you hurt."

"You sound like my father," Maggie said with anger.

"I will take that as a compliment," Cole said darkly.

"I did not mean it as a compliment," Maggie roared back. "You treat me like some dumb girl, like those in the village."

"That is not true Maggie and you know it!" Cole yelled back.

Maggie jumped back with surprise. Cole never yelled at her. Sure they had crosswords with one another, but never had he yelled at her.

"I am not a child Cole. You cannot treat me as such!"

"Then you should stop acting like one," Cole said harshly. Tears had returned to her eyes and were falling down her cheeks.

"You beg to go with us Maggie," Cole said, now more calmly, "but if you only knew what waits in the shadows, what waits in the dark, then I think that you would be glad to stay."

"Glad that I am left here, while you have an adventure," Maggie snarled.

"This is no game, Maggie. These are no make-believe monsters like we used to imagine," Cole said urgently.

"I know it is no game. Remember I was there when the Reapers attacked, but I will not be left here to wonder if you and my father are still alive," cried Maggie again.

"You are not coming," Cole voiced forcefully.

Angry tears fell down Maggie's face as she threw another punch at Cole. This time it connected, hitting Cole in the mouth. Maggie was about to throw another, but Cole caught her arm.

Suddenly there was an explosion of light. When the light cleared, Cole found himself caught in a world of shadow. There was no darkness nor was there any sunlight, just a blank land drenched in an un-natural eerie grayness. There was a constant feeling of fear in the air. It was like a mist, always surrounding, always following, and never leaving. But there was also joy and happiness mixed in that at moments over-powered the feelings of terror. It was wonderful when those mere seconds of joy would take over and that was the only feeling that Cole would feel. Yet it would only last for a short time before once again dread and fear would set in and wash out the joy and happiness.

There was another flash of the bright familiar light and Cole stared at Maggie and she stared back. Cole still held on to Maggie's arm. Slowly he let her go and she stepped away from him. Her face was pale in the lantern light and her eyes were wide with fear. She was breathing heavily and shaking all over.

"What was that?" Maggie asked in a soft whisper.

"You saw it?" Cole asked shakily.

All Maggie could do was nod.

Somehow, Maggie and Cole had shared the vision. She had seen everything that Cole had. She felt the fear and the joy.

"It's what awaits me on the journey," Cole said, turning from Maggie, so he no longer had to look at her terrified face.

"That is what you were speaking of?" Maggie said breathless.

Cole nodded.

It suddenly went quiet, neither one spoke, neither one knew what to say.

Maggie didn't say anything as she disappeared from his room. She still seemed rather shaken by what she had witnessed. Cole stood for a long moment not knowing what to do. The expression that Maggie had given him was one of fear and Cole couldn't help thinking of the fear he had seen on her face. He worried that perhaps now that Maggie really knew what he could see and do, their friendship would be over. He wondered also how Maggie had seen the vision. He was so lost in his own thoughts and feelings that he did not notice Kaya entering the room.

"Are you alright Cole?" she asked with concern.

Cole looked up at the old women a little startled that he had not noticed her. She stood before him, holding in her hands long leather wrapped bundles.

"Sorry Mistress Kaya" Cole replied, "I was just thinking."

"There is no need to apologize Cole. I expect that there is much on your mind, for there is much on my mine," Kaya responded. Cole nodded his head and waited for Kaya to continue.

"It has been a long day Cole," she said softly.

"Yes it has."

"You are probably tired," Kaya commented.

"Just a little," Cole replied.

"I have something for you," Kaya suddenly said.

Kaya presented the first long leather bound package to Cole.

"You don't have to give me anything," Cole replied.

"I was instructed to give it to you," Kaya replied. "Plus I was told that you have no weapon. Yours, having been destroyed by a Reaper," Kaya said. Cole stepped forward and retrieved the bundle from Kaya's hands. It surprised Cole how heavy it was. He was not expecting such weight for a slender package so he nearly dropped it.

With excitement Cole undid the leathering binding and pulled the protective leather away. It fell to the floor revealing two, silver long knives. When the blanket fell away so did something else. It clattered to the floor and the sound echoed around the room.

Cole looked down and found that it was a small leather drawstring pouch. Taking note of it, Cole left it there and turned his attention to the pair of sheathed long blades. Strands of brown leather were woven together to create belt and scabbards for the knives. The belt allowed for the knifes to be strapped around the waist, the blades then would lay on the right side on the hip bone, one just above the other allowing for easy access. The scabbard's chapes, lockets and pack buckles were made of silver, which was wielded into a design like that of a small plant, reaching for the sun. With an amazing amount of speed Cole had the blades strapped to his waist. With shaking hands he drew one of the blades.

The dagger's pommel was silver with a white tree carved in the center. Streaks of silver ran down and wrapped themselves around the grips and connected with the silver cross-guard, while a marble like material was placed in between the bits of silver along the grip. The pommel was of thick steel, heavy yet perfectly balanced with the blade, the blade it's self was thin, easier to slip between a man's ribs. Cole sheathed his blade and retrieved the other one. It was decorated in much the same way, the blade however was heavier and thicker, balanced with the hilt and blade, it was perfect for throwing. Cole let out a breath of wonder as he hefted the throwing knife.

There was no firelight in the room, for the hearth had yet to be lit, but the setting sun beamed rays of sunlight in through the window. Its fading light reflected off the silver blades causing them to look as though they were on fire. They were perfect in every way. The edges were razor-sharp, so sharp that it could, no doubt, split a hair, and the points, fine and deadly. An endless braid of words had been emblazed along the fullers, never starting and never ending.

"Fire" Cole muttered, reading the old language that was on the blade.

Cole pulled the thinner fight dagger free. Holding it in one hand he held the "Fire" blade in the other. "Brimstone" was the word that was inscribed on the other knife.

"Are they the names of the blades?" Cole asked.

"Are what the names?" Kaya asked.

"Fire and Brimstone," Cole spoke.

Cole was all at once startled when "Fire" suddley burst into flames and "Brimstone" began to glow with a hot whiteness.

Cole dropped the blade out of surprise and the blade went out.

"What just happened?"Cole said picking up the blades and looking them over. They did not re-ignite.

"You called upon them?" Kaya said.

"Called upon them?" Cole questioned.

"Correct. When you said their names, you called upon their power to aid you," Kay replied, as if it were a normal thing to have weapons suddenly burst into flames and begin to light up with heat."They are fighting knives fit for a warrior," Kaya said softly,"an Elfain Warrior."

"They're Elfain weapons then?" Cole asked looking the daggers over.

"Yes. One of the few that remain," Kaya said.

"These are very fine blades," Cole replied.

With great effort Cole sheathed his sword and then picked up the leather pouch that had fallen to the floor.

The pouch was made of the same leather as the knife's scabbard, only it was not as hard, but soft and showed the signs of years of wear.

Undoing the string Cole opened the pouch and shook out the contents into his hand.

"Flint and steel?" Cole questioned.

"Mmm!" Kaya muttered.

"What am I to do with flint and steel?" Cole asked perplexed.

"I would think that you would take it with you," Kaya said, a bit amused at Cole's comment. "I believe you will need to light a fire once in a while."

Cole did not answer. He had suddenly been transfixed by the look of the flint. By the fading sunlight Cole saw that this was no ordinary flint. It was cream colored, with lightning streaks of pure white running though it. It was unusual flint, most flint was a dull gray or brown, but never white.

"It is strange," Cole said, still gazing and running his fingers across the flint.

"Strange! Yes it would be strange indeed considering who it came from," Kaya stated.

"What do you mean?" Cole asked, tucking the flint and steel back into its pouch and tucking it into the inside pocket of his jerkin.

"Have you ever heard the name Alleana?" Kaya asked.

"Yes," Cole replied. He was all too familiar with the name. "She was Kayden's wife. She was a seer like me," Cole muttered.

"She was a great seer," Kaya responded.

"Yeah until she went mad," Cole thought.

"She came to me one day and instructed me to give the package to the boy with hair as white as snow and eyes the color of the seas that would come to Aloria one day. She said, "*he will need it, for his journeys will take him into darkness and he will need a light to see by*. I assume that you are the boy that Alleana spoke of so many years ago," Kaya commented.

Cole didn't reply.

"There is still yet one more gift I have to give you," Kaya replied. From her shoulder she unslung the second leather bound package.

Cole knew the moment Kaya had pulled it from her shoulder what it was. With another wave of excitement, Cole pulled the leather cloth away to find what he knew it would be. It was a bow.

"Now this I know how to use," Cole replied.

Cole rubbed his hand across the wood. It was made from a solid piece of ash wood. The honey colored bow was smooth and well cared for. It was a straight piece of wood. Its wood had been rubbed down regularly with a soft wax that would keep the moisture from getting into the wood. Cole tested the draw of the bow by stringing it and pulling it back. Although it was a straight limb bow Cole could feel the power of the bow in the draw. Cole let out a breath of wonder and he released his draw.

"It's a fine bow," Cole replied.

Kaya smiled and nodded her head in approval.

"It is. I have taken great care of it."

"This is your bow?" Cole asked.

"It is," Kaya answered.

"Then why give it to me?" Cole asked.

"I can no longer use it, Cole, and you are in need of a bow. This bow still has its uses. It has served me well and now it will serve you. It was made by a friend of mine and he would be proud to see it in action again by a great archer such as you." Cole rubbed his hand across the smooth wood again.

"Thank you Mistress Kaya. I will try and bring it back to you," Cole said.

"Don't make promises that you cannot keep Cole," Kaya said with a sad smile. "Now the sun has faded Cole and now I think that I must leave you. You must rest yourself for tomorrow will come all too soon," Kaya said, taking a step towards Cole. The old woman took Cole's head in her hands, bent forward and kissed him on the forehead.

"May you and your companions always be protected Cole. And may you fulfill your quest, for you are our hope," Kaya whispered, and then departed from the room.

CHAPTER 26

COLE SAT UP in his bed suddenly awake. He grabbed at his face, frantically pushing the hair from his eyes and taking in long deep breaths as he felt like he was being suffocated. He sighed in relief when he felt the cold cool air coming in from the open window. Sweat covered him and was soaked into his nightshirt. Getting to his feet, Cole went to the washstand. He poured water into the basin and threw some of it onto his face. As he came up he suddenly froze. He didn't remember ever opening the window and it didn't appear that Chanlyn had come to bed yet. Cole walked over to the window, looked out and then closed it. He was on his way back to his bed when he was suddenly grabbed from behind. His hands were forced back behind him and quickly tied. At the same time a wet gag was pushed into his mouth that smelled and tasted bitterly of nightshade. With panicking breath Cole inhaled the fumes and instantly he felt groggy and lightheaded and he nearly fell over and passed out. In a half daze Cole felt someone grab his legs.

Somewhere with in his muddled mind Cole realized then what was happening. He also realized that there was more than one person, one holding his arms and the other holding his feet. Before Cole faded into blackness he managed to kick the person at his feet. There was a large crashing sound as the man fell back into the washstand. Cole slammed his head back against his captor's face, there was a cry of pain and Cole was dropped to the floor, then there was complete blackness. Within his half unconcious state Cole heard another large crash and then the echoing of breaking glass. Following came the hard bone-to-bone contact sounds of punches and kicks. Cole was sure he was hearing the sound of a fight going on. The fight only lasted a few moments then all seemed to go quiet. Cole felt himself being turned over and the gag being pulled from his mouth. He hands were free and he could hear the voice of Gildon calling his name.

"Cole, Cole can you hear me?"

Cole let out a moan and sat up, holding his head. His vision somewhat impaired, Cole looked around his room and wondered what had happened. The door to his room had been broken down, half of it hung on its hinges and the other half was on the floor on fire. His window that looked out over the waterfall was shattered to pieces. Cole could feel the wind and the mist that came off the waterfall blow into his room.

"Who are you?" a cold voice asked.

Cole sat staring at Wallace as he crouched down next to a body that lay on his back, on the floor. It was one of the men that had just tried to take him. The cloth mask that had hidden his face was gone and Cole could see blood running from the man's nose.

"Who are you?" Wallace asked again, lifting the man's head up by the hair and slamming it hard on the ground.

From what light there was in the room, Cole could see the man was middle aged with dark black hair. He was tall, well built and had a scar across his cheek. Cole looked for the other man around the room but there was no sign of him.

"Tell me who you are," Wallace demanded coldly.

"I am Helm," the man spoke.

"What was your purpose here tonight?" Wallace asked.

"My purpose…?" The man stuttered as if he were trying to stop himself from talking.

"Your purpose?" Wallace ordered.

"My purpose was to take the boy," the man nearly yelled.

"Take him were" Wallace demanded

"To my Master" the kiddnapper practically screamed.

"Who sent you?" Wallace interrogated.

The man bit down on his lips and held his breath trying to hold his tongue from wagging.

"Who sent you?" Wallace said more forcefully.

"The Red Cloaks," the man shouted.

"Your scum is still around?" Wallace spit.

"We have lived for hundreds of years and will continue to do so."

"Why do you want the boy? What are your orders," Wallace asked.

"He is a *Wildling*, an abomination, the worst of your kind. He is to be judged. If I cannot capture him then I am to destroy him," the man shouted.

Suddenly without warning, the man flicked his wrist and produced a small knife, which glowed with a slight green color. The kidnapper sent it flying towards Cole. Wallace jumped up and tackled Cole to the ground. The knife would have hit Cole had it not been for Wallace. Instead the blade passed by and vibrated as it struck the wall burning a black hole in the wood. There were more sounds of breaking glass and when Cole and Wallace looked back the man in black was gone.

"He jumped out the window," Gildon shouted in disbelief. "He jumped out the window, right over the cliffs and into the falls."

"Better dead than tell his secrets," Wallace said, stepping to the window to look down at the steep drop.

"Who was he?" Cole asked looking at the broken window.

"I don't know who he was," Wallace stated. "But if the Red Cloaks are behind this, you're in more danger than I thought."

Cole looked at Wallace with wide eyes then swallowed hard.

"I don't understand? Why try and take Cole?" Gildon asked.

"To judge him. Cole is an abomination to them. Plus he is a seer?" Wallace explained, as he moved about the room checking every corner, nook and cranny there was, to see if it was hiding any more masked assassins.

"Who are these Red Cloaks you spoke of?" Cole asked.

"The Red Cloaks are hunters, assasins. They are mortals that hunt wielders. They believe that wielding is dark magic and that all who are wielders come from the Dark King and that they should be exterminated."

"I have never heard of the hunters," Gildon proclaimed

"They are a secret cult. Born in the days of the Dark King. Once allies but now they are a dangerous foe. Red Cloaks are well trained and are obsessive. They do not stop until their target is eliminated or they themselves are killed. Now Gildon, go wake your father and

Mistress Kaya. Tell them what has happened but be quiet about it. Also if you meet anyone tell them that there was an attack on Cole and say that he was killed in it."

Both Gildon and Cole looked at Wallace with raised eyebrows, not understanding why Wallace wanted that rumor spread.

"Whoever ordered this kidnapping on Cole, was someone that attended the council. Which means there are spies within Aloria. If they believe that Cole is dead, then it will be better for us," Wallace explained. "Now go, do as I have asked and when you are done, wake all those that are to come with us. Tell them to meet in the stables, we are leaving within the hour," Wallace ordered.

Gildon nodded his head and took off from the room.

"Are you able to stand Cole?" Wallace asked.

"I think so," Cole replied as he rose to his feet.

He was a little shaky and he felt nauseated but he stood.

"Come it's not safe here, we'll take care of your wounds when we get to the stables," Wallace replied.

"My wounds?" Cole questioned unaware that he had any.

Wallace indicated Cole's wrists. Cole looked down at his wrists and saw that they had received small cuts and abrasions from the rope that had been used to tie them back.

"Gather your things, Cole. Be quick about it," Wallace ordered watching the door.

Cole threw his saddlebag over his shoulder, flung his quiver of arrows and bow over his other shoulder and went to grab his knives. With some of the nightshade still in his system, Cole wavered in his steps and the knives slipped out of his hands and landed with a clatter on the floor. Cole bent down to get them, but Wallace picked them up first.

"Where did you get these?" Wallace asked, in a shakened voice. Cole looked up at Wallace and saw that all the man's color had drained out of his face.

"Mistress Kaya gave them to me," Cole said swallowing hard. Wallace looked as though he was going to draw one.

"She...She said that Alleana gave them to her to give to me," Cole said, hoping that Wallace would believe him.

"She really did know everything," Wallace muttered. Wallace looked the long knives over then handed them back to Cole.

"Lets go," Wallace replied.

COLE FELT A LITTLE awkward running around in the dead of night in only his nightshirt and boots. Wallace had only given him enough time to pull on his boots, and gather his saddlebags and weapons before taking off towards the stable. When he and Wallace entered the stable there was no one about but the sleepy eyed horses. Wallace did a full inspection of the place and found it to be empty. He lit one of the lamps and ordered Cole to sit down on a bale of hay and show him his wrists. At first Cole had not felt any pain, but ever since Wallace had pointed out his wrists, he started feeling the hard sting of his raw wrists.

"They're not deep, but they will be sore for a while and bruised," Wallace commented.

Wallace finished cleaning Cole's wrists with water from the stable's well, then rubbed some salve on the cuts and raw skin then bandaged them with linens from his nightshirt.

When Wallace was done, Cole looked at the job he had done.

"Not as good as Maggie?" Wallace asked noticing Cole inspecting his work.

'No, I think it's actually better," Cole replied.

"Chloey didn't just teach Maggie the tricks of her trade," Wallace said with a small smile.

The smile faded and an awkward silence fell over the two of them. Cole didn't reply, he didn't know what to say. It was the first time that Wallace had ever mentioned his wife in front of him. Maggie of coarse talked about her all the time.

To avoid the awkward silence Cole pulled out a set of clothing from his saddlebags and went to the back of the stable to change.

"If I may ask Cole, in your vision at the council what did you see," Wallace questioned as Cole dressed.

"There was a garden with a statue of an archer, he was ready to fire an arrow. He watched over a city. Then I felt as if someone was pulling me backwards. I moved across a forest, and meadows, ran backwards through hills and glens, followed rivers and streams until I found myself back in Aloria," Cole cried.

"You know where to go then? Wallace questioned.

"I suppose," Cole muttered pulling his shirt over his head. "I can feel which way to go."

" Feel?"

"Yes. Like I'm being drawn towards it," Cole replied.

"And this "feeling" where is it leading you?" Wallace inquired

Cole turned in the direction he felt a strong pull, a desire to go.

"East" Cole said after a moment

"East" Wallace muttered "Cole I must ask that you not tell the others about your feelings. Just tell which direction we should go. It is for your own safety and for the others," Wallace replied.

"I understand," Cole replied then buckled on his knives and slipped his jerkin on.

When he came back from dressing, Wallace was busy saddling Brom.

"Saddle Gladadear, Cole. When you are done saddle Chanlyn's horse. We need to hurry," Wallace commanded.

Cole did as he was told and quickly saddled Gladadear. She gave out a snort when Cole threw her saddle blanket on her. She turned her head and looked at him with her black eyes as if she were saying, *are you joking. It's the middle of the night.*

"Sorry Glad, but we have to go," Cole told her as he threw on her saddle. The intelligent horse seemed to understand, for she let out another snort and nodded her head.

When Cole had finished he stepped out of Gladadear's stall. When he did a cry of joy reached his ears.

"Cole, you're alive," Chanlyn yelled.

Chanlyn ran over to Cole and bear hugged him with such a force that Cole couldn't breath.

"Chanlyn I can't… breath," Cole choked out.

Chanyln quickly let go of Cole and pulled away. When he did, Cole could see that Chanlyn had tears in his eyes.

"They said that you were killed in an attack. I didn't believe it so I ran to our room. I saw the door and the window and the blood.

I thought that you were really..." Chanlyn stopped and wiped the tears away. "I'm being a fool. Of course you're not dead. But what happened?" Chanlyn asked.

"The storytelling will have to be saved for later, Master Chanlyn. We have work to do." Wallace announced. "Chanlyn saddle your horse. Cole, move onto Gildon's horse." As Cole and Chanlyn rushed about pulling saddles and blankets, bits and bridals from the stable walls, Godfrey and Mistress Kaya came into the stables. Not long after Grayson came in leading his own horse, a brown and white giant of a stallion called Thor, and two others loaded with packs on their backs into the stables. Wallace, Godfrey, Grayson and Mistress Kaya stood talking. As Cole finished up with Gildon's horse a great voice of anger could be heard coming into the stables.

"What on earth is this all about?" Sir Arthur's voice yelled, as he and Artemis, followed by Gildon came in through the doors. "For goodness sake, we have a murderer to catch. We cannot let Cole's death be in vain. I was about to search the whole city from top to bottom looking for that scum and now I am ordered to come here to the stables with my saddlebags where..." at that moment Sir Arthur caught sight of Cole and his breath went out of him.

"There is no need to search for Cole's killer, Sir Arthur. The man is in his watery grave and Cole is still among the living. Now if you would, I would have you speak a little quieter for I would not have the whole city upon us," Godfrey spoke, just as loud as Arthur.

"Yes! Of course!" Arthur said, his eyes never leaving Cole's.

"You're alive Cole!" Arthur said.

"Yes," Cole replied.

"You really are alive? I do not behold a ghost?" Arthur asked.

"No, I am no ghost, Sir Arthur," Cole replied.

To prove that he really was alive, Arthur stepped forward and pulled on Cole's cheeks, which was slightly painful for Cole.

"By the heavens and the stars you are alive," Arthur cried joyfully.

"Sir Arthur, we are glad that you have proven that Cole is alive. But now is not the time for celebration. You and Artemis need to saddle up your horses, we are leaving now," Wallace commanded.

"We are to leave tonight?" Arthur asked in quiet surprise.

"Within the hour," Wallace stated.

"But that is impossible," Arthur exclaimed. "We must gather supplies, maps, and plan which course we are to take. We must know where it is that we are going."

"Sir Arthur, Cole was nearly killed in his bed by an assassin. The longer we stay the more chances our enemy will have of killing him or seriously hurting him. Right now the enemy thinks that his assassin has accomplished his task, which will give us time to disappear. But it will not be long before whoever it was that has betrayed us will find out that Cole indeed is alive and their man dead. The sooner we leave, the greater distance we will put between us and the enemy," Wallace announced.

"I agree with Wallace," Grayson said

"But what about food?" Arthur asked. "We cannot simply walk out with nothing.

"The supplies for your quest have already been gathered," Godfrey interrupted. "Along with gold and silver to help you along your way, when the food supplies have run dry."

"All is prepared," Mistress Kaya explained. "All you have to do is ready yourselves." Arthur looked around him and saw that everyone was ready but for him and his son.

"I see the wisdom in your words. Artemis and I will be ready in less than half an hour," Arthur replied.

Artemis and Arthur left those gathered and went to saddle their horses.

"Mistress Kaya," Wallace said, turning to the woman.

"Yes Master Wallace."

"Would you do me the honor of granting me a favor," Wallace asked, "would you tell Maggie that I love her and that I will one day see her soon. Also tell her that Cole is alive when you think the time is right and we are out of danger. I know it will hurt her to hear that her best friend has died, but it is not only for Cole's sake in keeping the secret but for hers as well," Wallace spoke.

"I will do as you ask Master Wallace."

Wallace nodded his head then left Kaya to go and check over Brom. Cole was leading Gladadear from her stall when Kaya stopped him. "Take courage Cole and know that you are not alone. The Gods are with you and have a plan for you," Kaya said, patting Cole on his shoulder." Cole nodded his head and passed over the threshold of the stable and out into the night.

Two hours after Cole was attacked, six men and nine horses passed through Aloria unheard but not unnoticed.

CHAPTER 27

AS AGREED, Cole only gave the simplest instructions. They were to head east. Wallace suggested that the company take a path that started near the lake along the valley floor. Although the path did not start out heading directly East, Wallace assured them that eventually it would.

Reflection Lake poured out into a stream that they then followed. The stream grew wider as the day's travel progressed and soon the stream turned into a river that then took them further into the rugged wild landscape. The sandstone cliffs that Aloria was built from, continued to surround them as they traveled, and as they went deeper, the red and tan colored peaks grew taller into dramatic formations, stretching upward, reaching for the sky. To Cole, the towering mountainous peaks reminded him of the mountain range in Kells and memories of home flooded his mind. Two months had passed since that fateful day, but to Cole it felt like it had happened just days ago. Cole shook his head trying to push back the thoughts of home. His hate for the Reapers still burned like a fire within him and he had to swallow several times to quench that fire.

The morning came and went as they moved through the valley. They saw deer, hares and squirrels run from them as they approached and Cole even caught sight of a wild cat turning tail and running up a mountainside to hide. Even though Cole saw many new sights and heard familiar and new sounds, he couldn't help feeling a little nervous. He felt like someone or something was following them. Having learned from experience to trust his instincts, Cole mentioned his uneasiness to Wallace, who went back and retraced their steps. He was gone for half a day but found not a trace of anyone following them. Even though Wallace said that he couldn't find any sign that they were being followed, the feeling stayed with Cole. Several times he had touched the ground to trace behind them but he couldn't see anyone following them. He was glad that there were plenty of trees and foliage growing in abundance along the valley floor. The company could hide within them if any thing should happen and there were also boulders of rock that they could use to position themselves behind should they have to defend themselves. Cole tried to push the feelings of uneasiness to the back of his mind and concentrate on his feeling of where they were supposed to go.

It seemed strange to Cole that Wallace was leading them. He would have thought Gildon or Grayson would have taken the lead, seeing how they were the ones that grew up in and around Aloria and would know the area best. Yet whenever Cole told them which direction they were to go, Wallace found a trail or path that would lead them safely in that direction. It amazed not only Cole how much Wallace knew about the part of Albavar they were traveling through. Wallace even asked Grayson whether a pass was open or if it was still blocked by the winter snow, a pass that Grayson knew nothing about.

It was apparent that Gildon was impressed with Wallace's knowledge for he asked him about it that night when they had made camp along the riverbank.

"It seems that you know a lot about this place Master Wallace. Far more than I, and I was born in Aloria," Gildon commented with curiosity. Wallace sat near the fire with his knife out skinning a couple of long thick tree branches. Wallace didn't say anything at first. Cole got the impression that he didn't want to talk about it and was just ignoring Gildon's inquiries.

"This isn't the first time I have been to Aloria," Wallace finally replied.

Cole was very surprised and his facial expressions showed it. He wasn't the only one, Sir Arthur had suddenly stopped what he was doing and Artemis just stared. Chanlyn who was writing in a book had dropped his quill to stare at Wallace with an open mouth. Gildon raised an eyebrow and waited for Wallace to continue.

"When I was ten years of age my parents were killed in a raid.

I myself was injured and nearly died, but I was saved by a man named Elrin, who brought me to Aloria." Wallace explained then fell silent.

"And…" Gildon asked.

"And what?" Wallace said, running his knife along one of the branches.

"I believe that there is more to the story," Gildon said, prodding for more information.

"I left Aloria when the war between Kayden and Shelrin broke out," Wallace said. "End of story."

"Is that when you joined Kayden's army?" Chanlyn asked.

"Mmm," Wallace grunted.

"There must be more than what you have told us," Gildon responded. "For Mistress Kaya said you can no longer hide your past, for it will come out."

"I have told you my past," Wallace said, with a tone that said the conversation was over.

Gildon shrugged his shoulders, "It will all come out one day Master Wallace and I hope I will be there when it does."

Dinner was fresh caught quail, shot by Cole. The company had reasoned that it was better to save their supplies of food for when they would really need it. Since there was plenty of fresh water and game around them, and they had the means to catch it, there was really no need for them to use up the food supplies right away. The rest of the night was spent in almost utter silence. After dinner Cole sat down next to Chanlyn and watched him scribble in a bound book of paper.

"What are you doing?" Cole finally asked.

"Writing down our adventures. Mistress Kaya said I should keep a record, so that others could read it."

"Who would want to read about us looking for some fabled weapons?" Artemis asked with distain.

"Our descendants," Chanlyn voiced.

"Hah. Like my great-grandson would want to read about me following a stable boy that says he can see the future and thinks he can find old weapons of power." Artemis mocked.

"I would," Chanlyn muttered, and then went back to his writings.

...

THE NIGHT WORE ON and Cole's thoughts mulled over the events of the day. He wondered what Wallace's life might have been like and it kept circling around his head. He had never known that Wallace had lost his parents, in fact, now that Cole thought about it more, he really didn't know anything about Wallace. The only facts that he knew about Wallace were that Wallace was Maggie's father, that he was a farmer in Kells and that he was married once. It was difficult for Cole to think that Master Wallace had been a young boy at one time, a boy that lived through the time when Albavar was under the rule of Shelrin. Wallace had said that his parents had been killed in a raid. Cole wondered if they had been killed by one of Shelrin's men that had been ordered to kill all the young boys in the mountain villages. He thought of his dream he had had about William and the attack on his village. He wondered if Wallace had experienced something similar to it.

THAT NIGHT Cole's dreams were filled with black cloaked Reapers that hid in the shadows and the boy William. He woke to find himself running along side an older looking William as they ran though a maze. Steep rock walls enclosed around them and it seemed as they ran further and deeper the walls seemed to grow closer together. A sense of danger and death was in the air. A thin mist swirled around them, which began to grow thicker as time passed, blocking out the moonlight that lit William's way. Cole was sure William couldn't see him. He was positive that he was in a dream of the past and was now sure that William had lived through the attack on his village. The question was how?

Together William and Cole turned a bend in the maze of rocks and found that they had come to a dead end. A rock wall at least a hundred meters high blocked their way. Out of breath and taking in deep panicked breaths, William sought for a way out. He tried to climb, but the walls were sheer with no handholds or foot holds to hang onto. A deep-throated laugh came from the mist filled air. Cole felt the marrow in his bones suddenly freeze when he heard the cold cruel laugh. He had heard it once before. It was the laugh of death. It was the laugh of a Reaper.

William spun around to face the Reaper. The Reaper sat on a black horse its cloak falling about its form and the mask of steel was cold and hard as moonlight fell upon it. William drew his sword and stood ready to defend himself. His sword hand shook with fear as he stared up at the Reaper. The Reaper dismounted from his horse and took a few steps towards William.

"It is foolish to go up against a Reaper, boy," the Reaper's raspy voice echoed inside William and Cole's heads. "If you put down your weapon, I will not hurt you, too much. "

William swiped his sword at the Reaper for his answer. The tip of the sword nicked the Reapers mask, sending bright sparks flying. The Reaper hissed and was on William with unnatural speed. A gauntlet covered hand grabbed William by the neck.

"I am not allowed to kill you boy, but I can take a few years from you, you just have to be able to talk," the Reaper voiced, lifting William up, his feet kicking out. The Reaper lifted up its mask and leaned in towards William and placed his other hand where his heart was. William's body suddenly went stiff.

"No! Let him go!" Cole screamed, running towards William and the Reaper, his own swords drawn. But before Cole could get there a bright blue bolt of lightning flashed in front of him and then exploded. A horrible scream erupted into the night, echoing off the walls a thousand times over.

COLE BOLTED UPRIGHT and looked around, expecting to see something on fire. But all that was around him was the dark of the night. It was cold, cold enough that Cole could see his breath as he breathed to settle himself down. A familiar yet distant sound caught Cole ears and he looked over to where the sound was coming from. He got to his feet and moved towards the sound. He found Master Wallace sitting near the camp. His sword was drawn and stuck into the ground next to him. In his hands was one of the dried out branches that he had been skinning earlier that night. Now he had a flat stone and was rubbing it across the wood. Cole recognized that Wallace was smoothing out the wood.

Cole came up behind Wallace, snapping a twig under his boot. In a matter of mere seconds, Wallace had hold of his sword and was on his feet, spinning around to face whoever it was that was behind him. Cole's hands went up and stared at Wallace like a scared deer.

"It's me Master Wallace," Cole said.

"You should never sneak up on someone when they have a sword close at hand." Wallace complained, as he returned his sword back to its spot in the ground and went back to his smoothing. "You should be asleep," Wallace replied in his soft-spoken way.

Cole took a seat next to Wallace.

"Couldn't sleep," Cole answered.

Wallace merely nodded his head and continued his work.

The two sat without speaking to one another for a while until Cole broke the silence. He cleared his throat intending to ask Wallace about his life in Aloria and had the question on his lips and took a breath.

"Can I ask you…what it is that you're doing?" Cole asked, chickening out at the last minute.

Wallace stopped then tossed his project over to Cole. Cole tried to catch it but missed and it clattered to the ground. Biting his lip from embrassment, he picked it up and examined it by moonlight. The shape of a thick dried out branch was no more. Now it was beginning to take the shape of a double-edged short sword, much like the ones that Kaya had given him. Cole suspected that the other branch that Wallace had been working was the sword mate.

"Who are they for?" Cole asked, handing it back to Wallace.

"For you," Wallace answered.

"But I already have a sword," Cole muttered.

"Yes, you have a sword, but do you know how to defend yourself with it?"

"No," Cole admitted.

"Hence the wooden ones. We can't have you cutting off your own head, now can we? Once you have managed to master one sword we can then move on to the pair of Whicka blades."

"Whicka?" Cole questioned.

"Your knives that Kaya gave you are called Whicka's. Named so because of where they came from. The Isles of Whicka," Wallace said.

"Where are they?" Cole asked.

"To the far north and across the Whitecap Sea," Wallace said.

"How do you know this?" Cole asked curiously.

"Aloria is not the only place I have lived," Wallace said, taking back the wooden sword from Cole and again starting the smoothing process. It fell silent as Cole stared at Wallace with wonder. He wanted to know more about this man that he had grown up with.

"Would you tell me about the Isles of Whicka?" Cole asked finally.

"Not much to tell. The islands are cold in the winter and hot in the summers. The people believe that they are descendants of Dresden and Feona," Wallace explained.

"Why did you go to there?" Cole asked.

"No reason. Just wanted to see them," Wallace said.

Cole got the feeling that Wallace was hiding something from him, but by the way he answered Cole's questions, he sounded like he didn't want to talk about it. It seemed that Merryrick wasn't the only one that had kept his past a secret. Wallace had secrets of his own.

Cole let out a smirk as he thought. The laugh made Wallace lift an eyebrow.

"What do you find so amusing?" Wallace asked, looking over at Cole.

"Nothing! Just that it's a bit ironic, you and Merryrick," Cole answered.

"Oh and how is that?" Wallace asked.

"Merryrick didn't tell me about his past and now I find out that I really don't know anything about him. And you don't want to talk about your past either."

"Facing and remembering your own past can sometimes hurt," Wallace muttered.

"I suppose you're right. But I would like to know my past. I would like to know who my father and mother were and where I came from," Cole muttered.

"You will one day Cole. I am sure of it," Wallace answered, but said nothing the rest of the night.

...

THE NEXT DAY'S travel was hard and the going was slow. They had come to a point where the rock walls of the sandstone cliffs had enclosed around them. Hundreds of years of wind and water had carved a slotted canyon, with twists and turns that confused Cole to no end. Pillars of sunlight streamed in through the cracks and broken rocks above them. Cole marveled at the layers of rock that seemed to be pressed together, creating different colors of sandstone. Water had collected at the bottom of the canyon from rains and from winter's snow, creating small stream-like waterfalls and pools, which the company had to trudge through. Some of the pools were short and shallow, only going past Gladadear's ankles, while others were long and deep, spanning several yards, the water reaching up to Gladadear's belly. Whenever they had to cross through a deep pool of water, Cole's nerves were tightened to a point that they would shake and only when they were a good ways away from the previous collection of water, did his nerves relax.

Night came early in the canyon. Once the sun had sunk to the west, the shelves of rocks prevented any sunlight from reaching them making traveling dangerous and almost impossible. They pulled to a stop in the late afternoon and found a cave like formation of rock with pools of water so clear that one could see the bottom. Chanyln, thinking that he could reach down and touch the bottom, plunged his hand into one of the pools only to discover that the bottom was much farther away than it appeared to be.

"What is this place?" Chanlyn asked, his voice echoing off the rock walls.

"This place does not have a name," Wallace said. "Never been here before. But the path we follow through the canyon is called Thayeden's Maze."

"Oh and why's that?" Cole asked, undoing the cinch around Gladadear's belly.

"Because a man named Thayeden went in and never came out." Grayson said, "or so the legend goes. They say you can hear the man's cries of despair at night, as he tries to find his way out," Grayson explained, as he unsaddled his own horse.

"Really?" Chanlyn asked.

"Mmm." Grayson mumbled, throwing his saddle to the ground. "I heard it once. I'll have to tell you about it tonight after supper."

"Speaking of supper why don't you boys go gather wood for the fire. We'll need a fare bit. I expect the nights get cold with all these rocks about us," Gildon said. After Chanlyn and Cole had finished unsaddling their horses they headed out to get the firewood.

"Not too far boys," Wallace warned.

"We're not children," Artemis stated.

"May I remind you, young Artemis, that some of us were nearly killed in our beds a few nights ago!" Arthur said angrily.

Artemis said nothing but stormed out of the campsite.

Cole, Chanlyn and Artemis found plenty of dead branches off trees that had fallen down between the rocks from trees above. They filled their arms full of the dried wood then started to make their way back to camp. As Cole followed Chanlyn, he suddenly got the feeling that they were being watched. Turning around in circles, Cole looked about him to see who it could possibly be, but there was no one, besides Chanyln and Artemis. He froze, his heart feeling like it was about to jump into his throat when he thought he heard a deep moan.

"Did you hear that?" Cole whispered.

Chanlyn being the last in the line hadn't realized that Cole had stopped. He ran into Cole, who ran into Artemis, who was knocked forward, making him loses his balance, which made him fall forward.

His armload of branches and twigs went flying as Artemis flung out his hands to catch himself.

Artemis let out a few curses in anger when he landed. He got to his feet and dusted himself off then turned his anger on Cole and Chanlyn.

"What are you cow brains doing?" Artemis yelled.

"You didn't hear it then?" Cole asked.

"Hear what?" Artemis asked.

"The moan," Cole replied, his eyes darting back and forth trying to figure out where the moan had come from.

The three boys stood in silence for a moment but heard nothing.

"I don't hear anything stable boy. Now let's get moving. I don't want to get caught out here in this maze in the dark," Artemis said curtly.

As Artemis went about picking up his share of firewood a deep and sickly sounding moan echoed off the wall of sandstone.

"There! You heard it that time?" Cole said.

This time Artemis did hear it and it sent a chill up his spine. The three of them stood frozen in place, hugging the bundles of sticks they had collected to their chests. The moan came again and the boys took off, dropping their bundles and running for the safety of the camp. When they came running in out of breath, the others looked up at them with quizzical expressions.

"There's something out there," Artemis cried.

"What is all of this," Arthur spoke, "are you telling lies again boy?"

"He's not fibbing Sir Arthur," Chanlyn spoke, "there really is something out there. It gave out this horrible moan."

Wallace seemed to be convinced that Cole, Chanyln and Artemis were telling the truth for he picked up his sword and headed out to check the situation himself. The rest of the men followed each taking their sword and bows with them.

"Where did you hear the moan?" Wallace asked.

"Over there," Cole said, pointing in the direction they had come.

The group walked for a few minutes until they came to the spot where the boys had dropped the wood. Wallace, Grayson and Gildon searched around the area but found nothing that would explain the reason for the moaning.

"Are you sure you didn't just imagine it." Gildon asked, "We did just tell you about Theyeden."

"All three of us imaging the same sound at the same time," Chanlyn spoke up, "not likely."

"He has a point," Grayson stated. "What do you think we should do?"

"It is more than likely the boys heard an animal of some sort," Sir Arthur pointed out. "Let us go back to camp and have some supper. The sun is sinking and before long we won't be able to see what's in front of our faces." Everyone seemed to be in agreement and started to make their way back to camp, Wallace however stood where he was with his head cocked to one side.

"Are you not coming Master Wallace?" Cole asked.

"You go ahead Cole. I think I'll stay a little while and take a look around," Wallace replied.

"Are you sure? " Cole commented.

"I'll be alright, I can manage. There will be a bit of moon tonight, it will be over us soon," Wallace said, taking a seat on a nearby rock. "You might as well take back the wood you gathered. I'm thinking Sir Arthur is right. Nights can get pretty cold."

Cole bent down to pick up his bundle of sticks when he suddenly became aware that he was being watched. Cole dropped the branch and spun around, his eyes looking into the darkness, but he couldn't see anything. The feeling was strong, stronger than it had been before.

"What's the matter Cole?" Wallace said, seeing Cole's stiffened body.

"Someone's watching us," Cole whispered.

"Do you know where they are?" Wallace asked, as he unsheathed his sword.

"I don't know," Cole replied, as he bent down and touched the ground.

The familiar sensation of running forward like the wind came to him. Within his head he saw the same path that they had just traveled that afternoon but it was dark now and the world had fallen under the curtain of shadows making visibility within his trace almost impossible.

"See anything Cole?" Wallace asked.

"There's nothing, just…" Cole started to say then stopped.

Just as Cole was about to shift his gaze to another direction he caught the slight hint of movement out of the corner of his eyes, like a shadow shifting.

"What is it Cole?" Wallace asked.

"There someone behind us!" Cole replied. "There's more than one. I can't make them out. It's too hard."

Cole felt an alarm go off in his head as the reason for why he couldn't see whoever it was that was following them came to him.

"They're covered in cloaks, black cloaks…" Cole stammered out.

Cole pulled his hand away from the ground and the vision was lost.

"Reapers," Cole whispered.

"Reapers. How in the world did they find us?" Wallace cried. "Cole which way are they coming from?" Wallace asked.

Once again Cole placed a hand on the ground and he rushed forward, running like the wind until he found his target. His sight was a little clearer now and he could make out the figures as they moved through the dark.

"There are two of them, horses too," Cole yelled. "They're coming from the west, they are almost right on top of us," Cole shouted, pulling his hand free of the ground.

The others must have heard Cole cries for they came back looking alarmed.

"What the matter?" Gildon asked.

"We've got Reapers behind us," Wallace announced, "two of them."

"Reapers! How in the hells did they find us?" Gildon asked.

"I don't know. But they're coming," Wallace answered.

"What do we do?" Sir Arthur asked.

"You run. Take Cole and the others and get out of here. I'll try to hold them off." Wallace said.

"You can't fight two Reaper's alone," Cole said.

"He won't be alone, I'll stay and help," Grayson said, pulling his own sword free.

"You can't do that!" Cole hollered.

"Merryrick did," Wallace replied.

"And Merryrick's dead," Cole said coldly. "Besides the Reapers are mine."

The groups stood in silence staring at Cole. His voice was full of anger and hate. The sound of a horse whinnying echoed around them. The Reapers were close.

"This isn't the time to argue," Wallace voiced. "Gildon, get Cole and the others out of here."

"I'm staying," Artemis said, pulling his bow free from its case and then stringing it.

"None of you are staying" Wallace announced.

"I won't leave," Cole shouted.

Without warning Wallace step forward in front of Cole.

"I'm sorry about this Cole," Wallace said and then gave him a sharp punch to the gut. "Gildon, Arthur get the boys out of here."

Cole bent over holding his stomach as he fell to the ground. His hands went out to catch himself. Only seconds passed but in those few seconds he rushed forward.

Not too far in front of the company, Cole saw the two-cloaked figures riding on horseback moving towards where Wallace and the others lay in wait to attack. They moved with caution so as to avoid rocks that could trip their horses.

It struck Cole then that these two riders didn't act like Reapers and the horses weren't as tall or as black as Cole remembered the Reapers horses being. If fact he saw that one was rather short, the other being a little taller. The last of the setting sun sent out a ray of light and it shone off the cloaks of the riders. They weren't black like he thought but were a deep green.

"Green cloaks," Cole whispered.

Time rushed forward as the future played out in front of him. The two riders came around a bend in the rock and they were totally visible to the company. An arrow was fired and it struck the first rider. The rider fell from the horse with the arrow piercing the heart. When the body hit the ground the hood came off the rider's head revealing who was under it.

Cole felt himself being picked up off the ground and flung onto Gildon's shoulder. His hand came free and was pulled back to reality.

"Stop!" Cole tried to cry out, but the breath that was knocked out of him from Wallace's punch had yet to come back. He tried again and all that seemed to come out of his mouth was a wisp of air.

He could hear Wallace saying to get ready.

"No doubt they will come around that bend, fire when you see the first hint of them." Wallace ordered Grayson

Cole was being carried further and further away. He had to do something. He took in air as fast as he could to try and work up a yell.

"Here they come. Fire Grayson fire now!" Wallace yelled.

In a matter of seconds a hot searing pain burned across Cole's arm and he let out a scream. At the same time he saw Artemis let his arrow go. He saw the first of the riders come around the bend of rock.

"No, wait!" Cole yelled hoarsely. But it was too late the arrow was in the air and heading straight for the first rider. Panic rushed through him as he saw the arrow arch across the sky. He wiggled free of Gildon's grasp and toppled to the ground bringing Gildon with him. Cole bolted to his feet and took in a breath and screamed.

"AYLA STOP!"

His voice echoed off the walls of the canyon a hundred times over and then slowly faded. There was a silence that fell over the company. The only sound that could be heard was the shifting of the wind.

"Please, please don't be dead," Cole begged getting to his feet and starting to run forward but was caught by Artemis hands.

"Why did you call out stable boy? You gave away our position," Artemis muttered angrily.

"They're not Reapers," Cole breathed. "I made a mistake. It's Ayla."

"That cannot be," Gildon replied. "No one knew that we left Aloria except Mistress Kaya and my father."

"Who in blazes tried to kill me?" Ayla's voice rang out of the dark.

Everyone's attention was pulled away from Cole and they all turned to look at the two hooded riders that came around the bend of rocks to stop in front of the six companions.

"Ayla?" Gildon asked, stepping towards the first horseman, "is that you?"

"Of course it's me, you nincompoop," Ayla said, pulling the hood from off her head and then sliding off her horse. The other horseman still sat remaining on its horse. Even in the dark Cole could make the white star on Buttercup's forehead.

."Thanks for the warning Cole," Ayla said, then turned to face her horse again.

"Ayla how did you get here?" Gildon asked.

"We followed you," Ayla responded as if it were easy.

"We were careful not to leave a trail young lady," Wallace said politely, but had a hint of anger within his voice.

"She led me," Ayla said, point to the hooded horseman. Cole knew instantly whom it was that was hiding under the cloak but that still did not stop a cry of surprise escaping from his lips when the rider pulled her hood off.

"Maggie!" Cole and Chanlyn cried out together.

"Hello Cole, Chanlyn, Father," Maggie replied nodding to each man in turn. Cole's head turned to look at Wallace. His arms were folded about him and he did not look at all happy to see his daughter. Gildon looked at his little sister in much the same way.

"For an outlander she's not half bad at tracking," Ayla said.

"Thank you Ayla. I was taught by my father and Cole," Maggie replied, getting down from Buttercup.

"Now is there a camp nearby? I am rather tired and cold," Maggie said, "and I could go for a hot drink."

There was a bit of awkward silence as everyone looked at everyone else to see what each would do or say.

"This way," Wallace finally said, leading the way to the campsite. When they reached the camp, Wallace ordered a small fire and said that no one was allowed to ask any questions about the new arrivals until they had all eaten and clean up was done.

In a hurry to hear the story, supper was prepared in hast and eaten in the same manner. Everyone helped with the clean up and before long all sat around the fire waiting for the story to be told.

"I guess I should start at the beginning," Maggie said, and then took a sip of her honeymaid tea, a hot drink that she was introduced to in Aloria.

"Two nights ago I woke to find that you were all gone and there was this daft rumor that Cole had been killed by an assassin the night before. I found Mistress Kaya and she told me the truth about what happened and which way you went," Maggie said, as she took another sip of the honey and cinnamon tea and began again.

"Then I simply followed your trail," Maggie replied.

"And what about you Ayla, what about your story?" Gildon asked.

"I found out the same way as Maggie, from Mistress Kaya, and she told me that I should find Maggie in the stables and that she shouldn't go alone, that it would be good for her to have some company," Ayla replied.

"That's it then?" Gildon asked.

"That's pretty much the way it happened," Maggie commented.

"You didn't meet any danger or wild animals on the way, or had any exciting events take place?" Gildon asked eagerly, the storyteller in him looking for an exciting tale.

"Well Ayla did stub her toe back there and moaned about it quite a bit. Sounded like an old man dying," Maggie reported.

"It really hurt. I thought that it was broken," Ayla complained.

Cole and Chanlyn looked at each other from across the fire with embarrassed expressions on their faces. Artemis would not even make eye contact with anyone.

"Excellent, I can make it work," Gildon said with a wink.

"Don't go exaggerating the story," Ayla said, "you always make your stories sound like some tragedy."

"I won't I promise," Gildon said.

"So I have a question for you gentleman," Ayla asked, "why did you try to kill us, or more pointedly why did you try to kill me?"

"That's because the stable boy thought you were Reapers," Artemis said bluntly.

"Why would you think that?" Ayla asked.

"Because all I saw of you were your black cloaks which turned out to be green," Cole tried to defend himself.

"Saw us. How could you see us? You didn't even know we were following you?" Maggie voiced.

"I had my suspicions," Cole said, "but every time I did a trace I couldn't find you." Cole replied.

"I'm really confused?" Alya reported. "What is a trace and how could you mistake us for Reapers?"

Cole opened his mouth to explain but no words came out.

"Ayla you know Cole is a seer right?" Maggie said, stepping in for Cole.

"I suppose," Ayla stated, looking at Cole with suspicious eyes.

"Cole has a unique gift of tracking. If he touches the ground he can see a league behind or in front of a path that he has already traveled or will travel," Maggie explained. "That is what he calls a trace or tracing."

"Oh so that is why you made us stay behind a few leauges. It was so Cole couldn't see us," Ayla replied, suddenly making the connection. Cole looked over at Maggie feeling a little hurt. She knew about Cole's gifts and she exploited it so she could achieve what she wanted.

"So when you got close enough to us and I did a trace all I could see was two hooded black cloaks riding towards us," Cole responded.

"But how could you mistake us for Reapers. We weren't wearing black cloaks, we were wearing green," Ayla asked.

"Squint your eyes," Cole instructed. All of them did, even Artemis and Sir Arthur.

"See how everything is blurry and out of focus," Cole asked.

There were nods of agreement and understanding.

"That's how I see when I'm tracing. My sight gets clearer the closer I get to things or when something comes closer to me. I saw that you were following us and saw a blurred vision of two hooded black cloaks heading our way. Only when you got close enough did I see you more clearly," Cole explained. "I am sorry that I did not see you more clearly earlier. Hopefully I can do better the next time," Cole said apologetically.

"There won't be a next time," Wallace said, speaking for the first time since Maggie and Ayla were discovered. "In the morning you Margaret will be escorted back to Aloria and you will stay there," Wallace said, in his soft angry voice.

"No. I have made it this far and I will not turn around on your command, even if you are my father."

"Do not defy me girl. You will go back."

"Oh and are you going to make me? You cannot send me back alone and you cannot send a man with me. You need everyone here and who is to say that I will not lose my escort and turn around and follow you again. Admit it father, you cannot send me back," Maggie said, with a smirk at her father. "All you can do is go forward."

"She has a point there," Grayson said. "You cannot possibly send her back now. None of us knows which way to take, not in this maze.

You are the only one that knows the way. We cannot go back and we cannot go forward without you Master Wallace."

Wallace let out a breath of air and looked at his daughter. He was defeated and he knew it. He looked at Maggie and she knew that the two would be having a long conversation later.

"All of you get some sleep. I'll take first watch. Gildon I'll wake you in four hours time," Wallace muttered.

Wallace turned from his daughter and went to take up his guard-post a short ways off from the camp sit. Chanlyn went off and pulled out his book, his ink and pen and began to write. Maggie saw him writing and asked Cole what he was about.

"He writing about our little adventure," Cole replied shortly, stoking the fire for the night.

"I wouldn't say it's a little adventure," Maggie responded.

"You're right," Cole muttered. "Why did you follow us Maggie? After what you saw when…after what you saw when we touched, I figured that you would never want to see me again."

"I did not want to be left out," Maggie said, "on this little adventure."

"Seriously Maggie, why?"

"What I saw and what I felt scared my very soul and I wanted to lock my door and hide behind it," Maggie explained, "but then when I remembered those moments of pure joy and happiness I wanted to experience them. I want to feel those emotions so badly that the fear I felt seemed to diminish and I found that I could stand and face what was to come. It was because of what I saw with you that made me come," Maggie said, looking over at Cole. "I knew that you would need everyone's help in conquering this task and I am willing to help in anyway I can."

"Even with all the fear and pain that awaits us?" Cole asked.

"Fear and pain are a part of life. But so is joy. We cannot have one without the other."

Cole stared into Maggie eyes and knew that she was not lying. Her eyes were full of determination and will power. She would see Cole through this task even if she had to give up her own life. And that was what scared Cole the most.

CHAPTER 28

"ARE YOU READY?" Master Wallace asked.

Cole adjusted his grip on the hilt of his wooden swords, nodded, and then waited for Wallace's attack. Cole did not even have time to take in another breath before Wallace's own wooden swords came down upon him. Cole quickly raised his left hand in defense, blocking Wallace's blow while sweeping his right hand across Wallace's chest, but Wallace sidestepped the strike and the two separated.

"Good!" Wallace said as he struck again. This time Cole felt the sharp pain in his right arm as Wallace's blow came down on it.

"If these were real swords you would have lost your arm," Wallace said, stepping in front of Cole, who was rubbing his already throbbing arm.

Again and again Wallace attacked. Cole tried to do his best to guard himself and he succeeded a few times, but most of the time he felt the sharp smack of wood hitting his arms, legs and head. In less than half an hour Cole was sweating. His muscles started to quiver and he was breathing as hard as if he had been running over three leagues. He had never fought like this before. Wallace's blows came down as hard as hammer blows and they were like trying to guard oneself against a massive tree falling on you. Wallace also moved quickly. It was impossible to know where he was going and what attack he was going to make.

The company spent two more days winding through the maze of rocks and caves until they came out to gaze across a land of rolling hills, rugged wilderness and a sea of heather. Ever since the almost Reaper attack, Wallace would have them make camp two hours before the sun set and would put Cole and the others through drills of swordsmanship.

Wallace explained one night after a workout, that it was important to learn how to defend oneself with more than one weapon. Although many of them were excellent archers, there may come a time when they would have to fight hand to hand. Besides learning to fight with a sword, Cole was also learning how to use his knives with Grayson, and Gildon was teaching him to not only use his fists, but to use the rest of his body as a weapon.

Each night Wallace would line them all up and call out the names of drills. "Head cut. Right flank, left arm, left flank, right arm head, left parry, right parry, cross block."

They would follow through the drills, moving their swords in the right movement. They used real swords when practicing drills, but when it came to fighting one on one, they only used the wooden swords.

Master Wallace attacked swiftly and Cole managed to block the blow that was aimed at his torso. Again he blocked Wallace's blow but failed to guard himself against a sweeping arch that caught Cole on his other shoulder.

"Watch your opponent, Cole, observe his movements. If you're watching you can guess your opponents next move," Gildon cried, watching the match from the sidelines. Cole tried to do as Gildon suggested. He watched Wallace as they circled each other.

"Attack Cole, always be on the attack," Wallace said, giving Cole a chance to press forward. Cole ran forward and used a head cut, but Wallace easily defended himself with a left parry. Again and again Cole came at Wallace, using the different techniques that Wallace had taught him.

"Don't be afraid to mix up your fighting techniques," Grayson called out.

Taking Grayson's advice, Cole locked one sword with Wallace and tried to use one of his knives to jab the end into his ribs. But the attack failed when Cole's sword arm buckled under Wallace's weight. He lost his balance and fell forward. Wallace's sword came down onto Cole's head with a loud crack. Cole hit the ground seeing stars and feeling dizzy. He soon felt a warm liquid running down the side of his face and then everything went black.

...

COLE SIGHTED THE TARGET in front of him and pulled back on his bowstring.

"Now take it slow, you don't want to spook him," Merryrick's voice whispered in his ear. Cole slightly turned his head to look at his master from the corner of his eye.

"I know," Cole's ten-year-old voice muttered. Merryrick had told him the instruction a hundred times over whenever they went hunting and on this trip there were no exceptions.

"Then you should know to keep your eyes on your target. Never assume that they will stay where you last saw them."

Cole pulled back his arrow until the feathers of the notch touched his cheek and concentrated on his target. His target was a buck that had a bad leg. It had somehow managed to break it and the poor thing was suffering from it. Both Merryrick and Cole were surprised that a bear or a wolf pack had not gotten it first. Merryrick said that it was their duty to put the creature out of its misery.

Cole took in a breath and let it out as he let go of his arrow. The arrow flew through the air heading straight for the buck. But the buck wasn't there any more in its place was the hard scaled body of a Hellhound. The thing turned and its deep red eyes stared at Cole, while it licked its upper lips and then it ran at Cole.

Ten-year-old Cole's heart felt like it would burst from his chest with fear as the hound let out a deep menacing howl, calling the others to him. Cole ran then, racing through the woods, not knowing which way he was going.

"Merryrick," Cole called out. "Merryrick where are you?"

Everything around him blurred into smears of greens, browns and yellows and Merryrick had disappeared and there was only darkness and a strange blue light around him as he ran. Suddenly something hit him hard on the side of his head and fell forward. He could feel the warmth of his own blood run down the side of his face. Drops of it fell on the ground, sinking into the dirt. Where the drops fell, a mist began to ooz up and around him. Next Cole felt a sharp pain stab him in his hand. Looking down he saw blood pool in his palm and run over, the droplets falling to the ground. More blood fell and more mist came, wrapping around his legs like a snake wrapping itself around its prey. It soon surrounded him and within the mist there were shadows. In utter horror little Cole spun around in a circle counting the dark hooded shadows of the Reapers.

"Nine," Cole muttered, "nine Reapers."

They stood all around Cole, encircling him with no way out. They glided slowly forwards as they took their time. The howls of the hell-hounds grew louder as they echoed through the night never stopping. Cole searched for a way out, his eyes darting all around him.

"You cannot escape boy," the voices of the Reapers echoed in unison inside Cole's head. "We've found you."

No longer the age of ten but six, Cole cowed on the ground, crying for Merryrick with his hands covering his ears, trying to cut out the voices that burned through his head.

"We can smell you. We can smell the life blood that leaks from your mortal body."

Cole felt his head burn with the sharp pain from his head.

"We follow your trail of blood and tears and soon we will find you. And your friends, your friends will perish, they will die by our hands. It is only a matter of time. So run little rabbit, run as fast as you can. We are coming for you," the voice declared.

The Reapers charged forward and surrounded Cole in their black cloaks and he was swallowed up in darkness.

COLE BOLTED UPRIGHT, heaving in gulps of air. He was shaking badly as if he had chills from a fever.

"Oh good you're awake," Alya said, looking at Cole with one eyebrow up. "Master Wallace will be glad."

Cole ignored her as he ran towards the nearest tree and threw up. He was looking down at his hand. A clear clean scar shone in the firelight. His hand went up and touched his head. He felt the soft touch of linen and realized that Maggie must have bandaged his head.

"Cole?" Ayla questioned, seeing Cole's terrified eyes.

Cole turned and forced himself back away from her.

"Don't touch me Ayla," Cole ordered, shying away from her touch. He moved past Ayla back to his bedroll and began rolling it up. Ayla seemed to be the one on guard duty for the rest of the camp was fast asleep, and Cole was glad of it. That meant he could make his escape.

"Cole what are you doing?" Ayla asked.

"Leaving," Cole whispered.

"You shouldn't really get up, you did just get knocked unconscious."

Cole said nothing but just continued to pack his saddlebags.

"What are you doing, Cole?" Ayla asked, watching Cole's panicked moves.

"I told you. I have to leave," Cole muttered. "Right now!"

"Why?" Ayla asked.

"The Reaper's they are coming," Cole whispered in a hurry.

"These Reapers again," Ayla breathed out.

"Ridicule me all you want," Cole spoke coldly. "But the Reapers are real and they are coming."

"How?" Ayla asked. "Gildon said that you lost them in the mountains."

"The hellhounds. They can smell my blood."

"If you're leaving then I'm coming with you," Ayla said.

"No you're not." Cole retorted.

"I believe I am," Ayla replied.

"No you are not," Cole shouted.

"Yes I am," Ayla shouted just as loud.

The sudden shouting match woke everyone from their sleep.

"What the devil's is going on?" Sir Arthur asked in a yawn. "Is Cole alright?"

"No! He's not alright," Ayla stated loudly. "He's gone completely mad."

Cole gave Ayla a cold hard look.

"Cole, what is the matter?" Maggie asked.

"Nothing Maggie go back to sleep," Cole said.

"He said that the Reapers are coming and that they're coming for him. Something about how they can smell his trail by his blood so he's leaving. He's running away and leaving us to these Reapers."

"Is this true Cole?" Wallace's voice asked.

Cole let out a breath of frustration. Now that Wallace was awake, there was no escaping now.

"I wasn't leaving you to the Reapers," Cole snarled.

"But you were leaving?" Wallace asked, getting to his feet.

"The Reapers are after me. If I leave, they will follow me and leave you alone. I can't…" Here Cole choked up a little. "I can't lose any one else that I care about. I can go and find the weapons on my own. Please go back to Aloria. I don't want anyone else getting hurt because of me," Cole replied.

"Cole," Wallace stated, stepping in front of the young man. "I laid down my sword and swore an oath that I would help defend you. I cannot go back on my word. One day we will face the Reapers and we will have more of a chance of surviving if we fight them together."

"Wallace is right. Together we stand, alone we fall," Sir Arthur cried.

"Very well said, Sir Arthur," Gildon replied.

"Well now, if the boy is sure that he sees Reapers we had better get moving," Grayson said, rising to his feet.

"In the middle of the night?" Artemis protested. "The last time he saw Reapers, they turned out to be two misfits."

"What was that about misfits?" Ayla questioned coldly.

"Then you can stay here and wait to be proven right or wrong," Grayson said. "I, for one, don't intend to sit on my duff and see if those souless black riders come calling."

Everyone agreed with Grayson and within less than an hour's time the camp was cleared and any signs that there had been a camp had been wiped away. Yet as they rode through the darkness, Cole knew that it was already too late. The Reapers had found his trail.

CHAPTER 29

WALLACE LOOKED OUT across the wide stretch of grassland before him. In the distance he could make out thin wisps of smoke rising up and then disappearing.

"There looks to be a village over there," Arthur said, taking notice of the smoke.

"That would be Woods Hollow," Gildon replied, surprised at the direction Wallace had led them. "Amazing! You do know your way around Master Wallace," Gildon said, praising the man. "The way I would have taken you all would have taken at least two weeks and we have done it in ten days. Yes I'm sure that is Woods Hollow. Although I do not know why they called it Woods Hollow. There are not any woods around here. Mostly grass lands with sheep. Must be a name from ancient times. There is an inn there. They serve up a nice rack of lamb with carrots, turnips and spices. Oh I can smell it now. I've often stayed there when I'm out and about on Alorian business."

"Did you say Inn?" Arthur asked, looking out towards the distance smoke columns.

"Oh, it will be nice to have a proper meal and a bed to sleep in after sleeping on such hard ground and eating stale bread for ten days straight."

"We are not staying," Wallace grunted. There was an outcry of disagreement from Arthur and a few others.

"Come now, Master Wallace. A few nights stay with a proper bed cannot do any harm."

"May I remind you, Sir Arthur, we have Reapers on our trail, we cannot afford a few nights."

"Just because the stable boy said it doesn't make it true," Artemis muttered.

"But surely we can afford one night? "

"Sir Arthur," Wallace interrupted, "we can not even afford one night, not when it comes to the Reapers," Wallace replied in a way that said the conversation was over.

"Father, I must ask you to reconsider," Maggie's soft voice asked, as she came to stand next to her father. Wallace turned and looked at his daughter full on in the face. In her eyes he saw strength and determination, yet he also saw concern and sorrow.

"Margaret..." he said shaking his head.

"Father, look at him," Maggie said, her voice raising an octave. Wallace turned once more and his eyes fell on Cole.

The hood of his cloak was pulled over his head as if the boy was trying to hide himself away. He sat slumped with his head falling towards his chest. The boy was exhausted; they all were yet Cole seemed to be taking a beating of late. Ever since he woke from his recent dream, the boy had changed. No longer did he smile or laugh. He flinched at sudden movements and became nervous and tense with the smallest sounds. His eyes no longer held the brightness in them but they were dull and gray. He would not eat nor would he sleep. Wallace would watch him pull out his food like the rest of the company, yet while the others would wolf down their supper Cole would just sit looking at it, pretending to eat. Sleep eluded Cole. He would fall asleep only to be woken a few hours later, drenched in sweat and breathing hard. Dark circles had started to appear under his eyes. Even Artemis who cared little about Cole looked at him with weary eyes. Practice with the swords became an obsession with him. Wallace's sparring sessions with Cole were intense and often ending when Cole was struck hard and could not continue for the rest of the night.

"He needs to sleep father. A person cannot survive without some rest," Maggie whispered.

"The girl is right Master Wallace," Arthur replied, taking part in the conversation.

"I agree but how are we to get him to sleep?" Wallace asked, his eyes leaving Cole to look at Maggie. "I believe Cole fears it."

"I think that I can help you there," Maggie said in a whispered voice.

"How?" Wallace asked.

From Maggie's little waist bag she pulled out a small container that held a white powder. "It's nightshade," Maggie whispered.

"Isn't that poisonous?" Arthur asked.

"Yes, but only in large amounts. In small amounts it acts as a sedative," Maggie said, seeing her father's eyebrows arch up in concern.

"How long have you had this nightshade?" Wallace asked.

"Mistress Kaya gave it to me when I left Aloria," Maggie replied.

"Then why haven't you given this to him before if he it needs so bad?" Wallace asked.

"I offered it to him but he won't take it. It is as you said, I think Cole fears to sleep," Maggie replied.

"Then if he won't willingly take it, then we'll have to trick him into taking it," Arthur said. Both Maggie and Wallace looked at Arthur with shocked expressions.

"Like you said Maggie, one cannot survive without sleep."

Wallace took in a large breath and looked back over at Cole.

"He's right," Wallace muttered. "All right Maggie," Wallace said, letting out his breath.

"Then can we stay? It will be far more comfortable for him," Maggie asked, pleading softly.

"One night, that is all that we are staying," Wallace said.

"Maggie, you had better do it," Arthur said. "You know what to do and the amount to give him."

The idea of slipping something past Cole made Maggie feel horrible. But Cole needed sleep and Maggie was determined to give it to him. Maggie went back to where Cole and Chanlyn sat resting on their saddles.

Wallace then turned toward the others. "We are staying only one night. That is it. We will gather supplies today and leave early in the morning."

The cheer from the others was a whole lot happier. Cole, however had suddenly shot straight up, his back rigid as a wave of uneasiness hit him.

"Cole, what is the matter?" Maggie asked, looking at Cole with concern.

"I don't think we should stay," Cole said, looking down at the village.

"Why not? It looks rather nice," Maggie said. "And just think of the soft beds they might have."

"How do you know that the beds are soft?" Ayla injected. "They could be as hard as the ground that we sleep on," she replied.

Maggie gave Ayla a hard stare, but then turned her attention to the village smiling, her eyes sparkling in the sun. Cole also looked down at the village but no smile crossed his lips. A small voice he heard in his head kept whispering a warning, *be wary, there are dangers unseen.*

"There are dangers unseen," Cole said softly.

"I think you're just tired. I know I am. It will be nice to be able to sleep indoors once more, instead of on the cold hard ground," Maggie's voice echoed above the small voice.

"Cole do you have any water in your water skin? I drank all mine and I'm quite thirsty." Without taking his eyes from the village, Cole handed his water skin to Maggie.

"You really think we should not stay?" Chanlyn asked. He sat on the other side of Cole, his own weary eyes looking down at the town as well.

"There's something about it that doesn't seem right."

"Maybe you should tell Wallace about it," Ayla spoke.

Cole's eyes moved towards where Wallace stood, his gaze stopping on the faces of the others as he sought out Wallace. They look tired and worn out. They had been pushing hard, waking early in the morning, before the sun even had time to rise and then kept on going until they could no longer because of exhaustion. Surely one night would not do any harm and he hadn't had a dream about the Reapers of late. Cole convinced himself that the others deserved a good night's sleep. Even the horses deserved a rest from their saddles.

The news that they would be able to sleep in a real bed and eat something different than old crusty bread, dried out meat and moldy cheese lifted their spirits so high that Cole did not want to crush them with his feeling of uneasiness. Everyone else seemed to be fine and Cole felt perhaps he was just tired and the awkwardness he was feeling was the result of stress.

As Cole watched his companions from under his hood, Maggie slipped some of the dried nightshade into Cole's water skin, and then capping the top she shook it so it would dissolve into the water. Ayla caught Maggie slipping the drug into Cole's water and she stared at Maggie with raised eyebrows. Maggie shook her head as a warning to Ayla. Ayla took a breath as if she were going to tell. Maggie started to panic but when Ayla let the air out in a huff and then rode away, Maggie breathed easy.

"Thank you Cole," Maggie said, handing it back to him, wiping her mouth as if she had just taken a drink.

Cole took the water skin and started to tuck it back in his supply bag.

"Aren't you thirsty Cole?" Maggie asked.

"No," Cole replied.

"Are you sure? You look like you're thirsty and it's really cold and refreshing," Maggie said.

"I'm fine Maggie," Cole replied annoyed.

"It will do you good Cole," Maggie insisted.

Cole looked over at Maggie and he could see in her that she was concerned for him. He knew he was worrying her. So just to make her happy Cole pulled the cap off the water skin and took a large swallow. With that one swallow Cole discovered how thirsty he was and before long he had drunk up all the water in his water skin. When it was empty Cole looked at the skin and then at Maggie.

"Something wrong?" Maggie asked.

"No it's just that this water tastes kind of bitter," Cole said.

"I thought it did too. The spring that we got it from must have had something in it to make it so," Maggie said, feeling her face turn red as she lied.

"Mine doesn't taste bitter and I got it from the same spring," Chanlyn said.

"That is rather odd," Maggie said, looking at Chanlyn with hard eyes.

"You must have been awfully thirsty," Maggie said, looking at the flat waterskin.

"I guess I was," Cole replied softly, giving Maggie a smile that never touched his eyes.

...

WOODS HOLLOW was larger than Kells. Its whitewashed, thatched roof buildings ringed around the village square and they looked warm and inviting to the weary travelers of the company, except to Cole. His uneasiness had been growing steadily stronger as they drew closer to the village. His eyes darted back and forth from under the hood of his cloak, as he tried to capture every movement and sound that might give warning to dangers unseen.

But something was happening to him that he could not explain. He felt a great weariness suddenly come upon him and the world started to blur around the edges of his vision. He knew he was tired, but the fear of the Reapers suddenly appearing from out of the darkness and taking the lives of his friends had frightened him to a point that he could not sleep even if he had the notion to. He had taken the watches for three nights, too frightened to close his eyes. Nightmares were waiting for him in the dark and were possibly waiting for him in the future.

His eyelids felt heavy as they entered the village. Cole rubbed them to try to wipe the grit of sleep from them, but it was no use, his vision was becoming unclear. He felt groggy and heavy headed. Out of the fuzziness Cole saw that the group had stopped in front of a building. Through his half closed eyes Cole read Travelers Inn.

"We have to keep going," Cole heard himself say, yet it seemed far way.

"Nonsense Cole," Maggie's voice said, as though she were some distance away.

What is wrong with me, Cole thought as he looked over at Maggie and she smiled at him. Suddenly Cole felt his world fall out from under him and he plummeted into the shadowy world of unconsciousness.

SHAFTS OF MOONLIGHT seeped in through the planks of a rooftop. Cole pulled his gaze down and was greeted with the familiar scene of a stable. He didn't recognize his surroundings, he didn't know whose stables he stood in but he felt closer to home with the smell of straw, hay and feed. Turning he found to his delight that

Gladadear stood within one of the stalls. His smile faded however when Cole noticed that she dug at the ground with her hooves nervously. Concerned Cole went over and hopped over the stall's gate. He patted her and rubbed her down, trying to calm her, but he knew that there was something wrong. Gladadear always had a sense for knowing when something was wrong or was out of place.

Cole stood stroking Gladadear trying to take in his surroundings, for the lanterns that hung from the stable support beam, threw the stable into shadow.

"There is nothing here," Cole whispered, as he searched the depth of the shadows with his eyes. Just then the air suddenly became still and the birds that nested within the beams of the stable took flight, escaping out through the open doors or windows of the stable. The horses went wild with fear, their eyes rolling in their heads as they snorted with trepidation. Gladadear even reared up and kicked at the stall gate, almost hitting Cole on the shoulder as a cold screech echoed throughout the stable.

Quickly Cole jumped from the stall and spun around looking for the source of the cry. He found it. The cry had come from a bird or at least Cole thought it was a bird. It was perched on a beam just above the door, its dark eyes stared down unblinking at him. Cole got the feeling that the large black bird was watching him. The moonlight showed the creature to have black feathers with a deep purple-feathered head. Its auburn eyes watched Cole as he took a step back and reached for the hilts of his swords. His innards twisted into knots as a he realized that the bird was dangerous.

The moment that Cole's hands moved toward his blades the bird attacked. Cole tried to pull free his whicka knives but the bird came at him too fast and he felt the knife-like talons rip through his shirt and skin along his shoulder. Warm blood ran down his arm, soaking into his shirt.

Perceiving that the bird might come back for a second attack, Cole lurched himself forwards. He hit the stable's packed dirt and felt a gust of wind and feathers rush past him, letting him know that the bird had indeed come back for a second assault. He was on his feet again watching as the bird swept around him, its wings fully outstretched.

As the bird came in for another attack, its wings began to flare up with flames. Cole stared, not really knowing what to think or do.

The bird soared toward him, flapping its wings and as it did small flames fell from it wings and landed on the bales of hay and straw, which caught fire immediately. In an instant the stable was consumed. Great waves surrounded him, encircling him in a ring of fire. The flames grew bigger and taller until there was nothing but a wall of fire. Within the inferno he could see silhouettes of people and hear screams of humans and horses. He reached out for them, but when his hands reached out the shadows disintegrated as if they were nothing but ash. Cole reached out for one silhouette that stood within the flames. This time the shadow did not disappear, but instead it grew more solid. Cole pulled hard and out of the flames he beheld the remains of a girl, but she was badly burned. He let go of her and she fell back into the fire and then disintegrated into nothing.

COLE'S EYES fluttered open and he found himself staring into semi-darkness. Disoriented and confused Cole rolled over onto his back and gave out a groan as the pain of stiffness and soreness spread through his body. His head hurt with a horrible headache and he felt unsteady, like the room was spinning in several directions at once.

Closing his eyes against the dizziness, Cole became conscious that he was lying in a bed with blankets tucked in around him. Someone had removed his boots and stocking as well as his cloak and jerkin, swords and belt.

When the dizziness passed, Cole opened his eyes and eased himself up into a sitting position on the bed. The room he was in was small and had a low ceiling, yet it was warm and comfortable. A small fire danced in the hearth, across the room, throwing shadows on the white washed walls and the ceiling. The only furniture in the room was the bed and a washstand, with its pitcher and bowl; the rest of the room was bare.

Cole let out a sigh as he rolled to his feet. He gradually made his way to the washbasin where he filled the bowl. Taking off his shirt, Cole used the ball of soap to scrub the dirt and sweat he had accumulated during the ten days journey.

"It is nothing like a hot bath," Cole said to himself missing the bathhouse in Aloria, "but it's better than nothing."

As he scrubbed his thoughts turned over what had happen to him. He knew that he had been drugged, knew that Maggie had been the one to slip the crushed up nightshade plant into his water, that was why it tasted so bitter. Cole had made the connection right before the plant had taken effect. Kaya had given it to him back in Aloria that was how he recognized the taste.

He remembered riding Gladadear down the small hills and coming to a town. They had come to an inn and that's when everything went black and Cole was caught up in the terrible nightmare.

As he was toweling himself off Cole took notice of the little looking glass that hung on the wall over the washstand. He was surprised to find that the reflection that stared back at him was one that he did not recognize. In the four short months since he had left Kells, he had changed both mentally and physically. The youthful face of boyhood was gone and in its place was a thinned and hollowed face. With the hours of running and riding, along with Wallace's training exercises, his body had become lean and thin. His muscles were tight and taut and his silver white hair seemed to be almost opaque. Cole turned away from his reflection and headed for his saddlebags. He pulled out a somewhat clean shirt and put it on. He was just barely putting on his stockings and boots when the door to his room opened slightly, then fully admitting Maggie.

"You're awake," Maggie said, a little too brightly.

Cole stood up and pulled on his jerkin without saying a word to her.

"You look better, now that you've had a few days of sleep," Maggie continued nervously, as she felt the tension that surrounded Cole.

Still Cole continued to ignore her as he pulled on his blades.

"Not going to talk to me then?" Maggie commented.

"What do you want me to say?" Cole muttered emotionless. "That was a dirty little trick you pulled on me."

"I know I shouldn't have done it and I feel awful about it but... but something had to be done."

"Had to be done huh?" he replied coldly. "I had to be drugged?"

"What else could I do?" Maggie nearly shouted. "Three days without sleep. You looked like you had just stepped out of your own grave, walking around like a dead man. You did not sleep, nor did you eat. I was not about to watch you drive yourself insane from exhaustion. I made you a promise. I did what I thought was right," Maggie spoke harshly.

Cole turned away from Maggie. He was angry, not only with her but also with himself for making Maggie worry.

"How long have I been *asleep*?" Cole asked more coldly than he intended.

"Two days," Maggie replied, her voice still a little high pitched from her anger.

"And where are we?" he asked getting his other shirt and stuffing it in his saddlebag.

"A town called Woods Hollow?" Maggie answered.

"I know that. That part I remember," Cole responded icily. "I mean what inn are we at?" he asked.

"Oh! It's called The Blackbird?" Maggie reported.

Cole suddenly stopped what he was doing as the image of a blackbird with steel feathers and a purple head flashed across his mind.

"It's a nice enough place. The beds are soft and free of bed bugs, but the food is somewhat questionable, doesn't seem to bother Sir Arthur though. He drank enough the night before and the last night to literally fill a barrel and then slept till noon today." Maggie chattered.

Cole spun around to face Maggie.

"Maggie," Cole cried, breaking through her nervous chatter.

Maggie stopped and raised an eyebrow to him.

"What did you say this place was called?" Cole asked.

"The Blackbird," Maggie replied.

"I think it's time we were leaving," he stated, scooping up his saddlebags and flinging them over his shoulder then moving for the door. He grabbed Maggie's hand and dragged her out with him as he left the room.

"Where are the others?" Cole asked, rushing down the cramped little hallway.

"I'd expect that they are in the commons. It is almost suppertime. That's why I came to check on you in the first place. To see if you were up and if you were, whether you wanted supper," Maggie rushed her sentences like she always did. "Why is there something the matter?" she asked as they came to a flight of stairs.

"Yes. Something is the matter. This place isn't safe. We need to leave and we need to leave now," Cole replied, taking the stairs two at a time. "There's going to be a fire that takes the whole town."

"If there's going to be a fire shouldn't we tell someone?" Maggie asked.

"I think I'm the one that starts it," Cole replied. "If we leave then…"

"Then you won't be around to start it," Maggie finished. "I understand now, but Sir Arthur is not going to like leaving." Maggie muttered.

"I don't care what he likes and dislikes. We need to leave!"

They had come to the bottom of the stairs and into the common room. The place was not unlike the White Rose back in Kells, with a large hearth, tables and chairs, and antlers decorating the walls. The room was crowded but not quite filled to its capacity. There was a hum of conversation with the sound of a minstrel woman singing in the back ground as Cole entered. He found Sir Arthur, along with Artemis, Ayla, and Chanlyn seated at a table in the far corner, enjoying a meal of meat pies and mugs of cider.

"And the dead has risen!" Arthur joked seeing Cole.

"Going somewhere?" Ayla asked, seeing Cole saddlebags hanging from his shoulder

"We need to leave," Cole said.

"Had one of your visions then," Artemis mocked.

"This place isn't safe," Cole remarked.

"I can assure you sir my inn is quite safe, I don't let any riff-raff off the street come in," said a rather large portly man, he, along with a young serving girl were there to drop off a few trays of meats and cheese, fruits and breads to the table and to bring more mugs. Cole eyes widened as he looked at the girl. She was the girl from his dream and the image of her badly burnt and fading away into the flames increased his desire to leave.

"We have to leave now. Please!" Cole pleaded.

"There is nothing to worry you Cole. All is safe," Sir Arthur said, taking one of the many mugs. "Right master innkeeper?" Sir Arthur said, bringing the mug to his mouth and taking a long drag.

"Right you are Sir Arthur, right you are," the innkeeper replied cheerfully. "Now everything seems to be in order, but if you need anything else do not hesitate to ask." Seeing that all was right with the dishes, the innkeeper patted his large belly and then left to tend the bar. At seeing Sir Arthur place another empty mug on the table, Maggie raised an eyebrow.

"Only cider my dear girl. Can't have what happened last night happen again," Arthur chuckled. "Take a seat Cole, you must be hungry after so many days of not eating,"

"What happened last night?" Cole asked, whispering in Maggie's ear as he slid in next to Chanlyn.

"He got a little drunk and started telling people about you and your...talents." Maggie whispered back.

"Now I think we really do need to leave," Cole said, looking about the inn to see if anyone was watching him and spotted two gentlemen at the bar that were looking at him. The hairs on the back of his neck were starting to rise on end.

"Father hopes that anyone that heard Arthur, might think that it was just a drunken rant," Maggie whispered.

"Why didn't we leave right then and there?" Cole asked.

"We couldn't wake you," Chanlyn whispered. "Plus if we ran, it might give the impression that you really are what you are."

"A seer. Yeah well I've seen something and it isn't good," Cole said.

Cole told Chanlyn about his latest dream, Chanlyn nodded and shrugged his shoulders not really showing any urgency about his dream.

"We'll just keep you away from fire and birds," Chanlyn said, as he bit into a meat pie. While Cole was talking to Chanlyn, the two men that had been watching him started making their way towards the table.

"You boy," one man spoke with a slurred accent as he pointed his thick finger at Cole. "Are you the magic user?"

Cole looked over at Maggie for an explanation.

"Sir Arthur last night said that you had the blood of the Elfain warriors running through your veins," Maggie muttered.

"Ah yes. I might have exaggerated a bit last night," Sir Arthur said, a little red faced.

"Show me a magic trick," the man said, looking at Cole with blood shot eyes.

Cole looked at the two men that stood before their table. One was huge with large broad shoulders. His arms were as thick as his legs and the other was thin and gangling with a smile of yellowing teeth.

"I don't know any tricks," Cole muttered, and then he turned away from the drunk.

"I am Magnus of the Northland. The best sword's master in all of Albavar and I want a magic trick," the man shouted, pulling out a knife and slamming it down onto the tabletops.

"Gentlmen please. Come let me buy you a drink, in fact let me by you several drinks," Sir Arthur said, trying to defuse the situation.

The inn had suddenly gone silent. All conversation had stopped. Everyone turned to look at what was going on and no one did anything to help. They just stood there, watching. The minstrel woman had stopped her playing and singing and the innkeeper stood behind the bar wiping down a glass and trying to ignore the drunken man.

"If you do not have a magic trick for me then perhaps one of your friends do?"

Magnus pulled his knife free from that table and took a step towards Ayla. Cole clenched his fist and hot anger began to course within him. He could feel the energy rush through him. He could feel the energy dancing in his toes and in his hands and fingertips. Laughter exploded in Cole's head as the voice he had heard once before echoed in his eardrum.

What a fool. What a fool indeed. Show him a trick. Burn him! Burn him away. Burn the place to the ground and all those within that do not help you. Let your true power show.

The vision of the whole town consumed in fire flashed through Cole's mind. He smiled to himself at the very idea of it. Of seeing the arrogant man that stood before him burn away, much like the girl he saw burn. He could feel the flames on his fingertips.

"Stop," Cole said his voice not his own. "You want a trick?"

"Uhh…yes," Magnus replied, his voice a little shaky.

Even in his drunken state, Magnus could feel the air around the boy change and he could feel the hair on the back on his neck stand up on end.

"Very well," Cole muttered.

Magnus and his friend, along with the rest of the common room, waited for something to happen, but nothing did save for the feeling of a little puff of wind pass just over his cheek.

"There. Your trick is done," Cole replied coldly.

Magnus felt a sharp sting on his cheek. His hand went up to his cheekbone. It felt wet and when his hand came way from his face, his fingertips were red with blood. He turned to look behind him and was shocked to see his knife jutting out of a barrel, still slightly vibrating. He wiped the blood away and turned back to see Cole standing there with another table knife in his hands.

"Leave now or my next little trick will go in your heart," Cole whispered quietly, but the whole room heard.

The room was dead silent as the stares of the onlookers went back and forth from Magnus to Cole.

"I would leave and rather quickly. For your own safety," Wallace's voice rung out from the doorway.

Magnus and his friend turned in the direction the voice had come from. What they saw was three men cloaked in black with their hands on the hilts of their swords. Magnus had to admit defeat; he knew that he could not go up against three grown men and this strange white haired boy. He lifted up his hands and backed away. Magnus and his partner moved past Wallace, Gildon and Grayson with a swift retreat. The rest of the common room seemed to settle down for they went back to their drinks and conversations.

Cole let out a breath and fell down onto the bench, his hands shaking slightly as he released his hold on the table knife.

"Are you alright Cole?" Maggie asked, seeing how pale Cole had suddenly gone.

"Mmm…fine," Cole muttered.

But he was far from fine. The moment he heard the voice come to him he felt the strangest feeling come over him, a sense of pure and unruly power wash through him. Nothing could touch him. He was invincible and had the power of the gods. He could have killed Magnus, with one swift move. He could have taken the man's life, burned him, he could see the flames, see how to call the fire spirit and bend it to do his will and for a few mere seconds Cole considered it. And yet within those few seconds a horrible feeling of fear struck him and it pulled him out of his power hunger trance and his vision cleared, free of flames.

"You did well, Cole," Wallace said, coming up behind him and patting his shoulder.

"I was terrified." Cole muttered.

"Mmm…only a fool wouldn't be," Wallace said.

"It nice to see you awake Cole," Gildon said with a wink. "Bright eyed and all that."

"However did you do that?" Ayla asked.

"I don't know," Cole replied. "I just got mad. And the next thing I knew I had his knife in my hand and I'm throwing it."

"Remind me never to make you mad," Chanlyn said, from under his hood.

"Wise words," replied Sir Arthur.

"And now my friends, I hate to be the barer of bad news but it's time we were leaving. Word in town is that we are not the only visitors here. It seems there are a few Red Cloaks here as well," said Wallace.

"Red Cloaks?" Maggie whispered with an intake of breath. "How did they know we are here?

"The Red Cloaks have spies everywhere. Word must have reached them of our arrival," Grayson said.

"We have been discovered and it won't be too long before they come looking for us here, considering what just happened. I can say for certain that rumors of tonight's events will reach the ears of every person in this town and beyond by morning's end tomorrow. Our time of relaxation and comfort is at an end."

Deep disappointment was expressed from the others but Cole felt a great weight lift off his shoulders at hearing they were leaving. He had managed to control his wielding and in that he felt that the town was safe.

CHAPTER 30

SHAFTS OF MOONLIGHT seeped through the planks of the rooftop as Cole entered the inn's stable. He had been assigned to saddle the horses as the others made ready to leave. Upon entering the stable, Cole found that it was not empty, a boy a few years younger than he was saddling a chestnut mare.

"I can help you, sir, once I get this horse saddled and ready to go," the boy said.

"Thank you, but if I may, I'll start preparing my horse and my companions horses while you work," Cole said, jumping over the gate that held Gladadear.

"If you wish sir," the boy said.

Cole's hands moved fast in saddling Gladadear. It was not hard considering he was well practiced at the task. He was bent down low buckling a cinch when he heard the clip clop of horse hooves on stone. When Cole finished and he stood up straight, the horse and the boy were gone.

He finished tying his saddlebag on to his saddle and situated his bow and quiver on his saddle. Once he was finished with Gladadear he hopped over the stall gate and made his way towards Brom. He suddenly stopped when he noticed the shafts of moonlight floating in through the cracks of the roof.

"No!" Cole whispered, "No! This cannot be."

Cole spun around and looked up above the stable doors, expecting to see a purple-headed black bird. But there was nothing there. His arm gave out twinges of pain, telling him that his vision was about to take place. He was about to take off running but was stopped short when a hand whipped out from the dark and covered his mouth and grabbed him from behind.

"Do you think you can make a fool out of me and get away with it?"

Cole immediately recognized the voice belonging to Magnus.

"I would kill you right here and now, but there is someone that wants you alive. So I will give you what you gave me and take what I am owed."

Cole then felt the hard tug at his waist as his Wicka knives were pulled free from their sheaths. He then felt the sharp sting across his cheekbone as Magnus cut it with one of his own knives. Once Magnus had the knives Cole was thrown to the ground.

"Those are mine," Cole yelled angrily, getting to his feet and charging Magnus.

Magnus watched Cole rush towards him and with a malicious smile on his face kicked Cole in the ribs and sent him to his knees,

"Not so tough any more. You may be strong with your spirit, but you can't hold onto it for very long," Magnus laughed, as did his friend.

"Gentlemen please don't harm my prize. The Lord Griffon won't pay for damaged goods," said a lovely and singsong voice.

"Megara, we did your little act for you. Now when do we get paid?" Magnus asked greedily.

Cole looked up to see the minstrel woman entering the stable. She was dressed in a silken dress and cloak of black with strips of purple that covered the head and skirt. The dim lantern light within the stable gave the black of her cloak a shine that almost made it look to be made of feathers.

"You will get paid when we deliver our little duckling to the Red Cloaks. So why don't you tie his hands and gag him? Then we can be on our way," Megera ordered.

Cole tried to fight, he tried to call up that rush of energy, but nothing was happening. Cole kicked and punched, he cried out but there was no one around to hear him. Magnus gave Cole a hard slap across the face that sent him reeling, so much so that he could do little as his hands were pulled behind his back and were tied with coarse ropes. A gag that smelled like rotting potatoes was forced into his mouth. All the while the minstrel woman Megara watched Cole with her intelligent and knowing brown eyes.

"I must admit you are quite a wonder. Your wielding is quite amazing for one so young. I could read the strength in you the moment you walked into the common room. A real *Wildling*, I am impressed. Although I don't think Magnus was impressed. He had a pretty good scare because of you. But what can I say? He does get paid for his little performance. And well Winston, he's there for effect. The poor man is dumb. But what can he do? He must make a living. Oh dear listen to me jabbering the night away, mustn't keep a captain of the Redcloaks waiting. Now where is that boy with our horses? Oh it doesn't matter. Magnus pick him up and let's get out of here."

Winston picked Cole up and roughly threw him across his shoulder. As he moved to follow the others, a cold hiss echoed through the air. An arrow came out of the night and stuck Magnus in the shoulder. He cried out in pain as another arrow hit Winston in the thigh.

Cole yelled, but the gag stopped any understandable sounds from coming out.

The giant of a man dropped Cole to the ground and pulled the arrow out of his thigh. He looked around scanning the dark night to see where the red-feathered arrow had come from. Two more arrows came flying, this time black feathers and they were headed for the Minstel woman. They nearly struck her but she moved just a few inches to the left. The arrows flew past her and stuck deep into one of the stable support beams.

Cole stared at the woman and she noticed his shock.

"Just a little trick of my own," Megara smiled.

The woman's smile never left her face even when Grayson, Gildon and Ayla came charging in through the stable doors and attacked the kidnappers. Gildon headed straight for Magnus, as Grayson headed for Winston and Ayla went for the woman.

Cole watched the deadly dances awestruck. He never knew how deadly they were, not until now. Even though Grayson was older, he was fast. He danced around the mute giant with amazing speed. Cole now understood where Gildon's learned his close quarters fighting technique. All Grayson used was his extremities; no matter how Winston attacked, Grayson had a counter attack with a kick or a punch. Winston tried to use a knife on him, but with one swift move Grayson had disarmed him and seeing he was disarmed bolted and fled for the door.

Gildon used his bow against Magnus, while Magnus attacked Gildon with Cole's own blades. Gildon spun his bow, deflecting Magnus' attempts to stab him. With a dastardly twist of the blades Magnus caught Gildon's bow between the blades and ripped it out of his hands and flung it away into the shadows of the stable, leaving Gildon open. Magnus stepped out for the striking blow but Gildon's reaction was a millisecond ahead of Magnus. When Magnus stepped out, Gildon caught his leg and swept it out from under him. With his support leg gone, Magnus fell back and the Wicka knifes flew from his hands out of reach. At that moment Gildon pulled an arrow from his quiver and went to stab the man in the shoulder, but Magnus seeing Winston flee followed after him as quick as he could get away.

While the two men were fighting, so too was Ayla. Ayla charged the minstrel woman who spun out with her cloak and in an instant had unsheathed two short swords. Cole knew what the minstrel woman was intending, because of the flaring and blurred layers of fabric from the cloak, they hid the two blades. And Ayla thinking that it was just a cloak would run right into them and be cut to ribbons.

Cole tried to shout out a warning to Ayla but the gag in his mouth prevented his warning from reaching her, still Cole screamed. It all happened in a matter of seconds and yet to Cole the world around him slowed as he watched Ayla run forward and at the last second before reaching the woman and her swords, she fell to her knees and slid right under the flaring fabric and the deadly steel blades. As she slid under she pulled an arrow from her quiver and nocked it to her bow then popped up onto her feet and swung around to face the bard. All three fighters now faced the minstrel woman with their bows. Seeing that she was out numbered Megara grabbed Cole by the hair and pulled him to his feet, using him as a shield.

"Let him go!" Ayla ordered through clenched teeth.

Megara's eyes darted back and forth from Ayla to Grayson to Gildon and then back as she moved walking backwards for the doors with Cole and one of her knives to his throat.

"Back up or I will slit his throat," Megara threatened.

"You injure one hair on his head and I shoot," Ayla said coldly.

"You won't shoot. You wouldn't risk it. You could hit him."

"You have a choice. Let him go and you may just walk out of here alive. If you don't you'll end up with an arrow in your eye."

"You can't make that shot, not without hurting the boy," Megara scoffed.

"I never miss," Ayla replied icily, pulling back her bowstring to a full draw.

Megara looked into Ayla's eyes and knew the girl was telling the truth. From the corner of her eye she saw that she was close to the doors. Taking her chances, she shoved Cole forward and as he was falling, she threw one of her blades at a lantern. The blade knocked the lantern from its hook and it shattered on the stone floor, spilling oil everywhere. Immediately the dry straw and hay caught a flame and it spread rapidly.

Megara turned and ran. She passed under the door just as Wallace and Sir Arthur came running in.

"Get her," Ayla cried.

Turning directly on his heels, Arthur ran after the woman.

Grayson cut Cole's hands free and pulled the gag from his mouth, and then they all turned to run after Sir Arthur and the minstrel woman.

"Wait!" Cole yelled. "The fire, we have to stop the fire."

"What about the Redcloaks, no doubt she is running to tell them where they can find us?"Ayla asked urgently.

"If we don't stop the fire, it will burn the whole town down," Cole yelled.

Looking into Cole's eyes they all understood.

"Gildon, help get the horses out, the rest of you grab anything that will extinguish the fire." Wallace ordered.

Horse blankets and buckets were grabbed and dunked in troughs full of water. Those with the blankets proceeded to slap at the flames and then run back to the water and start again. Gildon ran to the stalls of the terrified horses and opened each of the stall's gates and slapped the horses to get them running. Somewhere, someone shouted out an alarm of fire and more people came to help. Among them were Maggie, Chanlyn, along with others that were staying at the inn.

"Chanlyn," Cole called through the smoke as he coughed, his lungs feeling like they themselves were on fire. "Chanyln can you blow out the fire like you did with the candles back home?"

"This is a lot bigger than candles," Chanlyn called, as he slapped at the flames.

The flames of the fire were huge now. They were reaching up through the roof. The heat within the barn was intense and the smoke was filling the fighter's lungs, burning them.

"Please Chanlyn!" Cole coughed.

"If I do it wrong, I can make it worse," Chanlyn cried.

"I know you can do this," Cole said.

Cole watched through watery eyes as Chanlyn closed his eyes and took in a smoky breath. Then Chanlyn brought up his hands, spread out with palms up and slapped them together. A strong and overwhelming blast of wind blew through the barn. The fire was blown out save for a few sparks which were quickly put out by a few slaps from the wet blankets.

"My stable! My beautiful stable," the innkeeper wailed as he took in the damage.

The support beam where the lantern had hung had taken the brunt of the damage. The straw and hay had been burnt to piles of ash. Whatever else that had burned in the fire was scorched black by the heat.

"Ha, your beautiful stables. Be grateful that it was the stables and not the inn. In fact be grateful that the fire did not spread to the inn and then take the whole town. I told you not to build your stable so close!" a pudgy woman, who Cole took to be the innkeeper's wife, said stepping in front of the man and shaking a finger at him.

"Didn't I tell him?" the woman said looking at a girl who nodded her head in agreement.

"Yes you did tell me but how did the fire start?" The innkeeper wondered out loud. Cole took a step forward ready to explain but was interrupted by Sir Arthur's cry.

"I have him!" Arthur's voice came in from the darkness.

All turned towards Arthur as he came in dragging someone behind him. When Arthur entered the semi-circle that the fighters had formed he flung his prisoner onto the ground. Cole stared at the frightened boy that was the inn's groomsman.

"That's not even one of them," Cole said.

"What?" Arthur cried, "It has to be one of the culprits. He was the only one that I saw out there."

"James where have you been?" the Innkeeper cried and he looked down on the boy. Shaking with fear the boy looked up at his master as he got to his feet.

"I was waiting out front sir. I readied the horses as you requested and took them to the front for the riders to take the reins from me," the boy said. "I waited and no one came, then out of the darkness they came running from around the back. She shoved me aside and took a horse without paying. I was running after her when this man," the boy James pointed to Arthur, "tackled me to the ground and started dragging me back towards the inn and she got away without paying."

"This woman that I was to capture, why is she so important," Arthur asked.

"She said that she is with the Red Cloaks" Cole said. "She was going to take me to some Red Cloak captain named Griffon."

"Oh dear," Maggie muttered.

"Which means we don't have much time. The Red Cloaks are nearby. We must leave quickly," Wallace ordered,

"I gather then she is a bounty hunter. Then there must be a price for you," Gildon said with a worried expression.

"Aye, and no doubt he is wanted dead or alive," Grayson replied.

CHAPTER 30

"WE CAMP HERE for the night," Wallace declared as they approached a copse of willows near a small spring in the last rays of daylight. "Tend to your horses and quickly set up camp. Then we shall discuss where we are headed."

They had fled the inn two nights ago. The night they had left the inn had been a long one. It had been a blind race, a race that had not ended with the rise of the sun. Megara had obviously found Captain Griffon of the Red Cloaks and given him news about their location, for a group of about twenty horsemen appeared on the horizon the morning after the incident at the inn. At first they were mere specs of black in the far off distance, but gradually they became far more visible as they gained more ground.

Wallace pushed them from morning until they could go no farther from lack of light. They made their camp and hid themselves in a grove of weeping willows. The bending branches hid them and their horses out of sight and from the searching eyes of the Red Cloaks. Again he ordered them to build no fires and posted watches for fear of a surprise attack. The game of cat and mouse had lasted for two nights and three days, until on the third day when the last rays of sunlight began to peek over the western horizon the horsemen had disappeared.

"There is no sign of them," Sir Arthur said anxiously.

"Do you think they have given up?" Gildon asked, as he uncinched his saddle.

"I do not think so. They saw us as clear as we saw them. They would not give up the chase with their prize in their sights," Grayson said. "They are more than likely up to something."

"Whatever their intentions we will not stop our march," Wallace said.

"But surely we can take it easy. We need more rest than what we have been getting Master Wallace. We have been running all these days with little rest. I can hardly ride from weariness," Sir Arthur said.

"It is best that we put a few leagues between us and them while we still can," Wallace said looking discouraged.

"You will run us ragged and then where will we be?" Sir Arthur complained.

"We do not have to run much longer, Sir Arthur, we are almost there," Wallace answered.

"And where is there?" Arthur asked.

"Blackthorn Forest," Wallace replied, his head nodding to the still darkened horizon line.

There was dead silence as all the companions looked towards the distant horizon. Cole looked around him, wondering why there was such a stone cold expression on Gildon, Grayson and Sir Arthur's faces.

"You cannot mean for us to cross through that dreaded forest Master Wallace?" Grayson asked.

"Blackthorn is our destination," Wallace answered.

"You cannot be serious."

For the past few days, the "draw" Cole felt to the place where the weapon lay hidden was getting stronger. The feeling that Cole had followed did indeed lead them to follow streams and river, across hills, glens and meadows. Now he was led to the last phase of their journey, the forest of Blackthorn.

When Cole told Wallace which way they were heading, he did not seem surprised that they would end up in Blackthorn. He seemed to know where they were going.

"Within the forest lies the remains of one of the old cities, Aydrien or Ayden's city. It's suspected that it is nothing but ruins now. Shelrin destroyed it months after the destruction of Alorian," Wallace explained.

"And you think that is where we will find one of the seven weapons?" Gildon asked.

"Yes." Wallace answered.

"How can you be so sure that is where the weapon lies?" Sir Arthur asked.

"Cole feels it's there," Wallace said exposing the secret.

"He feels that its there," Artemis roared. "Well then if stable boy "feels" its there then it must be," he mocked.

"How long are you going to act like a giant jackass?" Ayla spat angerly.

Everyone turned and looked at her with shocked expressions on their faces as she got to her feet and stood in front of Artemis.

"You have been jealous of Cole for a long time. Probably since the day you met. I don't believe he has done anything to earn your spite. I hear he saved your back at Kells and has probably saved all our lives over and over again without us even knowing it," Ayla whispered coldly so the Red Cloaks could not hear her, yet the whispering seemed to give her rant more of a scarey effect. "If you don't believe that Cole can feel the weapons that's fine. But I believe that he can and will find the weapons. If you don't believe in Cole then why did you volunteer to come in the first place?" Ayla demanded. "Was it to see him fail? Because Cole won't fail, I'll make sure of that," with that she folded her arms and sat down.

The camp lay silent for more than a few moments. Feeling some-what awkward at Ayla's rant, Cole didn't know what to make of it. Ayla had defended him. He had always thought that Ayla didn't like him and here she was standing up for him. Girls just didn't make sense to him.

"Aydrien uhh," Grayson muttered breaking the silence.

"What about Aydrien?" Gildon asked.

" It is quite possible that there is a weapon there and I think that it's a bow we are looking for,"Grayson replied.

"How do you know?" Sir Arthur asked.

"When I was young, I was told the story by my Grandmother of a white tree growing within the great city of Aydrien and that it bloomed silver leaves in the years of peace. Yet when darkness threat-ened the land, the great stone archer, that watched over the city, would wake to fight and defend its people," Grayson spoke. "It might just be possible that Cole has led us to the right place."

"You would have us go into Blackthorn, believing in an old story you were told?" Sir Arthur asked in disbelief.

"Stories are what have led us here in the firstplace," Grayson spoke. "For Gildon is always telling us that there is some truth in all stories. But why not tell us that you suspected we were heading for Blackthorn?" Grayson asked turning to Cole.

"That was my doing Master Grayson," Wallace spoke up. "Cole did not know where we here heading, all he knew was that we were being guided towards a forest in the East. I told him not to say anything. If I would have told you that I suspected that Blackthorn was where we were headed, would you have come?" Wallace asked, presenting the question to all. "Also I did not know who I could trust. The Red Cloaks were and still are after us. They also have ways of finding out things. If the knowledge got out that we were heading for Blackthorn, the Red Cloaks or anyone else that wishes us harm could intercept us or be waiting for us, hence the secrets."

"I understand," Grayson nodded. "I believe I would have done the same thing."

Gildon and the others nodded their heads in agreement as well.

"Excuse me, but what is Blackthorn Forest?" Chanlyn asked curiously. "You talk of it as if it were a forbidden place."

"You have never heard of Blackthorn?" Gildon asked in wonder.

"No," Chanlyn said. "You must remember most of us grew up on the other side of the mountain. Blackthorn is not known to us."

"It's haunted," Ayla cried. "It's filled with ghosts and demons, left there by Shelrin to attack any who wander into the forest."

"Who told you that?" Gildon asked.

"Master Witkins."

"Master Witkins tells a lot of tales to scare younglings," Grayson commented.

"He said any who enter the forest are lost forever and never seen again," Ayla said shivering.

"Never seen again?" Gildon asked.

"Aye," Ayla whispered.

"Then where do all the stories about the ghosts and demons come from?" Gildon asked.

The company laughed at Ayla's confusion.

"Yes well, whether or not the forest is haunted it is still a dangerous place. One can get lost rather quickly. It is a place that has yet to be fully explored. How are we to find this ruined city? The forest is vast and we know nothing of it true dangers. We may lose our way and be lost forever. We may be the ones that are never seen again," Sir Arthur said.

"I do not think that we will lose our way, we have Cole after all," Maggie said happily. " As you said he can feel the way!"

"What do you think Cole, can you guide us?" Sir Arthur asked.

"Of course he can," Gildon said. "He's done it so far."

"Too true," Sir Arthur voiced disconcertingly. "Too true."

"We will leave at first morn's light. All of you get some rest. Tomorrow we will reach Blackthorn," Wallace announced.

COLE WAS SUDDENLY jerked awake as a leather-gloved hand clamped over his mouth. Thinking that the Red Cloaks had finally found them he fought his attacker, jabbing him in the gut with his elbow.

"Easy boy, it's me," Wallace's voice whispered in the dark.

Cole instantly relaxed and Wallace removed his hand.

"What's going on?" Cole asked. Wallace placed a finger to his lips telling Cole to keep quiet, and then with the same finger beckoned him to follow. Following his prompting, Cole followed Wallace to the edge of the willows. Artemis was there bent down low on one knee with the hood of his cloak pulled over his head.

"Is he still there?" Wallace asked in a soft whisper.

"Yes." Artemis answered.

"What's going on," Cole asked.

"Artemis spotted a Red Cloak," Wallace explained. "No doubt he's a scout of some sort, possibly one of the twenty that has been following us or possibly from a larger branch. I can't tell. I want you to use your tracing Cole and see what we are up against. We need to know whether we need to run or whether we can fight," Wallace asked.

"Where's the one that Artemis spotted?" Cole asked.

"Just there, about fifty yards from the way we came," Artemis answered, nodding his head in the direction he was looking. Cole looked out from under the curtain of the weeping willow vines that softly swayed in the wind. He looked out at the hill swept plain that they had crossed just a few short hours before. The moon was high and full, illuminating the top of the hills. He couldn't see the man that Artemis had noticed at first. But then a shadow moved and Cole caught sight of him. He bent down touching the grass-covered ground. Instantly he was running forward to where the scout lay on his belly, slowly crawling forward through the grass. He moved soundlessly and slowly, so slow that he did not make the tall blades of grass shift in his wake. Cole could tell by the man's skill that he was a true tracker. The scout stopped for a moment and turned his head to the left. Cole followed the man's action and saw that there was another Red Cloak scout, crawling through the grass the same way as his fellow Red Cloak. Again Cole's minds eye ran forward to where the other scout lay. There he spotted another Redcloak, moving slowly towards the grove of willows.

Cole rushed around the grove and counted at least ten Redcloak scouts making their way towards them. Wondering where the other men had disappeared to, Cole backtracked the trail they had ridden the day before. Reaching his limit of a league, Cole could see nothing out of the ordinary. As he was about to let go, he saw a flicker of orange out of the corner of his eye to the south. He ran forward, pushing himself a half a mile more until Cole had to stop. His head had begun to hurt and with every step he took the pain in his head grew in intensity. Yet through blurry eyes and the pain, Cole made out an infantry of Red Cloaks moving across the plains with hundreds of torches lighting their way. Cole counted at least a hundred marching towards their little camp.

Cole let go of the ground and made his report to Wallace.

"Artemis is right. They're Red Cloaks. At least ten of them are moving in. No doubt to try and capture us," Cole reported.

"Ten?" Artemis cried.

"Shh!" both Wallace and Cole shushed at once.

"Ten?" Artemis whispered, "Where did the other men go."

"There's at least a hundred men behind us," Cole remarked. "It is most likely they went back and joined them."

"Why so many following us?" Artemis asked.

"Cole, within their ranks did you see a coat of arms of some sort, a silver swirling bird. Its wings spread out, while the talons hold double bladed axes."

"I didn't see much. I had to push my limits in order to see beyond a league. What I saw was alot of blurry torches and a lot of shadows moving forward. I gave myself a bit of a headache."

"I see. It is more than likely a hunting party," Wallace reasoned.

"A what?" Artemis and Cole both asked in unison.

"Let's just say I would rather face a hellhound than a Red Cloak hunting party," Wallace answered.

Cole looked at Wallace with apprehension.

Nothing could be worse than facing a hellhound, Cole thought.

"Right now we have little time. Wake the others, but be quiet about it. We cannot fight this battle here. Our only option is to run. We need to try and make it to the woods. There we might be able to lose them. Go quickly!"

Artemis and Cole did as ordered and ran back to the camp. Wallace looked out across the grass-covered hills. He couldn't see anything but he knew they were out there and with every moment that passed they were getting closer.

When Wallace got back to the camp, Artemis and Cole had woken everyone up.

"What is it that you want boy?" Sir Arthur was almost shouting at Artemis. "It's not yet time to go. Away with you."

Wallace stepped past Artemis and looked at Arthur with such a cold glare that the man's next word came out as a stutter and then faded to a whimper.

"Sir Arthur," Wallace whispered. "The enemy has surrounded us and is now making their way towards us. If you continue to be as loud as you are, you might find an arrow in your heart. Now silently get to your horse without making so much as a peep."

Sir Arthur said nothing as he quietly followed orders. "There is but one chance for us to escape. We have to make it to the woods.

Understand? The Red Cloaks are not merciful or kind. You ride hard," Wallace whispered. "Now get to your horses. Do not stop until you are safe within Blackthorn. If we ride fast enough maybe we can escape before those who are sneaking in can follow us."

Cole breath's came in shaky rasps as he climbed atop Gladadear. The little mare seemed to sense that there was something amiss, for her ears were up and she dug at the ground.

"Easy Glad! Easy," Cole whispered into the mare's ear. They moved through the grove as silently as possibly. Once they reached the edge of the trees they stopped. Cole could see the blackened horizon in the distant. He wondered how far Blackthorn was from where they were. Five, ten, maybe even fifteen leagues. He feared that the range was too long for Gladadear to run after not having a whole lot of rest herself. He prayed that the shaggy mare would have the strength and speed to carry them both to safety.

Wallace looked around him, making sure all were with him and were ready to run. He nodded and with a great cry kicked Brom into a run. They all burst forth from the grove, all in a wild gallop for Blackthorn. At first Cole could see no one behind him. No doubt they had surprised the hidden scouts, rushing from the grove and getting a head start. But it was not too long before the thundering sounds of the Red Cloak's horses came echoing in behind them. Cole turned to look over his shoulder and by the light of the silver moon he could see the cloaks of the Red Cloaks flaring out behind them, as they were quickly gaining ground. As Cole turned back around he heard the sharp hiss of an arrow pass over him. He ducked low in his saddle, making himself as small a target as he could. He guided Gladadear in a zigzag pattern for Merryrick taught him that it's easy to shoot someone who is riding in a straight line, harder if they can't predict your movements. Another arrow flew passed, this time it came from ahead of him. Cole dared to lift his head and look between Gladadear's ears. Ayla had just fired an arrow and was getting ready to fire another one. Her arrow flew high and then suddenly dropped, hitting one of the scouts in the shoulder, knocking him from his horse. After Ayla's arrows, Grayson's flew next and then Wallace's. Although none hit a target it made the Red Cloaks pull back, out of the range of the flying arrows.

Time seemed to pass slowly. To Cole it appeared that no matter how long or fast Gladadear ran the thin black outline of Blackthorn was not getting any closer. Cole looked back over his shoulder one more time. The Red Cloaks were gaining on them again, their bows ready to fire.

Using his knees, Cole guided Glad as he pulled out his bow, glad that he had strung it earlier. Like everything else in his life, Merryrick had taught him how to ride and shoot.

"Riding and shooting is easy once you get a handle on it. The hard part is hitting your target not only while are you moving, but also when your target is moving. You have to be a kind of fortune teller, predicting where your target is going to be and that is when you shoot," Cole recalled. He nocked an arrow, turned and let it go. His arrow hit a Redcloak and he fell.

"Two down eight to go," he thought.

Ayla, Grayson, Gildon, Wallace, Chanlyn and even Maggie let loose a swarm of arrows at the Red Cloaks, who fell back slightly, out of range of the hissing projectiles and then returned fire when the others were nocking more arrows. Cole felt a wisp of air pass him and then felt a slight sting on his upper arm as an arrow nicked him.

They were close now, so close that the black horizon turned into individual shapes of trees. They just had to climb over one more hill-top and descend it and they would be home free. The closer they got to the rising hill and to Blackthorn the more arrows came speeding towards them.

"Just a bit more old girl," Cole encouraged Glad. "Just a bit more." Poor Glad was breathing heavily and sweat had started collecting in her hair at the neck. Gladadear snorted then took off up the rise. Reaching the top, Cole looked down and froze as he stared down at a white swirl of water, a river.

It was in those mere seconds, when the moonbeams illuminated Cole from behind, that it came out of nowhere. He felt the impact first, so great was it that it sent him forward, up and onto Gladadear's neck. Then came the pain. The fierce, agonizing pain felt as if hot metal had been shoved through his right shoulder. Cole let out a scream, and nearly fell from Gladadear. Pain and nausea enveloped him and half unconscious Cole kicked Gladadear down the hill, fighting to stay awake. He could feel warm blood running down his back and chest. Utter darkness was threatening to take over him as Gladadear reached the riverbank.

"Cole. Just hang on," Cole heard Grayson yell.

Arrows came whizzing down at them in a hailstorm. In his weakened state Cole heard Wallace give out a scream of pain. Someone must have grabbed Gladadear reins and led her into the river, for Cole was barely hanging on. His eyes were half closed when he barely registered that he was in water.

"He's not going to make it," Grayson yelled, noticing Cole. "It's bad."

The Red Cloaks had reached the top of the rise and were looking down on them. Then they too started descending towards the riverbank. The storm of arrows continued raining down on them as they tried to cross the river. Suddenly Gladadear reared up screaming as an arrow struck her in the rear. Half unconscious, Cole couldn't hold on and he slipped from her saddle into the river. He could hear muffled cries as the current pulled him under. The sharp edge of a rock came up and the last thing that Cole remembered before he was over taken by darkness was a loud CRACK and then he knew no more.

CHAPTER 31

COLE WOKE UP SCREAMING as every nerve within him registered pain. He screamed until he could scream no more, then turned over and threw up. Water spilled out of him and it seemed that it would never end. When it ended he fell back breathing hard. Half dazed Cole struggled to get to his feet. He managed to get up onto a bed of grass before a wave of sickness sent him to the ground and darkness took over again.

The next time he opened his eyes he was lying on his back, eyes staring up at an azure blue sky. He watched an eagle for a time before he sat up and looked about him.

He could see he was on the bend of the river and that he was in a forest, with giant black wooded trees surrounding him, but had no idea where he was. His head hurt terribly from a crack on the head, no doubt from the rock he had met in the river. His shoulder burned with a fearsome pain that comes from having muscles and tendons ripped and shredded. Cole closed his eyes and tried not to focus on the pain that hurt him so. He had to think of what to do.

The thought struck him that he was in Blackthorn Forest and that maybe his fellow companions were somewhere in the forest looking for him. It also struck him that not only might his friends be looking for him but also the Red Cloaks.

Common sense told him to stay were he was, no doubt Wallace and the others had the knowledge to follow the river down stream and find him there, but if the others could follow a river, so too could the Red Cloaks. He didn't know what to do. If he went deeper into the forest and got lost, his friends might never find him.

Perhaps they won't find you. Perhaps they are all dead, the dark voice whispered inside Cole's head.

"No stop. You can't think that," Cole told himself out loud. "They are alive and you know it." And he did know it. Cole didn't know how to explain it, but he knew they were alive.

The more Cole thought about his predicament the more he knew he was in trouble. Whether he stayed by the river or went deeper into the forest he needed a fire. His teeth were already chattering from the cold and his body shook uncontrollably from lack of body heat and shock. A fire was necessary to stay alive. But where there's fire there's smoke and smoke brings attention, unwanted or otherwise. It would be a gamble. A fire could help his comrades find him faster, but it could also bring the Red Cloaks just as fast. Letting out a breath of air, Cole made his decision and started gathering scraps of wood to make his fire.

When he had managed to gather enough wood to make a small but warming blaze, the realization that he had nothing to start the fire with set in. He literally had nothing. Most of his supplies had been with Gladadear, in his saddlebags. His bow and arrow were gone, washed away in the river. His two Wicka knifes, which he usually had strapped to his back, were also tied tightly to his bags. In despair and pain, Cole pulled his knees to his chest and softly began to cry.

"I should have never left," Cole muttered out loud. "I should have stayed in Kells."

"Do you mean that?" a voice asked. Cole's head popped up from his knees and gave out a cry when he saw Merryrick sitting next to him.

"Merryrick!" Cole cried. "How did you...what are you...your dead!" Cole stated.

"True. But so will you be if you don't get your fire going," Merryrick simply replied, nodding to his small pile of wood.

"I can't light the fire. I'm not a fire wielder and I don't have anything to light it with?" Cole replied, showing his empty hands.

"Are you sure about that?" Merryrick asked, looking Cole up and down as if he had something on him that could help.

"Yes," Cole said.

"Didn't Kaya give you a gift?"

"She did. But I don't have my knives," explained Cole.

"The knives were not the only gift she gave you," Merryrick said simply.

Cole thought back to the night that Kaya had given him the blades. Then he remembered that she had given him a small pouch and inside was flint and steel. He had put the pouch in his inner pocket of his jerkin and had yet to remove it.

"The flint and steel!" Cole cried.

Cole opened his eyes to find that there was no Merryrick sitting beside him, that he was alone by the riverbank. But the thought of the flint and steel stuck with him. Praying that the pouch containing the flint and steel was still within his pocket, that the river had not taken it, he felt for it, patting his wet jerkin and tunic. With a great sigh of relief Cole pulled the pouch out from the pocket and opened it up. The unusual color of the flint seemed to glow in the afternoon sun. As he looked upon the rock he remembered what Kaya had told him.

It will be a light in dark times, Kaya's voice echoed in his mind.

With shaking hands, Cole pleaded for the kindling to catch as he struck his flint and steel together. At once the mass of dried leaves and twigs began to smoke and with a little help from Cole, blowing at the small sparks the kindling caught fire and went up in flames after only one strike. The fire quickly grew as Cole added more fuel. He soon had a nice blaze going and he sat with his hands up to the flames trying to warm them.

Yet even with the heat from the small fire, Cole could not stop from shaking. He had taken off the wettest parts of his clothing and laid them near the fire, waiting for them to dry. He tore off part of his shirt and bandaged his shoulder as best he could.

As the flames licked up the scraps of wood and leaves, Cole watched the flames dance and he felt the warmth. He quickly sprang back however when the fire started to hiss and pop as it sent out sparks.

The fire grew in size and in heat. Large white flares were thrown up then disappeared into the air. The flames themselves were changing from a bright orange to a bright yellow until there was a burst of light, so bright that Cole had to look away. When his eyes could see again he turned back and found that the fire's flames now burned in pale blue flames. The fire settled and it continued to burn its blue flame, through the day. Yet even though the fire was there, Cole's condition became worse. His shoulder pained him greatly. The wound was turning a blackish color.

He struggled to keep his eyes open. He knew he had to remain awake, for once sleep took over he might never wake up. But after having his entire body shaking with chills, not only from the cold but also from shock, it was getting impossible to keep his eyes open. He was so very tired and weak. His body felt heavy, as if he were being pressed into the ground. His head felt as if it was an anvil and a large hammer was pounding upon it. He wanted it to stop to have the terrible pain leave him alone and yet it was the pain that was keeping him awake and alive.

The day began to fade and so did the pain. It faded away along with Cole's desire to remain awake. He didn't even care or feel any fear when he heard the howling of a hound and saw the pair of yellowy-blue eyes staring at him. All he could think as he finally let go, and fell into the blissful darkness of sleep was "it's over."

It would not be his friends or even the Red Cloaks that would be the ones to find him but rather the Reapers.

HEAT BURNED THROUGH Cole's body like wildfire. A delirious fever set in and he knew neither day nor night. He dreamed of his companions, seeing them only in glimpses. Often times they were alone, wandering around in a thick fog, with terror on their faces. He saw Maggie, her eyes red from crying. Chanlyn walked with his head down in despair. Wallace's face grim with grief, whispered to himself that he had failed. He dreamed of shadows that wandered through the fog following his friends. Their great black cloaks shifted around them when they moved, as if they were nothing but smoke and fog themselves. Cole cried out to them warning them about the shadows. But they would not or could not hear him and they would simply fade away into the fog.

When Cole was not burning up, he was shaking with cold. His teeth chattered and his muscles tensed and tightened up when his body was racked with chills. When that happened Cole felt a bitter sweet taste in his mouth and then a warm feeling that would slide

"Very nice to meet you, young Cole" the gentleman said, from his table of plants and roots.

"If I may sir, but how did I get here?" Cole inquired.

"I was going to ask you a very similar question myself," Eli said. "But since you asked first I can answer first. We saw your summoning fire and came to investigate. Well rather King saw your fire and he came to get me. We found you wounded and burning up with fever and since I cannot leave a wounded creature, animal or man to die, I carried you here and here you have remained for a week past." Eli explained, and he went around his home gathering and plucking dried leaves, flowers and roots. "Now I wonder how it is that you came to be within the realm of Blackthorn with a hole in your shoulder and a crack to your skull."

"I was shot by a Red Cloak scout, and as for the crack to my head I believe that happened when I fell in the river," Cole muttered, telling the truth but not revealing so much that he had to explain his whole story to Eli.

"A Red Cloak scout? I assume that this scout that you speak of is a human being and that they are not a friend to you," Eli asked, now at his table.

"No sir they are not?" Cole answered.

"Hmm...if I may ask why did this Red Cloak shoot you in the first place? Did you take something of theirs that was not yours?" Eli asked.

"No Sir. They shot me because they wanted to capture me," Cole revealed.

"Capture you? What on earth for? If you did not take anything of theirs as you say, then why would they want to hurt a lad like you?" Eli asked, coming back to Cole with two small wooden goblets, one he filled with hot water from a kettle that had been in the flames of the fire.

"Because of what my friends and I are," Cole stated.

Suddenly realizing the situation his friends had been left in when he was forced to leave them, made him panic and he felt the immediate need to run out and find them.

"I thank you sir for your kindness Master Eli, but I must be off," Cole said, rising to his feet, but found that his legs could not support him and he sank back down onto the soft bedding. Eli gave Cole a soft chuckle as he came back over to him carrying two small wooden cups.

"I fear you are not yet ready to be on your feet lad. There is still a bit of the fever in your eyes," Eli said, handing Cole one of the cup. "Drink this."

"But my friends and my companions, they are in trouble I fear," Cole said.

"If your friends are named Maggie, Chanlyn, Wallace and four others, they are safe within the village of Treetop." Eli replied.

"How do you know this?" Cole questioned his heart still in a rise.

"A little bird told me," Eli replied.

Cole looked up at the birds that were fluttering in and out of the cottage and he came to believe that a little bird literally had told him that his friends were safe.

"Now be so kind as to drink the remedy you have in your hands before it gets cold. It tastes far better hot."

Cole sniffed at the contents of the cup and found that it had an odd scent to it. Obeying Eli though, Cole took a gulp of the brown medicine and gaged on it as it went down. As the bitter liquid burned at his throat the taste reminded Cole of how wet leather smelled.

"I know it tastes like boiled bark but it will take the aches away and let you rest in comfort. You will need your rest if you are to rejoin your friends," Eli said, as he looked at Cole's face of disgust. Eli handed the other cup to Cole who looked at it with raised eyebrows.

"Tis only water," Eli responded. Grateful to have something to wash the taste down, Cole drank the water in large gulps. He didn't realize how thirsty he was until the cool spring water hit his lips.

"Now then," Eli said, when he had put away the goblets and returned to the fire. "What precisely are you referring to? What are you and your friends?"

"We are wielders," Cole whispered.

"Mmm...I see! So you and your friends ran here to Blackthorn not really knowing why?" Eli questioned. Cole felt the need to tell Eli the truth.

"We came here because we are looking for something," Cole told him.

"And this something that you and your companions have been searching for, I presume that it has some importance. Otherwise I do not think you would have been shot for some nonsensical item," Eli said thoughtfully.

Cole nodded. "It's a weapon. A powerful weapon."

"Ahh! I see now," Eli spoke. "You seek the bow of Ayden, don't you?"

Cole's mouth fell open and his eyes widened with wonder and shock.

"Why do you seek such a weapon young Cole? Do you wish for fame and fortune? Many, I'll have you know, have wasted their lives seeking something that only legends tell of."

"I do not seek it for fame nor fortune. But rather to stop someone from taking power again," Cole spoke, not wanting to look Eli in the eyes. He knew that if he did, he would tell the old stranger all that he had to tell. For a moment Cole considered running, but the moment that idea came into his head he knew it would be useless. He could barely stand, let alone run.

"And who is it that you have to stop?" Eli asked, tilting Cole's head up with a finger. "Who is it Cole?"

Cole looked into Eli's eyes. He saw in them warmth and kindness. Within him came the feeling that Eli was not the enemy, but a friend and that he could be trusted.

"Who Cole?" Eli demanded.

"Shelrin," Cole muttered.

Eli's demeanor changed immediately. His kind eyes changed. The birds began to scream and flittered around the room madly. King began to bark and bare his teeth. The temperature in the room began to drop dramatically. It became so cold, so quickly, that the fire in the hearth went out completely. Cole shivered in the dark and let out puffs of air that he could see.

Cole heard Eli take a great breath of air and the birds calmed and King ceased his barking. The room began to warm again and Eli lit another fire.

"I am sorry for the loss of my temper," Eli stated. "Perhaps you should start your tale from the beginning young master."

Cole obliged and ending up spilling his whole tale to Eli. He told Eli of his dreams, his ablity to trace, the Reapers coming to Kells and killing Merryrick. He went on to tell of fleeing to Aloria and having the capability to see the future, as well as seeing Shelrin wake from the stone prison. He unfolded his story of seeing the attack on White Guard City and finally seeing the grand garden where the Bow of Ayden lies, and the places all the other weapons of the Seven Elfain Masters lie. When Cole had finished his tale, his throat was dry and he could barely talk. Eli said nothing as he retrieved another goblet of water for Cole.

"Your tale would seem rather far-fetched to any other man," Eli said, when he returned to Cole. "But what you described to me of the grand garden I know to be true. For I have seen this place. Ayden's Garden it is called and it does lie within Blackthorn."

"Do you know where it is," Cole asked, his breathing becoming rapid with excitement.

"Aye I do," Eli said.

"You do not jest?" Cole asked.

"No. I do not jest," Eli whispered. "However, what you saw within your vision, young Cole is not what you will see. The city is abandoned, has been since the day Shelrin destroyed it. What you seek, you may not find. As I have said, many have gone looking for the bow and have wasted their lives in doing so."

"I have to try at least. Will you show me the way?" Cole asked. "Will you take me tomorrow?"

"Aye, I can do that, if you are feeling up to it, but know this my young friend. The city is nothing but a wasteland."

CHAPTER 32

THEY DID NOT GO the next morning or the next. Eli didn't want Cole suffering from a relapse of fever and the next day it rained. So it was not until four days after Cole found himself in Eli's cottage that they woke early and started their journey to the city of Aydrien.

They moved through the forest slowly, stopping frequently so Cole could rest. Eli led the way, following a small path as it wound its way through the pines, evergreens and firs. King moved through the thick trees like a ghost, disappearing ahead of them and then suddenly reappearing to walk beside them.

"I don't understand," Cole said sweeping his finger across King's back as he passed him to walk in front of Cole.

"What is it that you don't understand?" Eli questioned.

"What do you mean that King is a spirit holder? Is he not just like any other wolf?"

"King may look like any other wolf, but he holds a great amount of Spirit."

"Can he wield?" Cole asked.

'In a way he can. But not like you or I. He senses when there is something amiss in his forest, a strong capability to smell out wielders, good or bad. He can aid those in trouble if he wishes with providing large amounts of Spirit. He is by definition a baywolf." Eli explained.

"So are they like Hellhounds," Cole questioned.

Eli suddenly froze amd turned around to face Cole, the temperature suddenly dropping.

"Never compare King to those mongrols" Eli said coldly. So coldly that Cole felt a chill run up his spine. "King is and will always be a superior race compared to them."

Cole said nothing he only nodded agreeing with Eli.

The air around them rose in temperature as Eli nodded and turned back around and continued walking. "In a way bays are like the hellhounds. The have a heightened sense of smell of wielding. The are fast and have their own source of spirit,"

"Bays? You mean there's more than one species of Spirit holders?" Cole asked.

"Oh yes indeed," Eli replied. "There are horses, dogs, wolves, bears, and deer. Occasionally there are holder's that are inanimate objects such as swords, knives and bows."

Cole stopped for a moment to go over what Eli had just said.

Then he quickly ran forward to catch up with Eli.

"Wait, so Ayden's bow. Is it a Spirit holder or a bay as you called it?" Cole inquired.

"Not a bay," Eli commented. "Bays are living Spirit holders. The have the free agency to help if they wish. They also choose who they want to serve with."

"Like Master and servant?" Cole asked.

"In a way yes and no. The role of Master and servant are often flip-flopped. No one is really a master and no one really a servant. It's more of a partnership," Eli answered.

"So what are the inanimate objects called?" Cole asked trying to grasp all the information he could.

"They are called Sources," Eli replied.

"Why are they called that?" Cole asked

"I would have thought that was obvious. They hold Spirit. Wielders can use the spirit within the object to increase their wielding power. Wielder's can transfer Spirit into the object and save it for later when they themselves are running low."

"Is that what the seven ancient weapons are then?" Cole asked. "Are they sources?"

Eli stopped again to look at Cole. "The seven weapons maybe Sources, but I believe that their power sources come from Raw Spirit."

"What's raw spirit?" Cole asked, his mind bursting with questions. Everytime Eli explained one thing a hundred more questions burst into his mind.

"Raw Spirit is raw energy. It has no uniform energy like with Fire Spirit or Water Spirit. It can be wielded and turned into one of the uniform Spirits. But it is powerful stuff. Wielding it comes at a cost," Eli said his eyes no longer looking at Cole, but seemed to be lost in a memory.

"What kind of cost?" Cole asked softly.

"What? No more questions," Eli said pulling himself out of his thoughts. "If we want to reach the city before dark we must hurry," Eli expressed, then turned around and started walking at a quicker pace that Cole had a hard time keeping up with.

As they went deeper into the woods the trees grew taller and wider. Cole also took notice that they were getting closer to their destination. Here and there he could make out broken and cracked cobblestones that were at one point, roads. He could imagine walls and roofs that belonged to homes that were nothing now but rubble amongst the tall growing trees. He saw a few towers that still stood. But it seemed that at any moment the wind could come along and topple them with one simple gust. Eli moved through what might have been the main street of the city, for there were far more piles of rubble than before. Cole craned his neck to stare up at a shell of a building. The black eyes of empty windows stared at him as he passed. He wondered what it might have been, a theater, a church, or perhaps an inn. As they moved through the abandoned city it was eerie and a bit frightening to hear nothing but the sound of the wind. Cole jumped back when he was suddenly surprised by a flock of crows flying out of the darkened remains of a freestanding chimney.

By late afternoon Eli and Cole mounted a staircase that looked rather questionable. The stairs were made of stone and at one time there had been many of them. Now there were wide gaps and whole sections of the stairs missing. More than once Cole had to leap over holes and place his weight very carefully on crumbling steps. It wasn't until the sun was in the far west that Eli pulled back a curtain of creeping vines and Cole got his first look at the grand solarium that was once known as Ayden's Garden. But there was nothing grand about it, not any more.

There was nothing recognizable, nothing that told Cole that this was once the garden from his dreams. It was as Eli said. It was a wasteland. The green glass paneled roof was gone, shattered and the ionic columns that had once stood proud and strong, were gone. Destroyed. Their remains were scattered about, toppled over and broken. The once tamed and exotic creeping vines had grown wild long ago and now covered everything, choking out anything that struggled to grow. The white tree, with its silver leaves and white blossoms, was a broken and jagged stump. The lush island that it had grown on was covered in weeds and brown grasses. The spring that once flowed with clear spring water had dried up in years past. As for the statue of the archer it was nowhere in sight, lost amongst the rubble and debris. Cole stood for a moment, his eyes roaming over the scene until he gave out a grieving moan and then fell to his knees.

"There's nothing here," Cole wept softly.

"I told you that it was a wasteland," Eli reported, feeling Cole's grief.

"You did, but I thought that there would be something. Something that might be here," Cole replied, gathering a pile of sand in his hands and letting it strain through his fingers. What was he to do now? The loss of finding Ayden's Garden in this state physically hurt him. So much so that he felt his heart would break. Eli left Cole to mourn his loss and began making camp. He cut away an area of vines and made camp behind the remains of the fallen down ionic columns. Taking the vines he had cut away, he snapped them in half, allowing the oils from the vines to leak out, and then set them ablaze. The oils from within the vines caught quickly and when Cole finally came over, Eli had a bright and cheerful fire going.

"We will stay here tonight. Midday has long since passed and we will not make it home before dark. It is not wise to wander in the forest at night, at least not in this forest," Eli announced.

The rest of the day was spent quietly. Cole spoke little and that was only to answer questions Eli put to him. King went off for a while but returned bearing three dead hares that he had caught. Cole helped Eli clean and skin two of the hares and prepared them for the fire. King took his hare to some corner of the garden to have his dinner alone. As Cole helped, he noticed Eli had rolled up his sleeves, so they would escape bloodstain when they cleaned the hares, and had yet to roll them down again. Around Eli's upper arm were five tattooed bands, much like Merryrick's, yet they were different from Merryrick's seven bands. Eli's five bands were braided together and went around his arm, like an eternal braid.

"Are you an Elfain Warrior?" Cole asked, his hopes rising.

For a brief moment Cole thought that all was not lost. Perhaps he wasn't supposed to find the bow of Ayden but rather a warrior from Ayden.

"Why do you ask that?" Eli questioned.

"Because of your bands," Cole answered, his head nodding towards the bands.

"Master Merryrick had bands similar to yours. Only he had seven bands with a dragon's head placed in the middle of the bands. He never told me what they meant. Since I believe he was an Elfain Warrior I figured that it might have something to do with the Warriors," Cole commented.

"In a way the bands that your master and I bear are connected to the warriors. But as for me being a warrior, no I am not," Eli answered. "The bands I bare are the marking for the cavalry," Eli muttered.

"You were in the war?" Cole asked shyly.

"Aye," Eli muttered.

"So… Merryrick was in the war as well?"

"I would say so. From how you described his bands, he was a Ranger, a high ranking one as well, if he also had a green dragon's head. He was in an elite group known as the Green Dragons. They were those that were closest to General Kayden," explained Eli.

"A Green Dragon?" Cole wondered out loud.

"Mmmm. The Green Dragons were spies, secret mission men and women. They were Masters with the bow and knife. They were excellent hunters and they had a way of disappearing right in front of your eyes. It was said that if you ever spotted a ranger you only had a few seconds to live," continued Eli.

Cole thought about Eli's words. Merryrick being a ranger made sense. The years of Cole's life living with Merryrick passed before him as he remembered the skills and lessons his master had taught him. Lessons on how to hunt, how to use the bow, to track and follow a trail silently, and to kill without the animal suffering were all part of the lessons. It all came back to him in flashes of memories. Yes, Merryrick had to have been a ranger, as well as being a Warrior.

"You said that the bands also had to do with the warriors. What did you mean?" Cole asked.

"I have no doubt that you know the tale of the first Elfain Warriors that came from the Havens to defeat the Dark King right?"

"Yes," Cole replied.

"Well the Elfains were born with silver bands around their upper arms. As a child grew older and more experienced in wielding, the bands would become darker and more in number. They were known as the Elfain's touch."

"I still don't understand," Cole replied.

"I'm not done. Keep listening," Eli remarked. "After the defeat of the Dark King, the seven warriors decided to stay. The Warriors married each other, for example Ayden married Lochlynn and they had children. And then some of the Warrior's children fell in love with mortals and they had children."

"And those children inherited the ability to spirit wield," Cole injected, "and that's when the age of the Elfain Warriors was born. What does that have to do with the markings?"

"Those of a pure Elfain line also inherited the silver bands," Eli tried to explain. "If a child was born with silver bands, at the age of ten they were presented to the Warriors at the school in Alorian and taught how to use their powers of wielding. The bands were a great honor to have at one time. But after Alorian was destroyed and Shelrin took power, the bands were a curse. Any one tied to the Elfains were captured and forced to join Shelrin or die. So many began to hide their marking with tattoos. When the rebels came along, the marks were more of an identification of what military group and rank you belonged to."

"So that's where the tattoo bands come in?" Cole asked. "So the bands represented the years one served? Must have been a long war."

"Aye, it was," Eli answered.

Cole was lost in his thoughts for a time wondering why Merryrick never told him about being an Elfain Warrior or even a Green Dragon. He presented the question to Eli.

"Can you not think why?" Eli asked. "It is the same reason why many hide the Elfain's touch. They were scared of what might happen to them if they were discovered."

"But the war ended a long time ago," Cole muttered.

"Not so long ago Cole. Fifteen years may seem, like a long time to one so young like you, Cole. But for those that lived through those times, their memories are still very fresh in their minds," Eli stated, speaking from experience. "Those times were dark. People that had been neighbors and friends for years upon years, and even family would turn against each other. Anyone caught harboring a Warrior was condemned to death. Even now days there are still those that hold the warriors in contempt and would wish them harm. You are very much aware of that."

Cole nodded thinking of the Red Cloaks.

"But why?" Cole asked. "Why did Shelrin want to destroy the Elfains in the first place?"

"Because it is said that seven Elfain Warriors would return and destroy the darkness once and for all. If you destroy the Elfains then you have destroyed the foretelling and there is no possibility of it coming true," Eli answered.

"But..."

"I know you have many questions Cole. But I am tired and if I am tired you must be exhausted. There will be time to talk tomorrow. For now, I wish to sleep," Eli said tiredly.

A VIOLENT CRASH startled Cole from his sleep. He got to his feet and opened his eyes, but found a cloud of black smoke filling the air around him, burning his eyes and making them water.

"Eli what's going on?" he cried then coughed as the smoke filled his lungs.

Nearly blind, Cole squinted his eyes to see through the smoke and covered his mouth to prevent himself from breathing in the foul air. He could see people running around, rushing past him.

"Eli what's going on?" Cole screamed again, as he ran forward, following the people that had scrambled past him. He passed through the vapor of darkness and let out a cry of shock when he reached the other side.

He was in Ayden's garden, back to it before it had been demolished. The great white tree still stood, the ionic columns were still standing, the glass roof was still intact and the spring still flowed with clear water and the Archer stood on its pedestal, its bow raised ready to fire its arrow. It all looked the same, yet the atmosphere of peace and tranquility was absent. Instead there was terror and fear filling the air. A loud explosion rocked the earth and rattled the glass ceiling. Cole covered his head thinking that the glass would shatter and rain down upon him.

"They've reached the main gate," a cry echoed behind Cole.

Cole turned to where the voices had come from and his eyes widened with absolute dismay as he saw the whole city was under attack. There were thick black clouds rising up from fires that burned all over the city. It was a scene of complete devastation, people were screaming and running away from what Cole realized were battles. There were great winds and rains falling sideways. The earth shook, water froze and fire burned. Below him at the bottom of the staircase a whirlwind of ice and snow battled a blazing fire. Cole could see two men standing in the mist of the fire and ice, battling one another in hand to hand combat. To the north, a raging lightning storm was ripping through the sky. Red and blue lightning split the sky and intense claps of thunder resounded everywhere. Cole understood then that he was seeing the desolation of Aydrien. The city was falling to Shelrin.

There was more shouting and Cole turned towards it. A group of more than twelve men came running into the garden. Right behind them were thirty others, dressed in black bearing swords stained with blood. The men in black were strangely clad in armor that was sharp and jagged. Bits of black rock and shards of glass had been wielded together to form their suits of armor. Their helms covered their faces, yet Cole could see nothing of their eyes. They contended with the twelve men, violently attacking them with blows that would shatter any normal man. Most of the rock-armored men concentrated their numbers on one man. From what Cole could discover he was tall, black haired and quite young. The side of his face was smeared with dried blood and his chest rose up and down rapidly.

The once fine clothes of the twelve men, that bore the emblem of the Elfain Warriors were torn and stained with blood and mud.

With a sword the black haired man defeated a rock warrior, piercing the man in the heart. The rock soldier shattered like the shards of glass his armor was made up of.

"Remember the heart. Pierce the heart," the man shouted.

Three more of the black rock soldiers were shattered by their hearts being pierced by a sharp point of a creeping vine that was wielded by a dark haired warrior. Four other soldiers were destroyed by a spear of frozen water, wielded by the hands of a young man no more than fifteen or sixteen years old.

Although the Elfain Warriors destroyed half of the black rock men, their numbers were still greater than the warriors. Two warriors were gravely injured in the battle and they fell by the blade. Cole could do nothing as he watched the warriors become surrounded. The man with the black hair drew back to the statue of the archer. The black armored men moved in closer with their swords raised. Cole's heart beat fast as he knew that the men were about to be executed before him. He wanted to close his eyes against the carnage but he knew that he could not. Horrified that he was seeing this, he knew there was a reason for it. As the black men got ready to bring their swords down, there suddenly came a great flash of lightning. Then more lightning came, flashing as it struck the hearts of every one of the black armored men, who shattered like an exploding pane of glass. The warriors turned away from the lightning and the exploding men, as did Cole, not realizing that he could not be harmed. When the men and Cole turned back they discovered that their enemy was gone. The warriors stared in absolute astonishment.

The sound of a man slumping to the ground made the warriors turn. It was the black haired man that had fallen to the ground.

"Hayden! Your majesty!" one warrior called, and ran to his aid.

"I'm fine Elrin. Check the others," the young man ordered.

The one man named Elrin stayed to help Hayden to his feet.

Hayden rose and in his hands he carried with him a bow, which he placed back in the hands of the stone statue of the archer. Once the bow was back in the grasp of the statue, Hayden's knees buckled and he fell to the ground.

"Sir you are not fine, you're bleeding," Elrin cried, as he noticed a large stain of blood on Hayden's tunic, it growing larger as the seconds passed.

"Bernard! The king needs you!" Elrin cried in urgency, as he tore at the king's tunic to find the source of the blood.

Once he found the wound, he tore his own tunic and pressed it to the king's wound.

An older warrior came in from behind Elrin and took hold of the make shift bandage. Bernard looked the king over. The old man closed his eyes and took a breath, the room began to glow as little golden dust particles like beads flew from the plant life that was around them and settled on the king. Once done, Barnard moved away and Elrin took his place. As Bernard was healing the king, many of the warriors gathered around the young king, including the young ice wielding boy and Cole.

"Alright there young Eli?" the king asked, the young man that stood before him

"Yes sir!" the young Eli answered shyly.

"Master Eli?" Cole said in total disbelief. For a few moments Cole just stared at the very young boyish face of Eli as he watched the king.

"Are you able to stand your Highness? The enemy is fast approaching," Elrin asked.

"Commander Elrin?" his lordship spoke in a soft whisper.

"Sir, your highness?" the commander said, and got to his knees.

"Elrin, my wife and child, are they away?" Hayden whispered.

"Yes Sir! They are safe and hidden and only I know where."

"Good. It eases my mind to know that before I die."

"Sir you are not going to die," Elrin proclaimed.

"Elrin, you were never a good liar," the king smiled, "even when we were children, you could never tell a proper lie. You know as well as I that I am dying. I do not have much time left in this world," Hayden said, his once deep green eyes were slowly fading of light. "Wielding the Bow has cost me much."

Commander Elrin turned to look towards the old physician, who nodded his head.

"But you healed him did you not Master Bernard?" Elrin yelled to the old man.

"I did what I could commander. But he has lost too much blood and using the bow has take much from him," Bernard muttered.

"Lady Eleanora will wish to see you. She has ordered me to bring you to her," Elrin replied, his voice choking up.

"You will have to make my apologies for not returning to her," Hayden spoke, his voice fading.

"Please Hayden, my friend! "

"Raise him Elrin, raise him as your son. Be the father that I cannot be. Train him in the ways of the Elfains, like my father and grandfather, for he is an Elfain. Raise him to be a Warrior. Raise him to fight the dark."

"One more thing I must ask of you my true friend. Do not let them destroy the statue of Ayden. It now waits for my son to claim it. For if they destroy the archer, then Aydrien will truly fall."

It was then that King Hayden of Aydrien grasped Elrin's hand and made him swear that he would take care of his son and that he would not let the statue of Ayden fall. He then fell back and closed his eyes forever, and then his hand slowly slipped from Elrin's hand and in Elrin's hands was a crystal star.

The group stood in silence and then the whole room shook as red lightning licked the heavens.

"We have not time to grieve," the commander said, wiping a single tear from his cheek. He headed for the tree on the wall where he placed the crystal star into the carving of the seventh star. The great carving rumbled and began to crack in the center. The scene was all too familiar to Cole as he watched the two stone doors swing inward, revealing a stone stairway leading downward.

"Master Bernard and Young Eli go forward. Wilson, Cox, Helms and Roan go also. When you reach the bottom of the stairs, take the tunnel to the left. It will take you to the edge of the loch. Go quickly."

"And what of you commander? Do you not come with us?" Master Bernard asked.

"I will follow shortly. I must see that the last wish of King Hayden is fulfilled. Samson, Gideon, I will need both your strength," Commander Elrin spoke.

"Yes Sir," the soldiers spoke stepping forward.

"Wilson, if I do not make it, you will be in command. Go to the hidden fort in the trees. Be quick and I shall do the same."

Wilson placed his right hand acrossed his chest and bowed declaring he understood the order with a, "Yes, Sir." As Wilson rose, the solarium suddenly became very dark and black clouds rolled in, blotting out the sunlight.

"Go now! Samson, Gideon quickly," Elrin commanded.

Cole stood watching, as the small band of Warriors went forward and disappeared into the darkness of the passageway. Meanwhile Elrin, Samson and Gideon rushed to the statue of the archer and they managed to the carry the white stone man towards the passage. They were nearly to the opening when there was a sudden great explosion that knocked them to the ground. The green glass paneled ceiling shattered and shards of it fell down on them, cutting them.

"Quickly," Elrin yelled, as he felt a coldness begin to surround them. He visibly shuttered as a thin white mist began to creep in.

Injured the men dragged the Archer to the opening. With a great cry Samson picked up the archer and descended the stairs.

"Go, Go, Go!" Elrin yelled at Gideon telling him to get into the stairwell.

"Commander hurry!" Gideon yelled, as he entered the passage, only to fall to his knees as a black arrow penetrated his heart.

After that single arrow, a hailstorm of arrows followed, arrows rained down upon them. "Take cover!" Elrin yelled.

Even though Cole knew that he was caught in the past he ran and took his cover behind a column, as he watched the black arrows fly out of the mist

From his hiding place Cole watched as Elrin ran forward to the open doors, he fell when a black arrow caught him in the leg. But Elrin only stayed down for a moment. He got up and reached the wall.

Out of breath and bleeding, Elrin pulled the crystal star from the wall and the doors began to close.

"The door! Stop the doors from closing," a high-pitched scream sounded, shattering the remaining glass in the ceiling.

More men in black armor rushed out of the mist for the doors, but Elrin was there with his sword and he cut down any man that came near him. An arrow came and Elrin was shot through the back. He hit the doors as they shut and he slid to the ground.

A cold shriek filled the room and red lightning crackled, thunder roared and then all was dark.

CHAPTER 34

COLE'S EYES snapped open and he sat straight up. His head spun towards the remains of the back wall. He leapt to his feet and sprinted to the wall. He pulled at the thick curtain of vines that covered it. The thinner vines came off easily, however Cole had to hack at the thicker ones with Eli's knife as he cleared away the wall. His shoulder tingled with pain as he worked, but Cole ignored it and continued to clear the overgrowth from the ancient wall.

"Cole, what on earth are you doing?" Eli voice asked from behind him.

"Why didn't you tell me?" Cole cried as he pulled away a large section of vegetation. "Why didn't you tell me about the wall?"

"What about the wall. There's nothing to tell," Eli asked, moving out of Cole's way as he continued to chop at the vines.

"It's a passageway," Cole cried, working faster now that he had a section cleared and he could see a part of the carving. "You escaped from the city through it when Shelrin invaded."

"How would you know about that?" Eli asked in disbelief.

"I saw it! I saw it all," Cole cried. "I saw Hayden and Commander Elrin and all the others attacked by the rockmen. I saw Hayden use the bow. I saw Elrin opening the doors. I saw him fall, then everyone go into the passage. I saw the doors close," Cole shouted.

"You saw all that. Then you really are a seer," Eli muttered.

"Yes." Cole yelled. "Now please help me!"

"There's no point Cole. The doors won't open. I've tried more than once," Eli said.

"They will tonight," Cole cried with excitement.

Not really fully understanding, Eli stepped forward and began to help Cole. Even King pulled at the stubborn vines with his strong jaws.

After an hour of work, Cole and Eli stepped back, sweaty and out of breathe, and gazed up at the faded carving of the tree. It had begun to erode away in some places and it was hard to see. But what was most important to Cole was still very clear and visible to see. He stepped forward and wiped away the years of grim that had collected on the doors. The six crystal stars were still there, locked in place, and though there were signs that many had tried to retrieve them, for there were deep gouges in the stone around them, Cole continued to clean the stone until he found what he was looking for, the empty notch where the seventh star would have been.

Cole stepped back and pulled the pouch, which Merryrick had given him, from around his neck and let the star crystal slip into the palm of his hand. From behind him he heard Eli take in a breath of surprise. Taking in a breath of his own, Cole stepped back to the doors and placed the star crystal into the notch and pressed it in, just like Elrin did so many years ago.

For the first few moments nothing happened and then all at once the stars and the carving of the tree began to glow with the brightness of the moon. There was a low groan and then the grinding of stone on stone as the doors slowly opened. A gust of air, smelling like mildew greeted them when the door swung open. Darkness stared back at them. Torches were quickly produced by wrapping broken vines around branches of trees then the torches were lit on fire. Eli went first with a somewhat timid King by his side. Cole pulled the star from the wall and slipped in the passage as the doors started to gradually close behind them.

"Are you sure you wanted to do that" Eli asked, after the doors were completely shut.

"There is obviously a way out," Cole said, "you got out."

"There was a way out a hundred or so years ago. Now?" Eli stated in the semi-dark.

"I hadn't thought about that," Cole murmured.

"Well best foot forward," Eli stated and started descending the stairs.

They talked little as they moved downward and when they did, their voices echoed about them making them feel that they were not alone.

"Do you remember this," Cole asked.

"I remember the darkness and the terror I felt," Eli replied.

It seemed like ages had passed when they finally reached the bottom. By the feel of the cold air that surrounded them, Cole knew that they were deep under ground.

"Where do you think we are?" Cole asked using what little light he had from his torch to look around.

"Probably somewhere under the ruins of the castle," Eli answered, not really knowing himself. "It seems that we are in some sort of cavern," Eli's voice reverberated off the walls.

By the light of their torches, Eli and Cole explored their surroundings. There were strange-like rocks that looked like melting wax and spikes that hung from the ceiling and some that grew up from the floor, looking more like teeth. Water drops echoed around then as they fell into a pool in the distance somewhere.

Cole turned from examining a particular rock formation that looked more like a growing mushroom than a rock. He gave out a cry as a face loomed out of the darkness. Shocked, he dropped his torch and it rolled away.

"What is the matter?" Eli asked in alarm.

"There's someone in here with us," Cole cried.

Eli ran forward ready to pull out his knife, when the light from his torch lit the face that Cole had seen. Eli let out a chuckle at Cole's foolishness.

"So you are afraid of what you seek?" Eli asked with a smile.

Cole retrieved his torch and with the light of both flames Cole stared up at the statue of the Archer and opened his mouth. Beside a very thick layer of dust and a good many cobwebs the Archer appeared to be fine. He still stood with his feet apart, left arm pulled back with an arrow nocked to his bow ready to fire.

Cole cleared away the cobwebs and blew the dust from the white stone man. He moved around him, taking in the whole statue. It was very well crafted, the proportions were precise and the detail in the face were so correct that Cole felt that at any moment the statue would spring to life.

"Now that we have found the Archer what do you do now?" Eli asked watching the boy circle the stone man.

"I don't know," Cole replied as he rubbed his fingers along across the arrow. "Maybe there is a compartment or something that…Ouch." Cole suddenly pulled back his hand and he sucked in a breath.

"What happened?" Eli asked.

"The arrowhead cut me. It's real," Cole said sticking his finger in his mouth to clean off the blood.

"That's a bit odd," Eli stated. "It looks as if it were made of stone to me."

"It does to me as well. But the arrowhead is steel or I cut my finger on a very sharp stone."

"What if the…no that cannot be…but it might be," Eli muttered in the gloominess.

"What?" Cole asked.

"Oh I was just thinking. If you say that the arrow is real then maybe so is the bow?" Eli said stepping forward and tugging on the bow.

But the thing wouldn't budge.

"You try and take it Cole," Eli said "Maybe since you dreamed of it, you are meant to have it."

Cole stepped forward and took a breath as he placed both hands on the bow and tugged. It came away easily into Cole's hands. He didn't know if he imagined to or if it was a trick of the light, but he thought he saw the fingers of the statue loosen its grip on the bow and the statue smile.

The moment Cole had the bow in hand there came a resounding CRACK. His gaze came up from the bow and looked at the statue. It was beginning to fall apart.

"What is happening? What's going on?" Cole cried.

"The enchantment has been broken. Whatever spirit was holding the statue together is now gone. The heir of Ayden has claimed his bow," Eli shouted.

"The what?" Cole voiced.

But before Eli could answer a great groan echoed all around them. King began to bark as the earth below and above began to quake.

A large spiked rock fell from the ceiling and crashed to the ground. Seconds later, several more collided with the ground and broken into pieces.

"It appears that the archer is not the only thing that is falling apart," Eli hollered.

The groaning grew and the spikes rained down, the stairs completely collapsed when a very large boulder fell from above and slammed into them.

"Move," Eli shouted and shoved Cole into one of the tunnels, "King!"

The baywolf leaped in after the two humans and they ran. They only just made it through a few passages when they were suddenly knocked off their feet as rocks, dust and sand fell on top of them. The torches were extinguished and all went black.

CHAPTER 35

COMPLETE AND UTTER darkness surrounded Cole when he came to. The air was so thick with clouds of powder and dust that he struggled to breath. Dizzy and slightly confused, Cole managed to get to his feet after digging himself out from under a pile of rubble.

There was a sound that vibrated off the wall but Cole couldn't understand what it was. His head was spinning and his ears rang. He shook his head to try and clear away the mass of cobwebs that clouded his mind. After a few moments Cole's head became clear and he understood what he was hearing. It was barking, an urgent sort of bark that could only come from a Baywolf.

"King," Cole called, "Master Eli where are you?"

The only reply that Cole received was the howling cry of King.

"Master Eli," Cole called again.

No reply.

Something was wrong. He could feel it. There was something in the air besides dust and grit. It was a cold feeling, so much more than the dampness that surrounded him. It was a feeling of dread.

"Eli? Sir, are you hurt?" Cole cried, his heart beginning to speed up in pace.

There was definitely something wrong if Eli wasn't answering him.

Crawling on hands and knees over piles of smashed rocks and mud, Cole felt his way through the darkness towards the whining canine. It was slow going for Cole. He moved nauseously, feeling out and patting the ground for what was in front of him and around him before he moved forward, for it would do Eli no good if he got himself seriously injured.

"I wish there was some light," Cole thought, a tremor of fear rising up within him. It was too dark, but nothing like the darkness of night, for within the night there was always the light of the stars or the moon. The dark that surrounded Cole was just that, pure unbreakable blackness. There was no light to separate it.

As he reached out, his hand grazed across wood rather than stone. Cole grabbed hold of it to discover that it was one of their torches. Amazingly it had escaped being buried in the cave in, yet it would do him no good, for there was no fire to ignite it again. Cole was about to toss the torch aside when he had a vague memory of him putting his flint and steel striker back into the pocket of his jerkin when he was near the river. Cole patted the jerkin pocket holding his breath. He let it out when he felt the bulge of the fire starting steel and flint in his pocket.

He pulled them out, careful so as to not to drop them in the total blackness. He sent up a prayer that there was enough oil from the creeping vine on the torch that it would ignite and bring the torch to life. Cole brought his steel striker down onto the flint and several sparks flew but none caught on to the torch. Again and again Cole brought the striker down onto the flint but the torch did not light.

"Please," Cole pleaded, "Just one spark that's all I need." He tried again, this time there wasn't a single spark.

"Just light!" he screamed out in frustration and anger as he slammed the steel across the flint.

Bright blue flames burst out from the strike and caught the torch. They swallowed up the wood, nearly burning Cole's hand. The brightness of the fire blinded him for a moment and he had to look away until his eyes became adjusted to the light.

He spotted King frantically digging at the ground, whining loudly. Within the rubble, Cole could see a hand sticking out from under the pile of rocks and dirt.

"Eli," Cole cried, and bolted over to his aid.

Very careful, so as not to cause a landslide, Cole unburied Eli from what could have been his tomb clearing away the rocks and dirt. Cole carried the unconscious man further down the tunnel, away from any possible threat of another cave in. He lay Eli gently on the ground and by the light of his torch looked over him.

"Eli? Sir, can you hear me?" Cole asked

Eli gave no response and Cole's heart began to beat a little faster. Eli didn't look too well. Even in the firelight he looked paler than normal. His breathing was shallow and ragged. There was a very large purplish bruise across his abdomen and he was shaking uncontrollably from shock.

"What do I do?" Cole ranted.

His thoughts fell back to Kells when Merryrick had been ill. He could do nothing for Merryrick back then, and now he could do nothing for Eli. He felt useless, like nothing was in his control. He needed Maggie and her powers to heal.

"Maggie's not here," Cole told himself aloud, "but what would she do?"

He took a breath, closed his eyes and made himself calm down as he thought of Maggie. He had often seen her tending to the sick and the ill. She'd bandage wounds and wipe away tears. Her very touch seemed to calm people and heal their very wounds, both physical and mental.

"Touch," Cole whispered.

Maggie had touched him and if Kaya was correct that he could take on any spiritwielder's talents for his own, then maybe he could heal Eli.

"But how?" he thought.

He had done it before, by healing Thomas, but could he do it again? Merryrick had warned him that he was never to heal that way again, but what was Cole supposed to do, He hadn't learned any other way. Eli was dying. He had to do something.

Cole breathed in and out. He used the fading technique and let everything fade out until all he heard was his heatbeat slowing in his chest, No it wasn't his heartbeat he realized, it was Eli's. It was so soft and slow that Cole feared that it would stop at any moment. It was then that Cole felt the strange sensation that he had felt by the riverbank in Kells. He opened his eyes and saw the flames of life burning everywhere around him, flames that he could not see with his normal eyes. It seemed there was life growing and living even in the dark. The whole cave was burning with life; it glowed like fireflies in the night. Some tiny, not much bigger then a pinprick and others such as King's burned with a cold blue that was as bright as glowing stars. Eli's flame however was low and it flicked in and out.

Remembering the description that Maggie gave when she was healing, Cole tried to copy her as he let his life flame flow in to Eli. Slowly his own flame began to burn brighter and larger until it consumed Eli. Cole watched Eli's body stiffen, as the fire within him grew.

The bruise on his belly was fading, the head wound was rapidly healing and his breathing was returning to normal. Cole was careful not to let too much of his life flames flow into Eli too fast. Maggie had told him once that letting too much mana flow can overwhelm the body and can cause more problems. Cole figured the mana that she talked about was what Merryrick called lifeflames,

Cole suddenly cried out in pain as his right arm flared up. The pain grew stronger the longer he fed Eli's flames. But despite the pain, Cole held on until Eli's eyes fluttered open. Cole could feel himself fading, the blurring darkness crowded around him. Suddenly he felt a rush of energy flood over him. It was like falling into a pool of ice-cold water, shocking him awake. Cole sucked in a deep breath of air as his eyes snapped open to stare into the cold blue eyes of King. The baywolf stared at Cole with an intensity that told him that King had been the source of the chilling energy.

A bay is a free spirit and gives life to who ever is in need of it if it is not yet time for them to pass over to the other side. That is a bay's power, Eli's voice ehoed in Cole memories.

"Thank you King," Cole muttered, his breath coming in short bursts.

Cole staggered to his feet and back against the tunnel wall.

Even though King had given him strength, he was still as weak as a newborn and his arm still throbbed with pain. He slid down the wall's surface, ready to pass out. But King's barks woke him, telling him that he had to remain awake. Not for Eli's sake but for his own.

Cole pulled whatever ounce of energy he had together and pulled himself to his feet once more. He made sure that Eli was still breathing, then took the torch and turned back the way he had come. With the torch to see by Cole dug through the rubble he had once been buried under and found the grip hidden under a thin layer of dirt.

The quiver of arrows was not too far from where the bow had fallen. He carried it back to the makeshift campsite and sat down next to Eli, who had fallen asleep with King's head resting on his chest.

To keep himself awake, Cole examined the grip in the torchlight. It was about the length of his forearm. It looked like steel yet it was lighter than steel and felt very strong. There were strange markings cut into the metal, but he could not make heads or tails as to what they meant. He wondered how he was to bring the bow back. He pulled and twisted the ends of the rod but the shape of the bow did not return. Tired and frustrated Cole was ready to throw the rod back into the darkness. As he flicked his wrist to throw it away it suddenly snapped open and the bow appeared.

Surprised, Cole flicked his wrist again and the bow once again folded in on itself and became the grip again. Over and over again, Cole flicked his wrist to change the handle into a bow and the bow into a rod.

The bow itself was a silver color, the same as the grip, which shimmered in the torchlight. It was his bow in a way. The grip fit his hand perfectly. The blue veins still wove themselves along the bows limbs. Yet there were parts of it that were new and a little strange to him. The limbs recurved away from him, instead of curving towards him. The handle was thicker and was molded with teardrop holes along it. With little difficulty he strung the bow and pulled back on the sting. Cole could feel there was greater power behind the weapon even though he had not pulled it to full draw. He didn't even know if he could mange to ever pull it to its fully drawn capabilities.

With a deep sigh Cole relaxed the bow and flicked it into a rod and replaced the arrow back into the quiver.

SOMETIME DURING THE NIGHT Cole must have fallen asleep, because he woke with a sudden start. He looked around him and wondered what it was that had woken him. The blue flames still glowed brightly in the darkness, shining its light on King as he sat next to Eli, whining sadly.

"Master Eli? Cole said, his voice echoing around hin.

His heart fluttered when Eli didn't answer. It stopped for a beat when he felt that the old man seemed to be sleeping a bit too peacefully. Cole bolted over to Eli and violently shook the warrior.

"Master Eli!" Cole shouted.

This time Eli snorted awake and bolted up, his eyes wide and looking at Cole.

"What? What is it? What's happened?" Eli responded, his gaze darting from left to right. Cole fell back on his heels with a great sigh of relief.

"Nothing has happened per say," Cole replied. "I just thought that you were…I thought that you might have…"

For a brief moment Cole was silent. Eli looked around him and noticed the rubble of rock that had caved in on them. Eli's fingertips touched the side of his head and then he looked at Cole.

"I was trapped under the rocks wasn't I?" Eli asked. "You pulled me out and…did you heal me Cole?" Eli asked. Cole nodded his head.

"And the blue fire is your doing as well?"

"Yes," Cole simply replied.

"Well I thank thee, Cole. You are truly a gifted lad. But come now. I believe that I am well enough to travel. What say you to getting out of here? This darkness is oppressive and I have need for some sunlight."

Cole nodded his head again and the two rose to their feet and gathered what few belongings they had. Cole made sure that he had the bow tucked safely away in his quiver before picking up the torch and leading the way further down the tunnel with King in the lead.

"How long do you think we have been down here?" Cole wondered out loud.

"Hard to say," Eli answered. "There is no sun to help us keep track of the days. But from my calculation, which might not be accurate, I'd say a day, possibly a night as well."

"That long?" Cole asked.

"Give or take a few hours" Eli replied.

They wandered down the tunnel for what seemed like hours. The passage twisted and turned left, then right, then right again. Cole tried to keep track of the turns that they made but lost track when he could not keep up with the endless twisting. At times Cole was not sure that they were making any progress or whether they were just circling around in an endless underground maze. There were a few times however when the passage became a tight stifling tunnel, so low that both Eli and he had to bent over just to get through.

It wasn't until they came to an intersection that Eli let out a cry of surprise.

"Oh dear!" Eli cried, his voice echoing off the distant walls.

The tunnel they had been following suddenly opened up to reveal a chamber where the tunnel split up into three other passages.

"Which one do we take?" Cole asked, shining his torch down each one.

"That is a question that I do not have the answer to," Eli replied, loftily. "I have no recollection of this place."

"Um, what do you mean?" Cole asked, feeling somewhat nervous,

"Just as I said. I do not know which one to take."

"But I thought that you've been here before?" Cole asked.

"That was a long time ago and things looked so much different when I was young. Now be quiet and let me think. All this talking and echoing is giving me goosebumps."

Cole let out a sigh and sat himself down on a large boulder, while Eli went back and forth between the three tunnels muttering to himself. He watched Eli for a moment and then suddenly realized that King was nowhere to be found.

"King!" Cole called, wandering around the chamber looking for the wolf.

"Shh!" Eli shushed, putting a finger up to his lips.

"King!" Cole called again, this time it was more as a whisper.

King's barks echoed off the walls, which made it difficult to know where his howls were coming from and he couldn't figure where the baywolf had gone.

The chamber they were in wasn't very big. There were the three separate passages that led to who knows where and save for more piles of rock there was nowhere for the wolf to go. Eventually Cole figured King was behind one of the walls, how he got there Cole had no idea. Not unless the baywolf could walk through solid rock walls, which

Cole wasn't so sure the wolf could not do. It seemed however that King had not walked through solid rock but rather through a whole in the wall. The earthquake that had happened the day before had not only caused a cave-in but had also caused a section of a rock wall to collapse opening up yet another small passage.

Crawling on hands and knees, Cole pulled himself through the hole to retrieve King. When he made it through, he was greeted with the brightness of a stream of sunlight that flowed in from the outside world.

"Master Eli, Master Eli, there's a way out. Master Eli!" Cole shouted.

Eli appeared from the darkness of the hole and looked around him. It was then that Cole looked around his surroundings as well.

The sunlight from the opening illuminated a vast chamber with high ceilings. Lining the walls were elegant strone carvings telling stories of battles, celebrations and events. Within the center of the cavern was a carved white stone tomb. The white stone had long since started to turn gray and was covered in a growth of cave moss. Intricate carvings of horses and men of war adorned the tomb. Although withered and worn, Cole understood that the carvings told a story about a great battle. And that whoever was in encased in the tomb had won.

"I do not believe it," Eli muttered as he took a step closer to the tomb.

Eli swept a hand over the cover of the tomb, wiping away years of dirt, moss and film from the stone. Although faded and almost weathered away, Eli read out loud the name of who was enclosed within.

"Here lies the savior of Albavar, He who destroyed that Lord of darkness Gavin, Ayden al'Kell, King of Aydrien, Grand High Master of the Elfain Warriors, beloved husband and father. Do you know what you have found lad?" Eli asked flabbergasted. "You have found the tomb of Ayden, the great warrior that destroyed the Dark King."

"I didn't find it. King did. But is it really his tomb? Is it really Ayden?" Cole asked, looking at the tomb then at Eli.

"I dare say it is," Eli replied.

"So they really were alive at one time," Cole muttered.

"What do you mean, of course they were alive?" Eli questioned.

Cole shrugged his shoulders as he pulled away a bit of moss.

"I just thought that they might not have been real. I mean there are all these stories about the Warriors coming down from the Havens and doing these incredible things. Some of which are so incredible that they seem far-fetched," Cole replied.

"Far fetched!" Eli cried, with disbelif. "Far-fetched? Who was it that said he saw Ayden's bow in a vision and that it led him here? Who was it that used the crystal key to unlock the doorway and proceeded to find Ayden's bow and who was it that told me a story about their master being killed by Reapers? If I were to tell your story, lad, to anyone else, they would think it far-fetched and yet it is true, is it not?"

"Yes," Cole replied .

"Beside they had to be real because you are here," Eli replied, looking over the tomb more closely."

"What do you mean by that? Why does my being here prove that Ayden and the other Elfain warriors were real?"

"Because you're the heir of Ayden," Eli said, bending down to look at one of the carved scenes along the sides, "most impressive. Look at the artistry of these carvings, most impressive indeed.

Cole didn't hear anything else after Eli had announced that he was an heir of Ayden. He just stood there thinking that he had heard wrong.

"How do you know?" Cole asked, his voice a little shaken.

"What? How do I know what?" Eli asked.

"How do you know that I'm the heir of Ayden," Cole asked, a little bit louder than he intended making his voice echo around them.

"Oh! Well because of the bow. I don't think just anyone could have just simply plucked it out of that statue's hands. But you did. So my conclusion is, you have to bear the bloodline. Only the heirs can take the weapons of their ancestors. Did you not know this?" Eli continued.

"No," Cole muttered.

"Mmm, strange that your parents never told you about your bloodline," Eli muttered, as he walked, half bent, around the tomb.

"I never knew my parents," Cole replied. "I don't even know who they are or were."

"I am sorry about that lad. It must have been a hardship for you, but now you know where you come from."

Cole looked back at the tomb with curiosity, his thoughts reeling, wondering if what Eli had just said was true. He rubbed his fingers along the white stone tomb, thinking that somewhere there were answers he was seeking among the old carvings.

"There's something more written here," Cole said, as he pulled free a patch of moss revealing more lettering.

Eli literaly shoved Cole aside to look at his discovery. He pulled off more of the moss and wiped the dust away, reading out loud. "Upon this stone are the last words of Ayden, King of Aydrien," Eli read, running his finger along the carved letters. "And the days shall be numbered when the sun shall stand in the east and the moon in the west, the winds will come and darkness shall rise and that black dragon that once ruled will rise once more. The fields of wheat shall be stained red with the blood of man. Hope and light will seem lost to those dark nights but fear not my people of Albavar for upon the day that the dragon will rise, so too will the blood of my blood rise again, bringing with him the blood of my kin. And they shall bring forth the weapons of old to overcome that great darkness that took this land so long ago. And this shall be a sign unto you he will bear the name after mine own father, he who built a great kingdom among the stars. He too shall build a great kingdom among the race of man, uniting the seven lands together. His name shall resound through history both among those of the light and also those of the dark. Thus ends the last foretelling of Ayden the great ruler of Aydrien," Eli spoke, reading the last line.

"I've never heard this one before," Cole remarked.

"Very few have," Eli said.

"It kind of reminds me of a poem that Merryrick made me memorize," Cole remarked. "It was called something like "Rise of the Warriors'."

"Oh and how does it go?" Eli asked with interest.

Cole took a breath in, as he thought about how the poem began.

"West of the Moon, East of the sun,
The winds doth whisper when darkness comes.
Dark be the dragon that will rise again,
Seeking out the light and wanting revenge.

Black be the wings that cover the sky,
Red be the ground where dead men lie.
Long will the birds cease to sing their songs,
And the rays of sun will seem far-gone.

All joy will seem lost all hope will be gone,
Cold is the night that wanes too long.
Fear not my child, for night doth not last,
Look to the old stories that have come to pass.

The great warriors of yesteryears,
Defeated a darkness that many feared.
Sent from the Haven's they did fight,
Wielding weapons with power and light

And when that Dark Dragon comes again,
So too will the warriors to fight and defend.
Sleep sound my child, and dream tonight.
The warriors protect you with truth and light," here Cole stopped trying to remember the rest of the poem. "I can't *remember the rest,"* Cole admitted.

"And the days shall come when they that are named
Shall step forth from the mount to rule and to reign.
Darkness shall fall and peace will be won,
And the warriors' heirs will bring a new dawn," Eli finished.

"You know the poem then?" Cole asked astonished.

"You'll find that many know the poem, but hardly anyone knows the meaning behind it. The foretelling reminded you of the poem because the poem was created to remind people of Ayden's last foretelling."

"Why is that?" Cole asked. "Couldn't they just say it they way it was written?"

"No. If your master taught you that poem, it is the same reason many teach it to their children, to remember the foretellings. Speaking the foretellings out loud back when the black dragon ruled would have landed you in a black hole of a prison," Eli muttered.

"You mean Shelrin? The black dragon was Shelrin?" Cole questioned.

Indeed!" Eli replied. "So no one landed in a prison, the poem *Warriors Rising*, was created to give many a way to remember the foretelling, a sort of secret message. Many of the other foretellings were also turned into poems, songs and ballads as well. You would be surprised at how many of the songs that are sung today come from Ayden's foretellings. *The Spider and the Princesses* is referring to one of King Ayden's earlier foretellings. The sad thing is, is that many don't even know what the words within the songs mean."

Cole stood silent for a moment as some of the songs Merryrick use to sing to him raced through his head and he wondered how many of them referred to a foretelling.

"How many foretellings did Ayden have?" Cole asked.

"Hard to say," Eli answered. "His visions had been written down at one time. But most were destroyed when Shelrin came to power."

"Why do that?" Cole asked.

"Come on boy. Use your head. To destroy someone you must take away any hope they have. The foretellings of Ayden gave people hope because they prophesied of one coming to save them. If you get rid of what allows people to hope, the people are easier to control. Shelrin sought out the foretellings to destroy that hope."

"But then there were the stories that were told so people wouldn't forget," Cole remarked.

"Correct. And that might be the reason for the belief that Ayden and the others are considered myths and legends to some," Eli explained.

They spent another hour in the cavern. Eli roamed around the carvings along the walls and tomb, as if he were committing every detail of the carvings to memory. It wasn't until the sun started to descend to the west and light shifted within the cavern that they slipped through the small opening and stepped out into the dusk filled air.

Cole took a deep breath of fresh air. He caught the scent of black pine, the fresh earth and clean summer air. It was refreshing after spending so many days in the dark, dank underground and he was glad to be out, in the land of the living, one could say. Grabbing hold of his hand, Cole reached upward, stretching out muscles and bones, working out the soreness he had received while in the cramped confined space. He felt the warm setting sun on his face and was glad to see it not only in the sky but the reflection of the sun on a large lake.

"We've come farther than I thought," Eli responded, when he saw the lake. "Lake Eastwood, I believe."

Once King was out of the underground, he took off towards the woods and soon was lost amongst the dense trees.

"Wonder where he's off to in such a hurry?" Eli wondered, watching the wolf go. "Well whatever it is he'll be back. If it's all right with you Cole, I'd like to make camp just near the lake. There's plenty of trout to catch and eat and fresh water to drink," Eli explained. "I'm as thirsty as a fish. Come on I know a stream not too far from here"

"I'm all right," Cole muttered.

"Boy, we've been without water for a long time. You need a drink."

Eli led the way and he was right. There was a stream about a quarter of a mile up from the lake. It was small. The water flowed up from underground and collected in a pool. Cole bent down and cupped the water in his hands and brought it to his lips. Once Cole felt the clear water touch his lips a powerful thirst came over him and he brought the water to his lips faster. After Coke had quenched his thirst he splashed water on his face and scrubbed the layers of dirt from him.

"I'll start a fire to warm ourselves, it's going to be a cold one tonight" Eli announced. "When you've finished we can see about getting some dinner"

Cole washed the rest of the dirt from his arms and hair. He sat there on the bank of the stream thinking about his previous conversation with Eli. The question, "was he really Ayden's heir", kept repeating in his mind over and over again. He would have to talk to Wallace about it if he ever saw Wallace again.

As Cole rose to his feet, the stream bank's mud caught hold of Cole's feet and threatened to pull him down. For a moment his arms windmilled out as he tried to keep his balance. For a few seconds he managed to stable himself. Feeling confident that he was safe from falling he stook a step and his feet completely slipped out from under him and he slid right into the spring pool. Cole burst out of the water and made a dash for Eli.

"Decided to take a bath with your clothes on?" Eli asked with a raised eyebrow as Cole came into the camp dripping water.

" We're surrounded!" Cole cried running for his newfound bow.

"What do you mean we are surrounded?" Eli asked.

"Surrounded by cloaked figures that carry long bows and sit in the tall grasses and watch us," Cole announced.

"And how do you know this?" Eli inquired perfectly calm as he fed the fire.

"I saw them by tracing. When I fell in the spring my hand hit the ground as I was trying to stop myself."

"It all fits now. You didn't decide to take a bath then."

"Master Eli, what are we going to do about the people watching us? They could be Red Cloaks," Cole cried out in frustration.

"Do? We'll invite them in of course," Eli announced very loudly.

CHAPTER 36

"COME ON OUT. We know you're out there."

For a few awkward moments it remained silent.

"You had better come on in and share our fire. My friend has found himself a new bow and has a desire to use it," Eli called out.

Still there was nothing.

"My name is Eli of Blackthorn and my friend is Cole from Kells, we will not harm you unless you intend us harm."

They rose up out of the reeds and long grasses like shadows, stepping forward out of the dark and into the firelight. There were six in all coming in from all sides, surrounding them. They moved in, gliding forward like ghosts. All of them had their own bows, all of which were drawn and ready to fire given the order. Cole whirled around with his bow, wondering who he should take aim at. Eli gripped his knife with a tight fist. Cole's mind could not help but return to the images of the Reapers.

"Stop, if you would please," Eli ordered, "come no farther until you reveal yourselves."

"You needn't fear us, Master Eli," one of the figures spoke, as he pulled his hood back away from his face and stepped closer to the firelight. The light from the fire revealed the youngish sort of face of a man. Apparently he was the leader of the band of shadows. He looked at Eli and then at Cole with hard eyes. Without so much as a word, but rather a shake of the head the other cloaked forms withdrew their bows and replaced their arrows back into their quivers. Cole remained holding his bow drawn.

"Seth? Is that you dear boy?" Eli asked.

"Aye Master Eli. But I would not go as far as calling me boy," the leader Seth replied.

"Oh you have given us quite a scare there," Eli said wiping his forehead with his sleeve as he put away his knife. "What brings you so far from Treetop?" Eli asked, gesturing for Seth and the others to take a seat around the fire.

"Wait! You know this person?" Cole asked.

"Yes I do. May I introduce you to Master Seth, Lord of Treetop and Master and Commander of the Rangers of Treetop," Eli replied. "Seth may I present to you…"

"Cole I presume," Seth answered.

Cole looked at the ranger master with suspicion.

"Maggie and the others have been most worried about you," Seth answered seeing Cole's question in his face.

"Maggie?" Cole said, finally lowering his bow. "How is she? Is she alright?" Cole asked, his questions coming out one after another.

"She is well," Seth replied.

"And the others? Ayla, and Chanlyn. What about Master Wallace and Grayson? Sir Arthur and Gildon? And…..?"

"They are all well," Seth replied. "They are all well and safe back in Treetop."

Cole let out a breath of relief. The last thing he remembered before falling into the river and being swept away was the Red Cloaks attacking.

"Then can we go there right now, to Treetop?" Cole asked in a rush.

"Sorry lad we will have to wait until morning. I do not wander the woods at night, even if there weren't any unwanted visitors roaming Blackthorn." Seth answered.

"Visitors?" Eli asked.

"Men in red cloaks. They wander through Blackthorn looking for something or rather someone," Seth said, his eyes looking over at Cole. "Besides the men in cloaks, there is also something else that is in Blackthorn. It's a kind of feeling, a silence that has not been in the forest before that gives one the feeling of dread. So I'm sorry lad you will have to wait until the morning before we journey to Treetop. So if we may Master Eli, might we share your fire and your company for the night" Seth asked.

"It will be a pleasure and a delight," Eli answered. "You wouldn't happen to have anything to eat? Would you? Our supplies disappeared in the depths of a cave."

"We do indeed," Seth said then turned to two of his hooded rangers, "Marcus, Will, you two have the first watch. Alecia, Lily, you have next watch. Tragen and I with take last watch. Is that agreeable?" Seth asked his fellow rangers.

"Aye," all agreed.

Not much was said during the evening. Seth and Eli talked, mostly about the recent events in Treetop. The four rangers that were not on watch whispered quietly amongst themselves.

Cole kept to himself for most of the night. He sat in front of the fire, drying his clothes and himself. Exhausted from the day's events and the increasing warmth of the fire, Cole found it hard to keep his eyes open.

COLE TOOK A DEEP BREATH. The air smelled of nothing. There wasn't even a hint of wood smoke in the air. The lack of scent told him that he was in a dream and what he beheld wasn't real. Or perhaps it was real. The images and events that he dreamed about often turned out to be real or would come to pass in the living world. He just hoped that what he saw now was just a dream, one that he would wake up from.

He stood in a thin cloud of mist as rain fell and lightning was striking. Yet even as the rain fell he could not feel it. Looking through the rain, he could see that he was surrounded by hooded shadows, dressed in the green and brown cloaks of the Rangers. Every one of them had their bows drawn and an arrow loaded to their strings. Among them Cole could see Ayla, Gildon and Grayson their bows drawn as well.

"You have to stop, Cole," Maggie's voice cried out through the mist.

Cole turned to see Maggie and the others looking at him with terror in their eyes.

"Cole! You have to stop! Please!" Maggie pleaded, taking a step towards him. She was quickly grabbed and pulled back by her father.

"No Maggie," Wallace cried.

"We have to help him," Maggie begged, tears flowing down her cheeks. "Please Cole stop!"

Stop what, Cole thought.

Searching his surroundings Cole sought for an answer. Not far from where he stood he saw Artemis, lying on the ground. His face was bruised and blood ran down the side of his face and the rain washed it away. He looked very pale in the rain and Cole thought him dead. Cole fell to the ground and shook Artemis and that is when he saw the blood in his shaking hands. He pulled them back away from Artemis, staring at the blood.

"Did I do that to Artemis?" Cole questioned.

His dream shifted then. He still remained by Artemis' side but he realized that someone was standing over him. When he looked up, he saw himself staring back at him. But the Cole that stared back at him was a self he did not recognize. The self that stared back at Cole had no expression. That Cole stared out through cold eyes that had changed in color, no longer blue but silver. In his hand was Ayden's bow, which seemed to be a glowing, pale-blue arrow.

"Cole, please! You have to wake up," Ayla cried.

Both Coles turned their heads to where the call came from.

"I don't want to shoot you, but I will. We all will," Ayla yelled out into the rain.

Cole watched himself bring up Ayden's bow and pull back on the fletching of the arrow and aim it straight at Ayla.

"What are you doing?" Cole yelled, jumping to his feet to stand in front of the bow and arrow.

"Wake up!" Cole screamed at himself. "Wake up. You can't do this."

The glowing eyed Cole did not register that there was another Cole, he just pulled back the string farther.

"They all have to die."

"No!" Cole cried and balled his fist. "I SAID WAKE UP!" Cole screamed and slammed his fist into the silver-eyed image of himself.

...

COLE SNAPPED OPEN his eyes and bolted up right.

"You alright lad?" Eli's voice came into Cole's ear.

Looking up he found Eli standing over him with a hand on his shoulder.

"You alright lad?" Eli repeated the question.

"Yes. Fine I think," Cole responded, running a hand through his hair.

"Bad dream I take it?" Eli asked.

"Something like that," Cole said, blowing out air, feeling his heart slow.

"Well take a minute and catch your breath, but make it quick we leave for Treetop in half an hour's time," Eli announced.

Blackthorn Forest was the most unique forest that Cole had ventured into. The deeper he and the others went, the denser the trees grew, as well as taller and wider than the trees in the forests he had passed through during his journey. Even the trees in Kells could not compete with the ones in Blackthorn. The trees were so tall that Cole had to tilt his head all the way back and even then he could not make out the tops of them. Unlike many of the woodlands that Cole and his companions had passed through, that held an atmosphere of tension and misgiving, Cole found that Blackthorn was nothing like the rumors that the others had told him. Although the forest was dense and seemed to be cluttered with trees and foliage there was a constant source of light. The sun rained down in beams and rays. The place was filled with noises from the animals. Birds sung, squirrels chattered, frogs croaked and every so often Cole caught sight of a deer or two grazing on long bladed grasses that grew around the trees.

Yet, even though the forest was teaming with life, Seth and his rangers were careful and always on guard, as they moved through the forest. The arrival of the Red Cloaks had made the rangers wary of the outlanders and that had no doubt concerned them. They followed no trail, at least none that Cole could see. They were well organized. There were two scouts that went ahead to check for any danger. Cole soon came to recognize the signals that the rangers used when signaling that the coast was clear or when there might be danger ahead. The rangers used whistling as their way of communication, sounding like birds. The call of the Skylark was the sound that let the rangers know that all was well. But when the cry of a nightingale echoed around them, Seth suddenly stopped and held up his hand, indicating that everyone should do the same.

"What is it?" Cole asked in a whisper.

"The call of the nightingale means that there is something amiss."

As if they had suddenly been turned into statues, all of the rangers froze and quickly drew their bows and fitted arrows to their strings and waited in silence. Feeling the distinct change in the ranger's mood, Cole strung Ayden's bow and hid in the brush with the others. It seemed that a good half an hour passed before there came the high musical whistle of the skylark, telling the others that it was safe to move again. Cole let out a breath as the serious mood of the rangers seem to defuse a little. The two scouts that had gone ahead, Tragen and Marcus, Cole thought it was, came back. Seth spoke to them and to the other Rangers that gathered around to hear what the scouts had to say.

Clearly there was something the matter for both Tragen and Marcus were shaken up. As Cole listened he caught a few words of the conversation.

"It's dead! All of it," Tragen was saying.

"Show me!" Seth ordered.

Tragen and Marcus looked at each other, apprehension apparent on their faces. However they followed their leader's orders turned and retraced their steps. Whatever had frightened the two Rangers had left not only a mark on them but also in the air. As the rest of them followed Tragen and Marcus, Cole had no doubt the others noticed a sort of thinness around them, as though there wasn't enough air for them to breathe. Like the energy of life and living had gone. Even the plant life seemed to feel the lack of energy. Stopping, Cole observed that the foilage and greenery had begun to wilt and had begun to turn brown. It wasn't just one or two plants that were dying from lack of rain or sunshine, it was wide spread all around him.

A sudden scream broke the group's unnatural silence. Lily let out a cry of horror and suddenly froze as tears began to fall from her cheeks. The other Rangers, along with Cole and Eli came to her aid. Lying at her feet were the remains of a red tailed fox, or at least that was what Cole thought it once had beem. The was nothing left of the thing but skin and bones, and it was completely white, As Cole looked at the poor creature he ran a hand though his hair, thinking that this was all too familiar.

"Master Seth, sir. If you please we wish to not go any farther," Marcus said.

"Oh and why is that?" Seth replied.

"What we described to you is up ahead. We will wait here and comfort Lily. And we would also request that Will and Alecia remain here. They are young and I don't think they need to see what is ahead," Marcus replied.

"Very well, Will and Alecia remain here and keep watch. I will return momentarily," Seth responded seeing that Tragen and Marcus were truly afraid.

"Master Eli. Will you come with me? I may need the advice of a wiser man than I."

"Certainly!" Eli replied.

"And what about me?" Cole asked.

"I have no right to tell you what to do. Stay or come, it is up to you," Seth stated.

"I'll come if you don't mind," Cole answered.

"Then lets be about this," Seth responded and marched forward.

It didn't take them long to find what it was that had sent chills of fear up Tragen and Marcus' backs. They had come to a part of the forest were there was a steep incline and had to be overcome to go any further. As they rose upward, climbing over rocks and boulders, Cole shivered with cold and his breath came in puffs.

"Something is not right," Cole replied.

"Aye lad, there is a coldness to the air. A coldness that is darkness," Eli said.

"By all the stars and magic in Albavar what could have done this?" Seth let out his voice clearly filled with anxiety. He had reached the top of the incline first and stood frozen with his back stiffened.

Cole came up after him and his own mouth dropped in dismay. What he saw was a land of nothingness. The land was dead. All of it was dead. The trees, the brush and the ground cover were all dead. But it wasn't dead as if a fire had come through and burned everything black. No it wasn't black, but white, an unnatural gray white, the color of ash.

All of it was ash. The trees were ash, the leaves were ash, the very ground was ash and when Cole walked upon it, it crumbled to dust and into a fine powder, for the ground was ash, and he realized that everything that was the color of ash, was ash.

The remains of the fox were not the only remains that were found. Littering the ground were the remains of other forest creatures. Rabbits, birds, squirrels and chipmunks were dead and all had been turned to ash.

"What could have done this Master Eli? What is the cause of this?" Seth inquired.

"This my boy is what happens when life is ripped from you. These poor creatures have had their lifespark stolen from them. Something dark has come to Blackthorn."

"What could it be?" Seth asked, the fear showing in his eyes and voice.

"Reapers," Cole whispered.

"Reapers?" Seth asked. "You mean the Shadowmen. But are they not just stories."

"Some stories are very true," Eli responded.

"We need to leave," Cole muttered his eyes darting about him, fearing that out of the whiteness would come the dark decayed robed figures that were the Reapers.

"I would have to agree with the lad. This place is not one I would like to stay much longer," Eli said

"Yes, there is much that needs reporting to Lady Merida," Seth agreed.

With the swiftness of the wind they turned and ran back down the incline. Reaching the others, Seth ordered that they were to run as fast as their feet could take them back to their home in Treetop.

They all ran, even Eli. They ran together, never leaving anyone behind. They ran it seemed for hours into the deepest, darkest part of the woods until they came into the center of the forest where black giant oak trees grew.

The oaks were massive. The trunks were as wide as they were tall. Cole figured that not even a hundred men standing with arms outstretched would be able to surround one tree. The closest branches were at least a hundred feet up. It was here they stopped and heaved a sigh of relief.

"Should we not keep going?" Cole asked.

"We're are here," Eli breathed, "at Treetop."

Cole looked around. He saw nothing that signified that there was a village. There were no buildings or homes or people, not even a sound that a village was close by. He turned to pose the question to Eli.

"Not all villages are built on the ground," Eli replied. "And with a name like Treetop where else do you think the village would be?" With a very large smile on his face Eli point upward into the thick canopy of branches and oak leaves.

A high-pitched scream of a whistle escaped from Seth's lips. Cole tilted his head back and watched as a platform of wood came falling out of the tree and landed on the ground just in front of them. The Rangers climbed aboard the platform without fear and waited for Eli and Cole to join them.

Cole stood for a moment staring at the contraption then up into the treetops and then back at the platform.

"It quite safe Cole," Eli replied, stepping on after the Rangers.

Trusting Eli, Cole took a breath and stepped on. With another shrill cry from Seth, the platform began to rise, sailing upward through the air.

"How does it work?" Cole asked, watching the ground grow farther and farther away from him.

"It works by a series of ropes, pulleys, cogs and gears," Eli replied. Cole lifted an eyebrow, having no idea what Eli had just said to him.

"At the top there are men winding up the ropes that are attached to the four sides of the lift that we are standing on. The ropes are threaded through the gears and cogs to make it easier for the men up top, as well as pulled through a pulley system then wrapped around a very large spool. When the ropes are pulled upward, the lift goes up. When the ropes are unrolled from around the spool the lift goes down. Understand now?" Eli asked.

"I suppose so," Cole replied, not really understanding what Eli was trying to explain.

"It's a rather simple yet ingenious system," Eli said, getting ready to go into detail about how every cog and gear worked. But before he could get into any real details and confuse Cole even more, the lift came to a stop and all the Rangers abandoned the lift.

"Master Seth, Sir!" a young woman called out to Seth.

"Catavale what is it?" Seth asked.

"Lady Merida wishes to see you at once. You are to report to her immediately," The young ranger called.

"I'll come now, at her request," Seth answered and then turned to Will.

"Will, see that Cole is led to his companions. Master Eli, I am sure the Lady Merida will wish you to report the goings on in the outbound forest. The rest of you, return to your families," Seth ordered.

Seth and Eli clambered back into the lift and disappeared when it went even further upwards. The Rangers, being dismissed, dispersed, each of them, going different ways and Cole was left with Will.

"Come on, follow me," Will said, and stepped forward onto a wooded walkway and under a branch.

Cole ducked under the branch when he was clear of the oak leaves that had obscured his view. Suddenly the world opened up revealing the village of Treetop. It was like nothing he had ever seen before, and yet it was familair to him. Treetop was like any other village. There were the shops of the baker, the butcher, the tinsmith and the blacksmith. There was the market, a tailorshop, the tavern and the homes, yet unlike the villages that were built on the ground, Treetop was a village built within the boughs of the trees. The little town was connected together by levels of wooden bridges, stairs, rope swings and lifts. As Cole followed Will through the village, among the trees he noticed that not one tree house was the same.

There were some tree houses that had only one level. They were spread out along large and thick branches. Others looked as if wooden boxes had been stacked on top of one another. They all came in various shapes and sizes. They were all different and unique. As he moved through the village his head turned this way and that, his eyes darting all around to try and see everything. Men, women and children moved about across the bridges, climbing up spiral staircases that wound around the trunks of trees, as they went about their daily lives. He saw vegetable and fruit patches growing in containers on the decks of homes. The Rangers and others swung on ropes and whizzed through the air on something that Will called a zip-line. The whole environment was new and exciting to Cole.

So lost was he in his amazement that he did not hear the calling of his name or the running footsteps along the bridge. It was only when he was nearly knocked to the ground as a small thin body ran into him and wrapped its arms around him, was his attention drawn away from the village.

"Cole! Cole!" the muffled voice of Maggie came as she hugged Cole so hard that he could feel his spine and ribs cracking.

"Maggie," Cole said, breathless, "Maggie I can't breathe."

''I don't care," Maggie said, holding him tighter.

"Come on lass, you don't want to kill him, just when we got him back," Master Grayson said from behind her. Along with Master Grayson stood, Chanlyn and Gildon. Ayla and the others were nowhere in sight.

MAGGIE TOOK A BREATH and finally let go, wiping her tears away.

"You had us so worried," Maggie said looking up at him with red puffy eyes.

"Aye you gave us quite a scare there lad," Gildon agreed.

"Where are the others?" Cole asked

"Out looking for you mate," Chanlyn said stepping forward and taking his hand, shaking it quite heartily then pulling him into a bear hug.

"I was so close to believing that you were dead," Chanlyn whispered "But Ayla insisted that you were alive," Chanlyn pulled back and slapped him on the back. This caused Cole to stiffen up in pain.

"Your shoulder, the arrow, I forgot," Chanlyn replied.

"Cole, what happened to you?" Maggie asked.

"What happened to you?" Cole replied seeing that all his companions had some type of bandage, scrap or bruise upon them.

"After you fell in the river and were swept away, the Redcloaks came upon us. It was a fight that nearly ended Master Wallace's life and severely injured some of us. If it had not been for Seth and his Rangers interceding and bringing us to Treetop the outcome would have been very different."

"Where is Master Wallace now?" Cole asked his voice shaking slightly with emotion. He could not lose someone else.

"He is at home resting," Maggie answered, "he is quite alright."

Relief flooded Cole and he showed it.

"So answer my question Cole, what happened to you?" Maggie nearly shouted.

"Might I suggest we take our conversation back to our lodgings? We are in the way here," Grayson answered as a rush of people tried to push past the gathering.

"Then I shall leave you in the safety of your companions," Will spoke. Cole turned and looked at the Ranger, realizing that he had quite forgotten about him.

"Thank you Will, and thank your friends for all that you have done for us."

"Yes, thank you Will," Maggie said stepping towards the Ranger and giving him a kiss on the cheek. As Will turned away Cole could see that Will had suddenly gone red in the cheeks from blushing.

"You better gave me a kiss like that because I was the one that nearly died!" Cole teased.

"Oh do be quiet," Maggie replied hotly as her own cheeks turned pink.

"Shall we go then?" Gildon asked signifying the way with his hands.

...

MAGGIE WAS THE ONE that led the way to a small two-story tree house that looked as though it was ready to fall apart. But Maggie and the others assured him that it was quite safe and very comfortable. Upon entering Cole found the first floor bigger than he had expected. To his surprise there was a small firepit in the middle of the room, lit with a blazing fire, keeping the room warm. There was a table tucked in a corner and a few chairs with feather down pillows to sit on. There was also a dry sink with a few shelves above it. Cooking utensils hung in the walls near the shelves, while small white clay pots, no doubt containing herbs and spices sat on the shelves. Across from the front door were glassless windows that opened up onto a deck. There too were chairs to sit upon to watch the sunsets. The tree house had apparently been built around part of a very thick and solid branch, for within the center of the house were the very large and straight pieces of the tree, and built around it was a stairway that wrapped around the support branch that lead upward to the second floor. Maggie was right the house was small but comfortable.

As Cole was examining his surroundings the sound of footsteps coming down the stairs made him look towards them. It was Wallace. When he reached the last step he caught Cole's eyes and held his gaze. Cole had only been gone for about a fortnight, yet to him, he felt that Wallave had aged five more years in that short time.

Linen bandages were wrapped around his mid-drift and his left arm. There were several bruises that were a yellow-green color and under both his eyes were heavy black circles. Cole's own eyes caught the glimpse of the war bands that were tattooed around Wallace right arm.

He was in the war, the thought flashed across Cole mind.

"Father what are you doing out of bed, you should be resting?" Maggie complained.

"I have rested enough," Wallace said looking at his daughter then turned his gaze back to Cole.

"What of your adventures Cole, there is much I need you to tell."

Cole was about to begin his tale when the door to the tree house suddenly swung open. There in the doorway stood Ayla.

"Is it true, is he here?" Ayla voiced loudly. Ayla marched into the room and right up to Cole. Her eyes were ablaze with anger as at first she just stared at Cole without blinking. Great huffs of air escaped her lips and then her mouth opened as words of anger exploded, and hit Cole in the face.

"Where in the world were you? I have been looking everywhere for you," she shouted. "For nearly a week we have been scouring the forest for you. From sun up to sun down we looked. And here you are, safe and sound while I have been tromping through the forest looking for you. Kaya said protecting you was going to be hard. Boy was she right. When I found that campsite of yours there was blood everywhere and…" she stopped and was quiet for a moment.

"What's she doing?" Grayson asked looking at Ayla with his head cocked to one side in interest.

"I think she's crying," Gildon said, awestruck.

"I've never seen her do that," Grayson replied.

"Neither have I," Gildon responded, watching Ayla's eyes fill with tears.

"Stop gawking at me. And I'm not crying. I've got something in my eye."

"If you say so," Gildon replied, taking a seat in one of the chairs around the table with the others.

"It's the truth," Ayla shouted.

"Do you mind," Maggie hollered. "Cole was just about to tell us what happened to him."

Ayla hurried to her seats at the table and looked up at Cole, waiting for him to begin.

"Well I guess I should start with this," Cole said, placing the handle of steel in the center of the table for all of them to see.

They all looked at the steel grip with interest and then back at Cole.

"What is it?" Ayla asked.

"I found it, I found Ayden's bow," Cole said.

They were all silent for a moment, their eyes darting from the steel rod to Cole and then back.

"It doesn't look much like a bow, does it," Maggie pointed out.

Cole picked it up from the table, flicked his wrist and the limbs of the bow snapped up and out, with it already strung.

A cry of admiration escaped from everyone's lips as Cole showed off the weapon.

"Is that all it does?" Gildon asked, looking the bow up and down.

"What do you mean, is that all it does?" Ayla said flicking one of Gildon's ears out of annoyance.

"Well the stories of the warriors say that their weapons were powerful, I was just wondering if it did more? If this is Ayden's bow well, shouldn't it do something more?"

"He has a point there," Grayson said. "The old stories do say that a weapon of a warrior increased his strength. Have you tried it out yet Cole?"

Cole shook his head "I've only pulled the string, I haven't fired an arrow from it yet."

"Then what are we waiting for. Let's test it out," Chanlyn cried.

It seemed that all of them were in agreement for they all rose from the table and went out onto the deck. Ayla handed one of her arrows to Cole, who strung it to the bowstring. He pulled the arrow back, looked down the shaft and chose a target safely away from the direction of the village. With a deep breath, he let the arrow go. The arrow zipped through the air whistling as it went. Nothing out of the ordinary happened. The arrow struck its mark in the center of a tree and and stayed there.

"You must have done something wrong," Ayla remarked.

"I didn't do anything wrong," Cole said mildly.

"Let me try then," she said.

Thinking that nothing was going to happen, Cole handed the bow over to Ayla. She took her stance and carefully strung an arrow to the string. She struggled to pull back the bowstring, but managed to hold the bow with only slightly shaking hands. She took aim for the mark in the center of the tree and fired.

"Ow," Ayla cried as the string backlashed and burned into her wrist. She dropped the bow. "Gees that stings," she said through clinched teeth.

"My turn," Maggie cried and picked up the bow.

"If I can't do it, you most certainly can't," Ayla replied, blowing on her red and throbbing skin, just above the wrist.

Wanting to prove Ayla wrong, Maggie did the same as Ayla had in picking one of her arrows and carefully placing it in the the string. She pulled back, aimed and let go.

Maggie howled in pain because she also was burned by the string.

"I told you," Ayla mocked.

"At least I got my arrow closer to the mark than you did. And you supposedly never miss."

Chanlyn was the next one to try the bow with the same result as the others. His right wrist was as red as a fire burn after he took his shot. Gildon and Grayson tried, and all ended up with angry looking welts just above their right wrists.

"Try it again Cole," Wallace advised. "It seems that you are the only one that can handle the bow without being harmed."

Ayden's bow was given back to Cole along with another arrow and he took his aim. But instead of aiming for the tree that he had used for the target previously, he focused his aim on a tree that he was barely able to see, a mere twig in the distance. He knew he would never make it. The tree was nearly three hundred yards away and there was a wind coming in from the east. It would certainly be knocked off course. Yet he pulled back on the bow a little more and waited for the right time to let it go. He could feel the strain on his sore shoulder and knew that he had to let go soon. The moment came and the arrow was released.

Mouths fell open as the arrow flew straight and true, hitting the tree with an echoing thud.

"So that is what it does?" Ayla said, breaking the silence. "It lets you shoot long distances."

"I would have to say that that tree is at least three hundred yards or further," Grayson said, impressed with Cole's shooting.

"And all done without snapping the bow. This must truly be Ayden's bow," Gildon replied with excitement.

"To tell the truth," Grayson said. "I did not think that the weapons of the Seven Warriors could be found. I believed in them but never did I think that one would be found." His eyes fell on the bow in Cole's hands. "If I may Cole, might I examine it?"

"Of course Master Grayson," Cole said, giving over the bow to him.

"It is a strange sort of bow. It is not made of wood but rather a metal, a light metal, yet it is strong and I cannot find how it folds in upon itself, there's not even a seam. It is a strange bow indeed," Grayson said, handing the bow back to Cole.

"Explain to me again how you came by it," he asked.

Cole started the story but was soon interrupted by a half knock on their door. They all clambered back into the treehouse to see who it was after Wallace had answered the door.

"Who was that? " Gildon asked taking notice of the scroll that was in Wallace's hand.

"A messenger," Wallace replied, breaking the seal on the scroll and unraveling the parchment. "It is from Lady Merida. She wishes to see us immediately. All of us are to come to her at once, specifically Sir Arthur," Wallace announced.

"Where are Sir Arthur and Artemis?" Cole asked.

"Artemis went out with a group of Rangers in search of you and to investigate the Red Cloak's camp," Ayla said, "as for Sir Arthur, he's probably in the tavern drinking away his sorrow and grieving for you. So he says."

"Chanlyn, Gildon go and find Sir Arthur. If he is in the tavern try and sober him up then meet us at Lady Merida's Manor. Go now if you please," Wallace ordered.

Chanlyn and Gildon were off and out the door quicker than a jack-rabbit. "The rest of you make yourselves presentable."

"May I ask who Lady Merida is?" Cole asked, to anyone that would answer him.

"Lady Merida is the ruler of Treetop," Maggie said.

"I guess you could say that she is the queen," Ayla remarked as she undid her braid and ran her fingers though her hair only to rebraid it again.

"She's not a queen at all, not really. She is just the Lady of the village," Maggie replied, in a rush of words.

Cole barely had time to change his clothes, scrub his face and hands and comb his hair before it was time to go. A group of Rangers came to the little treehouse to escort them to Lady Merida. They wound their way across bridges, climbed winding staircases and were carried up on lifts to stand before the manor of Lady Merida.

Cole stood on a wide deck before the doors of the manor, looking upward. Lady Merida's manor house was built in the high canopy of branches. There were at least four floors, along with a watchtower that peeked up out of the treetops. The whole manor house was built and supported by several large tree branches.

Chanlyn and Gildon were already there with Sir Arthur, who looked a little disheveled with his shirt untucked, his hairs sticking off in several directions and his face flushed from drinking. When Cole stepped off the lift with Wallace and the others, Sir Arthur let out a cry and ran to Cole and flung his arms around the boy's neck. He was clearly drunk.

"My dear boy," he weeped, "I am so sorry that you are no longer with us. Your death has caused my heart to break and I grieve for your lost soul every morning, noon and night."

"But Sir Arthur I am not dead. I stand before you," Cole responded.

"Hush! I weep for you everyday," Sir Arthur said, his gaze falling on Cole with crossed eyes. "We shall all…" Sir Arthur started to say, but then he let out an incredibly loud burp.

"Sir Arthur," Wallace voiced. "Pull yourself together. Cole is not dead, nor has he ever been. We are about to enter into the Lady Merida's company and I would not have you bumbling about like a drunken fool"

"Even though he appears to be one," Grayson muttered under his breath.

"Lady Merida has specifically asked for your company here today. You are the Mayor of Kells, now act like it."

"You are right Master Wallace," Sir Arthur replied straightening his jerkin and making himself presentable. He tucked in his shirt, buttoned up his jerkin and flattened his hair then presented himself to the Ranger that guarded the doors to Lady Merida's manor.

"Sir Arthur and company, my good man. I believe that the Lady within has asked for us," Sir Arthur said with a slight slur to his speech.

The guards at the door had obviously been informed of their coming for they were ushered inside and then presented to another set of double doors. One of the Rangers knocked and then the doors were open.

"My Lady!" Sir Arthur and his companions," one of the Rangers announced as Sir Arthur stepped over the threshold and entered a garden.

Cole was temporarily blinded by the shafts of sunlight that fell in through the thinner branches. It was a little garden with hanging baskets that spirited bright and colorful flowers, hung around the garden's walls. Herbs and vegetables grew within the same kind of containers that were so common in Treetop. They were scattered around the garden.

"Thank you Mayvis. You may go," the sweet and soft gentle voice of Lady Merida said to the ranger who had opened the door.

"Yes my lady," Mayvis the Ranger said, before bowing, and then left the garden.

"Please come forward my dear friends," Lady Merida called to them.

Because the walkways were slender and small, the visitors had to walk in single file then they spread out around the base of the pool.

Lady Merida was a lot younger than Cole imagined her to be. She was no more or less ten years his senior. She sat on a bench that was placed in front of a small pool of water. Her long chestnut colored hair fell over her shoulders and her hazel eyes stared at each of them as she greeted them with a soft smile. Both Master Eli and Seth stood on each side of her. Cole nodded, his head to Eli, wondering what he had told the lady but the old man looked cold and grim and he stood with his arms folded.

"Master Wallace. I see that you are up and about," the lady said after getting to her feet to stand before them. "Gildon, I'm looking forward to another one of your entertaining stories," She smiled at the young storyteller.

"Maggie, and Ayla, " Lady Merida said greeting each in turn. "And this must be Cole. The heir of Ayden, the boy that was lost and now has been found," she said looking Cole up and down. "Master Eli has told me of your underground adventures. We must talk later, just you and I. I would like to know you better as I have come to know your friends."

"My lady, I do not mean to be rude, but there is much that must be said," Seth interrupted,

"You are right Lord Seth. There is much to tell," Lady Merida replied, taking her seat back on the marble bench. "No doubt you already know why I have called you here. This morning a group of Rangers were sent out to investigate the northern part of the woods because of some smoke that was seen rising near a place we call, Windswept Hill. We thought that it might have been a forest fire. Instead they met a group of these Red Cloaks you have told us about and were taken captive. One of..."

"Excuse me my lady I do not mean to be rude but what does your men being captured, have to do with us?" Sir Arthur asked.

"Then you do not know Sir Arthur?" Merida asked alittle surprised. "I fear for my men, Sir Arthur, as well as for your son Artemis," the Lady replied slowly.

"My son? Sir Arthur asked, as if suddenly realizing that he was not among them.

"The reason I have called you here is not only to ask for your help, but to also inform you that your son and companion Artemis was among the captives."

CHAPTER 37

SIR ARTHUR'S KNEES suddenly gave way and he crumpled to the ground, completely passed out.

"Oh dear," Merida cried, ringing for her guards. "Take him to a room and have Meris look him over," she ordered her men as they carried Sir Arthur from the garden. "The news must have been too much for him to handle."

"Probably the drink that he couldn't handle," Grayson muttered.

Once the guards had disappeared from the garden room with Sir Arthur in tow, Lady Merida turned back to her guests.

"I fear that the news of Artemis being captured is not the worse news I have for you. There is more that I must tell you. One of my Rangers was set free to give us a message. They know that we have been helping you and are sheltering you. If we do not turn all of you over by nightfall they will execute all of my men. Master Wallace you have told me about these Red Cloaks, is there any way that I can negotiate the release of my men and your companion?"

All heads turned to look at Wallace for his response.

"It is possible my Lady. If you were to take their offer of a trade," Wallace answered. "Us for your men, your Ladyship," Wallace replied. "All but the younger ones"

"That cannot be the only way," Merida cried.

"Your Ladyship. We led the Red Cloaks to your forest. It is our fault that your men have been caught up in our affairs. I see the only way to rescue them without causing bloodshed to your people, would be to trade us for them," Wallace spoke.

Cole felt a lump of fear growing in his throat and he was finding it hard to swallow. After being hunted and shot, Cole's fear of the Red Cloaks was sound, and here Wallace was offering to trade his life for men that he didn't even know.

"Do not put all the blame upon your shoulders my friends. I share as much of the blame as well. It was I that saw you and I told my men to go to your aid. Now there is no time for blaming anyone. And I will not trade a life for a life. There must be another way."

"I cannot see one my Lady. There is not much time left before nightfall," Wallace explained.

"Do you think they will kill the men at nightfall?" Seth asked.

Wallace took in a breath and let it out slowly before he went on.

"They will not kill them, at least, not right off, but rather torture them. This party of Red Cloaks is not just any party. They are known as the Hunters. They are a cruel and bloodthirsty sort that pass judgment on any that they think is a servant of darkness, any they deem unworthy to wield."

"How is it that they judge them? What right do they have to condemn another man?" Lady Merida asked.

"They believe that they have the right. They claim that they are blessed by the gods to do so my lady," Wallace replied softly. "When nightfall comes men, women and even children are taken to suffer the seven judgements. If one can survive the seven judgements then you are condemned to be executed for having dark spirts within. If you die from the torture then you were not guilty of any darkness," Wallace explained. "The Seven judgments are also used to gather information as well".

"That is ridiculous," Merida cried out, her face going very pale as the color drained from her.

"I would have to agree with you," Wallace stated.

"How can such a group exist or be born?"

"They were born in the days of war my lady. They were meant to root out Shelrin's spies and to judge those that were founded to be traitors. They were just men and women at first, but then after the Great War was over, their leaders became fearful of any that bear the gifts of spirit wielding that did not believe in their ways. They did not want another to take Master Shelrin's place and so they became as hard hearted and as cruel as the dark lord himself."

"And you say that my men will be put through these seven judgments at nightfall? Why nightfall?"

"It is said that the dark spirits are more noticeable then, therefore it is easier to pass judgement," Wallace continued.

"And these seven judgments, what are they?" Seth asked.

"They are not pleasant things to speak of Master Seth. All I can say is that is it very painful and just as painful to watch," Wallace said, through gritted teeth, as if he had witnessed the Red Cloak tortures before. "Make no mistake my lady, your men and mine are in danger," Wallace spoke.

"What would have us do my lady?" Seth asked.

"I will not abandon my people to heathens like the Red Cloaks. But I have no plan as to what to do."

"Lady Merida. If I may?" Eli said, speaking for the first time. "Perhaps we should trade them for our men," Eli spoke.

Cole looked at Eli with shock as the man suggested that they betray him and his friends right in front of them.

"Master Eli what do you mean by this?" Merida demanded.

"I have a plan brewing your ladyship," Eli replied.

"Then let us hear it," Merida exclaimed.

AN HOUR OR SO later Cole slipped out from behind a black pine tree and entered into the Red Cloak's camp. Dressed as a Ranger, in the mottled green and brown cloak and with a full quiver of arrows, he crouched down within the shadows of a near by tent. Not long after, Ayla slipped in next to him. With Ayla's ability to slip into shadows and become invisible, he and Cole were selected to scout the camp and return with information on how the camp was layed out.

"The sun in descending. There will be more shadows and it will be easier to move about the camp," Ayla whispered.

Cole said nothing but nodded his reply. He hadn't said much more than two words since he and the others had left Treetop. In truth he wanted to scream and shout but he knew any noise might put himself and his friends in danger. While he watched the camp within the shadow of his hiding place, his gut twisted into knots as he thought of Master Wallace, Gildon, Chanlyn and Grayson bound with their hands tied behind their backs, being marched into the Red Cloak camp defenseless. And then there were Maggie, and the other Rangers he had come to know. They waited back on the western side of the forest waiting to attack the camp.

Even though he knew it was all a ploy and all part of Eli's plan, it still did not stop his mind and nerves from worrying. Eli's plan was a good one but it wasn't a worry free plan. There were risks as there were with any plan. But Cole hoped that they could pull it off. All they needed really was time. As Cole and Ayla moved to another shadow the memory of the council ran through his mind over and over again.

"MASTER WALLACE my plan does involve you and your comrades being turned over to the Red Cloaks. But it is to get the attention of the Red Cloaks, a distraction if you please," Cole recalled Eli saying. "My plan is simple yet I think that it will be effective. Seth and a few of his Rangers will escort you to the campsite of the Red Cloaks. There he will demand to see his men," Eli said, as he turned to Seth. "It is most likely that they will take you to them rather than have them brought to you."

Seth nodded his agreement.

"Also I do not believe that they will simply let you and the men leave, but will take you and the others captive as well. Am I right in my thinking Master Wallace?" Eli asked.

"You are correct. The Red Cloaks do not keep their word and are not ones that will let you simply leave." Wallace answered.

"While this is taking place myself and the rest of the rangers will sneak in and surround the camp. There we will wait for the signal that tells us when to attack the camp. Hopefully this attack will distract most of the guards enough that you can free yourselves and the men and escape to safety," Eli said, as he finished explaining his plan.

"It is a good plan," Wallace replied, "but how are we to send a signal that you are to attack. I believe that the Red Cloaks will think something amiss if we have weapons or anything else upon us and without doubt they will search us and will make Lord Seth leave our weapons."

"You are right Master Wallace," Eli replied, then turned his attentions to Cole.

"Are you willing to help us Cole?"

"Yes. What do you want me to do?" Cole asked.

"I need you to start a fire. A blue fire."

"COLE WE MUST MOVE," Ayla's voice whispered in Cole's head, thereby disturbing his concentration.

The sun had shifted in the sky. The shadow they had been hiding in was disappearing. Soon it would be gone and they would be revealed. Cole nodded in agreement and both he and Ayla slipped into another shadow between two tents. They had just barely made it when two sentry guards passed by them. Both Ayla and Cole stood stone still, too afraid to breathe, for fear of being discovered. The two-sentry soldiers passed without a pause. As soon as the sentries were gone, Ayla made ready to move. Cole stopped her though when he held up his hand across his chest and shook his head. Mere seconds later another set of guards appeared on the other side of the tents, moving in the opposite direction.

"How did you know?" Ayla asked, after the guards had gone.

"I saw them," Cole replied, as he pulled his hand from the ground. They stayed between the tents a few moments more before moving on. After that they never crossed paths with another guard.

The Red Cloaks camp was formed with the lower ranking men's small two man tents being set up on the outshirts of the camps circle, while the higher more noble ranking men had larger tents in the center. Ayla and Cole slid past one layer of tents after another without any trouble. The camp almost appeared to be abandoned. The closer they got the more nervous Cole became. In his gut he knew something wasn't right.

"They know we're here," Cole whispered to Ayla.

"How do you know that?" Ayla asked.

"We haven't met another guard or soldier in a very long time," Cole whispered.

"Maybe we've just missed them all," Ayla said.

"We're not that lucky. No. It is mostly likely that we are walking into a trap and they are waiting for us," Cole muttered back.

"What do you want to do?" Ayla asked. "Do you want to turn back?"

"We can't!" Cole replied. "Eli is counting on us, not to mention Wallace and the others. We still might be able to pull it off if we are careful."

"Right then. Is it safe to go?" Ayla asked.

Cole put his hand to the ground and his mind raced forward

"We're safe enough," Cole whispered and they slid out of their place.

It only took a few moments more to reach the center of camp. By that time the sun was almost set and purple and blue rays of light flittered through the gathering clouds.

"There's not much time left," Ayla whispered as she and Cole melted into a deep shadow of a large tent.

"You don't think that they will start the judgement right at nightfall?" Cole whispered.

Ayla did not have to give an answer for as the sun disappeared over the western horizion the battering of drums echoed thoughout the night. Cole and Ayla slid deeper into their shadow as torches and bonfires were lit, causing the cover of the night to dissipate.

"Night has fallen and the darkness has covered us. The judgement time is upon you." A deep and gravely voice cried out. "All ye that are servants of the dark shall confess and be judged for their sins," the voice continued.

Cole felt a coldness rush up his spine. The voice that was shouting the words of condemnation seemed to be familiar to him, but his memories could not place the voice to a name or face. Slightly fearful and curious he dared to peek around the tent's corner to see who it was that was speaking.

No more than ten meters in front of him sat the captured Rangers. They sat on the ground with their hoods off their heads, hands tied behind their backs, looking up at the man who spoke. He stood before the Rangers, his head covered in a red cloak. The hood was pulled up to hide his face from view. He held a staff of wood in his one hand while the other was stretched out over the group of prisoners. Surrounding the Rangers were guards, dressed in their red tunics with a silver firebird emblazened upon their chests and swords at their waists. There were others that stood without the ring of guards and fires, covered in travel stained robes of red.

"The old ancients of this world said that by your deeds ye shall be judged. And so shall ye be judged and so shall it be," the leader cried out. "Bring forth the first blasphemer so he might be presented to his jury."

Cole's heart jumped into his throat when Artemis was dragged forth from a tent and placed in front of the leader and then forced to his knees. Cole's breath came in deep huffs as he saw the condition that he was in. His face was bloodied and bruised. One eye looked to be swollen shut and his nose broken. Within the light of the bonfires, Cole could see that Artemis' face wasn't the only part of him that was black and blue. His body showed signs that he had been beaten.

The Rangers went mad and started to fight against their bonds. The guards rushed in and beat the rangers down. One Ranger managed to get his hands free and ran forward to grab the boy, but was struck down by one of the guards and was knocked to the ground. The guard stood over the Ranger, ready to pierce the man with a short sword. Cole's heart jumped up into his throat as he realized that it was Seth. Cole's eyes darted around the camp looking for the others. But they were nowhere in sight.

"Stop. Do not kill him for he will be judged for his crimes against us," the leader cried.

The guard looked at the leader with disappointment on his face, but still sheathed his sword. Instead of stabbing the man, the guard punched him in the gut and then brought his knee to Seth's face. Seth went down and the guard continued his assault. When the guard had exhausted himself from kicking Seth, he spit on the bleeding and unconcious man, then returned to his place.

"As I was saying, the boy was judged with the seven judgments and lives. He is found to be guilty for he is a wielder. He possesses the power to wield dark spirits for he can bring forth fire. And fire is the tool of destruction. He is a son of that dark warlord Shelrin, he, that ruled over us for a hundred years with blood and horror. Jury that stands before me is the boy guilty?"

"Guily! Guilty! Guilty!" the guards and the gathering crowd shouted.

Cole watched with horror as the crowd continued to scream and shout. He felt the familiar tingling in his fingers as his anger grew within him. Although Artemis was spoiled, selfish and unkind, he did not deserve to be treated with such hatred and mistreatment.

Without much effort Cole freed an arrow from his quiver and placed it on the ground. Snapping the arrowhead off, he quickly pulled out his flint and firestriker. Using the arrowhead, Cole cut away a piece of the tent and wrapped it around the broken arrow.

"Light!" Cole ordered as he swiped his firestriker across his flint.

"Cole what are you doing?" Ayla asked. "It's not time. The others might not be in position yet. We can't take on a whole army.

"Something has gone wrong, Ayla, the rest have also been captured. We are out of time. We have to try and do something, otherwise they are going to kill Artemis."

The tent cloth began to smoke.

"We just have to pray that the others are in postion. You don't have to help."

"I won't back down," Ayla told him.

Cole nodded his head.

"When the fire explodes go to help the Rangers."

"What do you mean explodes," Ayla asked.

Cole didn't answer instead he strung the arrow to his bow and took aim. Ayla also strung her bow and nocked an arrow.

"Get ready!" Cole whispered.

"What shall we do with him?" the Red Cloak leader cried visciously.

"Hang him!" someone shouted.

"Burn him!" another shouted.

"Take his heart!" a guard screamed, "take his heart."

The chant was taken up and the words, *take his heart*, echoed everywhere. The gathering crowd was so hysterical with shouting and screaming that they did not notice when more than one streak of blue light flew through the air and landed in the bonfires.

Screams of fear suddenly erupted into the night as one of the bonfires began shooting up sparks and then suddenly blew up and burst into very large bright blue flames. One after another the bonfires erupted throwing sparks up and out. The sparks touched down on the tents and soon they were ablaze. The Red Cloaks camp was suddenly in a mass of hysteria and confusion. Guards ran this way and that trying to put out the fires. The once gathered crowd was now running about as they ran from the fire.

As the bonfire began to ignite and the people started to panic, Cole and Ayla slipped out from their hiding place and moved into the crowd of Rangers, cutting their hands free.

"Run!" Cole screamed.

The Rangers didn't have to be told twice. They ran as fast as their feet could take them. They knocked guards down that stood in their way. They took up swords and fought their way free. Cole saw two rangers pick up Seth and run for safety.

He ran to Artemis, who lay on the ground, nearly unconscious.

"Artemis? Artemis, can you hear me?" Cole cried as he cut Artemis's hands free.

Artemis moaned but he opened his eyes.

"Cole?" He asked weakly.

"Yes. It's me," Cole replied.

"Get out of here!" Artems whispered.

"What?" Cole asked, not understanding what Artemis was saying.

Cole bent over Artemis trying to understand what Artemis was telling him.

"You have to leave. You have to go," Artemis muttered trying to shove Cole away from him.

"Not without you," Cole said.

"Leave. Leave now. It's a trap."

That was the last thing that Cole heard before he felt a hard sharp, thud on his head then everything went dark.

CHAPTER 38

COLE LET OUT A MOAN and he was pulled out of unconsciousness by the disgusting smell of rotting eggs.

"Come to little brat. Time to wake up. My master wants to meet you," a voice echoed in Cole's head. "Wakey, wakey. WAKE UP!"

A sharp, hard slap acrossed his face made Cole's head snap up from his chest. Opening his eyes, Cole looked around with unfocused eyes. From what he could tell, he was in a large and spacious tent with at least one hundred lit candles positioned all around him. Just in front of him was a table that had herbs, roots and a mortar and pestle scattered all over it. At first Cole thought he was back within the walls of Aloria, in Kaya's healing rooms. But then he noticed the cold steel knives and needles that were placed on a tray near his side.

"Welcome back to the living," a familiar voice said.

"You!" Cole cried, as his eyes cleared and he stared at the pretty face of Megera.

Cole snapped out his hands in order to grab at her throat but found that his hands were stopped and he could not reach her. He looked down to discover that his hands were strapped down to a wooden chair. Its arms were stained a dark red, the color of dried blood.

"Welcome to your judgement, *Wildling*," Megera said smiling with delight.

Cole jerked, kicked and fought the ties that bound him to the chair, but it was no use. He was tied down tighter than a drum.

"It is pointless to try and break through those straps. They are made of blackiron and no spirit wielding, not even fire can melt through those."

Cole said nothing but just stared at Megera without even blinking.

"Make him stop staring at me," Megera said, her smile gone. "Are you sure he can't use his powers?"

"The draft I gave him inhibits any wielding," a soft-spoken voice spoke from within the shadows of the tent.

"Yes, well, this one is not normal," Megera said, turning from Cole to the tent's shadows. "He's stronger than any of the others I have read."

"So you say," the voice replied, as it showed itself.

It was a woman, beautiful yet there was something unnerving about her. She was tall and willowy with graying white hair that fell off her shoulders and covered half of her face. She stared at Cole, with one visible blue eye. The other was hidden under her curtain of hair. Cole could sense there was something familiar about her.

"No it can't be. You look like him but you have her eyes" she cried as she rushed towards Cole.

"What are you doing witch?" Megera cried.

Not knowing what the woman would do, Cole tried to shrink back into the chair. He turned his head away from her as she rushed in on him.

"Look at me!" the woman screamed.

But Cole refused and closed his eyes against her.

"I said look at me," the woman cried again, as she took hold of one of the knives on the tray and placed it against his neck. "Look at me or I kill you here and now."

Breathing hard, scared out of his wits, Cole slowly turned his head back around and opened his eyes. She placed the knife under his chin and lifted his head with it so she could look directly into Cole's eyes.

Cole took in a sharp breath as he looked up into the woman's face. Half of it was normal while the other side looked as though it had been melted like the wax of a candle.

"Put down the knife, Ezmay," a rough, gravely voice spoke.

From the corner of his eyes, Cole saw the leader of the Red Cloaks step into the tent. His face was still hidden within the folds of his hood, giving Cole no clue as to who he was.

"Although he is the boy that burned half my camp down," the voice continued.

Even though Ezmay, as she was called, had had a knife to his throat, Cole would rather face her than the mysterious man that had just come in. There was a sense of darkness that surrounded him. The tent, with all its candles of light, seemed to get very dark and cold when he walked in.

"I said put the knife away," the man ordered.

Ezmay did as she was told and scurried away to hide in her shadow.

"Hello Cole," the leader said.

Cole physically jumped when his name crossed the man lips. He looked up at the man, but he had no recognition of him.

"I see you do not know me, that I escape your memory, even though we were at the same council at Aloria."

Cole tried to think back to the time he spent in Aloria, trying to remember the day of the council and who was there.

"Pray tell me, you have not forgotten me, for I have not forgotten you," the man spoke, as he pulled the hood of his cloak from his head.

"Cornwall!" Cole cried as he beheld the man's face.

"So you do remember me," Cornwall smirked.

"You were the one who sent the assassin after me back in Aloria." Cole cried in anger.

"Indeed!" Cornwall answered. "At first I had thought my man had succeeded. At least that was what I was told. But then he never came back and you and your comrades suddenly disappeared. It was then that I knew that you and your kind had escaped my grasp. But it did not matter for I knew that I would have you and so I have," Cornwall said happily.

"What do you mean by that?" Cole asked fearfully.

"Oh I think you know. But maybe I'll show you, just so you can see that there will be no one coming to save you," Cornwall turned away from Cole and turned to his attendents. "Bring them in."

With horror struck eyes, Cole watched as his friends were dragged into the tent. They were all there, Maggie, Chanlyn, Master Wallace, Grayson, Gildon, and Ayla. Tears began to well in his eyes as he saw them with their hands bound and gags shoved into their mouths. When their eyes beheld Cole, all of them went wild. They began to fight their bonds and the guards that held them. Alya managed to slam her head back into the guard that held her and he fell back with a broken nose.

"Stop now or I will slice the boy's throat," Cornwall called, as he held a blade to Cole's throat.

Defeated Ayla fell back and all the others stopped their fighting.

"Cornwall, you cad," Gildon shouted. He had somehow managed to get the gag out of his mouth. "You would betray your own people?"

"People! You and your kind are not my people," Cornwall replied with venom in his voice.

"Then what kind are you if you are not one of us?" Gildon countered.

"I am not a halfbreed. I am of pureblood, pure Albavarian".

"We are all Albavarian," Gildon shouted.

"Wrong!" Cornwall shouted." You and your kind come from him, that devil, the Dark King and his seven demons that came to our lands. It was your kind that bore that monster Shelrin, who rose up and covered our lands in a hundred years of darkness. And now that darkness is waking again," Cornwall shouted.

"You cannot blame the past on us. We are searching for a way to stop him and fight against him. Cole knows how to destroy him," Gildon cried.

"You lie. I will rid the world of your kind and that dark heathen Shelrin, once and for all," Cornwall replied. "I will judge this entire land and will be rid of the wielders and the boy, this abomnination, will be the first to go by my hands," Cornwall proclaimed. "Now get them out of here."

There was a great struggle as the guards pulled, beat and dragged their captives out of the tent. All the while Cornwall watched with a cruel smile on his lips. When the guards had gone, Cornwall turned his attentions on Cole.

"Tell me Megera, you called this one a *Wildling*?" Cornwall asked his eyes never leaving Cole's.

"Yes Master," Megera answered softly.

"Tell me! What is a wildling?"

Megara looked at Cole then at Cornwall.

"They are… They are wielders of raw spirits much like the Dark King so they say. They can take on any spirit and wield it. They. . . "

"I have heard enough," Cornwall said."Now tell me Megera, what color do they bleed?"

"I…I do not know sir," She replied.

"Then let us find out," Cornwall said, moving in closer to Cole with the knife in his hands.

Cole fought his hardest to escape the ironband that held his arms and hands, but it was no use. Cornwall grabbed one of Cole's hands and forced it back, exposing the veins of the wrists.

Realizing what Cornwall was about to do, Cole kicked Cornwall in the groin with all the strength that was in him. The Red Cloak leader went down to his knees. Moaning in pain, Megera ran to his aid and tried to help him to stand.

"Sir! Are you alright?" Megera asked.

"Don't touch me," Cornwall cried, as he rose to his feet.

Again Cole fought the bindings that held him. He tried to summon the energy within, but there was nothing there, he could feel nothing. The drug that they had given him was doing its work.

Pure anger rushed through Cornwall as he came upon Cole. He grabbed Cole's hair and slammed his head against the back of the chair so hard that he saw stars. Barely conscious, Cole felt little pain as Cornwall slit Cole's wrists and then dragged the knife up into his forearm.

"You'll die for that," Cornwall said in furious hatred as he watched Cole's blood began to seep out and drip onto the chair and then slowly fall to the ground. "In a matter of minutes you will be no more," Cornwall whispered into Cole ears, then he pulled back to watch the light start to fade from Cole's eyes.

"Sir what is going on?" Megera asked, her voice shaking in panic.

Cornwall turned around to discover that the tent was filling with mist and the candles were being extinguished. They felt the temperature drop and they could see their breath.

"What is this? What are you doing boy?" Cornwall turned back to Cole.

"First comes the mist that turns day into night," Coke whispered. "Then comes the howl that fills you with fright."

As the very words left Cole's lips there came a deep choir of howls that echoed all around.

"Sir, something isn't right, there is darkness in this," Megera cried in terror.

"Shut up!" Cornwall called in a panic. "You boy stop what your doing."

"Cold be the air that freezes the bone. Next comes the dead, which once were known."

The mist continued to fill the tent, growing thicker and thicker as the seconds passed. The light from the candles was completely gone and shadows started to flicker within the mist.

"You want to scream. You want to run and hide,

But it's too late for a Reaper is at your side."

A shadow moved out of the corner of Cornwall's eye and he began to hear whispers all around him.

"I said stop it boy. Stop it now," Cornwall shouted and then pommeled Cole across the face.

"How many souls will it take?

Will it be two, four, six or eight...," Cole whispered with a mocking laugh.

"I SAID STOP IT!"

Megera suddenly started screaming as she ran from the tent.

Her screams reverberated through the mist, then they just stopped. Ezmay the burnt witch fell back into the shadows and curled up into a ball, rocking herself back forth, sobbing like a little child.

"I am not afraid of you," Cornwall called as he unsheathed his sword and ran from the tent into the blinding mist. "Come and fight me."

As though it were an invitation the shadows within the mist thickened and began to surround Cornwall moving in closer to him. Cornwall swiped at the surrounding shadows but all he did was stab through the mist.

"What is this devilry?" Cornwall yelled, as sweat began to form on his forehead.

"You want to scream, you want to hide, but it's too late for a Reaper is by your side. A reaper is by your side, a Reaper is by your side," the line echo all around him, driving into Cornwall's head.

Again and again he swiped at the mist, yelling and cursing.

"What are you?" he howled.

"You know that answer?" a raspy voice replied.

"Show yourself," Cornwall demanded.

"Very well," the voice said.

The cloaked form of a Reaper appeared before Cornwall free of its metal mask,

Coldwell screamed as he beheld the deformed and decaying face. He continued to scream when the Reaper grabbed him, but his scream ended when the Reaper reached into his chest and pulled from him the glowing orb that pulsated like a beating heart. When the reaper was done, he threw Cornwall's body aside.

I'll get the boy!" the Reaper replied and then disappeared into the mist.

CHAPTER 39

"OPEN YOUR EYES COLE. Open your eyes," it was Maggie's voice. It echoed around him calling him back from unconsciousness. "Come on Cole you have to wake up."

She sounded frantic as if there was something after her. Cole eyes opened slowly and found Maggie standing over him.

"Cole, are you awake, Cole can you hear me? Come on you have to wake up. We have to hurry. They're every where," she sputtered out.

Cole let out a groan to answer Maggie.

"You're awake. Good! Now can you get up?" She asked in a panic.

"What's the matter Maggie? What is it?" Cole asked, not really sure what was going on.

"They're here, Cole, the reapers are here. We have to get away."

Through blurry vision, Cole saw Maggie standing at the tent door, looking out of it.

"Whom are you talking about?" Cole asked, climbing out of the chair that he was once strapped to. Maggie must have undone the bindings and had freed him. She must have also healed him for the cuts on his wrist and arms were healed, there weren't even any scars.

"The Reapers! Quickly Cole," Maggie said, rushing out of the tent.

"Maggie wait," Cole cried, feeling light headed and dizzy.

Cole took a step toward the tent door but his knees buckled and he almost went down but he caught himself on the table. He stood for a few moments and discovered Aydens's bow and his quiver of arrows as he looked around. It was disguised as the rod of plain steel. With a quick swipe Cole picked up the rod and ran, as best he could from the tent.

"Maggie," Cole yelled.

The world around him was covered in mist. The mist was so thick that he could not see anything in front of him. "Maggie," Cole called, running blindly into the fog.

"Cole, over here," Maggie called.

Cole ran in the direction that Maggie called to him from. He caught sight of her running ahead of him and he tried to push himself to go faster. But he was still tired from the loss of blood.

"Maggie wait, where are the others?" Cole called, "how did you escape?" he called.

"I'll explain later," Maggie yelled back, as she kept running.

The mist closed in around him, it seemed to be growing thicker, yet still Cole ran. He finally caught up to Maggie when he found her just standing in the mist, just waiting for him. Cole bent over forward, grabbing the ache in his side, as he took in deep breaths of air.

"Finally!" Maggie replied with annoyance.

"Where are we?" Cole asked, looking around him, out of breath. "Where are the others and how did you escape?" Cole asked,

"I told you that I would explain later," Maggie answered sharply.

There was something about Maggie's tone of voice that did not sit well with Cole.

"We should keep going and find the others," Cole replied.

"There is no need. The others are here. They are all around us," Maggie replied coyly.

The hairs on the back of Cole's neck stood up on end as shadows began to appear in the mist.

Cole suddenly snapped back away from Maggie and took a good look at her.

She looked like Maggie, with her strawberry blond hair and willowy frame and her blue eyes, but she wasn't Maggie.

"You're not Maggie," Cole said, stepping back away from the girl that stood before him.

"What do you mean? Of course I'm Maggie," Maggie spoke, yet even as he watched she was changing.

"No, you're not," Cole said. "What have you done with her?"

"Cole, you've known me all of your life. I'm Maggie, I'm standing right in front of you, talking to you."

"If you're talking to me, then why aren't your lips moving?" Cole cried out.

The girl that stood in front of Cole gave him a smile. It was a cold, mocking smile, one that showed the rotting, blackened teeth of a Reaper.

"Clever boy!"

It only took a moment for the imposter of Maggie to disappear and the cold, decaying form of a Reaper to appear.

"Who are you?" Cole asked. "What are you and where's the real Maggie?" Cole continued angrily.

"Who are we? That is a question that has many answers. We have been called many things. We are the Shadow Men, we are the Reapers, we are death made real."

"SHUT UP!" Cole cried, covering his ears in hopes that it would block out the voices.

"We were once warriors. We turned on our masters and slew our brethren and sisters for the sake of power. And such power we received from Shelrin, so much so that we could not die. No, never die!" the voices chanted together, reverberating around Cole's thoughts. "The power that we hold is great, but comes at a cost. It eats away at us. It eats away our bodies and our souls."

Cole fell to his knees. The voices were getting louder as they came in from the mist and started to enclose around him.

"But we will be restored. Once our master is restored so shall we be restored. The great Master will restore us, if we bring an offering. He requires the heart of an heir and the soul of a Wildling. We shall bring our master your heart and then the great dragon will be fully reborn through you. As for this Maggie, she is dead. We killed her to take on her image," the reaper's voice echoed in Cole's head.

"NO you're lying," Cole screamed, as he whipped out the steel rod and flicked the bow into existence, sparks of blue light snapped out as the bow took its shape. The bow had changed, Cole didn't know how but it was surging with energy. It vibrated with power. He felt the power that it held run through his fingers causing them to tingle.

"Fool of a boy," the Reapers challenged, their voices resounded in Cole's head. "You well know that we cannot be killed with a mortal's weapons."

Cole stared at the Reapers, his anger and hatred for them boiled within him, as the bow seemed to feed him power.

It was not that Cole could see anything, the Reapers could not show emotion, but rather he felt it, that the Reapers were afraid.

"You took everything away from me," Cole bellowed. "You took my home, you took Merryrick, you've taken my friends, so now I'm taking everything from you. I'll free you from this world and send you to the underworld and to the realms of outer darkness where you belong." Tears ran down Cole cheeks as he screamed in anger.

The Reapers let out a mocking laugh as they moved in closer.

"You cannot kill all of us," the Reapers replied.

Cole pulled an arrow and nocked it to the bows string. He pulled back the string and let go. The arrow blasted forward, striking the Reaper that stood before him in the heart. The Reaper stood for a second or two with nothing happening. Then it let out a scream as its boney, thin-skinned hand started to turn black and then waste away into dust and ash.

"What have you done?" it screamed as it rushed towards Cole with its hand out streached, but before it even could touch Cole, the Reaper withered away into nothingness.

It fell silent as Cole stared at the remaining Reapers that gathered around him. The air had shifted. It was thick with an unnatural heat. To Cole, it felt like the air itself was being pulled out from around him, but it wasn't the air that was being pulled but rather the life. From the corner of his eyes Cole could see the grass, the plants and the trees withering away and turning white. The Reapers were pulling the life from them, killing the plant life around them while they grew stronger with their life force.

"Cole!" came a scream from someone near him.

For less than an instant Cole looked in the direction that the scream had come from. For a split second Cole smiled when he saw her. It was Maggie, standing there, alive and breathing, no more the fifteen meters away. But it was in that instant that the Reapers attacked. Cole felt his body being hit with something, something heavy and hard. He felt himself fall to the ground, heard the words of the Reapers.

"Take his soul and then his heart," the Reaper's voices echoed in his head, before he was swallowed up in a blast of light.

MAGGIE STRUGGLED against the bonds that held her hands behind her back as she and the others were pushed forward. Maggie looked back over her shoulder at her unconscious father that was being dragged by two heavyset guards.

The gag that had been forced into her mouth prevented any of her screams from being heard. She had tried to fight, tried to reach for her spirit but there was nothing there. That horrible liquid that the woman had forced her to drink when they were first captured must have done something to block her power. Yet even without her abilities, she still had fought, she kicked at the guard that held her until he slapped her across the face so hard that the act made her head spin so that she nearly fainted. In a half daze Maggie felt herself being shoved forward into a darkened tent where she nearly tripped over something that lay on the ground.

As the rest of the guards dumped their prisoners, one of the guards lit a lamp. Maggie winced at the sudden brightness and had to close her eyes until they were accustomed to the light. When Maggie did finally open her eyes she let out a cry that was muffled by her gag. Her eyes widened in horror as she beheld what she nearly had tripped over.

It was Artemis. He lay on the ground in a crumpled heap. He had been badly beaten with half his face bruised, swollen and caked with dried blood. His arms and legs were cut in several places and one arm looked to be broken. His skin held no color and Maggie feared that he was dead.

Instinctively Maggie reached for her gifts of healing but found that there was a block, as if a brick wall had been put up between her and her power. She tried again. But the wall was still there.

"Blast that witch," Maggie cursed.

Maggie rushed to Artemis' side, then fell to her knees and placed an ear to Artemis' chest. His heart still beat, but his breathing was shallow and ragged, as if he were struggling to get air.

"Is the maggot still alive?" The guard that had shoved Maggie into the tent asked as he came over. He picked Artemis up by the hair and listened to his shallow breathing. "Won't be long now. He's a goner," the guard laughed then threw Artemis back to the ground.

Anger, frustration and fear for Cole and her friends filled Maggie with despair. She felt useless and lost. She couldn't do anything to help Artemis or Cole, not without her power. Tears began to well up within her eyes and they soon fell down her cheeks and onto Artemis.

"Your tears won't help him girl," the guard laughed. "But you can take comfort in knowing that you and your cohort of abominations will be joining him soon." The guards left then, taking the lamp with them and throwing Maggie and the others into the dark.

Maggie sat in the dark feeling cold and lonely. Even though she knew that the others were with her, she could not see them in the dark and so she felt alone. Her tears still fell, rolling down her cheeks as she struggled to get her hands free, but the knots were tied tight, so tight that she was starting to lose feeling in their fingers and hands. The fear that Maggie was feeling was building up inside her. She was scared not for herself but for Cole and the others. All she needed to do was get her hands free. But she couldn't do that without help and no one was going to help her. Hopelessness started taking over and new tears were starting to form.

As Maggie started to cry again, Artemis let out a moan and Maggie could have sworn that he had moved a little. Maggie tried to call to him but with the gag it her mouth it came out more of a groan. Working her jaw up and down, along with moving her head up and down Maggie managed to get the gag free from her mouth.

"Artemis, can you hear me?" Maggie called, her voice hoarse from lack of moisture.

Maggie licked her lips and called his name again. Artemis let out a moan in answer to Maggie's call.

"Artemis we need your help," Maggie called. Maggie let out a breath. How was he going to help her, he was the one that needed help, he was dying.

"Artemis, I know you're hurt and you need help as well, but I can't help you unless my hands are free," Maggie explained. "Please you have to try and get up. Please Artemis can you try and use your wielding to break my bonds," Maggie pleaded hoping that he wasn't drugged with the spirit blocking liquid.

Maggie let out a gasp and held her breath as she could hear movement. It sounded as if someone was dragging something across a dirt floor. Then after a moment, she felt Artemis's touch on her hands and she felt a warmth run across her wrist. There were several pops as the leather bands that held her hands broke apart and then one loud snap and her hands were free.

"Gildon, where are you?" Maggie whispered.

The sound of muffles came from her left and Maggie rushed over to where the sound had come from.

"Gildon I need light," Maggie ordered. "Are you able to connect with your fire spirit," she asked, after she had untied the fire master's hands.

A small flicker of light sparked to life and he held a small flame within the palm of his hands for a few seconds and then the light went out. He tried again and the flames burned for a few moments longer. Long enough that it allowed Maggie to see that there was a lamp that by providence had been left hanging on the tent main support beam. After Gildon had lit the lamp with a warm bright white light, he ran around to the others and untied them, setting them free as well. While Gildon helped the others, Maggie ran to Artemis and properly examined him. He was in a bad way, his breathing soft and nearly nonexistent. Once again Maggie reached for her spirit and found the wall there, banning her from healing Artemis. She fought the wall mentally, kicking at it with all the strength that she could muster and then when she was about to give up from exhaustion, the wall weakened and slowly it started to crumble and Maggie was able to grasp at her power.

She placed her hands upon Artemis' chest and carefully, so as not to overwhelm him, she pulled spirits from around her and forced them through him. In her mind she could see the injuries that Artemis suffered from. With the flames of life that burned through Artemis, Maggie concentrated on having the flames heal the internal wounds that Artemis had received. Maggie pulled bits of life that flowed through the ground and world around her and slowly let it flow to

Artemis, letting his flame grow in light and in strength. But as she was pulling the energy from around her, she felt a darkness begin to surround her. Maggie quickly stopped the flow and let go of Artemis just as Ayla let out a cry of fear.

"What it that?" She wailed.

As Maggie opened her eyes, she found that the whole tent was filling with a stange cold mist.

"What is going on?" Ayla asked again, "what is …" her cry of fear was suddenly interrupted with the echoing call of hounds.

"Reapers!" Wallace muttered.

"Father you're awake," Maggie cried, as she ran to her father. "Are you well?" she asked, looking him over.

"I am well," Wallace said, reassuring his daughter. "But I fear that we are in more trouble than the Red Cloaks have put us through."

"Father, what about Cole?" Maggie cried. "If they know he's here…if they find him first…"Maggie said, her voice shaking in fear.

"They won't!" Ayla replied, and then took off out of the tent with Gildon and Grayson right behind her.

"Ayla wait. You don't know what the Reapers can do," Gildon yelled chasing after her.

Grayson was next to leave and Wallace was ready to follow when he looked back at his daughter then at Artemis.

"Go father," Maggie commanded. "Go and find him. Bring him back."

"Do not leave the tent and do not, at all cost let the light go out. Light tends to keep the Reapers and the mist away. I will see you soon," and with that Wallace left the tent, leaving Maggie with the unconscious Artemis.

His breathing was much better, but Maggie dared not heal him anymore. Healing not only took a toll on the healer but also the recipient. Apart from using the life that was within the earth, the wounded also had to use their own energies to be healed, taking alot out of them. Maggie knew that the more she tried to heal Artemis the more harm she might do.

The mist that had started seeping into the tent seemed to be getting thicker. Maggie watched the mist as it swirled around, rising high up into the atmosphere. It did not take long for the whole tent to be swallowed up in thick smoke. The only thing that kept the mist from swallowing Maggie was the lamp. The mist appeared to dissipate wherever the light fell. The light was comforting and Maggie was glad to have it as she waited for her father and the others to return, hopefully with Cole in tow. Although Maggie had the lantern that kept the mist at bay, the light could not help extinguish the frightful thoughts that raced through her mind. Time ticked by with every second, and with every second that passed, Maggie imagined horrible things happening to Cole, and it only got worse when suddenly there was a burst of terrifying screams that echoed all around her. The screaming increased and Maggie felt tears in her eyes again. She scrunched up in a ball next to Artemis and covered her ears, hoping the cries would soon stop.

The cries did stop and all that surrounded her was silence. But the silence was more haunting and terrifying than the screaming. She was now more worried for her friends and family than ever. She felt like she would go mad at any moment. She thought she was going mad when she heard a faint voice call her name. For a second she thought that it was just her imagination that it was her need and desire to have something happen causing it, but then her name was called again and this time Maggie knew who it was.

"Cole?" she questioned.

"Maggie wait," Cole's voice called from somewhere nearby, as if he were just outside of the tent.

Maggie was ready to grab the lantern and step outside to greet Cole but she suddenly stopped herself. Her father had told her what the Reapers could do. How they used the mist to hide their true identity and also somehow make their victims believe that they were seeing the thing that they most desired or the thing that terrified them the most.

Maggie stood for a moment, with the brightly lit lantern in her hands. She stood at the tent's doorway looking out across a wall of thick mist. She could see nothing, not even the bright sky and the fog above the stars was so thick.

"Maggie stop. I can't keep up," Cole called as he ran past Maggie into the thick clouds.

"Cole!" Maggie yelled but he did not hear her. Looking back over her shoulder she looked at Artemis. He lay unconscious but he was still breathing.

"I'll be right back," Maggie called to him, and then threw herself into the mist after the boy she thought was Cole.

CHAPTER 40

MAGGIE PASSED THROUGH the mist easily enough. With the small pool of lantern light the mist physically recoiled from the light that surrounded her, thereby allowing her to see the world as it really was. It was quiet for a time then all at once Maggie heard angry shouting. It was Cole. He was shouting so loud it sounded as if he were in a lot of pain. Maggie rushed forward trying to follow the sounds of Cole's screams, but his voice echoed around her and she could not tell which direction she should take. She held her lamp high in front of her, trying to see past the pool of light.

"Cole where are you?" Maggie called out. But there was no reply. Then all at once, suddenly a blast of light exploded near her. The light was so bright that Maggie had to turn away from it to shield her eyes. When she looked back the mist that had once surrounded her was gone, burned away as a result of the blast of light. No more than a few meters away stood Cole. He stood tall and straight, his bow drawn in his hands, the arrow that was nocked to his bow, glowed with a slight bluish tint. Cole was ready to send it flying at the hoard of Reapers that surrounded him and were moving in closer to him. Cole let go of his arrow of light. It sprang from the bowstring not as an arrow but as a bolt of lightning. It struck a Reaper and went right through him, turning the Reaper into dust. Cole shot another Reaper and he too faded into nothing but blackness. But for all his shooting the Reapers were quickly closing in on him and it would not be long before they would completely over take him.

Seeing him in trouble, Maggie reached out for her spirit. It was there but far off. The light of life that she usually saw in all living things wasn't there. It wasn't like coming up against the mental wall that had blocked her from using her spirit, it just that there was nothing there. Desperately Maggie searched for the lifeline that would give her something to wield. As her mind searched for a source, she watched as a Reaper began to move his hands in awkward motions. He looked at if he were mixing the air. Maggie felt a tightness in her throat grow. She understood now why she could not find anything to allow her to wield. The Reaper was stealing the life around her. The plants, the trees, even the insects were being drained.

"Cole!" she screamed, knowing what the Reaper was doing.

She saw Cole, turn his head towards her, saw him smile and then saw him get hit with the Reaper's spell. Red lightning forked out from the Reaper's hands and hit Cole, square in the chest, flinging him in the air and back. Cole hit the ground and lay there, not moving. It was then that the Reapers fell in on him and Maggie screamed.

Desperate to help Cole in any way, Maggie took off her belt from her waist and picked a rock out of her belt pouch and tucked it into the pocket of the sling. With one quick continuous movement she whipped the sling around her head and let go of the knot. The rock flew fast and straight, hitting one of the Reapers. One after another Maggie flung her stones. The stones slammed into the Reapers, one after another. The impact of the stones on the Reapers, echoed throughout the night. One Reaper was brought down with a broken leg and the projectile smashed into the shadow man. Another was smashed in the face. The Reaper turned toward Maggie, its jaw broken.

"Another fool," the Reaper echoed, "Kill her."

Three Reapers suddenly turned from Cole and made their way to Maggie. Maggie's eyes darted from one to another trying to figure out which one she should try and take down. She knew that she could not take down all of them. Heart in her throat Maggie flung her stones, one after another. Rocks flew slamming into faces, legs, arms and bodies, but the Reapers still kept coming. Maggie slung a stone hoping it would hit one of the Reapers in the head, but as the stone came flying the Reaper caught it and crushed it to dust.

"Why don't you run little rabbit?" a voice touched her mind. "Why don't you run so the fox can chase you?"

Somewhere within her head someone was laughing a mocking laugh. They were laughing at her.

Yet Maggie stood her ground. She was not going to run, not going to shy away like she did so many times. Cole was in trouble and he needed her help. If she could buy him just a few more moments, then maybe...

The Reapers were upon her, so close now. One Reaper reached out to her, its fingertips nearly touching her cheek. All at once, three arrows came out of the dark, hitting one of the Reapers in the back. The Reaper turned, as did Maggie. Coming up behind her was Ayla, Grayson and Gildon. The three archers released another on slot of arrows, only this time the arrows caught fire in the air. When they struck the Reaper the decaying robes that it wore caught fire and was engulfed in flames.

"Don't just stand there!" Ayla shouted, "Run!"

Calls and shouts surrounded her. Maggie saw her father and she saw Chanlyn. There was Eli and what looked like a wolf at his side. They both stood in front of a Reaper. The wolf stood strong, baring its teeth and growling fiercely. The wolf was about to attack the Reaper, when the wolf itself, was attacked by a massive black beast. It was one of the Hellhounds. At first Maggie thought the wolf might be killed, but the white wolf quickly gained ground and it killed the hellhound, but there was another two to take its place. Eli fought with his powers of ice and Reapers fought with fire. Eli had managed to hold off one the Reaper by freezing him in a capsule of ice. The Reaper quickly melted the ice and Eli was forced to fight again. Wild winds blew this way and that, picking up rocks, clods of dirt, and broken branches and flinging them at the Reaper that stood before Chanlyn.

"Maggie," Wallace cried, as he battled with his own reaper. "Get Cole!"

Maggie nodded her head, seeing that all the Reapers but one were engaged in a battle.

Maggie ran to where Cole lay. The lone Reaper that had managed to avoid the conflict that surrounded him, moved in on the unconscious Cole. He knelt down beside the boy. His hand with its long fingers moved over to the left side of Cole's chest and curled its fingers into a claw.

As Maggie was running, she grabbed a stone out of her bag and wound up her sling ready to pitch the stone at the Reaper. As she did she felt her fear and anger focus on the Reaper as she aimed and let the stone fly. It hit the reaper with a great smack, the sound resounding, as though a clap of thunder had broken the night. The Reaper was tossed aside away from Cole and Maggie slid to a stop and fell on her knees. She quickly checked Cole over. He was breathing, at least she thought he was.

"Cole! You have to wake up," Maggie cried as she shook him. The battling that surrounded her seemed to be settling. The Reapers were captured. Wallace had snagged a Reaper in a twist of roots and vines, Eli had managed to freeze one in a block of ice and the one that Ayla and Gildon had shot with Gildon's fire arrows still burned. Grayson's foe lay on the ground, several arrows and a knife protruding from its chest. For a few brief moments it seemed that they had won, that the Reapers had been captured.

"You are all fools," a cold voice echoed in their heads and then began to laugh.

The world suddenly exploded and they were all thrown from their feet, landing on the ground. Out of breath and in pain from hitting the ground so hard, Maggie watched as the Reapers stood up free of ice, wind and roots. The Reaper that Grayson had put down stood and pulled the arrows and knife from his chest and for a moment they floated in mid air and then flew through the air towards Cole.

The Reapers began to gather in a wide circle around Cole. The one that burned walked toward the others still engulfed in flames.

"The boy is ours," the voice cried, as they turned and began to move in closer towards Cole.

Maggie quickly crawled over to Cole, to where he still lay unconscious. She tried using her gift to rouse him, but it was no use, she could still only feel the emptiness that surrounded her. Far off, she could feel some life, but it was too far away and she was not strong enough to pull it towards her.

"Please Cole!" Maggie cried.

The Reaper that Maggie had knocked out was back up again. Maggie watched as it moved in on her and Cole. Maggie used her sling to try and do what she had done before. But the Reaper had learned its lesson and used its power to blast Maggie's stones out of the air. The Reaper was getting closer, as Maggie stood over Cole and she threw her rocks to defend herself.

"Cole! You have to wake up," Maggie screamed.

"MAGGIE!" Wallace yelled to his daughter, where he lay on the ground.

They were close now, so close that all the Reapers had to do was reach out and touch her.

"COLE!"

The Reaper's fingertips were inches away from stroking Maggie's cheek when it was suddenly hit with a bolt of lightning. In an instant the Reaper disappeared in a cloud of dust. Maggie turned to see Cole standing with his bow in hand. The bow glowed with a pale blue, almost white, light that surrounded him.

"Cole?" Maggie asked, as she stared at him.

Cole stood proud, and tall, his face was set in a cold expression and his eyes, his eyes no longer held the blue in them but were silver.

"What are you?" the Reapers voiced in all their heads.

Cole took a step forward, moving past Maggie.

"I am death to you," Cole responded, not in his own voice.

As he pulled back on his bowstring and aimed at one of the reapers, in the bow string an arrow of lighting appeared. It crackled and snapped with enery as Cole pulled the bow to its full draw.

Cole's eyes watched the four Reapers that surrounded him as they pulled their black swords from their sheaths.

"Surrender to us boy," the remaining Reapers cried.

"Never!" Cole spat.

"You have no choice," they spoke."Surrender to us, or watch your friends die," the Reapers ordered.

"I Will Never Stand With You!" Cole stated firmly, as he released the arrow.

The arrow struck two of the reapers, striking one Reaper and oblitarating it and then slamming into the other Reaper that stood behind the first. Coke made ready to draw another arrow.

"Now! You will watch your friends die, by your own hands," both of the remaining Reapers ordered with hatred in their voices. With that, the Reapers twisted their fingers slowly together.

Cole suddenly bent forward, dropping his bow as he went to grab his head. He fell to his knees.

"Stop. Get away," he cried.

"Cole," Maggie yelled. "Cole what's the matter?" Maggie reached his side.

"Get away Maggie," Cole whimpered. "Get away NOW!"

Cole's head jerked up and his head turned to Maggie.

Maggie stepped back her eyes filled with terror.

Cole's eyes had changed again. They were blue again, a cold silver blue. Not his blue. Not his warm blue.

As Maggie stepped back, Cole rose to his feet and he picked up the bow. Immediately when his hand touched the bow, the blue, white light that glowed within the bow changed to red.

"Who are you?" Cole demanded seeing Maggie before him.

"Cole! I'm Maggie," Maggie replied.

"Maggie?' Cole whispered, as if he were trying to recall her from his memory.

Fear suddenly gripped Maggie when she saw that there was no recognition in his eyes.

"Maggie's dead, the Reapers killed her," Cole cried as he pulled back on his bowstring, bringing a red arrow into existance and pointing it at Maggie.

"No Cole. I'm right here. I am Maggie. The Real Maggie," Maggie spoke. "Would you believe the Reaper's words?"

"Do not speak her name," Cole grimaced.

"Cole what is wrong with you?" Ayla cried.

Cole's eyes were pulled from Maggie as he turned to look at Ayla. "Why do you not see what is in front of you?" She hollered.

"Everyone get back!" Wallace yelled. "He's being wrapped."

"What are you taking about Wallace?" Grayson yelled.